Two Halves of a broken Heart

Jade Royal

Chapter One

Her heart was beating so fast she was about ready to have a heart attack. She clutched her chest as if she would be able to feel her heart actually pushing against her chest. But all she felt was her heart beating like a thousand hungry butterflies. She couldn't remember a time where this feeling had ever overcome her body before. Sucking up air through her lungs, she reached with her shaking hands to pick up the slim white stick. She was so nervous, the moment her hands touched the slim item, she dropped it on the ceramic tiled floor.

"Come on Irys," She scolded herself. "Get your shit together." She heaved over, and picked up the stick.

"Please," She begged, closing her eyes and sending a silent prayer up to the heavens. Taking the leap, she opened her eyes.

"Oh my god!" Her scream was loud squeal. She jumped up and down and clapped her hands.

"WHAT THE HELL?!" Irys stilled when she heard the loud bellow coming from her room. She chuckled and covered her mouth. Wrapped up in her own excitement she forgot it was seven in the morning. She quickly got herself together and cleaned up the bathroom before leaving. Her man was sitting up in bed, confusion ripped across his face.

"Hell you making all that noise for?" He asked.

"Oh I just-"

"Never mind I don't even want to know," He grunted, throwing himself back into bed. "I'll save you the embarrassment of admitting you were masturbating." Irys rolled her eyes.

"I wasn't masturbating Derek. And if I was, I wouldn't be embarrassed to admit it either. Nothing wrong with that. Not like you were giving me toe curling orgasms anyways." Derek popped his head up and looked at her.

"Why you always gotta start with me?" He asked. She sighed and shook her head.

"I'm sorry honey. Forget it. I actually have something to tell you."

"Honestly Irys, I don't really care right now. All I want is some sleep."

"No babe this is serious though, and-"

"Irys!" He groaned. "Leave me be!" Irys sucked her teeth. Her excitement was slowly buzzing away. Of course she wanted to spill the news to her man that they were expecting, but clearly he wasn't interested. She should know better. He was a hell of a grump man when his sleep was messed with.

Derek rolled over and shut his eyes. He pretended to be asleep as he felt the bed sink with the heavy weight of his woman. He scoffed in his head. Yeah, 'his woman'. Derek never thought he'd get this deep with Irys, but yet here he was, sleeping in her bed. And now that he was seemingly in so deep, he couldn't find it in himself to get out of it. Or at least that's just what he told himself. Truly, if he didn't want to be with his whale of a girlfriend he didn't have to. He was here for a reason. So for now he just had to grit his teeth and deal with her until he did get what he wanted. And besides, Irys took care of him so he was going to take advantage of it for as long as he could.

He thought he'd won the battle with her, but that proved wrong when she pulled on his shoulder turning him over on his back. She swung her legs over his hips and sat on top of him. Derek grunted as her weight pushed against his hips.

"I said I want to go back to sleep," He told her.

"I know, but this is important Derek. And it's seven in the morning. I thought you said this morning you were going job hunting?"

"You love bringing up the fact that I'm jobless don't you?" He said. "It's like you can pick on all my shortcomings, and I'm supposed to ignore it and not fire back at you."

"No one is picking on your shortcomings," Irys snapped. "You said you were heading out to look for work and now you don't seem to care."

"I don't need to work right now. We have everything we need, and I don't see you struggling."

"Um no, you know that with my mom sick things aren't are easy and it'll help if you did have work. And besides, after a couple months I may not be working anymore for a little while."

"Why the hell is that?" He questioned.

"Because I'm pregnant. We're having a baby." As if the weight of his woman wasn't enough, her shocking news hit him like a ton of bricks.

"Whoa, wait," He said.

"I'm so happy I can't even believe it! I just keep imaging a little baby with your eyes and-"

"And no," Derek said. He used his strength and pushed her off him. He eased out of bed and stood.

"No what?" she asked.

"I don't want a baby with you Irys. We never agreed to start a family. How do you do this shit without talking to me about it?" Irys felt her mouth fall.

"How did I do this without talking to you?" she questioned. "What? You think I somehow got your sperm into a turkey baster and shoved it into myself and impregnated myself?"

"Well did you?!"

"You have got to be kidding me," Irys breathed. "Derek we've been dating for two years. How could you say something like that to me? And you know what, you did agree to get me pregnant!"

"How the fuck did I do that?!" He snapped.

"Last month when your horny ass was all over me like a maniac right here in this bed, I told you not to come inside me! And what'd you do? You busted your load in me. So right then and there you agreed to get me pregnant because you know I don't do birth control and you never wear condoms. So you had to know this would happen soon. Or what, you're just that stupid?" Derek had to hold back the urge to slap fire out of her. He paced in front of the bed trying to get his anger into check. He said he was deep into this relationship, but a pregnancy was not part of his plans. This was not the reason he was here and he wasn't about to be tied to this woman like that.

"Look," He said after calming down. "I thought we'd just take our time with having kids and just enjoy each other."

"Well yes, But what can we do now? It's already there? We can't take it back."

"Do you want to eventually be my wife Irys?" Derek asked.

"Yes I do," She replied hurriedly, as if she was expecting him to propose right then and there. But Derek would never propose to this whale. And honestly, she was a pretty woman, she was smart, and took good care of him, but he wasn't going to spend his life with her. That was just the reality of the situation.

"Well, I won't propose to you if you keep this baby. You'll never be my wife." Irys couldn't quite describe the feeling that came over her. It was as if a panic attack was slowly entering her body.

"So…what are you saying to me?" She asked with her voice shaky.

"Get rid of that thing inside you, or you're gonna lose me." Irys shook her head.

"Are you honestly telling me to abort our baby?" She asked, tears brimming her eyes.

"I'm not ready to have no baby with you Irys. And I have a say in this. So get rid of it, or you're gonna be a single parent. And I will by no means help you at all."

"Derek, you don't even help me now!" She snapped, her anguish turning into anger. "And you have the audacity to tell me what the hell I can and can't do?" Derek advanced towards her.

"You wanna get rid of it naturally, or you want me to do it for you?" He threatened, raising his fist. Irys looked down at his fist, and then back to his steely eyes.

"You know you don't have the balls," She gritted. Derek's anger tripped. Without another thought, he brought his fist back, and thrust it out quickly at Irys, punching her in the mouth. He followed up with a slap to her face.

The sting of the hits, blinded Irys. She was lost for a moment, not sure what to think or what to do. But the moment her daze began to recede she was left with the thumping of pain in her jaw that was an echo for what he'd just done. Irys gasped and touched her mouth. She looked at the blood on her fingertips. It all sunk in. He had hit her. Anger took over her conscience.

With fast hands, Irys punched him in the gut twice. The force of the hit backed him up, allowing her to get out of the bed. Once she did, she slapped him hard across the face, dragging her nails against his skin. He punched her in the head again, and Irys was no fool. She knew she wasn't gonna win a fight against him, but she wasn't going to go down without a fight either. So for the sake of surviving, she kicked him in his balls. When he doubled over, she brought her knee up straight into his face, satisfied when her knee hit the bone in his nose. He fell back, crying in pain.

"You of all people know I don't get down like that Derek!" She screamed. "How dare you hit me?!"

"You need to get your ass put in check Irys!" He snapped back, holding his nose. "I don't care what mighty horse you on right now, I'm not about to be the father of your baby."

"I won't just abort because you said so!" Derek got to his feet. Irys backed up just in case he was about to try and hit her again, but he didn't.

"So then you lose me," He stated. "But think wisely Irys. I'm the only man who'd give your fat ass a chance. There will be no man out there who's gonna fuck you like I did, who's gonna wanna be seen out in public with you like I am. You're lucky I gave you a chance and now you're gonna turn around and act like you the fucking shit. Newsflash Irys, you're nothing but a fat fuck with a good sex drive. So think about that shit before you throw all your chips away." Derek grunted at her before grabbing a pair of jeans, and his sneakers. He left the room abruptly. The slam of the front door startled Irys. There she stood, dazed and confused again.

Being fat never bothered her. She loved her body, and she was confident about it. But hearing those hurtful words coming from the man she thought she was falling in love with stung. It was true after all. She'd been single for a long time before Derek gave her a chance. There wasn't a man who wanted her. Getting Derek, and keeping him was hard. Was she just to throw that all away? But what kind of woman would she be to choose a man over her growing fetus? Sinking back into bed, Irys rested against the pillows, allowing her tears to stream free as an inner battle took place within her. Her baby, or her future with a man?

Chapter Two

The soft wails and moans of the golden retriever sounded at Lucien's ears. Through the pitch black room, he saw nothing but felt when the rough tongue of the dog swiped at his face. Grunting, Lucien pushed the dog away.

"Leave me alone," He ordered, turning over in bed. The sun was barely over the horizon and the last thing he wanted to do was to be bothered by a four legged animal. Sleep, he just wanted sleep. But as he pushed the dog away, the dog only hopped back onto his bed and persisted with its moaning and grunting. He used his wet nose and pushed at Lucien's chin.

"Salsa, get off me!" Lucien ordered. He tossed the dog a stern look, knowing she could see it through the darkness with her doggy vision. But the tone of Lucien's voice changed Salsa's demeanor. Lucien felt her get tense. Standing on his chest she barked down in his face. Lucien turned his head as spittle flew into his face.

"Alright damn!" Lucien shouted. He pushed the dog off him, but she didn't stop barking.

"Got some nerve barking in someone face with that rank ass breath," Lucien muttered. He sat up in the bed and grabbed his test meter from his night table stand. He didn't need the light to know where the small machine was. It was almost routine. But he turned on the lamp, bathing the room in its small light. Salsa sat in front of him watching him intently. She yawned and licked her nose.

"Satisfied?" Lucien asked. She only leaned her head to the side and looked at him. Shaking his head, Lucien pulled out his test strips then pricked his index finger. He cursed as he read the numbers on his meter.

"Guess you had a point," Lucien said to his dog as he stood. The dog followed him as he walked out of the bedroom. The patter of his bare feet, and of the four legged companion behind him sounded throughout his quiet home. With each room he entered, Lucien turned on the lights in his home. In the kitchen, he filled Salsa's bowl with food and water, but the canine ignored both. She trotted behind Lucien as he made his way to the fridge. It was as if she wanted to make sure he was doing what he needed to do, and she'd start barking heavily again if he didn't. She had a right to. That's what her purpose was. With a hard sigh he opened his fridge and peered down into it. He grabbed his insulin and trotted to the island in the middle of the kitchen where he sat down. Salsa sat down in front of him diligently to watch him. Taking out his syringe from the drawers attached to the island, he measured the right dosage of the cold liquid in that small vial. Something so small had managed to be the only thing that could keep him alive, ever since he was 10.

The sting of the needle going into his abdomen was barely noticeable. Though it was a pain he knew too often. Depositing his medicine into his body was when Salsa finally walked away from him. Just weeks after he was diagnosed with type one diabetes, his parents had brought home a puppy they called his service dog. Lucien didn't understand at first, but after intense training, whenever he was too high or too low, Salsa was there to alert his parents. Lucien had a disdain for the dog at only 10 years old because at ten which boy wanted a female dog named Salsa? And while he always swore when he was old enough he'd get rid of the dog, Lucien never managed to give his dog up. So sure, he fell in love with the thing. But while she was persistently annoying, she in fact always managed to save his ass before he ended up in a diabetic coma, or worse.

With the sun coming up over the horizon now, Lucien figured he might as well just stay awake. He needed to eat anyways to keep his sugar in check before he would get started with work. He was completely used to having to take care of himself and his sickness, but his body and his mind was starting to get numb. Most days if it weren't for his dog, Lucien wouldn't take his medication or even eat. Countless times he thought about his life and he knew there was nothing to be depressed about. He'd graduated culinary school three years ago, and after studying abroad, he was back home in Miami preparing for the opening of his own restaurant. Growing up, all he wanted to do was cook. At first he just loved eating. But as he matured he grew to understand how foods were made and enjoyed helping his mother in the kitchen. It seemed ironic now that the very thing he loved was being taken from him because of his sickness. Or maybe it was because he loved food too much why he was diabetic in the first place.

Either way, he tried not to let his sickness ail him, so he went for his dreams. And now so close to it, it seemed like everything was falling apart. His mind was his worst enemy. Sometimes depression didn't have a reason. It was just there. And countless times his friends told him how envious they were. He was starting his own business, and he had a woman as gorgeous as they came. Little did they know things were not as perfect as it might have seemed. Lucien was trying to make the best of every situation to make things as perfect as other people saw it. He just needed to dismiss his depression as nothing but his mind being too overactive with negative thoughts. Doing the only thing that freed his mind from the prison of his dark thoughts, Lucien just began cooking.

The sun was well up, shining through his large kitchen just as he finished cooking the last of his breakfast. He opened the patio doors, letting the sound of the birds chirping happily infiltrate his quite home. The moment the doors were open, Salsa ran outside excitedly for her morning exercise around the backyard. A second pair of footsteps sounded throughout the house, as his woman finally made her way into the kitchen.

"You know, that dog is really working my nerves," She stated grimly. Lucien stared at his model of a woman. She was tall, and slender, supple in all the right places with shoulder length light brown hair. Her skin was a brighter caramel than his complexion, adding radiance to her beauty. Being a man with his sickness, he pretty much lucked out when it came to dating.

"Good morning to you too," Lucien replied. She rolled her eyes and went to sit around the island to eat. Her short silk robe rose up when she sat on the high stool, letting Lucien know she wasn't wearing any underwear. Sighing, he went back to the island and sat across from her, watching as she dug into the French toast.

"Why you be having that dog bark early in the morning when you know I hate being woken up that early?" She complained.

"I don't know what you want me to do about it," He said simply. "That's what she's supposed to do."

"Figure something out or else I'm going to move out of here Lucien. Do you want that?"

"You know I don't want you to move out Rosa. But just be a little considerate okay?" She only huffed in response. Lucien wanted to be with this girl, but her selfishness was sometimes hard to ignore. Lucien got up from around the island and went over to the sink to begin cleaning up.

"What are your plans for today?" Rosa asked from behind him.

"Um, just going down to the restaurant then I have to finish making up a menu, then I need to look about hiring people before the opening." Rosa stared at her man's back. His broad shoulders made his t-shirt fit him snug. His lean waist held up his pajama pants but just barely. She knew if she picked up his shirt, she would be able to see his delicious V line. Though she threatened to move out, Rosa knew she wouldn't go anywhere. She loved being with Lucien. He was sexy, and headed to being successful, and he was one amazing lover. She licked her lips just thinking about how he satisfied her. Any woman would be stupid to have him, and just give him up. And she was a lot of things, but stupid, she was not. Jumping down from the stool Rosa came up behind Lucien and wrapped her arms around his waist. She licked her lips as she dug her hands in his pajama pants and grabbed his heavy manhood.

"You forgot one thing," She said seductively. Lucien sighed and tilted his head back. Turning off the water, he dried his hands before taking her hands out of his pants. Thinking she had him won over, she moved back and untied her robe. The silk fell from her skin, revealing her nakedness. Lucien turned around and looked at the beauty in front of him. Her skin was smooth, and perfect. Her breasts were rounded and perky, her stomach was flat, decorated with a small belly button ring that Lucien found incredibly cute. Her womanly core had her signature thin line of hair down the middle. She was appetizing, standing there in front of him, but there was just one problem.

"Not right now Rosa," He told her. Disappointment set in her face.

"Why not?" She asked.

"My sugar was high this morning. I can't have sex right now." Rosa admitted that her man was perfect. He was sexy, he gave her good loving, he was kind, and loving. There was only one real issue.

"I can't even-"

"Please don't start with that overreacting," Lucien cut her off. "We had sex last night."

"But your sugar isn't high now."

"No it's not. But my body needs time to regenerate Rosa. Let me get back to normal and I'll give you what you want." Rosa grabbed up her robe from the ground and shoved herself back into it.

"You know what, don't even worry about it. I'll just use my damn vibrator or some shit since-" Lucien grabbed onto her arm keeping her from walking away. If there was one thing he hated about having his sickness was not being able to have sex with his woman when he felt like it. Each time they had sex it was because it was planned. That way Lucien could keep up with his sugar for the day in preparation for the activity. But on times like this where she wanted to make love to him randomly, he just couldn't give it to her. With his sugar being high just a couple hours ago, his libido was thrown off.

"Why you do that to me? As if I tell you no for no reason. Or that I don't want to be with you?" Rosa just shrugged her shoulders. Lucien kept hold of her arm and backed her up until she bumped into the island. He lifted her at the waist and placed her to sit on top of the island. He spread her legs wide before doing down for a taste of her.

Rosa threw her head back as Lucien got down to business licking at her insides. He used his fingers and spread her little lips apart to get his way inside. Her breathing became ragged as her pleasure rose higher and higher. He was an expert at using his mouth and his tongue to drive her body into a bout of immense pleasure. Though she hated having to deal with him and his diabetes, she loved the sex with him, including oral. Finding her orgasm within minutes of the licking and sucking of her clit, Rosa released her juices into his awaiting mouth. Her body trembled as he sucked it up like a vacuum before finally releasing her.

"Did I make it better?" He whispered.

"Only a little," She pouted.

"What else you want?" Lucien asked.

"I want to go shopping," Backing away from her Lucien helped her down off the counter, then proceeded to wipe it down with a wet cloth.

"You know I don't mind taking care of you Rosa, but you should know that I am investing a lot of my money into my restaurant. And I'm not exactly rich."

"It's not about being rich Lucien! Any man with a woman will take care of her no matter what. Lately all you've been doing is thinking about yourself."

"Alright fine," Lucien said. "You win. Get my wallet from the bedroom for me." She smiled and kissed him.

"Thank you baby!" Though he wanted to be wise about how he used his money, seen as he was opening up his business, he also did not want to make his woman unhappy. But perhaps she was right, he didn't have to be rich to take care of her.

"Here babe," She said coming back and giving him his wallet. He didn't have enough cash as he looked through it, so he gave her his credit card. The smile that came to her face when he handed it to her gave Lucien some comfort.

"I'm gonna shower and get ready to go. See you later alright?" She had turned her back and was walking off before he stopped her.

"Will you come down to the restaurant and help me out after you're finished?" He asked. Rosa rolled her eyes. She put on a smile before she turned back around to face him.

"You know I'll be useless there, I don't know about anything! And plus, I want to see my mom later on today."

"I wish you wouldn't feel like that Rosa. I'd love to have you there with me."

"And I will one day. But my mom is sick you know that. I should be seeing her every day really."

"I get it baby. It's no worries." Rosa smiled. She walked back up to him and wrapped her arms around his neck.

"Everything will be fine honey," She said, pecking him on the lips. But what started off as a peck developed slowly into a deep tongue kiss that had her walls becoming moist again. Moaning into his mouth, she grinded against his pelvis. He grabbed a handful of her ass as if he was ready to finally give her some action. But just as she reached inside his pants again, his watched beeped annoyingly. Knowing what that meant, Rosa grunted and backed away.

"I'm gonna get dressed," She said quietly before turning and leaving. Lucien stared after her feeling helpless. One of the main reasons his sickness was beginning to plague him tremendously in his adult life was because of what it did with his relationship. There was no woman who wanted him after he admitted he was a diabetic. For some reason, when they knew the truth, everything else they found good about him evaporated. Suddenly, how nice and caring he was didn't matter. How protective and supportive he was, didn't matter. How good he was in bed, didn't matter. All because he was 'sick.' Rosa was the only woman who didn't turn him away when he told her about why he had to keep poking himself with needles, and why he only ate at certain times of the day, and why he couldn't even find his sex drive when she was laying naked next to him.

Lucien angrily checked his sugar again, so he'd be able to know the amount of food he would eat. Just knowing that Rosa was willing to stick by his side knowing of his condition made Lucien feel lucky. Even though sometimes they didn't see eye to eye, and she was a brat when she didn't get what she wanted, she still committed herself to their relationship. And Lucien wasn't about to give that up. He already felt so depressed and nonexistent. But to give up the only woman that would accept him would make him sink even deeper into his darkness.

Chapter Three

"What the hell happened to you?" Irys knew her coworker and the woman who had kind of become her good friend would pin her with that question the moment Irys turned up to work at the large Spa. She was running a little bit late after taking care of her mother for the morning before the health aid came in.

"Sorry I'm late, I just had to make sure my mother was okay. Did Charles say anything?" Irys asked, speaking of their boss.

"Ain't nobody care about what Charles got to say. You're his best employee anyway."

"So what does that make you?" Irys grinned.

"Don't try to divert the conversation. Now tell Luna, what happened to your face."

"You know I really hate when you talk in third person like that." She rolled her eyes at Luna before continuing.

"I had a small incident with Derek, that's all."

"Small!" Luna shrieked. "Irys your mouth is swollen. Oh hell no! He fittin' to get his ass kicked, I don't know who he think he is." She rolled up her sleeves and began mumbling to herself. Irys grabbed her arm.

"Don't worry about it Luna. I took care of it." Irys reflected on how she whopped his ass.

"Oh shit," She said. "Is he in the hospital? Or is he…" She leaned close and whispered to Irys. "You need me to help you get rid of the body?"

"Luna!" Irys gasped. She pushed the woman away and began laughing. "You'd honestly offer to help me do that? To become an accomplice?"

"Shit of course I would. You know I'll have your back."

"Well don't worry. He's not dead. He's around somewhere I suppose."

"So I hoped you ended the relationship with that man. You can't be with someone who would hurt you like that."

"Yeah I know. But he's the only man that you know, I can be with."

"That's complete bullshit. And if he told you that, he's only hating." Irys smiled at her friend but she didn't say anything else. It was alright for Luna to say something like that. She was in perfect shape and she turned down advances from men all day long.

"We need to get to work," Irys said.

"Fine, deflect me for now. But we're gonna get to the bottom of why you keep yourself in a relationship that doesn't make you happy."

"Who says I wasn't happy?" Irys asked.

"Well, there's the fact that you dragged me to the sex store with you to get not one, but two vibrators, and one dildo. But besides that your eyes. They tell me you aren't happy." Irys had to break eye contact from her. She couldn't quite face the truth she knew Luna was speaking.

"You seem to know so much Luna," Irys said. "Maybe you should be a psychic instead of a masseuse," Irys chuckled.

"Fuck off," Luna smiled, as she walked away, heading to her first appointment. She envied the carefree nature of Luna. She really was Irys's only true friend and Irys needed that best friend advice right now but just the fact that she was thinking so heavily about the ultimatum Derek gave her, made Irys feel horrible. She shouldn't be thinking so much. But yet still, she was filled with confusion. At this point, all she could do was just work and forget her troubles until she had to deal with them later.

For her whole work shift, Irys didn't get any calls or texts from Derek. She figured that was a good thing because they both needed to cool off. Though any other woman would have immediately broken up with her man if he'd hit her the way Derek had hit Irys. But things were so much more complex. She wasn't entirely sure she could lose him just yet. She was indeed planning a future with him. Being married was something she always aspired to be. She just wanted to be a wife and a mother. Here was her chance at it. Just letting it go so easily wasn't in fact easy for her to do.

The moment she pulled up to the home, it was time for the health aide to head home. Irys hurried inside to thank the woman and take care of her mother. She was sleeping soundly after a round of medication for her ALS. Irys hated seeing the woman who was as full of life as she was growing up, be down and out for this incurable sickness. But while her mother continued to get weak, her attitude never died down.

"Oh, you're home," Derek said, walking up behind her. Irys turned to see him leaning in the entryway of the kitchen.

"Um yeah. It's seven. That's when I get home."

"Don't be a smart ass Irys," He said quietly. She fished under the cabinets for pots and looted through the fridge to make a quick dinner.

"Here to apologize?" Irys asked.

"Um, no," He said. "You hit me back too. I just need to know what you're going to do with that thing growing in you." Irys breathed in deep. She didn't miss how he refused to call what was growing inside her a baby.

"I don't see how I can just get rid of my baby," She admitted.

"And you do realize what I said right? That I wouldn't be with you if you were gonna be pregnant? I mean come on Irys at least lose some weight first before carrying a child, shit!" Irys slammed down the raw chicken in her hand.

"I'm tired of you cracking on my weight Derek. Because the last time I checked-"

"Helloooo, I'm here!" The sound of her sister's voice chimed through the house. Irys rolled her eyes and grunted. More trouble for her.

"I have arrived!" Rosa said, entering the kitchen. Irys looked at her sister. She was dressed expensively from head to toe and carrying an armful of shopping bags.

"Mom is sleeping," Irys said. "So please."

"Hey Rosa," Derek said smiling at her.

"At least someone appreciates my presence," Rosa said. "Hey Derek."

"Where you been all day?" Irys asked. "Thought you would have been here earlier to help take care of mom. You know that I am trying to make it so that we don't need that home aid anymore."

"Unlike you Irys, I have a life. And I told you already mom needs to be put in a home or something. I don't know why you bother."

"I bother because that's my mother you useless twat," Irys snapped getting angry. She and Rosa had two different fathers. Rosa's Hispanic dad, left her with long silky hair and an exotic look, while Irys looked the complete opposite, weight included. But ever since Rosa hooked up with some guy she'd been acting like she was better than everyone else. She refused to help with their ailing mother, and all she did was walk around like she was Kim K or something.

"Whatever Irys. Look, I bought you something." She set the bags down and rifled through one of them. She pulled out a large nightgown.

"Victoria secret was having a sale. And I don't know, maybe you can put it on for Derek one night," She said. Irys looked at the shapeless material. Yes, she was a big girl, but she wore lingerie. Sexy ones at that. And she felt as if Rosa did these things to her, just to screw with her, to press on the fact that Irys wasn't small.

"No thanks," Irys said simply. "And either way, Derek ain't getting none of these cookies so..."

"You shouldn't deny your man Irys. Anything he wants give it to him."

"Hear that?" Derek chimed in.

"Whatever," She mumbled. Suddenly not feeling like cooking, she put the chicken back into the fridge, washed her hands and left the kitchen.

"What's her problem?" Rosa asked.

"You know Irys. Always mad at something." Derek looked Rosa up and down. Man she was gorgeous. And dressed in a tight dress, Derek couldn't help but admire her body. When he first met Rosa, they'd had a one night stand. One night of pure bliss. Derek never forgot how this woman pushed him beyond the edges of pleasure. Only, when he went to get her back, he was cornered by her fat sister who seemed smitten with him. To Derek it seemed easy. The only way he could be close to Rosa, was to be close to Irys. And yes, he'd done it. He pretended that Irys meant something to him, only to have Rosa around him all the time, to perhaps one day convince her they belonged together. But he'd literally gotten lost with Irys. He actually had to 'date' her and have sex with her. And because of that, now she was pregnant and refusing to get rid of the thing.

"Why you looking at me like that Derek," Rosa teased.

"You know why," He said.

"You better behave," She smiled.

"How about a quickie," Derek said. "She won't come bothering us." Rosa sauntered over to him. She licked her lips and looked him up and down. She pressed her hand to his crotch where his manhood was hardening.

"Oh look at that," She said a small frown turning at her lips.

"All for you," He breathed. "Do you remember that night I fucked your brains out?" He said. "Let me do it again." Rosa tsked and backed up.

"We can't," she said. "And you know that."

"You know I'm gonna be here until you submit to me right?" Rosa only smiled and backed up. She was sexually frustrated by Lucien, but she refused to cheat on him with a man who wasn't matching in the same size department as Lucien. What was the point of cheating then, if she wasn't to get something better than what her man had to offer?

"You need to focus on your woman," She said. Derek's arousal wasn't going to go anywhere. It was primed and ready for release. He was frustrated he couldn't have Rosa, but he wasn't gonna stop. He knew how to get a woman.

"Speaking of her…" Derek said. "I want you to hear just what you've been missing." Rosa scoffed. She had already sampled Derek. She knew he was nothing compared to Lucien when it came to sex.

"Oh, show me what you got macho man," Rosa teased him. Only he took it very seriously.

"Listen," He said. Turning on his heels, he left the kitchen. Rosa wasn't about to let him get to her, but after standing in the kitchen alone for five minutes, she cursed under her breath and gave in.

Irys ignored the sound of the door creaking open. Fresh out of a shower, she was burning candles and ready to lay down with a good book. Even though she didn't pay attention, she knew it was Derek who entered.

"You know I love it when you burn some candles," He said. Irys ignored him. She snuggled deeper into the bed and opened her book.

"Come on babe," He said. Derek kicked off his shoes, and undressed. Still, Irys didn't look at him. That was fine. As long as he still had the image of Rosa imprinted on his brain, his boner was raving. And the fact that he knew she was listening to what he would do to Irys, empowered him. He snaked over to the bed and got in behind her.

Irys sucked in a deep breath when she felt his arousal embedded against her ass. How could she ignore him if he was blatantly hard? He rubbed up against her, reaching around her body to hold her close. He pressed his lips against her neck, kissing her softly.

"Are you serious right now?" Irys whispered. He ignored her and sucked on her skin, He rubbed her ass and grinded against her. Irys was ready to push him off until he began playing with her nipples. A soft moan escaped her mouth as she tried to move away from him.

"No," She groaned.

"Stop playing," He said. He snatched her book from her hands and flung it across the room. Spreading her wide ass, he tried to find her opening, but struggled. Not even bothering to continue trying to find her hole. He got up on his knees and tossed her large legs open. He stripped away at her underwear before bending her legs back to insert his straining arousal into her. Irys threw her head back and moaned as he entered her, slamming himself in all the way to the hilt. Derek hated Irys's weight, but he had to admit that she felt good as fuck. With his eyes closed he imagined he was fucking Rosa hard and deep, and the way Irys gripped him only made the fantasy more real.

Like a creep, Rosa leaned against the master bedroom door with her ear against the wood. Sure enough, Irys's moans permeated through the door and right to Rosa's ears. With it, she heard Derek grunting and groaning himself. She was intrigued by the sounds of sex, but she wasn't at all any more interested in Derek. All it did for her was make her crave Lucien even more. The headboard was slamming against the wall viciously as Derek's moans got louder and louder.

"You like it don't you!" He groaned. From her only time with him she knew he liked to amp himself up. And behind that would usually come his release. And with the loud shout of release and the headboard coming to a stop, she knew that's exactly what had happened. Rosa just giggled and walked away from the bedroom.

Irys took deep breaths as Derek rolled off her. He grunted in satisfaction and rested back in the bed. She looked over at him, and the bliss on his face was unmistakable. Have you ever felt like you were having sex with a person you knew for so long, but yet still it felt like you were with a stranger? Irys knew how Derek ticked. She knew what he liked and what he didn't. Maybe it could have been because of their argument this morning, or maybe not, but Irys didn't feel as if she was having sex with a man she knew. His thrusts were different, his eyes remained closed the whole time, and he grunted things under his breath that were seemingly out of character. It wasn't hard for Irys to notice these things because while the sex felt good, it just didn't feel *right*. There was no orgasm to blind herself to what was happening. So she noticed everything. And laying there, completely unsatisfied, she couldn't help but let those thoughts consume her. Sleeping with a man who'd just put their hands on her this morning and then allowing him to have sex with her at a moment of weakness made Irys feel horrible.

"Do you see," Derek breathed.

"See what?" Irys asked.

"What you stand to lose if you don't get that abortion." Irys was shocked.

"I can't even believe you," She whispered. Getting out of bed, she snatched up her clothing and went for another shower. She blew out her candles, her mood completely ruined. And if Derek was going to be breathing down her neck about this situation, then she did not want to be around him. After her shower, she dressed in a t-shirt that was large, but hugged her curves. Throwing on a pair of shorts, and her favorite fluffy slippers, she left the bedroom. Derek was passed out on the bed, drawing loud snores.

Irys thought Rosa would be gone, but she was in the kitchen looking through all the things she'd bought.

"Oh didn't think you'll be coming back out," She said. Irys only grunted. She sat across from her sister and looked at all the things she had. From jewelry, to makeup, lingerie and some clothing.

"Why do you buy all this stuff?" Irys asked her. "You have all these things already. But when I ask for help with mom, you act like you're broke." Rosa looked up at her sister.

"Because I am broke Irys. I don't work. All this is because my man takes care of me." She raised her brows.

"Are you his woman, or his daughter which one?"

"Irys please," Rosa scoffed. "It's not my fault that I have a man that likes to make sure I have all these things. If you wanted those things you should have gotten you a man that could do that for you."

"Yeah well getting a man for me has nothing to do with his money. I guess that's where me and you are different," Irys said.

"So what you look for in a man? His package? How he works between the sheets?"

"No," Irys said.

"Funny you should say that just coming back from getting some." Irys rolled her eyes. Her and her sister weren't close at all, and these conversations were never supportive like it should have been when you were speaking to your sister.

"That has nothing to do with anything right now."

"It's alright. Because there's no shame in my game. Not only does my man take care of me, he puts it down in the bedroom!!" She groaned. Irys just stared at her as she clearly wanted to gloat.

"He has a whole 10 inches of thick, pure pleasure girl! And when we get into it, lord we get into it." She batted her eyes.

"How is Derek?" She winked.

"Why do you always feel the need to do that?" Irys asked her.

"Do what?" Rosa asked innocently.

"Every time you come here you show off all this shit your man buys for you and then talk about how he's a sex god. And I don't know what for? Are you trying to make me jealous? Trying to prove you're better than me or something? I'm not sure. But that shit is getting tiring. Meanwhile, you could give a damn about our mother." This was why Rosa hated coming over here. Irys found any reason to pick at her. Sure enough she was jealous of Rosa's life, but that was not for Rosa to deal with. It wasn't her fault that Irys was miserable.

"Maybe for once you could actually be happy for me," Rosa said. "When you and Derek started dating and I was alone, I wasn't acting all jealous."

"I could care less about your relationship Rosa. I just care about the fact that I'm dealing with the burden of our mother when I have you."

"Because I told you to put her in a home. And you didn't. So, your burden." Irys sighed. She couldn't have this conversation anymore. She had never made dinner and she knew her mother would wake soon and she'd probably be hungry.

"Okay well, I'm gonna make mom some food. You're welcome to leave."

"Bitch," Rosa mumbled. "Not my fault your fat, and miserable." Irys just ignored her. Rosa had called her fat all throughout their childhood, into their teenage years, and now as adults. At first Irys used to break down in tears because she didn't understand how her sister could be that mean. But as she grew older, and began loving her body, she realized some people were just made to look different. So what, she wasn't skinny, she was curvaceous, loved to cook, loved to eat, and she wasn't embarrassed about her body. Rosa couldn't possibly understand how she could be happy about her body, but Irys left that alone. She didn't show any more emotion to being called fat. The first time she'd done that in a while was just this morning when the man she thought she loved made it known that no man would want her.

Rosa snatched all her things up and left the house in a fit. Irys just shook her head and continued cooking. She could care less about being called fat. But she knew at least one thing Rosa said was true. Honestly, Irys really and truly did feel miserable.

It was around 9 when she heard her mother calling for her. Irys was in the living room, continuing her book not wanting to be near Derek. She hurried off to her mother, making sure to bring the platter of food she'd made for her.

"Hi ma," Irys greeted. All that confusion and sadness Irys felt for the day seemingly dripped away when she saw her mother's bright eyes.

"Hi baby girl," She smiled speaking choppily from her illness. Irys put the platter down and helped her mother to sit up being careful not to rattle her aching bones.

"I know my baby girl made me an amazing dinner," She smiled weakly. Though she was so weak, Irys loved the fight she saw in her mother's eyes. It inspired Irys, and while Luna was her close friend, her mother was just as close too.

"You know I did," Irys smiled. She put the platter on the rolling table and brought it over to her mother. She sat next to the bed to help her mother eat. Though she was bed ridden most of the time, she still loved the sun and being outside. Her skin was still bright from all the time Irys took her for walks, and the aid let her bask in the sun. So while she was sick, their golden complexion still matched.

"So, did you and Derek make up from this morning? Or what?"

"No we really didn't make up. Things aren't that good with us, I'll be honest."

"When did you figure that out?" She asked.

"This morning in fact. You know. I always thought we were okay. But today he just said something to me that I can't let go. And I don't see how I could ever see him the same again?"

"Clue me in dear, I'd love to know." She took her mother's comforting hand.

"Mom, I-I just found out I'm pregnant." Her mother gasped and clasped her hands over her mouth.

"Oh my goodness that's so great. You know I've wanted to see grandkids before I left this earth. And your sister, well your sister is a little bit too selfish for kids right now, ain't she?" Irys managed to chuckle at the face her mother made.

"Well yes that is most certainly true. See, I was so happy this morning. I thought Derek would be too. But ma, he told me that if I wanted him to stay in my life then I needed to get rid of the baby."

"That son of a bitch!" She snapped weakly. "Please tell me you did not listen to him!"

"No! I didn't listen. But for a moment I was caught in this web of weakness. He told me that with my weight no one would ever want me. He's the only man that gave me a chance and if I wanted to be in a relationship it would never happen again if I let him go."

"Now let me ask you something," She began firmly. "Are you ashamed of your body?" Irys looked away from her sparking eyes.

"No. Look at me. Are you ashamed of your body?" Irys looked at her.

"I'm not ashamed no. I love my body and I'm confident about it."

"Exactly. There are a million men out there Irys. And just because Derek won't want you, doesn't mean no one else will. Fact of the matter is, you love yourself, and you love your body. Why would you do something as hateful as an abortion to suit a man who clearly doesn't appreciate or love you enough in the first place? Forget him Irys. He ain't shit anyway." Irys snickered but she couldn't hold in her laughter.

"Now all of a sudden he ain't shit," She laughed.

"Hell yeah. And I see the way your mouth looked this morning, I just hoped all that commotion was you fucking him up. I know I ain't raise no punching bag."

"Oh trust I got him good. Luna thought I would need help burying his body," Irys laughed.

"You see her. I like her. Clearly she knows what's up. And if I wasn't so sick, oh I would have-"

"You would have what?" Irys chuckled at her mother. "Calm your old behind down." Kendra Black laughed so hard tears sprung from her eyes. She knew well her condition wasn't improving. But she was happy to go any day because she was fully content in the way she was able to connect with her daughter. She loved both Irys and Rosa, but they were two completely different women and she knew she'd never be able to connect with Rosa like she did with Irys. She was satisfied because she would always attempt and make sure she spoke with Rosa to build any connection and to show that she loved that woman. But if Rosa refused her advances, there was not much else Kendra could do.

"But in all seriousness," Kendra said. "When I was with Rosa's father he made it seem like he was the best man in the world. When he left me and Rosa high and dry I truly did believe I lost the best thing to happen to me. But then I met your father Irys. He was truly the love of my life. And he wasn't perfect no. But I wouldn't trade him for any other man. That's a complete fact. He showed me true love. And now I'm just sitting here waiting to join him in the afterlife. So seriously, don't take what Derek says to heart. If he's not the one for you, there's always going to be someone else who just might be the one." Irys took her mother's words seriously. She knew for certain what would be her next move.

"He's actually not that great in bed," Irys admitted. Kendra laughed.

"If you still need a vibrator after the fact, just throw the whole man away." Irys and Kendra both laughed with each other. After having her dinner, Irys cleared her plates away then settled into bed next to her mother where they talked and joked with each other until the both of them fell asleep.

Chapter Four

Lucien's watched beeped repeatedly just at the sun began to set. He looked at the time, not even realizing it was already past seven. The ground work for his restaurant was just about complete, and today the place had retrieved its last coat of paint. Shipment of all his cooking equipment had arrived and he'd been sorting through everything all day. He'd hired line cooks, sous chefs, and a restaurant manager who was in charge of hiring servers, and hosts. Things were coming together nicely, and the excitement of finally being able to open his own restaurant was finally coming to fruition. The hard part was going to be trying to manage his diabetes while he was behind the line. The kitchen itself was open to the actual dining room so the customers would be able to see him actually cooking and dressing their food before it got to them. It was a part of the eating experience that he wanted all his diners to have.

"Okay guys, thanks for coming in," Lucien said, pressing the button on his watch to get his alarm to go off. His line cooks and sous chefs had been vital in helping him set up the kitchen, and he appreciated them coming to help. In fact, there was a lot of people that came to help. Except his own girlfriend who didn't respond to any of his messages. Lucien was not a controlling, or possessive man. He phoned and sent his girlfriend texts but if she didn't answer, he wasn't about to lose his mind and call her repeatedly. Whenever she got back to him, they'd speak. It wasn't for lack of concern, it was just that Lucien wasn't going to be overbearing. And getting him angry wasn't an easy feat. Nowadays the only thing that truly upset him was when his sugar was out of control. And at that point, his wavering sugar would dictate his emotions.

Shaking hands with all his cooks, he said his goodbyes and watched them leave. Just before he was going to close the doors and lock himself inside, he saw his sister running across the street trying to catch him before he locked the doors. He smiled at the face she was making. She looked as if she was running a 10k mile race instead of just crossing one busy street.

"Sorry I'm late," She breathed, coming to a stop in front of the doors. Lucien moved to the side as she came in. She bent over with her hands on her knees.

"Whew!" She gasped. "Man I am tired as hell."

"Oh shut up," Lucien teased. "You work around the damn corner."

"Lucy don't play with me." Lucien cut his eyes at her. She knew she hated to be called Lucy. But that was his big sister. She did shit to annoy him just because she could.

"How did it go today?" She asked.

"It went well actually I just-" His watch began beeping again. "Let's go to the office, I need to eat something," He said. Locking up the doors, Lucien led the way back to his office. Once inside, he began heating up food for the both of them.

"You didn't even check your sugar," She said.

"I don't need to. I just know its low." She gave him a saddened look and it always broke his heart.

"Luna please don't do that," He said. "You're my big sister. Be strong for me, not upset."

"I just hate this, that's all." She ran her hands through his hair like he was ten again.

They sat around his desk once the food was warm and had dinner together. Most nights no matter where, Luna always wanted to have dinner with him. She said it was because she just wanted to spend time with him, but Lucien knew it was because she wanted to check on him. When he was away for his cooking, she positively went mad at not having him around.

"So, I have good news," She smiled.

"Yeah?"

"I finished the hiring of the servers. They are elite and professional. Plus, I ordered all the uniforms, AND I hired a staffing supervisor to just watch over the servers. The supervisor will be the link between the servers and us."

"Wow Luna, you're amazing," Lucien said, taking the folder she handed him. He looked through it, seeing pictures and information on all the servers.

"I'll help you set up all their information in the system for direct deposit, and then for them to be able to clock in and out for their shifts." Lucien was a little wary of her being his manager at first, but this restaurant meant just as much to her as it did to Lucien, because she knew this was his childhood dream.

"Thanks for doing this for me sis," He said.

"Don't even mention it. If I wasn't here who knows how shit would play out. Seen as your little girlfriend ain't been around yet."

"Here we go," Lucien rolled his eyes.

"I'm serious little bro! Since you bought the building and started working she ain't been helping you do shit but spend your money."

"Don't all women just spend money?" He teased.

"I'm not playing around Lucien. I don't like that little girl."

"First off, you never like any of my girlfriends. And second, we're only three years apart which means she's not that little because I'm not that little."

"Mom and dad invested this money for you to open this restaurant. They worked hard to see to it that you'd be able to do all the things you want. You and me both. I haven't opened up my spa yet but I'm working on it. You worked hard for this Lucien, and you just give the money our parents work hard for, to a woman that doesn't even come down here to help you in the slightest." Lucien pushed his food away.

"So I guess this would be the wrong time to tell you I want to marry her." Luna gasped.

"You what?"

"I was going to propose to her." Luna shook her head.

"Nope, no. I don't think so."

"Luna she's-"

"NO Lucien!" She shouted. "She may be your little fuck toy, and she may be what you want now. But she's not wife material." Lucien crossed his arms. He knew his sister would not approve.

"Not all women can be like you Luna," He said. Besides his mother, Luna was one of the most amazing woman he knew. She was the kind, but whacky in her sense of humor and she loved to have fun. He would love to have the approval of his sister because she was the only person he had now.

"You're right," She said. "There is no woman like me. Luna Ray is one of a kind. But that doesn't mean you settle for any little thing that comes your way and shakes her little butt at you." Lucien snickered

"That's not how it is," He smiled.

"Why do you think you have to marry this girl?" Luna asked.

"Because I don't want to lose her. In my condition, who's to say that I'll get another chance to share my life with a woman?"

"Oh please! You act like it's the apocalypse or something. And you're only 30 Lucien. Not 55 and on your last leg looking for love. There's plenty of time to find the right woman. That doesn't mean you should be selling yourself short on the women you choose to be laid up with. And I swear Lucien Ray you betta had been strapping up when you fooling around with that chick because if she turns up pregnant I don't know what I'm gonna do with you." Lucien laughed out loud this time. He pulled out his desk drawer to get out his test strips and his meter.

"All you'd have to do is just be an aunt simple."

"Lucien please don't give me a heart attack," She gasped. He was grateful for the laughter as he checked his sugar.

"Relax," He laughed. "I wear protection." Luna held her chest as if she'd almost truly had a heart attack.

"Thank the lord," She breathed.

"Come on. Don't be a drama queen." She made a face before smiling at him.

"Are you okay?" She asked once he began putting his meter away.

"Yes I'm all good. Come on, let me take you home."

"My knight in shining armor," She teased. Lucien stood and cleaned up their dinner. Once it was all done, he wrapped his arm around his sister's shoulder and walked with her out of his restaurant.

Lucien still hadn't heard from Rosa, but the moment he pulled up to his home he saw her car parked out front. All the lights were off in the house as far as he could tell. It was normally way too early for her to be going to bed but perhaps she was tired from all that damn shopping she was doing. Thinking of that, he knew his sister was right. Lucien was going to have to put that woman on a stricter spending regimen. If they could come to a compromise then it would ensure that she wouldn't be too upset at him.

Entering the dark house, he looked through the mail left on the mantle in the foyer. He was surprised when Salsa didn't come running to meet him. No matter what she was doing, she didn't miss when he got home. Lucien entered the kitchen and flipped on the light. Her food and water bowl were full. In fact, it looked just as it did when Lucien filled it before he left. That alarmed him.

"Salsa!" He called out for her. He didn't hear her paws on the floor, but instead he only heard whimpering. Following the sounds, he came to the patio doors. Sure enough, Salsa was outside tapping at the door weakly with her paws. When she saw Lucien, her tail wagged harder as she barked loudly.

"What are you doing out here?" He asked opening the door for her. If he wasn't home, he didn't leave her outside, especially with the heat of the summer. She jumped up onto him, licking at his arms and his face. Lucien scratched behind her ears, petting her. She gave his body a good sniff, and if checking his sugar for him before she padded away and hurried to her food. He watched as she ate hungrily, and lapped up water. With a grunt, Lucien left the kitchen and headed straight for his bedroom. The only person who could have locked her outside was Rosa. He entered the room and stopped in his tracks. The lights were off, but the room was lit with candles. Rosa was laying in the middle of the bed wearing a red teddy. She was sipping on a glass of champagne.

"I was waiting for you," She said seductively. Lucien's brain temporarily fizzled. He had to think hard about what he initially was going to say to her in the first place. He shook his head.

"Hey," he greeted. She took a long drink of the champagne. "Did you lock Salsa out?" He asked. Her facial expression dropped.

"So I'm here practically naked, and with candles burning, lights out, and you got the nerve to ask me about a dog?" she asked.

"It would seem as if that's what I'm doing ain't it?" he asked.

"Well if you want to know, I was trying to prepare all this for you, and the damn dog wouldn't leave me alone, so I put her outside to play."

"Don't do that again okay?"

"Are you going to get in bed with me and give me some loving or you just gonna stand there and scold me over your pet?" she asked annoyed.

"I need to take a shower," Lucien said. "I thought you were going to come down to the restaurant," He said as he undressed.

"I got tied up with my mother, and then I just came home. Can you get in the shower please? I'm horny as hell. You owe me from this morning."

"I know Rosa. I know." He was healthy enough to please his woman, but her lack of care she was displaying was doing its job at turning him off. He took a long hot shower, cleaning both his body and his mind. He was thinking too much for his own good and he needed to cut it out.

"Just live in the moment Lucien. Not today, not tomorrow. Just now." Turning off the shower, he stepped out of the stall and gave himself a quick wipe down. Without even putting on underwear, or covering himself, Lucien headed straight back for the room. Rosa sat up, gawking at his nakedness.

"This what you wanted right?" he asked. She swallowed and nodded. Grabbing a square package of protection from his night table drawer, he joined her on the bed. Splitting open her legs, he only had to get one look at her pretty insides before he was hard, and all his negative thoughts disappeared.

But when he entered her body, sharing this form of intimacy with her, he felt completely lucky to be able to share this kind of thing with a woman like her. Having Rosa was his way to be normal. To not be a man with his sickness. To not have to prick his fingers ten plus times a day, and inject needles into his body. Her loud moans in his ears, and her nails embedded in his back was a reminder of what he could stand to have with this woman forever.

****

Irys was jamming to 'Fool in Love', by Tina Turner as she was cleaning her bedroom. The morning sun shone through her room as she happily packed Derek's shit. When she awoke that morning he wasn't in bed with her. Like the diligent girlfriend she was, she phoned him to make sure he was alright. And you know what he said?

"Why you always breathing down my neck Irys? Go have a snack and leave me the hell alone." Then he'd hung up in her ear. After that talk with her mother, she realized she didn't have to put up with his shit. The only thing she needed to take care of was her mother, and her growing baby. Not some grown ass man who didn't realize how good he had it. So she made it her mission that morning to pack up all his things and put his ass out. Unlike what he thought about her being unhappy and alone if he ever left, Irys felt content and happy. It gave her joy to take over her life and not let him control it with his negative thoughts. It did hurt her that he would deny their baby and say those mean words to her, but it was sort of a blessing. Now she knew if he cared about her at all, he could never ask her to abort something they created. And then he would never tell her that she would have nothing if he left. But he was wrong. Irys would have her sanity, and she'd have her baby.

"What the hell is going on?" A large smile came to her face when she heard Derek's shout. Fixing herself up, she went downstairs to see him in the living room gawking at his things in the corner of the room packed up.

"Hey," She smiled.

"Irys what you doing?" He asked.

"What I should have done a little bit sooner. I'm keeping my baby so…I took the liberty of packing all your things for you. I expect you to be gone by the time I get home from work tonight."

"Excuse me?!" He shouted.

"I'm breaking up with you," She said.

"Oh hell no," He snapped. "Your fat ass does not break up with me. Who do you think you are?"

"I think I'm the woman that's been taking care of your ass. And I think I'm the woman that's tired of it."

"Look, I don't care if you break up with me or not. I don't wanna stay with your fat ass anyway. But you had better get rid of that baby. I will not-"

"You will not what?" She snapped. "You can't do shit! So there's all your stuff. Get the hell out of my house or I'm calling the cops. You choose." Anger getting the best of him, he reached out and pushed her hard. Irys fell back against the couch. She was ready to defend herself but he didn't attack further. He simply slid past her and grabbed as much of this things as he could and left the room. Gulping, she tried to catch her breath and calm her racing heart. She kept her guard up since he came back into the house to take more of this things. On his third trip he stopped and glared at her.

"Good luck ever finding a man who'd want your fat ass," He snapped. Irys just crossed her arms.

"Just fuck off," She retorted. Seeing he wasn't going to make her weak, Derek just grunted.

"I'll be back for the rest of my shit another time," He said.

"See ya," She said. She pointed to the door. Seeing that shit eating grin on her face was pissing Derek off. Sure, he didn't want to be with her but he didn't want that fucking kid around. She followed behind him to the front door. Derek could feel her body heat close behind him.

"You won't get rid of that thing? I'm only asking you one more time," He said.

"No I'm not," She said firmly. Seeing no other way out of it, Derek stopped in his tracks. He thrust his elbow back hard, hitting her in the stomach. She let out an 'oomph' and fell to the ground. She gripped her stomach as the pain of the hit resonated.

"Hopefully that'll do the trick," He mumbled looking down at her. Irys just stared up at him holding her stomach. His eyes were emotionless as he left her laying on the ground, slamming the door behind him.

Chapter Five

Rosa sat in the main dining area of Lucien's restaurant while he and his chefs were sitting around another table going over the menu. The place was pretty much done up and it would be ready for the grand opening in a month. So ready in fact that Rosa didn't even know why she was needed here. Lucien had barely paid her any attention, but he did ask her to come. Since he'd given her multiple orgasms the night before Rosa was obliging him by showing up with him. Not like she had anything else to do. She wasn't staying at home to cook or clean, and she didn't have a job. None of her friends were free either, so this was her only choice. But she didn't think she was about to be here all damn day with him. They'd arrive at 10 in the morning, and now going on seven they were still here.

"Lucien...." Rosa groaned. He looked up from his papers and looked over at her. "I'm bored."

"Well you're always on your phone. Why don't you set up social media accounts for the restaurant?"

"Which social media?" she asked. Lucien shrugged.

"All of them." Rosa grunted, but she pulled out her phone to begin the task. But after setting up a Facebook, she was bored again.

"I don't wanna do this," She said. "I'm bored again."

"Then I don't know what you want me to do," Lucien said, agitation rising in his voice.

"I know you don't have an attitude with me after I-"

"Lucy I'm here!" Rosa scoffed when she heard Luna's voice at the front door of the restaurant. Lucien got up promptly to let her in.

"Just my fucking luck," Rosa whispered. She hated that girl. With a passion. She watched as Lucien let Luna in, but she didn't come in alone. Behind her there were about ten people, a mix of both male and female.

"Hey sis," Lucien greeted hugging her briefly. She was all smiles until she saw Rosa sitting there. She rolled her eyes but didn't say anything.

"These are ten of the servers I hired for you Lucien, plus the supervisor. You'll be able to meet the other ten workers tomorrow." Lucien greeted each server with a shake and learning their names, before introducing the servers to the kitchen staff.

"Let's go for a tour," Lucien suggested. The servers were excited about the start of a new restaurant, and Lucien's place wouldn't work if he didn't have staff willing and ready to perform. He couldn't run a restaurant by himself. So he gratefully showed them around. He had cooked a large meal for the kitchen staff for working the day, and there was plenty left, so he invited the servers to stay and eat after the tour.

"They seem real professional," Lucien said to his sister as the servers were talking amongst themselves while enjoying their food.

"You know I only bring the best for my brother," She said. "And get this. The supervisor is trained in hospitality so he will be hosting a training session before the opening to make sure everyone knows the right way to do shit."

"Honestly I don't know what I'd do without you," Lucien said.

"Yeah me either. Since your woman only sits there looking like Dumbo." Lucien slapped his forehead. He knew this was coming pretty soon.

"If you got something to say, say it to my face," Rosa snapped.

"Oh you must have thought I was scared of your ass-" Luna was ready to lunge for Rosa, but Lucien grabbed her by the elbow and held her at bay.

"Come on Lu, not in front of the workers." Luna snatched her elbow from his grasp. She straightened her shirt and walked away. Lucien let out a deep breath, happy he avoided that collision. But when all the workers went home, leaving the three of them there, tension was running high.

"Are you ready to go home yet?" Rosa asked. The three of them were sitting at a table in the dining room together. While he and Luna kept planning, Rosa showed no interest. It was a little annoying if he was honest. But Luna was on it before he could answer.

"We're working," She snapped. "If you don't want to participate you can walk your ass home." Rosa gasped but she didn't respond.

"What were you saying before?" Luna asked Lucien.

"Do you think I need a host?" He asked his sister. "We did want people to make reservations you know. So we need a host perhaps?"

"Oh my god yes. I can start looking for one." Luna cut her eyes to Rosa. "Or maybe someone can step up and take the position," She said.

"The hell you looking at me for?" Rosa asked.

"What is the point of you being here?" Luna asked her. "In all seriousness."

"I don't see why I have to explain myself to you."

"Okay, let me put it this way. My brother told me he was opening up a restaurant. So because I love him, and I want to see him succeed, I'm doing everything I can to help him out. That's why I accepted his offer to be his manager. I've hired all these people to make this restaurant work. He has a perfectly capable and might I add, jobless girlfriend who's actually smart enough to be a hostess. Why aren't you volunteering to help him out?"

"This whole restaurant is his thing. I don't care about you being miss goody and helping him out. Just because he's doing this shit doesn't mean I have to be part of it." Luna couldn't believe this. And this was the woman his brother wanted to marry? Oh hell no.

"You're out of your mind," Luna said. "This is his life. So if you're in it, you need to at least care that he's doing this."

"What I do and don't do is none of your business Luna. And as mad as you may be about me and Lucien, I'm the one laying with him at night. Not you. This will be my last time telling you to butt out of our relationship before I remove you from the equation permanently."

"Hey!" Lucien said cutting into their banter. "Rosa don't ever talk like that about my sister," He ordered his woman. There was many things she could easily get away with, but talking to Luna like she lost her mind; Lucien wasn't going to let that go.

"Hold up. She gets to talk to me however and you say nothing. But I defend myself and you ready to come at me?"

"She's not threatening you Rosa. And you know how I am when it comes to her. Ya'll can argue all you want but she never crosses the line. You always do."

"I just don't get why I'm being ganged up on. This restaurant has nothing to do with me."

"It has something to do with you when you're out spending his fucking money though," Luna responded. She was seriously irritated with this clueless woman.

"Lu," Lucien whispered, trying to get his sister to relax. "If I won't allow her to talk to you in a certain way then you can't talk to her in a certain way either. The both of you need to respect each other."

"Some things need to be said Lucien. She wants to spend all your money but don't want to be a part of how you make that money in the first place."

"I've had enough," Rosa snapped. "You're always ready to pick a fight when you see me and I know why. No matter what you do Luna, you'll never get rid of me. Lucien will never leave me and you're jealous of that. Why don't you just stay out of our business and worry about your own man? Oh wait, I forgot that's because you don't have one. And because you can't get one to take care of you like Lucien takes care of me, you're trying to ruin what me and him have. So get a life and maybe you'll find a fucking man that wants your plain Jane ass."

Lucien didn't know his sister was that fast. The second Rosa shut her mouth, Luna dove out of her chair, tackling Rosa to the ground. Lucien had reached for her but like butter she slipped out of his fingers. She only managed to land one punch before Lucien grabbed her, pulling her off of Rosa who was just lying there trying to cover her face.

"Put me down!" She snapped. Lucien held onto her writhing body, taking her clear across the room in case she decided to jump Rosa again.

"I said put me down!" Lucien let her go and stood in her way.

"You need to calm down Lu," He said.

"You gonna let her say that to me?" Luna asked.

"No Lu, but you can't go attacking my girlfriend."

"Girlfriend? You call that a girlfriend Lucien? So quick to spend your money but not quick to support your dreams?"

"You know that it's more-"

"It's nothing," Luna snapped. "And imma tell you the truth Lucien. I'm not gonna sit around and watch this woman suck you dry. So if you wanna be with her, that's fine by me. But I won't be sticking around no more."

"So what are you tryna say? You realize that we only have each other right? You can't let one woman come between us."

"I'm not doing anything," She said. "You're doing it all yourself." She pushed past him angrily. Rosa was sitting in her chair again, holding her jaw. Luna just grabbed up her purse and stormed out of the restaurant. Lucien cursed under his breath and looked at his woman.

"Is that all?" She asked. "She fucking hit me Lucien!"

"Well if you would have shut your big mouth then she wouldn't have had to hit you. I can't defend you Rosa if you act like that."

"You know Luna hasn't liked me since day one. She's always trying to pick a fight with me."

"What do you expect? When you say things like you don't care about me or my business, how do you think my family would react?"

"Forcing me to be in this business is not right Lucien. Just because it's your dream doesn't mean it's mine. You don't see the wives of doctors becoming doctors just because their husbands are."

"No one wants you to become a chef Rosa. We're just asking you to care a little."

"Can we go home now?" She asked. "I'm sick of this shit."

"Yeah sure."

Lucien locked up the place, and led the way out. This whole argument put things in a new light for him. He could understand where Rosa didn't want to be in the restaurant today because she was bored, but not caring at all about this place or his dreams cut like a knife. And because of all of this Luna was mad at him. She was right. How could Lucien propose to a woman who wasn't willing to care about what he wanted to do? Being married meant they would share more than just the same last name. But now, Lucien was having second thoughts. He couldn't go through with something that would cost him his sister.

"You're going to have to apologize to her," Lucien said to Rosa as they drove.

"I ain't doing shit," She snapped. "Got some nerve telling me I gotta apologize after that bitch-" Lucien swerved the car to the side. He veered off from traffic and pulled up to a curb harshly. He shoved the car in park.

"What the hell are you doing?" Rosa gasped. Lucien stared at her.

"Don't you ever, for as long as you're in my life, ever call my sister a bitch."

"But she-"

"No. I don't give a fuck what she does Rosa. It's not your place, or your right to call her that. And I will not tolerate it." Seeing she lost the battle, Rosa just turned and crossed her arms.

"Like I said, you're gonna fucking apologize to her and the two of you are going to talk like ya'll have sense."

"Whatever," She huffed. Lucien shook his head before putting the car back in drive and peeling off.

"I just hope you know that it's me you laid up with and not her. She shouldn't have a say in our relationship and that's what I'm not going to tolerate," she added. Lucien didn't answer her. He couldn't deal with any of this anymore. Luna was going to be in his life. That was a given. But while he wanted Rosa in his life he wasn't going to sacrifice his only living relative for a woman that was starting to show him she really only cared for herself.

****

Irys tossed and turned all night, unable to be comfortable enough for sleep waking up feeling just as tired as she did when she laid down for bed. For the past couple of days, her nights had been restless because she was worried over the hit Derek had given her to her stomach. She was paranoid so much that she'd taken multiple pregnancy tests again. To her relief they all came back still positive. She knew she was psyching herself out but she couldn't help but worry.

Now as she was getting ready for work, she was trying to put makeup on to cover her bags. Taking a look at her belly she smiled and convinced herself that Derek's actions didn't harm her in any way. Before leaving for work, she cooked breakfast for her mother, and they both ate watching TV. Afterwards, Irys left her with the aide. Though she was worried about her pregnancy, Irys was happy with her new single life. Nothing really changed except the fact that she didn't have an annoying man at her side. And now she could focus on taking care of her mother and her growing baby.

She walked into work feeling energized despite the fact that she hadn't gotten a good sleep the night before. But work always seemed to cheer her up. Plus, she loved seeing Luna every day. Only today, the woman was at the front desk fuming. She was filing away folders and getting the place ready for opening.

"Hey," Irys greeted, not sure how to approach the woman just yet. Luan slammed down the folder she was holding.

"Hey," She responded dully.

"What happened?" Irys asked. She shook her head.

"I had an argument with my brother's girlfriend a couple days ago. He's been trying to call me and get me to meet up with them and talk, but honestly I just can't." She rubbed her temples.

"Does that make me a bad sister?"

"Come." Irys took her hand and led her over to the chairs where the customers sat. She held Luna's hand.

"Is his girlfriend arrogant and hard to deal with?" She asked.

"She's more than that," Luna said. "And you know I love Lucien like nothing else, but I can't be around that annoying little twit."

"I know it's hard but that's your brother Luna. He wants you to be in his life. You can't make him choose between you and his girlfriend."

"Why couldn't he choose someone that I would approve of?" She questioned.

"Because that's the way life is," Irys laughed. "And speaking of, guess who's a single bitch now." Luna gasped.

"Finally! Now we can do single shit together and I won't feel left out."

"Yes," Irys laughed. She didn't want to let out any news of her pregnancy until her 8 or 12 week mark.

"And even though I'm mad at him, I can't miss the grand opening of Lucien's restaurant. And you know you're coming with me," Luna said. "It's in a couple weeks."

"Okay you know I'm down. I haven't even met Mr. Lucien yet either."

"Just promise me if his bimbo girlfriend starts with me, you'll have my back. Because I just cannot deal with her."

"I always have your back Luna. No worries."

With that conversation, they were both ready to work for the day. Luna noticed the change in Irys. While she didn't seem completely happy with her breakup, she did look way better than she did before. In time she would only get better. The first customers came in, a couple and Luna went to greet them promptly.

"No English…Italian," The olive colored woman said. Luna got that she was trying to say she only spoke Italian. It wasn't strange they received customers like this because of the high tourism, and coming to the spa was one of the many things they did.

"Oh um-" Luna was about to get her boss when Irys intervened.

"Ciao!" Luna's mouth fell open as Irys continued speaking Italian with the couple and guiding them through their options for massages and facials. After situating them, she led them to the back and gave them a room.

"Okay, so Mrs. Bagatelle wants a facial and a hot stone massage and Mr. Bagatelle will have the same thing."

"Wait hold up. You speak Italian?" Luna asked her.

"Um yeah," Irys said.

"Since when?!"

"College," Irys laughed.

"Anything else I should know?" Luna asked. Irys shrugged.

"Um, I can speak French, and Spanish, a little bit of mandarin, haven't perfected it, but it's in the works. Come on let's get to work." Luna just stared after her friend. She knew Irys was smart, but she didn't know the woman was carrying language skills. When Luna thought about it she realized that Irys and Lucien were kind of the same. The only person she knew that spoke all those languages was her brother. Maybe now it was obvious why she and Irys became close so quickly. Luna was happy that a woman as smart as her wasn't being held down by a toxic relationship anymore. And while Irys thought her weight played a role in her relationships, Luna knew that any man would be proud to have a smart woman like that at their side, and soon Irys would find the perfect man for her.

Chapter Six

Lucien felt Salsa nipping at his fingers that were hung over the edge of the bed. When that didn't catch his attention enough, she rose up on her back legs and used her teeth to pull at the sleeve of his t-shirt before letting out a loud bark. Rosa shot up from her slumber.

"Fuck!" She shouted. "Lucien get your damn dog!" Lucien got up slowly, rubbing his eyes.

"Relax," He said lowly. He knew his sugar was low because he felt weak and he hadn't had any dinner before going to bed.

"I swear, you and this dog get on my nerves," She huffed. Salsa jumped on top of the bed. "Oh no, get down," Rosa ordered. Salsa bared her teeth and growled at Rosa.

"Salsa no," Lucien ordered. "Come girl." Lucien got out of bed so Salsa would follow him. But she was still growling at Rosa. She probably wasn't too fond of her anymore since Rosa locked her out of the house.

"Let me ask you something," Lucien said to Rosa.

"Get your dog away from me first," She said, visibly scared. Lucien whistled getting Salsa's attention. She hopped over to Lucien, jumping down from the bed.

"What?" Rosa asked. Lucien looked at his watch.

"It's three in the morning. What if I went comatose and Salsa was barking to wake you up to alarm you that I needed help. What would you do? Actually check on me or just run her away or lock her out?"

"Why are you asking me this?" She questioned.

"Because each time Salsa comes in here and barks you just get mad. You never ask me if I'm okay, or wonder why she's barking."

"You seem pretty fine to me," Rosa snapped. "Don't tell me this is going to be another argument like we had about your restaurant. Your situation has got nothing to do with me okay?" Lucien's brows raised.

"Nothing to do with you?" He questioned.

"Yes. That's what I said. Now I would like to get my beauty sleep." Lucien just hummed then turned and left the bedroom with Salsa at his side. Great. His girlfriend didn't care if he went comatose with his diabetes or not. She just cared about her beauty sleep. Shaking his head, he made himself a quick sandwich then went to sit in the living room to find something to watch on TV. Luna hadn't said much to him despite his efforts to have her and Rosa talk things out. He figured she needed a couple days to get over what happened in the first place and cool down. Unlike him, Luna could get hot real quick and she did not play games. And when it came to him, she would not tolerate a whole bunch of mess. But now Lucien was feeling like an idiot for admitting he wanted to marry a woman that was beginning to show him she was having a tough time caring about anyone but herself. He didn't even go back to bed. He spread out on the living room couch with Salsa at his feet. She didn't fuss at him, so he concluded his sugar was at a normal, and that was enough to get him to go back to sleep.

The repetitive ringing of the doorbell had his eyes popping open. This time, the sun was well out and shining bright through the house. Lucien fell out of the couch, falling on his face.

"Ouch," He groaned as he got up slowly. He rubbed his nose and headed for the front door. Curse words were on the tip of his tongue, ready to lash out at whoever was at his door. Only the words didn't quite leave his mouth when he saw his sister standing there with bags of groceries and two cups of coffee.

"Good morning," She greeted. Usually he'd chew her out for showing up this early on a Saturday, but being how they'd last left off wasn't good, Lucien was happy to see her.

"Surprised to see you here," He said opening the door wider.

"Sure," She winked at him. "I'm still mad at both you and that chick but I'm tryna be the bigger person. So here I am. I know you hate takeout, so I just brought groceries and I'm starving. When was the last time you actually made me a meal?"

"Two weeks ago," He supplied. She stuck her tongue out at him not expecting him to know when he'd actually cooked for her. He took the bags from her and led the way to the kitchen. Salsa came bounding in, bum rushing Luna and taking her down. Luna laughed and hugged the dog, petting her viciously.

"How's my Salsa!" She greeted. Lucien rolled his eyes. The only reason his dog was named Salsa and not something like Hunter, or Onyx, was because his sister was the one to pick out the dog who'd already had on a dog tag at the shelter with the name Salsa. So instead of changing it, they'd kept it. Lucien had tried ditching the dog with his sister, but somehow whenever it was time for him to go home, Salsa followed him unwilling to stay at Luna's house without him.

"What you want me to make Lu?" Lucien asked her.

"Chocolate chip pancakes, with whip cream. Very simple for you. You can whip that up in like three seconds."

"You are right my dear," He said, unpacking the groceries.

"That woman of yours isn't awake yet?" Luna asked.

"No not yet. I was low at like 3am, Salsa woke us both up. I don't think she was too pleased."

"She'll get over it. Or would she rather wake up next to your dead body?"

"Don't be so dramatic Luna."

Lucien was halfway through breakfast when he heart Rosa coming into the kitchen. She was dragging her feet in those slippers she always wore.

"First the dog, and now you have company at the crack of dawn," She said as she entered the kitchen. But when she saw Luna her facial expression got hard.

"What are you here for?" She asked Luna.

"He's my brother. I can show up when I feel like it."

"Actually no you can't. I'm the woman of the house. I need to know when he's having company and I need to be okay with it. I'm not okay with you being in our space."

"Rosa," Lucien warned. "Be respectful."

"Have a seat Rosa and enjoy breakfast with us," Luna said. She was being nice, but Lucien knew it was only to tease her. Rosa sat down and proceed to be quiet as she ate. It felt odd to be having breakfast with two women Lucien knew hated each other. But as long as they weren't fighting he wasn't going to say a thing.

"What are you doing today?" Rosa asked him.

"Restaurant work," he answered.

"Well if she ever leaves I'd like to make love to you," She said.

"Ew," Luna gagged.

"Then I'm gonna go and see my mom and get my nails done. So I'll need some money."

"He doesn't have any money," Luna spoke up. "So no nails for you."

"How do you know what he has and what he doesn't?" Rosa asked. "Because last I checked I was the one fucking him. And not you."

"Look you gold-"

"How much is it?" Lucien interrupted. The last thing he wanted was an argument. He couldn't take it anymore.

"200," She said.

"200 dollars to get your nails done?" He questioned. Rosa didn't answer. "I'm only giving you 50. It's in my wallet," He said.

"Fine," She huffed. She left the kitchen then, leaving Luna and Lucien alone.

"Can I have 50 dollars?" Luna asked him.

"Of course my dear," Lucien smiled at her.

"Good because I'm going to need an outfit for the grand opening. Me and Irys-"

"Who's Irys?" He questioned.

"My friend that I work with at the spa. I invited her to the opening."

"Okay. If she's with you then she doesn't have to pay for the food. I won't charge you Luna. Not when you're the one making all this possible."

"You're an amazing chef little bro. You're smart and ambitious. I'm just helping you live a dream that's all. And when I open up my own spa, I expect you to be my first client."

"You ain't lying," He smiled at her.

"Lucien!" Rosa called from their bedroom.

"Go on, I'll just watch TV and wait until you're ready to head down to the restaurant," Luna said. Lucien smiled at his sister and ruffled her hair before going off back to his bedroom.

Rosa was sitting on the bed, fully clothed in a tight red dress and heels. When he entered the room, he couldn't help but whistle at her sex appeal. She was truly gorgeous.

"You like what you see?" She asked. Lucien just nodded.

"Come over here," She said. After closing the door behind him, Lucien went over to the bed, sitting next to her. She got up but leaned in and kissed him lightly.

"I'm so sorry for my attitude lately. But you know I want to be here for you, and I want to make things work out. I just been so wound up." Lucien rubbed her back as she leaned forward and pecked his lips.

"I'm so afraid this restaurant will change us, and I don't want it to," She added.

"Don't think like that Rosa. You know I'll be the same. But you acting out this way, it's making Luna doubt us. Hell, it's making me doubt us."

"Well let me fix that." She kissed him deeply, shoving her tongue into his mouth. As she was kissing him, she pushed him to lay back. Wrapping his arms around her waist, he held her as he kissed her deeply. Her hands traveled down to his crotch. She pulled his shorts forward, putting her hands inside and taking his member out.

"We can't possibly do this with my sister downstairs," Lucien breathed.

"She's grown," Rosa said. "She can handle it." Rosa shimmied down his body until she hovered over his aching arousal. Taking hold of the base, she sunk her mouth onto him. Lucien couldn't help but groan loudly at the feel of her warm mouth consume him. She hadn't given him this attention in a little while, so he was going to enjoy this.

"Damn, you taste sweet," She whispered licking at his pre-cum. Wanting more than her pesky licks, Lucien took her head and guided her back down. She gagged but took him in and bobbed her head at a steady pace, sucking him softly. Her cheeks hollowed out as she sucked, drawing a release out of him. As her pace quickened, his breathing became labored. Grabbing a handful of her hair, he let out a deep moan as his released rocketed out of him and into her mouth. She gagged on it, but she didn't spit it out. She swallowed it down, and rose up slowly looking at him.

"Did I make it better?" She asked sweetly.

"Almost," He smiled at her.

"I can easily make it up to you tonight. Just be ready." Lucien sat up, and tucked his soft member back into his shorts.

"I'll be thinking about that while I'm working," He said.

They walked out of the room hand in hand after Rosa fixed herself back up. When Luna saw them together, she gagged a little. Rosa only winked at Luna then kissed her man goodbye before leaving the house.

"That's nasty," Luna said.

"When was the last time you had sex? Cause I think you need to get some to get off my back."

"You had better watch your mouth!" Luna snapped. "I get plenty action. Now go get dressed so we can go."

****

Even though things were a little rocky with Rosa, Lucien tried to put that to the side and just focus on his restaurant. With the opening coming up he was putting things in high gear. If he wasn't in the restaurant, he was around town marketing and getting the word out about the opening. Luckily he had a good team of cooks who were doing more than just showing up to cook. Along with that, he'd set up his website, and gotten his social media profiles finished. So far, the restaurant had 15 reservations, and they were two weeks from the opening. The maximum amount of reservations were 45, and Lucien wanted to go all out. He wanted to double his reservations for the night for both the 6pm and the 9pm dinner services. He just had to work to make it happen and he was willing to do so.

The start of a new week didn't stop his momentum. His menu was created in full and now it was time to actually start cooking. He wanted to do a couple test runs with his staff to make sure the food actually tasted as good as he imagined and to go over plating options and designs. Waking early Monday morning, he dressed and was ready to start his day. Turning off the alarm on his watch, he chopped up some fruits and had that with yogurt for his breakfast. Rosa came down to the kitchen stretching.

"No breakfast this morning?" she questioned.

"Um no sorry. I didn't know you would wake. What do you want I can make something quick before I go."

"An omelet," She said. As she sat around the island, Lucien quickly made her a perfect omelet with peppers and cheese. Finishing it up, he plated it and handed it to her with a glass of orange juice. Since he was planning to be in the restaurant for most of the day again, he went back to the fridge to bring his insulin with him.

"Oh crap," He breathed. He only had one more vial left. That would only last him half the day.

"What's the matter?" Rosa asked.

"I'm running out of insulin," he replied.

"Just get some more," She said.

"I'm on automatic refills at the pharmacy. They don't open for another two hours, but I won't need any insulin until later, but I'll be really busy in the kitchen today. Can you go and pick it up for me and bring it down to the restaurant?" Rosa rolled her eyes.

"Sure, why not."

"I mean it Rosa," He said sensing her hesitation. "I can't miss my shots, and I don't want to be in the hospital so I'm counting on you."

"Okay, okay," She said. Lucien nodded. He went over to her and pulled her in for a kiss.

"And don't lock Salsa out again," He warned.

"I will if she starts growling and shit." Lucien plucked her nose.

"See you later," He smiled.

Lucien arrived at work with all his cooks waiting for him. He greeted each one, and then let them inside.

"Your sister's not coming to watch over us like hawks?" His sous chef asked. Lucien smiled at the man. Joe Moore was the first to apply to the job once Lucien had posted it, and his experience spoke enough for Lucien to hire him right away. Though Lucien was the boss, everyone knew his sister played a role in the restaurant too.

"No, thankfully," Lucien joked.

"Damn sucks for you Joe," One of the line cooks joked, slapping him on the back.

"Shut up," Joe snapped.

"Oh wait a minute. You want to see my sister?" Lucien asked. Joe crossed his arms.

"No disrespect to you or anything. She's just really pretty." Lucien stared at the man. Though Luna was older than him, Lucien didn't play when it came to men that liked his sister.

"Oh that's very disrespectful," Lucien said. "Because my sister ain't pretty. She's gorgeous." Lucien watched as Joe let out a deep breath.

"Yes you're right. She is gorgeous. And a little bit annoying, but still gorgeous all the same."

"As long as you know," Lucien smiled. "But you're not gonna use me to get to her. You wanna talk to her, you better make your own moves."

"I hear that," Joe responded. Joe was a good enough guy for Lucien to let slide. If he wanted to talk to Luna, Lucien was comfortable with that. But he was going to make sure he kept a good eye on him.

In the kitchen, time seemed to go fast. At first it was a little shaky getting everyone's timing and making sure they were finishing up meals at a good time and talking it out. But after applying a system, everyone listened to him and they were able to operate smoothly. And then after figuring out garnishes and how to plate up, each cook tasted the dishes so they knew how it was supposed to taste no matter what.

It was 3pm when his watch went off. He'd been eating constantly because he was tasting all the food but that's when he realized that was probably a mistake. Leaving the kitchen he retreated to his office where he pulled out his test strips. His sugar was high. It wasn't too bad, but if it stayed untreated for too long, it was going to be bad. Lucien quickly dialed Rosa, but her phone rang out to voicemail.

"Hey Rosa, just calling to remind you about my insulin. I'm going to need it in a little bit." He left the voicemail, but the moment he hung up he could feel a headache coming through. He'd probably need it sooner than he thought.

After waiting another 20 minutes and not hearing from Rosa, he called her again and sent her a text. When those went unanswered, he checked his sugar again. He knew it had sky rocketed because not only was he sporting a headache, things were getting hazy for him. His vision was blurry and there was no way he was going to get into a car and drive anywhere. And he couldn't stand passing out right now. Not as things were going so well for him and the restaurant. Plus, none of his cooks knew he had diabetes and he didn't want to have to tell them. There was only one person who he would always be able to call on no matter what. And it wasn't his girlfriend.

"Check out the buns on that guy," Luna whispered to Irys as her client left. She'd just given him a full body massage and he was packed with muscle. She had just as much fun giving him the massage as he had receiving it.

"So that's what you do?" Irys joked. "Lust after each man you service?"

"Irys, we are single. I mean why not? And I know you're new to this so I'll give it a pass, but when a hunk lays on our table, we lust!"

"You should have just gotten his number or something," Irys said. "What's the use of lusting when you don't go for your shot?"

"Oh, so we're confident now? That's what we're doing?" Irys burst out laughing as Luna's phone rang.

"Hey Lucy," She greeted. Irys watched as Luna's smile faded.

"Luna I need you right now." Lucien's voice was low and sounded choppy as if he was sick.

"What's the matter?" Luna asked, alarmed.

"I asked Rosa to bring me my insulin and she said she would but now I can't get in contact with her. I need my insulin now Luna and I can't drive to get it, I'm getting dizzy."

"You sit tight you hear me? I'm on my way." She hung up the phone and quickly grabbed up her things.

"What's wrong?" Irys asked.

"I gotta take care of something important. Tell Charles I have to go it's a family emergency, no time to explain." She didn't care if her boss wouldn't be happy about her leaving. She wasn't about to leave Lucien in trouble like that. But there was more than worry in her bones. She was angry. And the moment she saw Rosa, Lucien wasn't going to be able to hold her back from whopping that girl's ass.

Thankfully the pharmacy was a quick visit. She was in and out in no time and on her way to the restaurant.

"Hey Luna," Joe greeted her once he unlocked the door for her.

"Hey Joe. Where's Lucien?" She asked.

"In his office," He supplied.

"Okay. I'll um, see you later." She smiled at the man and hurried to the upstairs office. As she figured he would be, Lucien was laying on his couch with his eyes closed.

"Lucien!" She called, afraid he was already passed out.

"Lu," He answered lowly. "I had to lay down I'm so tired."

"I know, I know. But just stay awake a little bit longer." Luna closed the door. She got down on her knees next to him on the couch, and fished around her purse for his insulin. She didn't know if he had a pack of needles or not so she just bought a new pack from the pharmacy. Filling the needle with the insulin, she rolled up his shirt and pinched the skin on his stomach in her fingers before sliding the needled into him. He winced only a little but he relaxed as he injected the medicine. Luna had learned not to be squeamish a long time ago when it came to giving her brother his medicine.

"How's that?" she asked, rubbing his forehead.

"I love you," He said lowly, closing his eyes. Luna smiled at him.

"I love you too. Can you walk? I want to take you home so you can rest."

"Yes. Just give me a minute. Actually, can you bring the cooks up here? I think I should tell them about this. I need to be able to trust them so they have my back."

"That's a good idea," Luna said. She left her brother and went down to the kitchen. The cooks were there just waiting for Lucien to come back to give them some direction. Instead it was only Luna coming to tell them their boss wanted to talk to them.

Back in the office Lucien was able to sit up as the cooks came into the office. They could all see something serious was up.

"Before we open the restaurant I feel it important to come clean about certain things."

"What's going on?" Joe asked.

"When I was ten I was diagnosed with type 1 diabetes. So the reason I left the kitchen was because my sugar was too high and I didn't have any insulin." There were collective gasps around the room.

"I don't want this to hinder me in anyway, but sometimes it will. And I need to trust my cooks. At times I won't be able to taste the food we put out and I have to trust that you guys have made perfection."

"You don't need to worry about it," Joe said. "We'll have your back and we know you'll have ours."

"Thanks," Lucien smiled weakly. "I've gotta go and get some rest, I can't really do too much right now."

"No problem. We'll clear down, clean up and lock up. I can bring you the key later Luna," Joe offered.

"Sure," Luna smiled at him. "Come on Lucy, let's go."

Lucien was grateful for his sister. She'd left her job to come to his aide when she should have had to. She didn't say anything about Rosa, but once he realized she was driving him back to her house instead of his, he knew she didn't want him anywhere near Rosa.

"Watch when I get my hands on her," Luna gritted as she drove. Lucien didn't say anything. There was no defense he could give to Rosa. She'd caused this on herself.

Lucien was strong enough to walk up to Luna's house, but the moment he fell into the bed in her guest room, Lucien was ready to take a nap. After a large glass of water, Lucien was knocked out.

Luna paced her house while Lucien slept. Now that he was okay, her anger took over her body completely. She was enraged that his own girlfriend would lack competence enough to do something as important as simply getting Lucien's insulin. At least to call and say she wasn't going to do it, Lucien would have known and wouldn't have waited around for her.

It was a little after seven that Luna heard Lucien's phone ringing endlessly. He was still asleep, so she dug his phone from his pants pocket and answered it.

"What you want?" Luna asked Rosa.

"Where's Lucien I been calling him forever. I went to get his insulin, they said someone already picked it up."

"You're damn right someone already picked it up you twit! Lucien asked you to get it for him earlier and he kept calling and calling you and texting you and you haven't responded and now hours later you wanna call talking about you went to pick it up?"

"I didn't have no service I was out!"

"You listen to me. Lucien trusted you to do something, and you didn't. You let him down tremendously, and on top of that he could have went into a coma. This is serious Rosa! My brother is sick and he needs someone who's gonna give a damn about him when he needs help!" Luna brushed at the tears in her eyes both from her anger and her sadness over Lucien's condition.

"This isn't a game Rosa. And if I lose my brother because you were too far up your own ass to care about anyone else oh trust and believe you're gonna have to do a whole hell of a lot to be able to get away from me."

"When is Lucien coming home?" She asked. Luna just sucked her teeth and hung up the phone. She wished she had a flip phone again just so she could have the satisfaction of actually banging the phone close on that bimbo. Rosa irked her nerves so bad and she wished Rosa would just disappear from Lucien's life.

"So you're gonna keep me hostage here?" Luna jumped at Lucien's voice.

"Didn't know you were awake," She breathed.

"I heard you screaming."

"Sorry. Rosa called. I just had to give her a piece of my mind. I want you to stay with me tonight. Just to make sure you were all good."

"I don't mind. I don't think I want to be around her anyway."

"Good. You go back and relax. I will make you dinner this time."

"Thanks sis."

Rosa was beyond agitated. This is what she was talking about. Why should she be responsible for Lucien's sickness? She was doing her own things with her friends and she had to be worried about Lucien and now she was being cussed out. So she was going to spend the night alone in the house with a dog that was pacing around the house and barking. She locked herself in the room for the night but that didn't keep the sound of the barking dog out. She'd had it with that damn dog. Even though she knew he'd be mad, she kept trying to call him in hopes that he would answer but he never did. She went to bed, angry and upset but she knew she needed to do something before she lost him.

By the morning, she was back to calling him, but he didn't answer still. She'd barely slept because Salsa hadn't stopped barking. When Rosa opened the bedroom door, Salsa was pacing and she seemed restless.

"Go away," Rosa snapped. She kicked the dog to get by it. Salsa yelped and skidded out of the way. Rosa went to get dressed planning to pop up at Luna's house to get her man back. But again as she left the bedroom, dressed in her jogging tights and tank top, Salsa was back barking in her face.

"Lucien's not here! Go away!" This time when she tried to kick the dog, Salsa reared back and bit Rosa on her leg. Rosa screamed out in pain and that must have scared Salsa. The dog let her go and ran away.

"You fucking animal!" Rosa snapped. She limped after Salsa who was now at the front door clawing trying to get out. Rosa shoved her feet into her sneakers, and grabbed Salsa's leash. She clipped it to Salsa's collar before opening the door.

"Time to get rid of you for good," She snapped at the canine. Thankfully she wasn't bleeding but the bite still hurt. Rosa wasn't going to live with a dog that vicious anymore.

After spending the night with his sister, Lucien knew he had to get back home in the morning. He couldn't hide out from the situation anymore. He had to have a serious talk with his girlfriend. At this point, he no longer trusted her and he needed to have that if he was going to be with her. He saw all the missed calls on his phone but decided to just talk to her once he got to the house. Luna of course would not let him come alone. He obliged her by letting her come but he told her to wait out in the car first before coming in. He knew she wanted to do more than talk to Rosa.

When he entered the house, he knew immediately things were going to be different. The smell of food permeated through the house wafting from the kitchen. That should have been a warning sign for him because Rosa never cooked. And he literally meant NEVER.

"Salsa," He called, whistling to the dog who failed to greet him at the door. Shrugging, he went into the kitchen. Standing at the stove, Rosa was hovering over the hot pan. He stood there watching her for a moment, her inexperience in cooking evident. She went to chop up some peppers but her strokes were slow and uncertain and then she went to throw the chopped up peppers in the pan. When the oil popped she screamed and backed up. Lucien couldn't help but laugh. She turned and looked at him.

"It's not funny," She pouted. Lucien crossed his arms.

"The fire is too high," He said. "Turn it down." She turned down the fire and looked at him.

"I was hoping you'd come back. That's why I'm trying to cook you something nice."

"Food won't make up for the fact that I could have been seriously sick yesterday."

"Well what you want from me? I apologized already so..."

"Things aren't that simple Rosa. And you should know that." He looked over at the spot where Salsa's bowls should have been, but the space was clear. Looking at back Rosa, he whistled again for his dog.

"Your dog bit me," Rosa said. "She wouldn't stop barking and acting crazy last night."

"Maybe because I didn't come home or something. And even though she doesn't like you, Salsa doesn't bite unless she's provoked."

"Well she bit me Lucien!" Rosa raised her leg, showing him the bite mark. There was no blood and it wasn't deep. If a dog purposely attacked you, sure enough they would latch on and draw blood. Lucien whistled again.

"The mutt isn't here," Rosa said. Lucien gave her a look.

"Meaning?"

"Once she bit me I didn't feel safe here anymore. I can't live with that kind of vicious animal."

"Rosa," He said firmly. "What did you do with my dog?" He asked slowly.

"I took her down to the shelter," She shrugged. Lucien felt his eyes widen.

"No. You're joking." He shook his head unwilling to believe that. But Rosa stood firm.

"Rosa!" He shouted. "That is my service dog! You can't just drop her off at a shelter because you felt like it! In all the time you lived here she's never bit you! That means you did something to her for her to defend herself! I can't even believe this shit!"

"I'm doing us a favor Lucien. You've always wanted to get rid of her so I just did it for you. And how do you care more about a dog than fixing our relationship?"

"Relationship?" Lucien asked. "If you could care less about the things that matter to me, then there is no relationship. First you didn't give a damn about getting me my insulin after you said that you would, then you obviously don't care about my restaurant, you just want to spend my goddamn money, and then I come home and you're telling me you gave my service dog to a fucking shelter? Do you know how many times that dog has saved my life when I wasn't ever aware I needed help in the first place? And you think that this is alright?"

"Lucien I hooked up with you. Not your restaurant, and certainly not your damn dog. All this extra shit is weighing on me. Why do I have to deal with it? Huh?"

"I am all those things Rosa. You can't have me without my dreams and aspirations. You can't have me without my dog. That's like telling a woman I won't be with her because she had a kid. If you accept me, you need to accept what I come with Rosa. And I made it completely clear when we started dating all the things that I wanted from life."

"I'm tired of accepting it!" She snapped. "I can't deal with a degenerate ass man who has an excuse for ever-"

"Wait," Lucien stopped her. With brows raised he pointed at his chest. "Are you calling me degenerate? Because I'm a diabetic?" Rosa crossed her arms and looked at him defiantly.

"You know what," He said. "It's not gonna work between us. We're over."

"Huh?" Rosa's heart dropped. "No Lucien, I-"

"You what?" He asked. "What have you done besides spend my money and nag at me? You know I was so blind to all that shit because I desperately wanted a woman. But you don't accept who I am, and I'm not gonna deal with you anymore." He walked by her and cut off the stove completely.

"I'm gonna get my damn dog. So you need to pack up your things and go." He turned away from her then, and began to leave the house. Rosa followed after him begging him to stay in the house. But he didn't stop. He opened the door and thankfully, Luna was leaning against his car, waiting for him to come back out. Rosa grabbed onto his arm.

"Please Lucien don't do this!" Lucien snatched his arm out of her grip.

"Don't touch me," He snapped. Luna perked up quickly, watching the scene in front of her.

"I mean what I said Rosa. I want you out."

"You think you gonna just get rid of me? That you're just gonna kick me out like I haven't been dealing with your ass for all this time? We can't eat sometimes because of your sugar. You can't fuck me when I want it, your dog barks all hours of the damn night, and you always complaining when I ask you to be a man and take care of me."

"What in the world have you done for me? Besides lay on your fucking back?" Rosa slapped him hard across the face. Luna jumped. Lucien turned to her.

"She just hit me!" Lucien said. Luna charged at Rosa. Once she was in her face, Luna slapped fire out of Rosa. She wasn't scared to put paws on any woman who touched her brother.

"You hitting him because he can't hit you back. But hit me. Go head. I dare you."

"Lucien...get her," Rosa said, her voice quivering. Lucien only crossed her arms.

"Luna I just told Rosa me and her are over. So she needs to pack her things and get out of my house. I have to go down to the shelter because this chick put Salsa in there!"

"What?!" Luna shrieked.

"So just do me a favor sis. Stay with her and make sure she gets the hell out of my house, and if she doesn't beat her ass!" Luna smiled at that, clapping her hands together. Lucien only cut his eyes at Rosa before hopping back into his car and heading to the closest shelter in town to get his dog back.

Chapter Seven

Irys sat outside in front of a coffee shop sipping on an iced coffee. She was taking her lunch break so she'd decided to walk a little bit before sitting down for coffee. Luna hadn't come into work again, she said she was still dealing with her emergency. Irys didn't push her to give details so she just let Luna know she was around in case she needed anything. But now that Luna was doing her thing, Irys seriously felt alone. She talked to Luna every day, and now without her, Irys didn't know what she was going to do with herself. So she had an hour of lunch break to linger around before she went back to work. After finishing her iced coffee, she left the coffee shop and just began walking.

It was crowded at this hour of the early afternoon but it was just the perfect temperature. Irys was wearing yoga pants and a tank top that was garnering her attention from people as she walked by. It took her a long time to get used to the stares, but now she didn't even pay it any attention. If they wanted to look, then they were free to do so. She refused to let anyone's insecurities make her uncomfortable. It was her body, not anyone else's, so she wasn't going to be told what to feel or how to look when it came down to it. Caught up in her thoughts, she forgot the street was crowded, so when someone pushed her, she snapped from her daydreaming and paid attention to where she was going.

"Looking to adopt a pet today?" Someone asked. Irys looked around realizing a man who worked in an animal shelter was standing out front holding a small cat. Apparently he was trying to get people inside the shelter.

"No," Irys smiled. "But I love animals."

"Come in and see some. At least take a look you never know what might happen." Irys shrugged. Not like she was doing anything else.

"Sure I don't see why not. I'm not doing anything anyways." Irys knew walking into the shelter was a bad idea. Because the moment she did, her heart was melting at each animal she laid her eyes on. One of the workers let her into one of the pens filled with puppies. Right then and there Irys thought about adopting a dog. She did need another friend. Besides Luna she didn't have one!

Holding onto the brown and black puppy, she pet and cooed at it. A streak of gold caught her attention across the room. A golden retriever was pacing up and down in its pen, seemingly restless.

"What's his story?" Irys asked one of the workers.

"Actually it's a she. She was dropped off this morning. A little strange but we don't turn animals away."

"She looks restless. Maybe she needs to be comforted?" Irys said. "Can I go in with her?"

"We've tried to comfort her but she only backs off. You can go near the pen but not inside. We're not sure if she might get angry and retaliate." Irys nodded and put the small puppy down. She left the pen and went over to the retriever. She whistled at the dog who kept pacing. After a moment she looked at Irys and came to the edge of the pen slowly. Sticking her finger inside, Irys reached for her, rubbing her finger on the dog's head. In return the dog licked her finger.

"Aw, you're not so bad," She said. The dog had a collar around her neck so Irys was wondering who would have given her up. Staying by the pen, Irys got comfortable and kept petting the dog who seemed to relax more and more with Irys near her. As she sat with the beautiful dog, the shelter door burst open and a man rushed in. Irys looked over her shoulder in time to see him as he approached the front desk. Wearing a pair of jeans and a simple t-shirt he blended in easily enough but for some reason he caught Irys's attention for longer than he should have. Standing at about 5'8, his slender but fit figure filled out the t-shirt he was wearing but his muscles were not overpowering. They were just right. His hair was cut low in the back, but on top he had light length that was only long enough to display his tight micro curls. Irys stared at him, feeling as if she couldn't look away. But then the dog next to her barked. Irys yelped from getting caught off guard. Everyone turned to look at her, including the man who had her captivated in the first place.

"Shit," Irys whispered. She quickly turned away, giving him her back and just looked at the dog, afraid to look anywhere else.

Lucien saw Salsa immediately when he entered, but it was when the dog barked that Lucien saw the woman sitting in front of the pen they were keeping her in. Lucien only caught a quick glimpse of the thick woman before she turned around. Something about her distracted him and he was craning his neck to actually be able to look into her face.

"How can I help you sir?" The woman at the desk asked. Lucien popped his head back around.

"Oh um. This morning my dog was actually brought here by accident and I'm just coming to get her back. She's right there," Lucien said.

"I'm sorry for the mix up sir but you understand that before I can hand her over to you I need proof that she is yours. Otherwise I can't let her go." Lucien had rushed here so fast he didn't have any proof really.

"Well how about this." He pulled his dog tags from beneath his shirt where he always kept it tucked under. On the dog tags was his name, the name of his service dog, and that he was a type 1 diabetic. That was in the case he passed out on the street and the person who found him would be able to know what was wrong.

"The dog has the same tags attached to her collar," Lucien said.

"Let me check on that," She said. She left the counter, and Lucien followed her.

Irys's throat was about to close shut when she realized the man was walking over to her. Out of all the dogs in this place, he had to choose this one? Having an inner panic attack, her heart nearly stopped when she heard him clear his voice.

"Excuse me little miss," He said from behind her. Irys took a deep breath then stood from her crouching position. She turned and looked at him.

"I know you don't see anything little about me," She responded to him. When their eyes locked, none of them looked away. It was strange for Irys because for a long time no one had ever looked her in the face. The only place they did look was her body, and then they refused to look in her face as if they were embarrassed to make eye contact. But this man, with his cool chocolate eyes only looked in her face. There was something oddly familiar about him, but Irys could place it. Surely if she'd met him before, she wouldn't have forgotten.

"Sorry," Lucien said lowly. "With you crouched down I didn't realize." He stared into her face, mesmerized by her butter scotch complexion and honey dew eyes. Her cherry butter glossed lips were pouty and looked so sweet. Her hair was a large afro framing her face with curls that looked soft to the touch. It reminded him of Tracee Ellis Ross. Glancing down at her body he saw that she was thicker than a goddamn snicker, and that just made him lick his lips. Damn.

"Let me bring her out," the worker said, opening up the pen for Salsa. She opened the pen but held onto Salsa's collar.

"Call her to you," She ordered. Lucien backed all the way up not breaking his eyes contact with the woman in front of him. When he was far enough, he whistled. Salsa fought out of the woman's hold and came running to Lucien. Lucien finally broke eye contact with the woman to look down at his dog and pet her.

"I can show you something else," Lucien said. He led Salsa back over to the worker. "Stay," He ordered Salsa. Salsa sat down and watched him.

Irys looked as the man moved away from the dog slowly. After giving her another glance, he turned around and walked like he was leaving. When he was far enough he lowered himself to the ground and just laid there. Irys was confused as to what he was doing. But then the dog barked and jumped into action running over to the fallen man. She sniffed all around him, barked into his face and bit at his t-shirt. When he didn't respond to her, the dog came running back to Irys. She used her head to push at the back of Irys's legs trying to get her to go towards the man. When Irys began moving, she continued pushing at Irys not stopping until they were next to the man again. Irys reached out and slowly helped him sit up.

Lucien knew that Salsa would get him help if he'd fallen and not responded to her. What he didn't expect was for her to push the woman to come to his aid. Lucien stared into her eyes as she helped him off the floor.

"See," Lucien said turning to the worker. "She's mine."

"That's proof enough sir. Sorry for the mix up."

"No worries at all. It wasn't your fault." Lucien looked back at his dog who was walking circles around the woman.

"Come Salsa," He whistled. The woman chuckled, causing the creamy mounds of her breasts to shake.

"You named your dog after Mexican sauce?" she giggled. Lucien smiled at her. Despite the argument he'd just come from, her innocence made him smile.

"Don't be making fun of my dog," He smiled. "And besides, when I adopted her, that's what her name was. She wouldn't answer to anything else."

"Well you'd better take good care of Salsa before she winds up back in here again. If you would have arrived five minutes later I would have adopted her already."

"Looks like you've got to find another dog to adopt," He said. "Even though she has a liking to you," Lucien added just as Salsa sat next to the woman's feet.

"Eh, perhaps she can sense who I really am underneath my skin unlike what humans can do."

"I'm human and I can see that you're a sweetheart." Irys was trying not to blush. But she failed miserably.

"Thanks," She smiled looking down. "I should um, I should get going. Time is running out on my lunch break."

"Oh, oh yeah sure," Lucien stammered. Irys pet Salsa, scratching her behind the ears. Lucien stepped forward, inadvertently invading her space. He was only trying to reach forward to grab Salsa's collar to lead her out, but when he was close to Irys all he smelled was peaches and cream. Oh my god it was intoxicating.

"Holy shit," He whispered to himself. Irys heard him curse but she wasn't sure why. She backed off immediately. He looked at her intensely. Damn she was a snack. Actually no, she was more than a snack. She was a goddamn meal that would satiate his appetite forever.

"I guess…I guess I should go now," She said.

"Yeah, yeah me too." She gave him a smile that stunted his heart temporarily before she hurried out of the shelter. Lucien could only stand there basking in the afterglow of her presence before the reality of his life smacked him in the face again.

"Come on Salsa. Let's hope that girl got all her things out my house," Lucien said.

Luna watched with her arms crossed as Rosa slowly stuffed her clothes into a suitcase. It wouldn't be taken so long if the woman didn't have so much damn clothes in the first place.

"When is Lucien coming back?" Rosa asked. "This isn't over, I need to see him."

"Trust me honey. It's over." Luna stated. She looked at her watch.

"You have another 20 minutes to get your things out."

"How do you expect me to get all these things out of here that quick?" Rosa snapped.

"Oh you need help? Say no more." Luna grabbed the second empty suitcase and opened it on the bed. She grabbed everything from the dresser that belonged to a female and dumped it into the suitcase. Then she went to the closet and grabbed as many shoes as she can and continued to dump it into the suitcase, making several trips until the closet was bare of shoes. Luna pushed Rosa out of the way and continued packing all the clothes. When both the suite cases were full, Luan closed them and began dragging them to the front door.

"So simple," Luna said. "You just tryna prolong this shit so you don't have to leave. But you gotta another thing coming if you think you bout to stay up in here."

Rosa saw now that it was useless. No matter what type of fight she put up, she wasn't going to be able to win. She decided it was best to just give in. But she wouldn't give up. Lucien was going to take her back. So instead of fighting Luna, she just carried her things outside. As she loaded her things in the car, Lucien's car pulled into the driveway slowly. Luna stopped what she was doing to look at her man. He came out of the car and opened the back door. Salsa hopped out happy to be back home. But when she saw Rosa, she growled and took off, getting away from her. Lucien had hoped Rosa would be gone, but knowing her, she would do anything to stall.

"Lucien!" Rosa called when she saw he wasn't going to even acknowledge her before he went inside. Stopping in his tracks, Lucien slowly turned around to look at her.

"Do you really think this is over between us?" She asked.

"Yeah I do actually."

"Well I don't. Because you're going to see that you won't be able to have any other woman. The life you want, you won't be able to have. I was here and I haven't left your side. I'm sorry for all of this Lucien but you will see that if you don't want to be single forever then you need to be with me. I'm waiting for you Lucien. All you have to do is call." Lucien didn't say anything. He just looked at her and watched as she got into her car and pulled off. Crossing his arms, he felt glued to where he was. Luna saw the contemplation on his face.

"You don't believe anything she just said do you?" She asked. Lucien shrugged.

"Yeah. What if she's right? I couldn't land a girlfriend before I met her."

"That's because all you did was have sex with them and then disappear. Those girls would have easily taken you as their man. You were just too blind. What you see in Rosa is her body and her features. Beauty is only skin deep little brother. And that woman does not have a beautiful heart. You are selling yourself short and I don't care that you're living with diabetes you deserve just as much as any average man."

"Luna," Lucien groaned. "I get it okay? You say that all the time."

"Don't brush it off Lucien. I am trying to help you out. Come inside. I can cook and we can just relax."

"Ah no. I just want to be alone right now. And I need to think about more things for the restaurant. You'll be a distraction I don't need."

"Lucien you know I don't like it when you push me away. I don't want to see you hurting over this."

"I'm 30 Luna. Not 13. Stop trying to baby me."

"It's not about babying you!" She snapped. "I just-I just want you to be okay."

"And I will be. I always am." He kissed Luna on the cheek. "Talk to you later." Though he said he was okay, Luna didn't believe him. And her gut feeling was right because after her brother ended his relationship, he just wasn't the same.

Irys pulled up to her home after her long shift at work. She was happy to be home and couldn't wait to see her mother. She'd bought some candles that she knew her mom would love to burn. As she walked to the front door she received a text from Luna saying she was alright and would be back to work tomorrow. Irys was thankful she was alright and thankful to have her friend back at work to share her day with. It was all normal stuff until Irys unlocked her front door and pushed it open. There were two large suitcases in the hall, blocking her way in.

"What in the hell?!" Irys said. "Diana!" She called out to the aide. Diana quickly appeared and helped moved the cases to the side so Irys could actually get into her house.

"What's all this shit?" Irys asked.

"I thought you knew! And I really couldn't tell her to leave it's not my place."

"Tell who? What are-" Irys's question was answered soon enough. Rosa came out into the hall eating ice cream out of the container.

"Why are you here?" Irys asked. "And that's mom's ice cream." Irys snatched the container from her.

"She's sick and you're fat. None of you need to be eating ice cream." Rosa grabbed it back and continued eating.

"Imma need you to leave," Irys said. "I'm not dealing with your shit tonight."

"Well that's too bad for you," Rosa said. "I don't have anywhere else to go....so."

"Sooo what? When did your problems become my problems?"

"Just cut it out okay. I don't have a place to stay so I need to stay here."

"Wait," Irys chuckled. "Does that mean that your man put your ass out? The one that puts it down in the bed?" Irys laughed.

"Shut up! This shit is not funny!"

"It's hella funny," Irys said. She shook her head and continued in the house. "Diana thanks for staying a little bit longer today. Let me write you a check."

In the kitchen Irys wrote Diana a check for her services before the woman left. Once she was gone, Irys looked at Rosa.

"Are you seriously wanting to stay here?" She asked.

"Does it look like I'm joking?" Irys huffed. Even though Rosa was annoying, she was still Irys's sister. She wasn't going to leave her out on the street if she truly had nowhere else to go. And besides, Rosa would choose to go anywhere but here if she had a choice.

"If you're gonna stay here then you need to pitch in and help me out."

"You know I'm not working Irys so I don't know what you want me to pitch in."

"Okay well since your so called boyfriend ain't taking care of you no more you need to start looking for a job."

"This is only temporary," She said. Irys sighed.

"Whatever you wanna call it. For the mean time you need to help take care of mom, and keep the place clean."

"Whatever." She tossed the carton in the garbage and the spoon in the sink. Irys had to admit that her sister actually looked sad about her breakup.

"You know you can talk to me about it," Irys offered. "I am your sister." Rosa looked at her contemplating on if she should tell her sister anything about Lucien. There was but so much she wanted to share.

"We just had a big fight. So we decided to take a break and after a little while we'll see what happens."

"What was the fight about?" Irys asked.

"I don't want to talk about it. I had a long day. I'm gonna get some rest."

"Okay fine," Irys said. "Move those cases into the guest room. I'm going to lay with mom for a little bit then head to bed."

"Knock yourself out." Since she didn't look like herself, Irys didn't want to bother her anymore. They'd talk in the morning about how she could help take care of their mother since she was going to be there. It would be a big help financially. She just had to actually live with her sister, something she knew wasn't going to be easy.

****

"Luna!" Irys greeted, jogging over to her friend. They hugged each other tightly. "Is everything alright with you?"

"Yes girl I am good. Just had to nip something in the bud really quick. Anything good happen while I was gone?"

"Luna you know it's boring when you're not here!"

"Oh gosh, we need to spice up your life a little. And speaking of spicing, don't forget about the grand opening of my brother's restaurant. We're already reserved and it's in two weeks. Just know that I am coming out to slay so I expect you to do the same." Irys hesitated.

"Well I mean I can try."

"That's complete bullshit. Don't play games Irys. Anyway, are you sure nothing happened to you while I was gone?" Irys tapped her chin.

"Well…there was this guy."

"Guy?! What guy?!" Luna shrieked.

"I just saw him yesterday. It was just a fleeting encounter but he was really handsome."

"Sooo, did you do anything about it?"

"No," Irys giggled.

"Wait. Weren't you the one who said there was no point in lusting if you weren't going to do anything about it? What happened to all that shit?"

"Okay fine I guess it's different when you're actually in the situation. But what did you want me to do? Ask for Jerry beads and then flash my boobs at him."

"I mean…it would have gotten his attention." Irys pushed Luna playfully. She had thought about that man a couple times after their encounter. She was surprised at herself for even doing that when she knew she would probably never see him again.

"I just became single. I can't be entertaining any other man."

"Why not?" Luna asked. "You know there is a thing as friends with benefits right?"

"So I guess that's what you have?" Irys teased. Luna crossed her arms. She didn't have that or a boyfriend but she was cool without it.

"Don't worry about me," Luna said. "Just because you single doesn't mean you can't have a good time when you want to."

"I just can't do that," Irys said.

"If this is another thing about how you look Irys I'm gonna scream." This time, Irys wasn't thinking about her weight. She was thinking about the fact that she had a baby inside her.

"It's not about that," Irys said.

"What is it about?" She wasn't going to tell Luna but at this point she had to tell someone. And if there was anyone who was going to support her through the pregnancy it was going to be Luna and her mother.

"It's because I'm-"

"Ladies, ladies," Charles said walking over to us. "We run a spa, not a daily talk show. Come on, get to work." Irys and Luna rolled their eyes at the same time.

"We'll pick up on this later," Luna whispered. She smiled at Irys and walked away to get ready for her clients.

The day was going normal for her until she got an alert on her phone for a card charge of 200 dollars. She immediately reported it wasn't her and Irys thought that perhaps someone got a hold of her card information. But then when she saw the place that person was using her card, anger filled her body. If she knew anything about her sister, she knew that the woman loved getting her nails done, and buying shoes. Both of which she'd done with Irys's money. Irys wasn't balling out. Her own nails only cost 20 dollars, why should she spend 200 dollars on her sister who had just forced her way into her house just last night? Clearly Irys needed to set some rules because she wasn't about to be taking care of no grown ass woman.

By the end of the day, it seemed that both Luna and Irys's mind were taken over by something. For Irys it was her sister.

"You look upset," Irys said to her.

"It's just Lucien. He's kind of giving me the cold shoulder."

"Why would he be doing that?" She asked.

"I know he's not doing it on purpose. His relationship with his girlfriend went south so now he's just trying to cope with it. And in that process he's not really talking to me or letting me in. I'm just worried about him."

"Just give him a little space. He'll come back. But if you keep forcing him, maybe he'll pull away only more."

"I guess you're right. Even though it kills me not to be in control of this. Why do you look so mad?" Luna asked.

"My sister is spending my damn money without asking."

"You know you never really talk about her," Luna said.

"Trust me, there isn't much to talk about and we aren't that close like you and Lucien. She just feels entitled to everything, including my money. So I need to go take care of that."

"Good luck with that," Luna smiled.

"Trust me. I'll need it."

****

Rosa was annoyed already and she'd only been at Irys's house for a day. Since she was there, the stupid aid kept asking her to do shit, and her mother was forever calling her. All Rosa needed was a place to stay. She didn't come to work and be bothered, but it was as if she couldn't get away. Locking herself in Irys's room, Rosa raided it until she found a credit card. At first she was just looking for some loose cash to get away for a bit but a credit card was just as good too. Finally escaping the house she went shopping and did her nails. That was the only thing allowing her to survive right now. Dealing with the heartache of losing Lucien, shopping therapy was the only thing that calmed her down somewhat.

She didn't care how long she stayed out. She just needed that time to herself. But her constant thoughts were all of Lucien. After shopping, she couldn't help but to drive down to his restaurant. He was there of course, she could see him through the glass windows working his butt off inside there to get things ready. Even though she wanted to talk to him, she didn't let herself be seen. She just watched him. She was fine with doing that until her phone began going off repeatedly. Of course it was Irys calling her. And of course Rosa ignored it.

"What are you doing?" Rosa grimaced at Luna's voice. She turned around slowly.

"I wanted to see Lucien," Rosa replied.

"I think he made it pretty clear he didn't want to see you Rosa. Leave him be."

"You know, this shit is all your fault. You planted this seed in his head that I'm this bad woman and all of a sudden now he's pulling away from me. You wanted him to be single because you're single and miserable."

"I'm not gonna feed into this bullshit," Luna snapped. "Just go away." Rosa stomped her foot, and huffed off. She would let Lucien decide in the end if he wanted her or not. She knew he only needed time before he realized he wanted to be with her again.

Since she couldn't hold off any longer, she hopped back into her car and drove off to Irys's house. She knew what would be waiting for her when she got home, and sure enough it was.

Irys was pacing when she heard the front door open. She stayed in the kitchen until Rosa came inside carrying a load of bags. Irys couldn't believe it.

"I know you didn't just spend my money for all this pointless shit!" Irys snapped.

"So what?"

"Look, I'm not gonna be in no big fight with you Rosa. I'm just gonna tell you the rules. This is my house, one I work hard to keep. You're gonna live here, you need to pull your weight, or you're going to get out." Rosa just crossed her arms.

"You need to get a job, or you need to stay at home to help take care of mom. You're going to clean up after yourself, and you will not be spending any of my money without even asking me first. Understood?"

"Yeah sure whatever Irys."

"You say that now Rosa but I swear-" Rosa turned and walked off not willing to hear anything else she was going to say. But just as she did that the doorbell was going off. Irys stormed angrily by Rosa to get the door. To her dissatisfaction, Derek was standing there.

"Oh lord," She sighed. How could her night get any worse?

"I need the rest of my shit," He said pushing his way through. He stopped short when he saw Rosa standing there.

"Back again?" he asked her.

"Unfortunately," Rosa sighed. "Where were you last night? You never came in."

"Oh, your sis didn't tell you she kicked me out? Some nerve of her ain't it?" Derek said.

"Wow Irys. No wonder you're being so bitchy. You should be lucky Derek even gave your fat ass a chance in the first place."

"I know you ain't talking Rosa. Because you the one that just got kicked out of her man's house. Stop worrying about other people and worry about yourself."

"Don't let her get to you," Derek said. "That guy obviously made a mistake." Rosa crossed her arms and looked at Derek. Someone as handsome as him shouldn't have given her sister a chance in the first place.

"I know she's just jealous," Rosa teased. Irys rolled her eyes.

"Derek get your shit and just get out. I'm going to bed, because unlike the both of you I actually have a fucking job. Make sure ya'll keep quiet. Mom is sleeping." Irys turned and left then, heading to her bedroom. Once she was gone, Derek looked back at Rosa.

"You okay?" he asked.

"A little bit annoyed and sad but I'm alright."

"Don't be sad Rosa. If you want you know I can make things better." With her arms still crossed she looked him up and down. She knew nothing would compare to Lucien, especially Derek but she was just in need of something.

"Come on baby. You know I was only with Irys because I wanted you. We can just try things out. If you don't like it then so be it. But I gotta have you."

"Alright how about this. You give me an orgasm and we can try. If not, forget about it. I need a man that knows how to fuck. Otherwise you're useless. And trust, my ex knew how to fuck."

"I'll get my shit later." He grabbed Rosa by the elbow and led her to the guest room where she was staying. He had a point to prove before he finally got the woman he really wanted.

Irys was listening for the opening and shutting of her front door that would tell her that Derek had gotten his things and got out. For some reason, the idea of having him in her home was preventing her from falling asleep. She knew he was sneaky enough to try and sleep on her couch instead of going to wherever it was that he was staying at. After taking a shower and throwing on a t-shirt, she opened her bedroom door and peaked out. The house was quiet and everything was dark. Irys was about to assume he'd left until she caught a glimpse of one of his tote bags. Shaking her head, she left her room and headed straight for the living room.

"Derek you know you can't stay here right?" Irys asked flipping on the living room light. But to her surprise the couch was empty. She stood there for a second. Maybe he wasn't there but he left his bag. That was plausible. She cut back off the light, and went over to the windows to peer outside. Nope, he was still in her house. His car was parked right out front. But now she had to figure out where he was, if he wasn't on the couch.

She walked through the house and checked the hall bathroom. Empty. Fear actually filled her gut for some reason, and she was uneasy. She hurried through the house and went straight to her mother's bedroom. Opening the door, she sighed in deep relief seeing her mother peacefully sleeping. If Derek was actually still in her house, there was only one other place he would be. Grunting, she closed her mother's door and walked through the house again until she came upon the guest room. She raised her hand to knock on the door, but stopped midway. The soft breathy moans that permeated the door gave her cold chills. She could only stand there in disbelief. Those familiar sounds of grunts and groans from Derek gave her flashbacks to when she would just lay in bed underneath him and watch him as if he was a stranger while he made love to her body. Maybe it was true, he was a stranger in those moments. But hearing him moan with so much pleasure in ways he used to moan for her, when she didn't feel as if he wasn't into her just made her question who her ex really wanted. Not that it mattered who he wanted now, but if he was sleeping with her sister that easy Irys had to question it. It did hurt that they had the audacity to do something like this right under her nose and in her own house.

Irys turned and was ready to just walk away from the room, but then she didn't. Clearly they didn't care if they got caught because they wouldn't have been doing it in the first place. And Irys wasn't just going to shy away and hide. She wasn't sure what came over her, but instead of just merely walking away, and turned the doorknob and burst through the door into the room. Of course she regretted her decision the moment she saw Rosa's legs high in the air with Derek pumping into her furiously.

"You might actually make me come," She was gasping, scratching at his back. Irys was quiet as a mouse, now afraid to say something. They hadn't heard her burst through the door because apparently their fucking was too good to pay attention to anything else. But she was already in the room and ready to confront them so she wasn't going to back out. She took hold of the door and slammed it shut, locking all of them inside. But the slam was effective enough to get their attention. Derek slipped from his position, falling on top of Rosa. She pushed him off and glared at Irys, not bothering to even cover her perky breasts.

"What are you doing?" Rosa asked.

"I can ask you the same thing," Irys responded.

"Oh I'm sorry because maybe you a little loopy from the chemicals you breathe in at work, let me break it down for you. I'm naked. He's naked. He's grinding on top of me. Obviously we're fucking Irys."

"It's very clear you're fucking Rosa. But why would you be fucking Derek?"

"Um, because I wanted to! It's not like you two are together anymore, so he's free to be with whoever he wants to."

"What would you say if you caught me with your ex?!" Irys snapped. Rosa laughed.

"Please don't flatter yourself plus size Barbie. None of my exes would even think about fucking you, especially after they had me. And I suppose Derek was tired of all that heavy lifting and wanted something light for a change. So if you don't mind, you're dismissed. I was about to come and you ruined it!" Irys ducked out of the way as Rosa threw a pillow at her. Speechless and feelings hurt, Irys just ran out of the room and shut the door. She hurried to her bedroom and locked herself in. She was questioning why she went into that room in the first place. What was it that she was trying to prove? All she did was make herself look like a fool. It also messed with her psych as well.

Instead of going to sleep, Irys laid awake in bed, imagining her ex and her sister having sex. Because they knew Irys was well aware of what they were doing now, their moaning and grunts escaladed. And it was just endless. Getting up from her bed, she went over to her stereo and quickly put it on, turning up the volume. Blocking out their pleasure was the only way she thought she would be able to sleep.

But while she couldn't hear them getting it on, just knowing they were was still enough to keep her awake. She did feel a little pathetic to be bothered enough by this that she couldn't even sleep. She was the one that ended their relationship. How could she care about what he was doing now? Was it because of Rosa? Either way, it was effecting her. She tossed and turned for most of the night, only able to get in a few minutes of sleep before she woke up again. It was exactly 5:07 AM when she heard the front door open and shut. She got out of bed and turned down her radio enough to hear the screech of Derek's car pulling away. She sighed in relief actually thinking she'd be able to fall asleep fully now that he was out of the house completely. She left the stereo off and went to the bathroom before she got back in bed.

Sitting on the toilet, she closed her eyes to prepare herself for bed, knowing well she needed to get her sleep. The relief she felt at Derek leaving was just so odd. Why did he have an effect like that on her when she knew she could care less about what he thought of her? Was it because she was only kidding herself and what he thought of her really did matter? Shaking her head, she opened her eyes. A loud gasp left her mouth upon her looking down. Red streaks painted against the crotch of her underwear surprised her into stillness.

"Oh my god. No…" She breathed.

****

Lucien sat alone in his house with Salsa at his side. He was nursing a small glass of scotch even though he knew he shouldn't be drinking. But it was probably the only thing that would get him to stop thinking so much. For each second that passed Lucien was trying to convince himself that he didn't need Rosa. That he shouldn't feel the need to have her in his life based on all the things she'd said to him. But now he was so lonely. The only person that was calling him all the time was Luna. Besides that he had no one. And what if he didn't have a sister? Did that mean he was to be lonely all the time too?

With his phone in his hands, he looked down at Rosa's number. Maybe they could talk it out. Maybe they could make things work. The both of them were upset when they had that conversation. What if it was only anger that caused her to say he was deficient? There was no way she could actually think of him like that. No way.

Succumbing to his thoughts, Lucien finally pressed the dial button, putting in a call to Rosa. While it rang, his heart fluttered. The line clicked on.

"Rosa, hey," Lucien said.

"She's a little busy right now," A guttural voice answered. Lucien was frozen.

"Who the hell is this?" Lucien asked.

"The man showing your woman a good time. Sucks to be the idiot who let her go doesn't it?" He teased. "Such a shame. I'll tell her you called after I finish giving her a couple orgasms or two." The line went dead. Lucien just stared at the phone for a long while. Sighing he slammed it down on the couch next to him in frustration. Salsa yipped at him, and brushed her nose against his knees. This time his sugar was just fine, but the dog was concerned about his emotional welfare. And that was in shambles at the moment. All he could think about was that he'd made a mistake. What she did with Salsa was uncalled for but Lucien should have just spoken to her. Maybe they could have resolved it, and Lucien wouldn't be sitting here alone.

Sitting there lost in this thoughts, the vibrating of his cell phone jolted him out of his daze. He grabbed up the phone and answered it quickly.

"Rosa?"

"Um no. Your sister," Luna said.

"Oh."

"Lucien are you still talking to her?" Luna asked. "Because I don't think you should be doing that."

"You don't know what I should and shouldn't be doing Luna."

"I'm just trying to-"

"So how about you stop trying Luna? When did my relationship become a three way? You kind of just butt your way in and you put these ideas in my head and I freaking listened to you and lost my damn girlfriend."

"But Lucien you know deep down you don't want her. You've said so yourself there were just things about her that you couldn't deal with. And then she calls you deficient and leaves your dog at a shelter? How can you be mad at me?"

"Me and her could have worked things out," Lucien said.

"No you couldn't have! And denying the truth about things isn't going to make things better. So you need to face things for what they are and not what you want them to be."

"What things are right now is that I'm sitting here without the only woman who was willing to be at my side. And all because of you."

"This-this isn't my fault Lucien," Luna said.

"Well it ain't my fault." Lucien snapped. "I'm going to bed okay? Night." Without hearing anything else she had to say, Lucien hung up the phone. Cursing at himself he went to pour himself a couple more shots before he actually settled down for bed. He was so upset he bypassed checking his sugar and just flopped down in bed after his shots and just went to sleep.

Luna was standing in front of Lucien's restaurant early before her shift the next morning. After her talk with Lucien last night, she was worried. No matter how angry he was Lucien had never spoken like that to her. Hell, Luna would never allow it. Not of her little brother. But she just knew deep in her gut something had to be wrong. She didn't want her brother feeling like Rosa was something he needed. He was the perfect man even with his condition and any woman would be able to see that and appreciate him.

By 8am, she watched as his car pulled into the parking lot. He left his car and came back around the front to get inside the restaurant. By just looking at him, Luna she knew she was right. Something was indeed wrong. He had dark circles around his eyes and he was a little wobbly on his feet.

"Lucien?" She questioned.

"Hey sis," He said. His tone was completely different from the one he had last night. It only made Luna more worried.

"I just wanted to check on you. After we spoke last night I was worried sick." Lucien nodded at her. He seemed dazed.

"Yeah um...I'm sorry for the way I spoke to you. I guess it was just the scotch." Luna gasped.

"Lucy why are you drinking?" She asked. "You know you shouldn't."

"Maybe I wanted to feel normal for once," He answered. Luna watched closely as he tried to open the door to the restaurant. But his hands shook and he couldn't quite fit the key into the lock. Luna took it from him and opened the door herself. When he stumbled inside she knew something was up.

"Did you take your insulin this morning?" she asked him.

"No," He answered.

"Well did you eat?" He shook his head. "Jesus Lucien!"

"Luna I'm fine."

"No you're not! You were drinking last night and you haven't taken insulin or eaten. Either your sugar is too low or its too high! You can't just ignore your health." She grabbed him by the shirt and led him up to his office. He was too weak to fight her so he just went with it.

In the office she pushed him onto his couch. Searching the bag pack he was carrying, she found his meter and test strips.

"Luna I don't-"

"Shush." She pushed him back roughly and pricked his finger to test his blood. Of course it was too low. Searching his bag again, she found his medication. Popping out two she shoved it into his mouth and gave him the water from her purse. He drank without question.

"Are you trying to kill yourself?" she asked him lowly.

"No," He said.

"So then don't do things like this Lucien. I have to get to work okay. Please be here when I come back later." She pulled a banana from her bag and handed it to him.

"I'll be here," He whispered. Even though she tried to hide it, Lucien saw her brush away her tears. She kissed him on the forehead before leaving the office and then finally the restaurant. She didn't know what she was going to do yet but she refused to allow her brother to be depressed over a woman who wasn't worth it.

****

"Hey, where's Irys?" Luna asked Charles when the spa opened and she realized Irys hadn't come in.

"She called out." Luna quickly got her phone out and went to the corner to call her friend. Irys didn't call out for just any reason. Only when she dialed her number the call went straight to voicemail. Luna decided to send her a text.

Hey, I'm just worried about you. Making sure you're alright.

Thanks Luna. I am ok. I will be in touch. Luna was grateful Irys answered but she didn't quite explain much. You ever just have a gut feeling that things weren't right? That's how Luna felt now. First it was with her brother and now it was her friend. Why were things so messed up?

Chapter Eight

Irys sat in the emergency room twiddling her fingers nervously. The hospital gown was scratchy against her skin. Her heart was beating rapidly as she awaited the doctor. Since early this morning after her discovery she was in a quiet panic mode. It was where she looked normal on the outside, but on the inside she was panicked.

"Hi Ms. Black," The doctor said, entering the room. Irys perked up and tried to smile at him.

"Hi," She responded. She tucked her hands under her thighs so she'd be able to stop twiddling them.

"How are you?" He asked, coming over to the bed. He pulled up a chair and sat down next to her.

"Um nervous I guess. Just want to figure out what's going on." He sighed and shook his head.

"I am so sorry to say Irys, but your HCG levels are going down. In pregnant women HCG is what we look at when we're testing for pregnancy. You told the nurse earlier you were about 8 weeks and around that time your levels shouldn't be wavering. I do not know if you'd like an ultrasound however. It might make things a little bit harder." Irys sensed the sincerity in his voice, but that didn't stop the trail of tears that trickled down her cheeks.

"So this is a miscarriage?" Irys asked lowly. The doctor nodded at her slowly. Putting her face in her hands, Irys could only cry as the one thing she was excited for in her life was now gone. He doctor wrapped his arms around her, holding her as she cried.

"How-how could this happen?" She asked, taking her face from her hands to look at him.

"There really isn't any reason Irys. Miscarriages this early have no cause. They just happen." He rubbed her back.

"So what happens now?" Irys wept.

"You may experience some cramping as everything passes. I advise against working for a couple days. Do you feel any pain now?"

"Just my back," She whispered.

"I'll order you some pain medication."

"How am I supposed to just continue on like this didn't happen?" She asked. "I wanted a baby, I can't pretend that I want to live knowing I won't have this special thing growing inside me!" She broke down again weeping into her hospital gown. Still she felt the presence of the doctor consoling her.

"No woman should have to go through this Ms. Black. But you're a strong healthy woman. Having babies in the future will not be a problem."

"Don't kid yourself. I'm not healthy. I'm fat and out of shape."

"I'm a doctor Irys. But I'm also a man. Listen to what I said." She looked at him, with tears in her eyes grateful for his support.

"After your medication someone is going to come and talk to you, just to make sure you're alright before we let you leave? Okay?" In other words, they wanted to make sure she wasn't suicidal. She was filled with great sadness, but it was the fact that she needed to take care of her mother that kept her from wanted to be gone from existence. So all she could do was lay there and cry silently for the loss of her baby.

****

"Can you help me with your mom?" The aide asked. Rosa gave her a look.

"What if I wasn't here? What would you do?" Rosa asked. Diana put her hands on her hips.

"I just need you to get her dressed while I get some lunch going."

"You get paid to take care of her so I suggest you do it. So don't ask me to help you do your damn job." The aide stared at her long and hard. If it wasn't because Diana cared for the aging woman and Irys, she would have left immediately. She thought Rosa was going to be here to help out a little but clearly she was just a leech. While Diana worked, Rosa just lounged around the house. She didn't mind that Rosa was there and not helping but when Rosa began adding onto the work she had to do, that's where Diana drew the line.

"That's not for you," Diana said, slamming the pot cover down as Rosa picked it up.

"Excuse me?!" Rosa snapped.

"I said that's not for you. I only made enough food for me and your mother. You want something to eat, you gotta make it yourself."

"Oh just wait until I tell Irys about this," Rosa said.

"Be my guest! Now excuse me!" Diana pushed her out of the way so she could put the steamed fish and veggies in a plate for Kendra and then for herself.

"Fine. I'll just order me some takeout." She gave Diana a fake smile before leaving the kitchen again to order herself some food. While she waited for it to come, Derek came by again like he said he would. Diana couldn't believe the type of relationship Rosa was carrying on with her sister's ex, but it wasn't her place to say anything about it. She could only watch and shake her head. She got the feeling that Rosa thought she was living some sort of luxurious life. Derek waited hand and foot on her, and Diana heard when they were in the bedroom humping the day away. She didn't clean up any of her dishes from the takeout and she left all her garbage out. Honestly, Diana was counting down the time until she would be able to leave. Usually Irys would be coming in when Diana was leaving, but this time she wasn't there. Diana wasn't willing to stay any longer to deal with Rosa. She made sure Kendra was comfortable and situated before she got her things ready to leave.

"I know you not fitting to leave the place like this," Rosa said, blocking her path. Diana took a deep breath to calm herself.

"Like what?" she asked. Rosa motioned to the dirty kitchen.

"Can you not see?"

"Oh yeah," Diana said. "What was it you told me this morning? That I should do my job? Well, I'm a health aide, not a maid. So you can clean up your own mess, and kindly get out of my way." Rosa gasped.

"Watch when Irys gets here! I am going to have you fired!"

"Good luck with that. Seen as you can't do a damn thing for you mother and Irys needs to work. Doubt she'd ever leave you in charge. I will ask you again, move out of my way or I'm going to put you out of my way." Rosa crossed her arms and stood there. She was being defiant but she didn't know that Diana wasn't going to take her crap.

"Have it your way." Diana pushed Rosa hard, moving her out of the way. To keep her away, she slammed Rosa against the kitchen wall and continued on her merry way out of the house. Throwing a fit, Rosa cursed every word in the book as she went to get her phone to call up Irys. Of course when she needed her, Irys didn't answer the damn phone.

"Relax your pretty little head," Derek told her as he was sprawled out on the couch.

"Shut up," She snapped. "As a matter of fact you can leave. I'll call you when I need some more fucking." Derek grunted and got up.

"Really?" he asked.

"Yes really," She said. "Go," She shooed. Even though he didn't want to he still got his things and left. He knew he laid it on her enough for her to be calling him back.

Alone in the house, Rosa was annoyed that Irys wasn't answering her phone, when she was supposed to be home already. That meant that if their mother was calling for Rosa, she actually had to go help her. Leave it up to Irys to be missing in action because she thought Rosa was going to be picking up her slack. Well, she wasn't!

Irys ignored Rosa's fourth call. She didn't want to speak to her sister at all. In fact, she didn't want to speak to anyone at the moment. Driving home from the hospital she was so numb. They'd kept her all day. After she slept from the medication there was a shrink in the room waiting to talk to Irys. They spoke for most of the evening and the doctor monitored her progress before she was allowed to leave. She didn't know what awaited her at home but she would find out soon enough.

Pulling up to the house, she got out of her car slowly. Her cramps were small because of the medication but she still felt them. She would be glad when she stopped bleeding and she could put this loss behind her. She had on a huge hospital pad and she was ready to shower, change and get into bed and just sleep.

Opening the front door, she walked through into the kitchen. Her mouth fell when she saw the mess of dishes in the sink and the garbage packed. Irys never kept her home like this and she knew the aide always cleaned up after preparing food for her mother so the only other person responsible must have been Rosa.

"Where the hell have you been?!" Rosa shouted, storming into the kitchen.

"I was dealing with something," Irys answered quietly.

"Yeah well while you off doing whatever the fuck you want to do, I was stuck here with that annoying ass aide, and now mom won't stop bothering me for shit! What do you pay her to do Irys? Look how she left the kitchen a mess!"

"It's not her job to clean up after other people Rosa. When she cooks she tidies up after herself but that's it."

"And she put her hands on me!" Rosa exclaimed. "She shouldn't be allowed back in here after that! What type of aid is she?!"

"Rosa just…" Irys didn't feel like arguing. "I can't fire her. I need her so I can do what I need to do during the day alright."

"Whatever. You just need to go look after mom, I'm sick of this. And I'm not here to play babysitter or caregiver. So think about that the next time you off doing your own shit and not thinking about anyone else!" Rosa shouted at her and bumped her hard as she walked by her. Irys just stood there. The last thing she had the strength for right now was arguing. So she continued onto her room and put her things down. Before she went to check on her mother she quietly washed the dishes, wiped down her counters, and took out the garbage. Diana had left dinner for her mother so Irys didn't need to cook again. Warming up the food, her mind was everywhere but within what she was doing. She never knew she was capable of even feeling this kind of numbness before. She could only imagine the pain a woman who carried her baby to full term but only birthed a still born would feel. It was all so terrible.

"Irys honey! Thank goodness you're home I was worried about you."

"Aw mom, don't worry about me. I'm okay," Irys attempted to smile weakly as she carried the food inside the room.

"I didn't want to bother your sister for help, she seemed so annoyed but I was just trying to talk to her you know. She just wouldn't have any of it."

"You know that's how Rosa is." Irys set the food down and helped her mother sit up. Kendra looked at her daughter deeply.

"Irys baby I know something is wrong what happened?" She questioned. Irys sat in the chair next to her mother's bed. Her warm concerned eyes were driving a hole through Irys's head. If there was anyone she could tell this to, it was her mother.

"I was a little late with coming home because I was in the hospital," She said lowly.

"For what?!" Her mother screeched. "Are you sick?!" Irys shook her head.

"No I'm not sick mama. But I um….I lost the baby." Kendra gasped loudly.

"Oh Irys baby!" Irys fell onto her mother's chest as she began weeping again. Kendra hugged her daughter as best as she could.

"Don't fault yourself for this," She whispered. "I know it hurts now but it will pass. You just have to remember that all things happen for a reason. And soon I know you'll be able to give me as many grandkids as I like." Irys chuckled as she wiped her tears.

"You not gonna be having me out here like Angelina Jolie with all these damn kids," She joked. Kendra held onto her child tightly knowing she would need as much comfort as she could get. The loss of a baby was nothing to be taken lightly.

****

Joseph opened the restaurant doors for Luna, letting her inside. She smiled at him but he could tell underneath she was worried about something. He hadn't really gotten the chance to know her, but her face always told you what she was feeling. She didn't hide that very well. Joe didn't think he could hide his expressions either when it came to this woman. When he saw her, he knew his eyes lit up and he could only stare. Her black long curls looked delicate to the touch.

"Hey Joe," She greeted.

"Hi Luna," He smiled. He wanted to hug her but he didn't know if it was appropriate. He hadn't even talked to her outside of the restaurant even though he wanted to.

"Lucien is in the kitchen?" She asked.

"Ah yeah, he is." Luna looked the handsome man up and down before giving him a smile and walking around him to get to the kitchen. While he wasn't looking, she turned back and looked at his ass in his jeans.

"Shame on you," Luna scolded herself. Shaking her head she proceeded into the kitchen. Lucien was hovering over a hot stove mixing something. His face was pulled straight, which it never was while he was cooking. That was a sign he was still stressing over Rosa.

"Lucy I got you some food," She said walking up to him.

"No thanks," He said firmly, not even looking at her. Here was his attitude again.

"What you mean no thanks?" She asked.

"I'm a chef Luna. I don't need you to bring me food when I have a place to cook it myself."

"Well, it's a fucking cheesecake. I know you won't make it here."

"I don't want a cheesecake."

"Looks like you need it," She said. He finally looked at her.

"Really?"

"Yes. Your attitude is on ten right now. Eat the damn cake and calm down." Even though he rolled his eyes, he took the bag from her and went over to the counter to open it. She watched as he cracked open the container and slowly ate the cake. She nodded in satisfaction. The cake would give him a little boost of energy that might counteract his sugar being too low, hence his sour attitude.

"No cake for us Luna?" Joe asked teasingly.

"Next time Joe. I'll personally deliver you a piece of cake." She winked at him, knowing her comment sounded sexual.

"That's what I'm talking about. I love a good piece of cake." Lucien cleared his throat.

"Joe, if you fuck my sister without marrying her first I'll kill you." The whole kitchen erupted in gasps.

"Lucien!" Luna scolded. He only shrugged his shoulders.

"I'm being honest with the both of you that's all. If you don't want my honesty, don't flirt in front of my face in my damn kitchen."

"Lucien nobody is waiting until marriage to have sex. You didn't."

"It's not about me. It's about you," He said. "You heard what I said Joe?" Joe stiffened up but nodded.

"Okay hold up. Did we forget you're my LITTLE brother? I appreciate your concern but I can handle my own relationships."

"That's funny. Because you can handle your relationships but won't let me handle my own. You always have an input in my business but I can't input in yours." Luna stood there for a moment. After gazing at her brother's blank expression, she grabbed her purse from the counter.

"You know what. I'm just gonna leave," She said. "When you have your head out of your ass then you can call me." Lucien groaned.

"Luna I'm sorry. You know that I-"

"I don't care for your excuse this time Lucien. If you want Rosa so bad, then go fucking get her. Forget about what I feel or what I said about her. Do what the hell you want to do. Because clearly my concern for you isn't wanted. I'm completely fine with that." Lucien only stayed quiet as Luna gathered her things and left. Joe went after her immediately.

"Hey Luna," He said grabbing her hand. He pulled her to a stop.

"What's up?" she asked.

"Um, I don't want to only see you or speak to you when you come here," he said. Could I have your number?" he asked.

"Sure yeah, you can," Luna smiled. She took his phone and entered her number then text herself so she'd have his number.

"Don't listen to Lucien okay? He's just in a sour mood from his sugar," She said.

"I gathered as much. That's why we're not sweating it. You shouldn't either. Because you know you'll be back tomorrow."

"Of course I'll be back. Who else is gonna annoy his ass?" Luna smiled. Joe cracked up at her and walked her to the door. Just as she exited, her phone buzzed. She looked at her screen to see a text from Lucien.

Love you sis. That's all it said. Even if she was a little mad at him, her heart softened at the text. She loved her brother to death and his happiness was her happiness.

Three days had passed where Irys hadn't come into work. On the fourth consecutive day when she walked through the doors, Luna jumped up and hurried over to the woman.

"Where you been at?!" Luna asked hugging her tightly. "Hardly any texts, no calls. I been lost here. What's going on?"

"Nothing I just needed time off that's all," Irys responded. Her smile was weak and there was something different about her eyes.

"Are you sure that was it?" Luna asked. "Because I can sense that wasn't everything."

"Here we go again with your psychic abilities," Irys said,

"It's serious Irys. I just know certain shit."

"Trust me Luna. I am okay. I had three days off to deal with it, I'm here to work that's all." Luna had to let it go. She didn't want to press anymore.

"How's your mom?" Luna asked.

"She's good. Asked for you a couple times. Had to tell her that you won't come see her."

"Do not do that Irys. You never invite me over!"

"I will soon. With my sister staying there with me now I never know what I'm gonna come home to and I don't want you to think I'm a pig or something."

"You know I wouldn't."

"I think I'm gonna need another job. With caring for my mother, and now having my sister living with me again, I just need the extra security. She doesn't have a job and I just don't trust her to get one. Is it awful of me to say that I want to kick her out?"

"Of course it's not Irys! She's a grown woman and won't act like it. You shouldn't have to bear her burdens. And besides I've been trying to move in with Lucien and he, in not so nice terms told me hell no." Irys had to chuckle at that.

"Why you wanna be up under him for?" Irys asked.

"Because I just want to," Luna pouted.

"I wonder if you're really older," Irys said. Luna rolled her eyes.

"Whatever," She smiled. She watched as Irys prepared herself for work. The usual energy she had was dimmed. She was rubbing her favorite lotion on her hands before she was looking through the computer at the reservations they had for the day. Luna wanted to ask again what was wrong but she didn't want to annoy her friend by asking the same thing over and over. But it was clear something was going on with Irys that she just didn't want to talk about.

"So the opening is coming up. We gonna go shopping for outfits?" Irys shook her head,

"You know maybe I shouldn't go," She said quietly.

"What? Why? You know this is big for me and my brother. I would love it if you came and supported him with me."

"I know Luna, but I'm just-" Irys let out a deep breath. "I'm just not in the best of moods and I don't want to rain on the fun at the opening you know?"

"That's nonsense!" Luna said. "If you're not in a good mood then you need to be at the opening to have something to take your mind off what's upsetting you. Please come with me. And if during you feel too sad or whatever you can leave. But at least try it out first." Irys stayed quiet and thought for a while. The last thing she wanted to do was celebrate anything after what happened to her.

"If you won't tell me yes I think I'm going to have to talk to your mother. I know you do anything she tells you to do." Irys rolled her eyes.

"Fine, I'll go. You lucky I just like to eat." Irys attempted another smile before she went on with getting ready for work.

****

Sitting at home again, Lucien was a pack of nerves. His opening was near and everything was finally just about ready. The reservations were piling up, giving Lucien confidence that the night would be successful. He of course just had to make sure that his food was good enough to get people to come back. His prices were reasonable for the demographics of the area, and it was fine dining food classics that everyone would enjoy eating.

In his bedroom he stared at his chef jacket hung up in his closet. To see the words executive chef written across the top on the right side with his name under it gave Lucien chills. This was all he ever wanted. His food dream never wavered and it was incredible that he was capable enough to fulfill his dreams. He wished his parents were only a phone call away so he could tell them about his restaurant. So that they'd be there in attendance to watch him cook his life away knowing that he didn't fail them or fail himself.

Even though he was ready for his moment he knew the issues he was having with Rosa not being around. His attitude towards Luna was out of control and it was partly because he was neglecting to take his medication. In his mind it seemed plausible that his body would revert back to normal if he just didn't take his insulin. That maybe insulin was just like an addictive drug. If he stopped taking it, his body wouldn't be dependent on it and he could function like normal. That was his depressed state giving him a conclusion to something that wasn't remotely possible. He did stop taking his insulin, and it backfired on his body and his mind. But instead of trying to do things he knew wouldn't work, he needed to go about fixing his situation the logical way. So picking up his phone again, he dialed Rosa's number.

"Lucien," She breathed answering the phone. Lucien was actually relieved it wasn't a man who answered this time.

"Hey Rosa," He greeted. "For a second I thought it would be a man answering your phone again."

"A man?"

"I called you some time ago. A man answered. Apparently you two were getting it on or something." Rosa was quiet for a moment.

"You have to understand that I was in grief over losing you and he was just there and I wanted to take my anger and grief out on something so I just-"

"You don't have to explain it to me Rosa. We're not dating you can do whatever you like."

"Have you-have you been with anyone else?" She asked lowly.

"No I haven't," He answered.

"Of course you haven't," She said. "That's probably why you're calling me. So you want to talk about us getting back together?"

"I just want to talk," He said. "And maybe it could work with us if we just discussed how things went down the last time we saw each other."

"What things?"

"What you did with my dog for one. And your feelings towards my diabetes." Rosa sighed long and hard.

"Lucien. I'm sorry about the dog. She bit me and the only thing I could do to feel safe was get her out of the house. And I know it hurts to admit your weaknesses when it comes to your diabetes but you have to see it for what it is."

"So then you really think I'm deficient huh?"

"You just can't do certain things like a normal man can Lucien. Don't fault me for being honest about it."

"I'm not faulting you Rosa. But there is a way to go about things. I know my lacks when it comes to my diabetes and I make up for it anyway that I can with you. But you don't seem to appreciate that."

"Let me come over there and talk to you. It's clear you know that we need to be together again, that's why you're calling me in the first place. Face to face we can discuss all of this. It doesn't matter what I think or what I say Lucien. Because in the end I'm willing to be with you. No other woman is gonna do that and you know it. Stop letting your sister trying to dictate what you do." Lucien stayed quiet. In his head he kept asking himself why he was doing this. Why was he on this phone with this woman who hadn't changed one bit? Why did he allow himself to feel like this was all Luna's fault and he needed to be with Rosa? He knew what he could and couldn't do regarding his sickness. But what he never considered himself was deficient. Why was he allowing himself to sink low enough to believe in her words, that he truly was deficient?

"Lucien? Are you still there?"

"Yes I'm here Rosa, just thinking."

"About what?"

"Why do you want to be with me?" He asked her.

"What?"

"You said you're the only woman who'd ever want to be with me. If I'm so deficient, why would you bother to be with me then?"

"Because you have the potential to treat me right. You give me what I want and when you're allowed to have sex with me, it's never a disappointment. I haven't had any other man to fuck me as well as you can. By far you're the best."

"Would you have my kids Rosa?" He asked.

"No," She chuckled. "Lucien I don't have time to take care of kids and I won't ruin this figure that you love so much." Hearing her words, Lucien just knew this was a mistake.

"This was a mistake," He said. "Calling you. It won't work. It won't ever work."

"What are you talking about?" Lucien took a deep breath.

"When you left at first I was okay with it. Then as the days went by I sort of sank into this depression because I was starting to believe in the things you told me. The same things you're telling me now. I thought that maybe I needed you because you were the only woman who I could be with. But then I can only wonder why in the hell a woman like you would want me if I'm so deficient? And your response is you want to stay with me because I can fuck you good? And then, I want to have kids at some point Rosa. You don't want that. What sense does it make that we be together?"

"No Lucien Do not do this."

"And I'm really offended that out of all this time we've been together all you can say to me is that I know how to fuck.

"What else can you do Lucien?!"

"More than you give me credit for. Bye Rosa."

"You're gonna be all alone! You watch! And then you're going to come crawling back to me begging!" Rolling his eyes, Lucien hung up the phone cutting off her rant. At a moment of weakness he did allow her words to be true. He felt he needed her and he was so depressed without her. But even if Rosa was the only woman who'd want him, he couldn't fathom living with a woman who was never going to fall in love with him. He knew Rosa wouldn't do that, because she loved herself too much to share love with anyone else. Maybe he would miss out on being with someone but his greatest dream was coming true. He wasn't going to allow himself to be weakened by his failed relationship.

"Come Salsa," Lucien said, as he left his bedroom. For the first time in a couple days he was actually going to willingly take his blood sugar and do what he needed to do to keep himself healthy for the opening of his restaurant.

****

Irys stared at herself in the mirror. Even though she said she would go, she was having her doubts now. But of course, it was her mother who kept reminding her she needed to get dressed and she needed to have a fun night out. On Saturday's Irys never went out. She stayed in, read a book, did some yoga and occasionally she drank some wine. Now that she was actually going out, she had to ask Diana to come by so her mother had proper care. There was no way Irys was leaving Rosa alone with their mother.

Dressed up, Irys went to see her mother to show her what outfit she'd chosen to wear. Kendra gasped.

"Oh my precious girl you look amazing," She smiled.

"You're supposed to say that, you're my mother," Irys smiled.

"Trust me, because I'm your mother I will tell you if you look broken down too."

"Actually, I believe you," Irys smiled.

"Now go, go have some fun. And please bring me back some of that food I'd love to taste it."

"I will." Irys kissed her mother goodbye and was ready to head out of the house. As she walked by the living room, she saw Rosa all dressed up as well.

"Where in the heck are you going?" Rosa asked, looking Irys up and down.

"The new restaurant opening," Irys replied. Rosa scoffed and laughed at her.

"Of course you'd be going to a restaurant. Too bad this one is booked all the way out. No way you're gonna get in." Irys knew in fact she would get in because she was rolling with Luna, but she wasn't going to gloat.

"I think I'll still take a chance," Irys said. "Is that where you're going?" She asked Rosa.

"Actually that is where I'm going." Rosa knew the last conversation she had with Lucien didn't go so well, and he thought he didn't need her. But she was convinced all he had to do was see her and he'd realized he wanted her on his arm. She was wearing a tight black dress, sleeveless with a deep V cut showing off both her boobs and her flat tummy.

"You taking yourself right?" Rosa asked. "Because you can't ride with me." Irys crossed her arms.

"Well why can't I ride with you?" She asked.

"Come on Irys, you expect me to want people to see us together? They'd think I was running a charity show being with you because clearly we're two different people who hang out in different crowds."

"You do know that we share the same blood right?" Irys asked. Rosa just crossed her arms. "Because no matter what I look like Rosa, or how much you don't care to be seen with me, we are blood sisters. Nothing can change that. And that has to amount for something." Irys backed out of the room.

"I don't need your ride I got my own. She should be outside any moment." Irys looked at her watch knowing Luna would be right on time. She wanted to be there when her brother cut the red ribbon for his front doors. Irys knew it was a proud moment for the both of them so she made sure she was ready and wouldn't have Luna waiting for her. Of course a big event like this her sister would be in attendance. The woman always made it to these things. She didn't know how Rosa played famous when she didn't even have a damn job to spend money as she'd like. Irys just shook her head and left the house to wait for Luna to pull up.

"Damn!" Luna exclaimed as Irys got into her car.

"What?" Irys asked clipping her seatbelt in.

"You look like a damn snack," She smiled. "Oh yeah I know some man is gonna want a taste out of your ass!" Irys laughed and pushed her shoulder.

"Shut up," She smiled. "I'm not no snack. Let's go I don't wanna miss the ribbon cutting."

"You?! Lucien would kill me!" She laughed pulling off and heading downtown.

As she expected, the front of the restaurant was packed with people waiting for the grand opening. The courtyard allowed for lots of people to wait and not have to worry about the street with traffic. Luna and Irys snaked their way around people, heading towards the front where the large name of the restaurant, *Toujours*, loomed.

Checking his watch, it was almost 6pm and Lucien was ready to cut the ribbon the on doors. He started to panic that Luna would be late until he saw her head of hair moving through the crowd. His sigh of relief was real. He didn't want to start anything without his sister there. He was already nervous enough.

"I'm here, I'm here!" She shouted finally escaping the crowd and walking up to him. Lucien hugged her tightly.

"What a turnout," She said. "It's so many people!"

"Tell me about it! But we're all ready." The servers were waiting inside, with the supervisor serving as the host until Luna found one. Only Joe stood next to him as his sous chef.

"Where's your friend?" Lucien asked her.

"Um…" Luna looked around for Irys. She must have lost her in the crowd. Just as Luna turned to tell Lucien, she saw a splash of red and curves.

"There she is. Irys!" Luna called her over. Irys pushed through the crowd finally getting through to the front. She looked up when Luna called her name.

"You forgot I can't slip through people like you?" Irys joked. Luna smiled at her and tugged on Lucien's shirt. When Lucien turned his attention back to his sister he was met with the radiance of a goddess. Irys locked eyes once again with the man she swore was so familiar to her when she'd spoken to him at the animal shelter. This time, he was wearing a black chef jacket with his name etched onto the side.

"You," Lucien said pointing at her.

"I remember you," She said. "From the shelter."

"Yeah, would you look at that? So this is your friend Luna?"

"Hold up you guys know each other?" Luna asked.

"Well we met at the shelter for like five minutes. He never told me his name, and I was saying he looked familiar in my head. It was because you two have the same eyes." Irys looked over at Lucien who was already staring at her.

"What are you staring at?" She giggled. Lucien blinked. He was staring at god's greatest creation, that's what he was staring at. She was wearing a red dress that matched her creamy complexion. The dress hugged her curves but it wasn't too tight and it went all the way down to just below her knee. It was an off the shoulder dress that showed off her creamy shoulders. And she topped it off with heels that had strings to tie around her calves. And her shape, Jesus she was thick and curvy and Lucien just wanted to wrap his arms around her hips and bury his head in her voluptuous chest.

Lucien cleared his throat, and tried to act like her presence didn't affect him.

"Nothing," Lucien managed to say. "Come Luna, we gotta cut this and get the show on the road." Irys stepped back a little and watched as Lucien and Luna stepped back towards the ribbon to get things started. He was staring at her, and Irys was now staring at him. His chef jacket fit him so perfectly she could still see those muscles she was intrigued by the first time she saw him. His black pants didn't sag off him either and Irys was there wishing he would turn around so she could look at his butt. Shame on her.

Instead of drooling over that man who was her best friend's brother, Irys paid attention to the host who had a microphone ready to talk to the crowd. He introduced Lucien as the head chef and then called out the name of the restaurant properly. With scissors in his hands, the crowd counted to three then cheered when Lucien cut the ribbon to the place. Irys cheered and clapped.

"See you ladies inside," Lucien said looking at both his sister and then at Irys. He gave her a small smile before tucking his hands in his pockets and walking inside before anyone else went in.

"Ready when you are," Irys said to Luna even though she was looking after Lucien.

"Sure," Luna said. She gave Irys a look noticing how the woman hadn't stopped looking at her brother. She didn't say anything about it however. She would just keep observing first.

Rosa knew if she was coming to this place what she needed to do was not bump into Luna. She didn't want that fight. And clearly Lucien listened to everything his dear sister said so if Luna didn't see her, she wouldn't be planting anything in Lucien's head for the night to make him turn Rosa away. She was tucked away in the crowd of people watching as Luna stood in line waiting to get inside. Rosa could only laugh at the fact that her brother had made her wait in line to get in like everyone else. But then standing behind Luna was Irys. Rosa was so sure Irys wouldn't be able to get in until she walked straight into the restaurant without even speaking to the host. She just smiled and waved then went inside. Sucking her teeth, Rosa pushed through the crowd and cut the whole line going straight to the front. Only when she tried to enter without saying anything, the host quickly grabbed onto her hand.

"Reservation?" He asked her.

"No, but I'm the head chef's girlfriend. I don't need a reservation."

"Well, Chef Lucien gave a precise list on who would be in attendance but not have a reservation. What's your name?"

"Rosa," She said. The tight lipped man shook his head as he looked at his list.

"Sorry Rosa, you're not on the list."

"What if he didn't think he had to put his own woman on a list?!" She snapped at him.

"Okay sure. Hold on." He turned his head and spoke into a small mike attached to his jacket. He listened and nodded to whatever the person on the other end said.

"Chef says if they aren't on his list and don't have a reservation they cannot be let in. We are booked full." Rosa's mouth just fell open.

"Now please. Other people are waiting to enter. If you do not want to go I'll have to get security to escort you away." With a stomp of her foot Rosa scrambled away. How could have Irys gotten in, but Rosa was left out? She was the one sleeping with the damn chef. Did that mean he was truly finished with her? Rosa really couldn't believe that. But there was nothing to do but go back home and just relax. She couldn't do anything because she didn't have any money. Then there was always Derek of course.

Irys had no words for the restaurant. It was just simply beautiful. All the furnishings were modern and cozy filling up the room with a relaxed atmosphere. The kitchen was open and stood against the back wall, facing all the tables so the diners could watch the chef's work in the kitchen preparing the food. It was actually pretty smart. Irys loved the whole thing. That plus their table was one of the closest to the opening of the kitchen. Which meant she saw Lucien very clearly. And with him standing there ready to cook he was poised and focused. Until he actually looked at her. His straight face broke and he smiled at her. Irys felt her cheeks warm as she smiled back at him. They were staring at each other until his attention was probed by the first server handing in a ticket. He took the paper then turned back to his kitchen staff. His voice was loud, in control, and authoritative. He shouted the order out and received a loud 'HEARD' from all his cooks as they confirmed they understood what the order was. The diners clapped as the cooking went underway for the first time. Irys was mesmerized. There was no other word for it.

"I'm going to have everything on this menu," Luna told the server. Since the server knew who Luna was she didn't question it.

"I'll just have the mushroom risotto for appetizer, and the filet, medium well please," Irys said.

"Um no, she's gonna have everything on the menu too," Luna said. "We're his guests but also his critiques. He won't mind making it all twice." Since it was fine dining eating there wasn't that many things to choose from and the menu wasn't long like a chain restaurant's menu. Still Irys was nervous about having him making everything for the both of them.

"Why don't we just share it all?" Irys asked.

"Actually that's a good idea," Luna said. The server smiled and poured them some wine before heading off. Irys watched as she gave Lucien the ticket. He read what it said and immediately looked up at her. Irys pointed at Luna telling him this was all her fault. He chuckled and turned back to his staff to read out the order.

Lucien knew Luna was going to order the whole damn menu. She was greedy plus her ass wanted to sample everything. She already told him that. But when Irys pointed the finger at Luna for her obvious lack of concern for him cooking all the food Lucien had to smile. She seemed such a sweet lady, but he could tell she was outspoken and full of spirit. Something about her drew him in. Was it her eyes? Was it her smile? Lucien didn't know. But even through the steam and the heat of his kitchen, every time he looked up he was drawn directly to her. And each time he did look at her, she was looking at him. For a split second that seemed to last a whole minute, they were just lost staring at each other. It was usually Joe who caught Lucien's attention enough for him to actually break eye contact with the woman. He finished off her and Luna's order and got it in a large platter for the servers to bring to the table. Lucien watched as the women received the food. They gasped at the enormity of it all. Lucien wanted to watch until they actually started eating. It was Irys who took the taste of her risotto first. Her eyes rolled with pleasure as she sampled the food. In just that, Lucien felt his own sense of pleasure.

Irys groaned as flavor erupted across her taste buds. It seemed like such a simple dish to create, but with the different types of flavor coming across she wasn't sure it was so simple after all. But either way, it tasted like heaven. Each item that she sampled, she was groaning and just in awe. She also would look at Lucien each time she did take a bite of something. If he wasn't looking at her already, she only had to wait a moment before he did finally look at her. He bit his bottom lip and watched her.

"You like?" He mouthed. Irys licked her lips and nodded at him.

"I know my brother can cook, but damn I forgot how skilled he really is!" Luna said as she stuffed her face with fried calamari.

"How do you like the food so far?" Luna asked Irys. Irys didn't answer her. "Hey I'm talking to you," Luna exclaimed picking her head up to look at Irys. But Irys was not even paying attention to Luna. She seemed dazed out and was looking over Luna's shoulders. Luna looked behind her to see that Irys was staring with at Lucien. And Lucien was staring right back at Irys. Luna looked between the both of them, not even realizing Luna had caught them staring. But it was clear they weren't staring at each other just because they wanted to. Luna turned back to Irys. She cleared her throat loudly.

"Um, hello!" Luna kicked Irys under the table. She jerked and looked at Luna.

"Oh were you saying something? Sorry I was distracted," Irys said innocently.

"Distracted my ass! Why are you eyeing my brother like he's a treat or something?" She asked.

"What? I am not-" Irys stopped her lie when Luna gave her a face. She groaned. "Okay maybe I am eyeing him like some hot melted caramel sorry Luna. I don't mean to." Luna crossed her arms.

"You know I am very protective of my brother Irys," She said.

"Yes I know. But he keeps looking at me too! And then you remember the man I told you I met while you were out of work?" Luna gasped.

"You were talking about him?"

"Yes! On my lunch break I was walking by the shelter and they got me to go in. Then he came in to get his dog. Which I find it completely hilarious her name is Salsa."

Luna was surprised the man Irys thought was so cute was her own brother. She didn't know what to think about it.

"See, he's looking again," Irys said, looking back over Luna's shoulder. Luna turned around sharply. Lucien made a face like a kid that been caught by his mother doing something wrong, and quickly turned away to get back to cooking.

"Interesting," Luna hummed. She looked back at Irys who was eating again. But during the night Luna noticed Irys was trying hard not to look back at Lucien. For the whole time Luna had known this woman, she didn't see Irys interested in anyone. That was partly because she was with Derek but even so Irys just wasn't the type of woman to be out there whether she was single or not. And it wasn't just Irys that was surprising Luna it was Lucien too. He was just torn up over his ex and now he was captivated by another woman?

After their dinner, they had to leave their table for the next set of reservations at 9pm. Lucien didn't want to kick them out while everyone left, so he invited them inside the kitchen.

Irys was nervous as she walked with Luna towards the kitchen. She hadn't had butterflies like this before with any man, not even Derek. It's not like she really knew Lucien like that in the first place. They hardly even spoke that much to begin with.

"How'd you guys enjoy dinner?" Lucien asked, opening the glass doors to let the women inside the kitchen.

"Oh it was great," Luna said. "But you know you're amazing Lucien." She hugged and kissed her brother. But his attention wasn't on her.

"Did you enjoy your dinner Irys?" He asked, crossing his arms and leaning against the stainless steel counter.

"Yeah, it was okay." Irys watched as his brows rose.

"Okay?" He asked. "Just okay? What was wrong with it?"

"The lamb chops were shaved down on the bones to the point where they look like dog chews, and the rice in the risotto was overcooked and tasted too much like wine. And there's no vegan options. I noticed that. You must know that someone will be a vegan when they come here." Luna gasped.

"Irys what the hell?!" Luna snapped. Lucien ignored his sister and kept eye contact with Irys. She winked at him.

"The actual meat on the chop was perfect, and there's no way we could have scraped the bone down enough to make it look like a dog toy. Secondly, the rice isn't overcooked because I made it myself and if you didn't know, risotto has wine in it. That's why it's a risotto. Thirdly, the zucchini pasta with quinoa balls are the vegan option, but just because its vegan doesn't mean it has to lack in taste. And that's why you didn't know it was vegan. Anything else?" Irys smiled brightly.

"You're good," She said. "I think you'll be able to handle any critic that steps foot in here."

"You're good too," Lucien said. "Almost believed you for a second." Luna looked back and forth between them.

"Well you fooled me!" Luna snapped. "I was about to cuss you clean out for coming at my brother's food!"

"You know I wouldn't do that Luna. I'm just testing him! Making sure he's ready for the critics. He kept a cool head and he made valid points." While Irys spoke, Lucien was looking at her breasts again. Then his eyes traveled down to her tummy. It wasn't flat, but it wasn't so rounded either. It was almost the perfect size for her hips, and those thighs.

"What are you looking at again?" She asked.

"Yeah, whatcha looking at?" Luna asked her brother. He gave Luna a look.

"Shut up," He murmured. "Anyways, there's a booth over there for you guys to relax. If you need anything don't hesitate to ask me." As they began walking towards the booth, Lucien grabbed onto Irys's soft hand stopping her. Luna turned to look back at them.

"Go on Luna, give us a sec." Luna scoffed and continued on. Irys stood nervously in front of Lucien not sure what he was going to say to her.

"You aren't mad I critiqued your food are you?" She asked innocently. Lucien smiled at her concern.

"No sugar, you're fine. That's not what I wanted to say." Irys couldn't help but blush at the endearment.

"What did you want to say?" she asked, not able to resist.

"I just felt it wouldn't be gentlemanly if I didn't comment on how lovely you look tonight," He said. Irys didn't know whether he truly meant that compliment or whether he was just trying to make her feel good about being a bigger girl.

"Is that compliment because you want to give it, or because you feel you have to give it?" She questioned.

"Have to?" He asked.

"Some people, especially men compliment me in attempt to reassure me that not everyone can be skinny and I shouldn't feel bad about my weight." Even though her words were unfiltered, her tone was still sweet. Lucien didn't like that she had to defend herself, but he knew it perhaps was engrained in her brain to do so.

"I'm complimenting you Irys because I want to," He said. "And if I compliment you in the future, don't you ever ask me that question again." Irys was both surprised and turned on by his ability to be nice one moment and then firm the next, all while retaining that cool, sexy attitude. She couldn't help but just look at him.

"Understand me?" He asked softly, with a slight edge.

"I understand," She replied. He jerked his head towards the booth.

"Luna's waiting for you," He smiled. She looked him up and down before walking away.

"What was that about?" Luna asked as Irys sat down.

"He was just complimenting my attire that's all." Even though Irys spoke to her, she was looking after Lucien dreamily. That look on Irys's face was so obvious to how she was feeling about Lucien.

"Excuse me," Luna said even though Irys wasn't paying her any attention. She scooted out of the booth and charged straight to her brother. She grabbed onto his elbow and dragged him to the corner of the kitchen.

"What?" He asked, tugging his elbow from her. He stuffed a piece of toffee in his mouth to keep his sugar at an appropriate level.

"Irys said you complimented her outfit."

"Yeah? Is that a crime?" He asked.

"And I see the way you two been staring at each other all damn night! What happened to you and Rosa huh? The woman you've been mad at me over?" Lucien rolled his eyes.

"Luna I already apologized for my behavior with that. And me and Rosa had a talk. It won't work."

"So this means what?"

"It means nothing Luna. I'm just as I was before just now I'm alone."

"You were never alone Lucien. You always have me."

"Sure Luna. Anything else you wanna drill me about?" He asked.

"Yes actually. What do you think of Irys?" Lucien shrugged.

"I don't know I mean she's nice," He answered. Luna crossed her arms.

"Get real," She scoffed. "You don't stare and be distracted by a female and just tell me she's nice." Lucien rolled his eyes.

"You always on my case Luna, I swear! People are coming back in I need to get myself together, I don't have time for this."

"Then just answer me then. What do you think of Irys?" She quizzed her brother intently. Lucien groaned in frustration.

"I think she's cute," He admitted. Luna smiled at him. He plucked her on the nose and turned to walk away. Before he got far he turned around and looked back at his sister.

"Really, really cute," He added. With a raise of his brow he turned and continued back to what he was doing. Luna smirked and hurried back over to the booth. She sat around the tablet and looked at Irys who was sipping from a glass of water. Luna smiled at her and began drinking out of her own glass. Luna had to admit, she was too protective of her brother. And in most cases, she always hated his girlfriends. But it was completely clear that Irys and Lucien saw something in each other. And what'd you know, they were both single and in need of someone to show them what real love was. And Luna was just the person to make them realize that. Luna laughed evilly in her head as she sipped her water.

Chapter Nine

"Oh you're here. I didn't see you inside the restaurant. Guess you couldn't get in?" Irys said as she entered her home later on the night of the opening and saw Rosa in the living room couch. Rosa sucked her teeth.

"No worries, I brought home some food. Come eat, I know you must be starving because you can't cook and there's nothing here to eat. Come, don't be shy." Irys didn't think Rosa would come, so she went to the kitchen to prepare a small plate for her mother to taste the food, but sure enough Rosa showed up in the kitchen. Diana also came into the kitchen ready to leave.

"Thanks for staying Diana," Irys greeted. "Give me a second." She went to her bedroom to retrieve her checkbook. Back out in the kitchen she wrote Diana a check for coming on a Saturday to look after her mom.

"Here you are, oh and I brought you some food too. This place was awesome!"

"Thanks Irys! If this is good as I keep hearing then I'll be going there myself."

"Trust me. It's amazing!" Diana and Irys embraced before she packed up her things, and took the plastic container with her as she left the house.

"Go on dig in," Irys said to Rosa, motioning to all the food she'd laid out on the counter. Rosa just stared bitterly at Irys. She didn't need Irys to bring her Lucien's food. She knew just how well her man could cook.

"Let me bring this food to mom. I know she'll love it." When Irys left the kitchen with the food to bring to their mother, Rosa just sat there in a fit. Yes, she was jealous and mad as hell. How dare Lucien just have her thrown away like trash? There was so many time where she could have cheated on him and left his ass down and out, but she never did that. And he'd turn around and just cast her aside? Rosa couldn't just let this go. She could easily call Derek and get him to do whatever she wanted but in the end she knew she wanted Lucien. His restaurant was going to be big and he was going to become a prominent chef. She needed to be at his side to reap all those benefits. She got up from the table leaving all the food untouched. She wasn't about to stop trying until she got her man back. If she had to stalk him, that's exactly what she was going to do.

She woke up early the next morning way before Irys had a chance to wake up. She threw on a pair of tight jean shorts, and a halter top, grabbed her purse and she was heading out of the house. She drove straight out to town and to his restaurant. There was still confetti on the floor outside the place from the opening. Finding a parking spot, she watched the building for a little bit. It was clearly closed and she didn't see Lucien's car in the parking lot of the building. While it was Sunday, she knew the place would still be open for late lunch hours, and then an early dinner. She just had to wait for Lucien to arrive. Leaving her car, she went across the courtyard to a small spot where she ordered herself a mimosa and waited for her man to get into work.

When she saw his Range Rover pull into the lot, she finished off her drink and stood ready to meet him.

"Hey, I didn't get your bill," The server said, blocking Rosa from leaving.

"Oh um yeah. How much for the muffin and mimosa?"

"15 dollars," She replied. Rosa went into her purse and ruffled around.

"Shit," She cursed. She'd forgotten that Irys had took back her credit card, and Rosa didn't have any cash. Lucien used to give her money that Rosa put in a separate account but that was empty now.

"If you don't have the money I'm going to have to talk to my manager. Then she'll decide what's next."

"Um I'm sorry I completely forgot my wallet. Can I talk to the manager please? Maybe we can work something out?" The woman nodded and walked away. The moment she did, Rosa took off, heading across the courtyard.

"Hey!" Someone shouted after her. Not looking back, she kept running but was stopped short by someone grabbing onto her arm. They stopped her momentum and dragged her back towards the place she was running from. When she looked up, a large man was holding onto her. Maybe he was their security.

"LUCIEN!" Rosa shouted as she fought the hold of the man. Lucien turned at the familiar shout of his name. He was just about to open the restaurant doors when he heard the shout. Looking across the courtyard he saw Rosa being dragged towards a little brunch spot. Lucien perked up.

"What are you doing?!" Lucien shouted, thinking the man was trying to hold Rosa against her will. He ran across the courtyard, charging towards them. In close range, he grabbed Rosa's arm, and pulled her towards him.

"Get the fuck off her," He growled at the man. He pushed him off Rosa and held Rosa to his side tightly.

"What the hell are you doing?" Lucien asked him. Before the man could answer, two women who worked at the place came running forward.

"She was trying to run off without paying!" The server announced. "This is our security, he was just stopping her!" Lucien looked at Rosa. Her head was down as if embarrassed to admit the truth.

"I was only trying to get my boyfriend to come pay it for me," She said. "You didn't have to come grab me up like that. He works right over there." Lucien groaned and let Rosa go.

"How much was the bill?" He asked.

"15."

"Here. Keep the change." Lucien pulled 40 from his wallet and gave it to the server. "Sorry for the trouble." Lucien took Rosa's hand and led her away from the scene. He didn't know what the heck was going on with her. He didn't say anything to her until they were safely inside the restaurant.

"What in the heck are you doing?" He asked.

"Meaning?"

"Running away and not paying a bill? Why would you do that?"

"I wasn't running. I was coming to ask you to pay for it," She pouted. Lucien crossed his arms.

"But why me?" Lucien asked.

"Because Lucien. You're my boyfriend. I-I didn't have any money and I thought you-"

"Stop saying that Rosa. We're not together."

"You still came running to help me," She said.

"Don't take my kindness for anything more than what it is. I thought that guy was trying feel up on you that's why I came to help you. Had I known it was because you were running out on a bill I would have left you alone so you could learn your lesson."

"Why are you doing this to me? I don't deserve any of this. You kicked me out of the house knowing I could have no place to stay, knowing I have no money. How can you live with that?"

"Whoa," Lucien backed up. Was she trying to pin this on him? "I know you have a place to stay with your mom Rosa. That's where you were before I invited you to live with me. That's the first thing. Second thing is, I tried to reconcile with you, but you ruined that with your blatant disregard for anyone but yourself."

"Lucien I want you back! What am I supposed to do without you? Without money?" Lucien's eyes bulged.

"Get a job Rosa! You care about money so much? Get a job!"

"A job!" She shouted. "I can't, I can't do anything!"

"Then I don't know what you want from me."

"You're obligated to take care of me Lucien. Especially if you know I have nothing because you used to give me everything."

"You weren't my wife Rosa. I'm not obligated to do anything!"

"Just take me back," She begged. She attempted to kiss him, but Lucien moved out of the way.

"No Rosa," he said.

"Lucien I-I-I love you," She stumbled. Lucien could only stare at her. The emotionless tone of her voice in those words made Lucien pity her. She stumbled on her words so much because it was difficult for her to try and make it sound real.

"You need to go Rosa." She seemed shocked that he still denied her at her display or affection or lack thereof. Instead of leaving like he asked her to, she lunged at him, wrapping her arms around his neck and attacking his lips. She kissed him feverishly. Lucien didn't kiss her back, but he didn't stop her either. He let her kiss him, and it continued when she reached to unzip his jeans. A small moan left his mouth when she palmed his manhood.

"You might not want me emotionally Lucien, but you want me sexually. Any man would." She kissed his neck while continuing to grope him.

"Stop," He groaned. He pushed her off gently. "I'm not having sex with you in my place of business," He said.

"So I'll come by tonight. Simple." He shook his head.

"Don't waste your time Rosa. If I wanted this to happen between us. It would have been happening already. Like I said before. You need to go." Anger swelling inside her, and being she was so close to him in the first place, Rosa socked him in the nuts. Lucien grunted and bent over in pain. As Rosa walked out of the place, he punched the wall knowing well he couldn't do anything to Rosa. Damn that woman had issues!

Rosa walked away from the restaurant angrily. She called Derek as she walked to her car. He answered promptly.

"I need money, and then I need you to come and fuck me," She grunted angrily.

"How much money baby? You know I don't have that much."

"I don't care. I need a shopping spree, and I need a fucking. You want to be my man Derek, you need to be able to handle it. I don't care what you do to get it, you just better get it."

The line went dead against Derek's ears. He wanted to keep Rosa, but there wasn't a lot he had to do so. The only person he was getting money from was Irys. Since she was acting like she was better than everybody, Derek had no problem using her. He still had access to her account, so he went in and easily transferred funds to his account then he set out to go and take care of his future lady.

Luna entered her brother's restaurant to work both her job as manager and as the temporary host on Sunday. Since she had her fun at the opening and was able to sample the food, she was ready to do her part at the place to help her brother out. As she walked to the back room to get things together, she passed Joe in the kitchen. He winked at her, and kept prepping. She lost her thoughts for a second, only staring at Joe. He was just wearing a t-shirt, and his strong biceps looked too good as he sliced up a piece of fish. Though her attention was gone, Luna kept walking.

"Oomph," Luna snapped out of her daze when she bumped into something sturdy. She looked up slowly into her brother's curious gaze. He leaned against the entrance towards the back rooms and stuffed his hands in his pockets.

"Whatcha staring at Lu?" He asked.

"Nothing," She scoffed. "And hi to you too. I brought you something to eat, come on."

"Why do you keep bringing me things to eat?" He asked. "I'm a chef for Pete's sake."

"Because you worry me and I don't think you eat enough. What was your sugar this morning?"

"100," He answered. Luna hummed then reached into her bag and pulled out a bottle of orange juice.

"Not too high not to low, but it could be better."

"I swear you need a husband so you can stop trying to take care of me," Lucien said.

"Whatever," She pouted.

"And speaking of husband, anything going on with you and Joe?" Luna rolled her eyes and continued past him, but he only followed her to the back.

"Nothing's going on. We spoke on the phone a couple times, that's all."

"Just don't give it up easily, okay?" Luna gasped. She threw an apron at him. "What?!"

"Don't talk to me about that! I'm your older sister!"

"Whatever Luna. You always be in my sex life. And I know you ain't no saint. Remember that time I caught you and that guy after your senior prom?" He snickered.

"I told you not to mention that again!" She laughed. "And I know your sex life ain't all that either." The smiled drained from Lucien's face.

"That's where you're wrong. You may not like her Luna, but Rosa knows how to fuck, I ain't gonna lie about that."

"I always imagined she'd just be a loose bag of goods." Lucien crossed his arms.

"She wasn't. I promise that." Luna looked at her brother deeply.

"I thought you were over her?"

"I am over her," He answered.

"Doesn't seem like it to me," Luna said.

"She was just here earlier." Luna rolled her eyes. "Luna am I supposed to be taking care of her?" He questioned.

"Excuse me?"

"It's just that, she didn't have a job while we were together. Then I kicked her out. Am I supposed to be helping her stay on her feet until she finds a job? Should I just be okay with the fact that she's struggling?"

"Oh no. Lucien none of this is your fault. She has a place to go. And the moment you broke up with her she should have been looking for a job, not complaining and running back to you. And I'm getting real tired of her coming up to you and putting this garbage in your head. You're not getting back with her right?"

"No I'm not getting back with her. She was just trying to fuck me earlier, and when I told her no she kicked me in the nuts and left."

"What?! Why didn't you call me to come whoop her ass?! You know I cannot take it when a female hits you!" Luna shouted.

"Calm down Lue. I'm over it."

"So why you look like that? I'm trying to believe you Lucien but you don't seem to be happy to be rid of her!"

"I'm not happy to be rid of her Luna."

"You confuse me so much Lucien. I don't fucking get it. I really don't. First you break up with her, then you start thinking you need her, then you tell me she ain't shit, but now you're not happy to be rid of her? What is it that's going on with you?" Luna watched as his eyes flickered down to the ground.

"Lucien?" She prompted.

"I'm heartbroken Luna. I don't know what else you want me to say. I can see she's not the woman for me, she's proven that. But I can't lie and say I'm not hurt realizing how much she didn't care for me. It just hurts thinking that I was going to marry a woman who could give two fucks if I went into a diabetic coma or not." Luna hated to be tough on her brother but she needed to be. It was a waste to have any type of feeling for that woman. He needed to move on.

"What about her do you like?" Rosa asked him. "You can't say she's a good person because she's not. She didn't support your dreams. She hated the fact that you're diabetic, and she was using you for money. But you said she's a really good fuck so perhaps that's what you really like about her. But newsflash, you can fuck any other woman on this planet and actually have feelings for them. You don't need to be stuck on her."

"She's not nice. And she didn't love me. And maybe she was using me Luna, but even if she didn't want to do something with me, she always did. So it wasn't just about the sex. She was willing to keep me by doing the things that I wanted to do."

"Well she ain't in your life anymore Lucien. So just drop all this shit."

"Next time I get my heartbroken, perhaps I'll keep it to myself since my sister makes me feel just as deficient as my ex-girlfriend said I was."

"Don't do that Lucien," Luna sighed.

"I checked the system when I got in and some of the servers didn't take their breaks. As manger I need you to ensure they take their breaks so we don't break any laws here. The tablet is at the front so you can check out the seating chart and look at all the reservations for the night." Luna got that he was ending the conversation by going boss mode on her.

"Yeah sure thing boss," She replied. He nodded at her.

"Thanks for the OJ." She watched him leave the back room, taking another sip of his juice.

"What am I going to do with you baby bro?" she asked herself. She needed to fix him.

****

Early Monday morning, Irys was up and making breakfast for her mother. Diana was due any moment, but Irys didn't mind cooking the meal. Rosa was still being her lazy self, cooped up in that bedroom. Hearing the doorbell, Irys knew it was Diana. She cut off the stove and went to open the front door. The two women greeted each other before returning to the kitchen.

"I made grits and eggs so don't worry about making any breakfast for mom."

"Got it." She smiled weakly at Irys. Clearing her throat she stopped Irys from leaving the kitchen.

"I don't mean to be rude Irys, but the check you gave me on Saturday, I tried to deposit it, and it um…it bounced back."

"What?!" Irys asked. "Bounced back?!" She immediately took out her phone to check her bank account with her mobile banking app.

"Oh my god." Her heart plunged into her stomach when she saw she had absolutely no money left.

"No...No…No…" When she checked her account activity she saw that the last of her money that was left was transferred into Derek's account.

"That fucking bastard!" Irys shouted. She looked up at Diana. "I am so sorry Diana. I didn't know that jerk went away with all my money. I'll write you another check." Irys was so mad she found herself shaking. But it was more than just anger that consumed her. The money in that account was what she lived off of. It wasn't much, just enough to pay certain bills and get her through the week before she got paid. So she had to dip into her savings account through her other bank that was primarily for her mother to make sure there was always enough money for her to take care of her mom in emergencies. As she wrote the check, she felt embarrassed and stupid that she'd been caught with no money all because her ex wanted to be vindictive. First it was her miscarriage that she thought he had a role in when he hit her in the stomach, and now he was doing this.

This was a big blow to her and she couldn't afford to use her emergency money when she had her mom to take care of. Rosa wasn't working and nowhere close to even consider getting a job. Everything fell on top of Irys. It just wasn't fair. Tears slipped her eyes as her frustration consumed her.

"Oh Irys don't cry," Diana said. She came up to Irys and hugged her. "I get how this happened. I'm sorry he did this to you."

"I just can't manage Diana. You do great work for me and my mom and you deserve to be paid on time. I just-I don't know why he'd do this to me."

"Men are dogs Irys. Don't worry about him. Then he would have won. Take this to fuel your next moves. When you make it Irys, he's going to be sorry he ever treated you like crap. Don't cry." Irys wiped her tears and handed Diana the check with shaking hands.

"He doesn't have access to this bank so it should work this time. I um…I'm gonna get to work."

"Thank Irys," She said softly. "See you later."

Irys packed her things up and headed to work. She dried her tears and stopped crying over Derek, but her anger wasn't going anywhere. She got that she was a nice person, but using her? That was uncalled for. She wasn't going to let Derek get away with it thought. She was going to do whatever she could to make sure he knew she wasn't to be messed with.

Before going to work, she went straight to Chase, to report the unauthorized transaction, and then she went about changing her account so if Derek tried again he'd hit a brick wall. After that, she didn't have any more time before work but once she got out of work she was going straight to the police department to file a report. Parking in her favorite spot, as she walked up to the spa she dialed Derek. Of course he didn't answer, but Irys didn't stop calling. It was about the 6th call where he finally picked up his phone.

"The fuck do you want?!" He snapped at her. "You got confident and put my ass out the hell you bothering me for? And you better not think I'm bout to take your ass back either."

"Oh please Derek! You wish I want your ass back! You fuck my sister in my own damn house and then you took my fucking money out of my account like you lost your damn mind!" Derek burst out in laughter.

"Man did you hear the way she was moaning for me?" He teased. Irys was just too shocked. She stood outside of the spa not wanting to go in so everyone wouldn't hear her conversation.

"I'm going to the police Derek. What you did was illegal and you're gonna pay for this shit."

"Go on you fat fuck. It's my word against yours. You could just be a disgruntled ex, and besides you let me have your account information."

"You fucktard I have the evidence that you transferred the money and I can easily say that it was unauthorized."

"Go right the fuck ahead Irys. I ain't scared of shit you gonna do. In the end we know that your soft ass not gonna go through with none of your little ass threats. So do us both a favor and just go eat a donut or some shit!" Irys's breathing contorted.

"Laugh all you fucking want to!" Irys screamed. "One day you're gonna regret this Derek! I will fuck you up if you continue to fuck with my life! Just leave me the fuck alone!"

Luna turned the corner just in time to hear her friend screaming hysterically into her cell phone. Luna had to pause and look around for a moment to make sure that truly was Irys. If there was one thing Irys didn't do it was shouting like that. The amount of pain in her voice gave Luna halt. She immediately felt like fighting her friend's battles for her just to get her to stop hurting.

Irys slammed her phone down on the pavement. Luna rushed over to her, picking up the phone from the sidewalk.

"What the hell is going on?" Luna asked. But instead of answering, Irys just paced. She could literally see the smoke coming out of that woman's head.

"Irys talk to me," Luna begged. Irys didn't stop her pacing, but Luna saw her begin to break down. She put her hands against her face and Luna knew that meant the tears were coming. She immediately went up to her to wrap her arms around the woman. Irys used Luna as a crutch until her eyes could no longer tear and sobs just left her mouth.

"Stop crying over his ass," Luna scolded. "He's nothing!"

"That's what he left me with. Nothing," Irys said. She was speaking of both her baby and her finances.

"That fucker took all my damn money and I have nothing. I just want to be left alone Luna. But it seems like no matter how good a person I am, I can't catch a damn break." Luna pushed Irys away so she could look at her in the face.

"Listen to me Irys. You're always going to go through some shit. But I promise that you will always be able to overcome it. Do not let this ruin your good heart. There are so many horrible people in this world. And you're a shining light Irys. Nothing can compete with that." Irys just held onto Luna for a moment longer. She believed Luna's words, but she just had to find the energy and the mindset to keep pushing forward.

"Come, let's go inside." Luna still held onto Irys as she led her inside. Once inside, Irys let her go and went about cleaning her face up so it didn't look as if she was balling her eyes out. Staring at her friend trying to get herself back together, Luna honestly felt helpless. First it was her brother and now Irys? Like someone flipped a switch, a sudden idea came to her head. Wait.

"Irys what are you going to do about the money? I can lend you however much you need you know that."

"No I couldn't take your money," Irys said.

"Um," Luna coughed. "Well, Lucien is looking for a host at his restaurant. I'm sure if I spoke to him he'll bring you on. Hell, I hired everyone but the cooks."

"A host? I don't know Luna."

"Don't be a Debbie downer. You're great with people. That's why you work here. Not to mention you speak three fucking languages. And this can be something you do after a shift here. All you'd need to do is talk about your pay with Lucien and that's it. Come on Irys. Besides, I'd be working there too." Irys thought for a moment. It was true, another job would be useful, especially now. She needed to make all her money back.

"Okay fine. I'll talk to Lucien about it. But you need to be there with me."

"Of course Irys. No matter what I'll always have your back." When Irys turned her back, Luna snickered. Her brother was a hot mess. Her friend was a hot mess. To fix it, Luna simply just had to get them together. Irys was an amazing woman. And her brother would appreciate her as such and needed a woman like that. They were eyeballing each other at the opening anyway. Plus, Lucien thought Irys was cute. Obviously this was the solution to everything. And having Irys work in the restaurant with Lucien? They wouldn't be able to resist each other.

Chapter Ten

The kitchen was prepped and ready to go for their Monday night dinner service. He didn't think the place would be fully booked out on a Monday night, but he figured it was because the place just opened up and people were still buzzing about it. So far, things were going well, and he was actually profiting. It would take a while to get things sorted out completely but in the near future he knew he would be able to live well off of something he loved.

While he lounged in the kitchen watching his staff eat their meals before service, he scrolled through the social media's he created for the restaurant adding pictures and liking more pages of other restaurants to get support from those places as well. He didn't feel like eating but he was sucking on a piece of ginger candy he'd made from scratch that he used to keep his sugar at an appropriate level during service. He should eat right now but he just didn't feel like it.

"You should eat," Joe said to him. He knew he and his staff was close but damn.

"I'll be okay," Lucien answered not even looking at him.

"You don't want me bringing you food, yet you still don't eat!" Luna's voice sounded through the kitchen. Lucien rolled his eyes.

"You always coming in here with something smart to say Luna. Damn, do you-" Lucien shut his mouth when he looked up and saw Irys standing next to Luna. She was holding her arms behind her back and looking around before she made eye contact with Lucien.

"Irys," He breathed. "Surprised to see you."

"Can't say I'm surprised I knew I was coming to see you," She answered innocently. Lucien looked her up and down. Like when he first met her at the shelter, she was wearing a pair of yoga pants, with a tank top and a simple sweater with a zipper down the front that she left open. She was curvy beyond reason. So much that Lucien couldn't even understand it. Rosa was nothing compared to Irys, but for some reason Irys kept grabbing his attention.

"Okay quit staring at her. We need to talk in your office," Luna snapped. Lucien blinked and came out of his head.

"Talk about what?" he asked.

"Just come on." Luna walked off first, passing him to lead the way to his office. Lucien stayed back and waited until Irys passed him before following them. Irys's heart leapt to her throat as she walked by Lucien. She caught the earthy smell of his body, but also something sweet. When she turned and looked at him, he smiled at her but she could tell something was in his mouth.

"What are you eating?" She asked him.

"Ginger candy," He responded. Irys immediately made a face.

"It's not that bad," Lucien laughed at the look on her face. Not everyone liked ginger or even considered that ginger should be candy, but it helped with his sugar tremendously.

"It's sweet ginger. Not the raw nasty ginger."

"Where'd you manage to find that?" She asked.

"I made it," He said. She gave him a look as if she didn't believe him. "I'm serious. I'll show you." They continued towards his office. Once inside, Lucien closed the door. He went to his desk, and showed Irys the bowl of candy on his desk.

"Here, try one," He offered. She took a piece of candy from the bowl slowly. Putting it in her mouth, she was surprised that the ginger candy was actually quite good. Lucien didn't know why it satisfied him when he saw her actually approve of the taste. Maybe because he was a chef and he wanted people to like his food. Or maybe because he was just a man looking to please a woman.

"It's pretty good," Irys said. Lucien winked at her.

"Anything I touch is more than pretty good," He smiled at her. Irys sucked on the candy, looking him up and down not hiding the fact that she took a longer glance at his crotch. The bulge there was slight and her fantasy began going.

"So I wanted to talk to you about Irys coming to work here," Luna said. Both Irys and Lucien looked at her sharply.

"I hire all the floor workers so I figured it would be no problem hiring her, of course I do need your approval first, and she needs to discuss her rate of pay and all that."

"For what position?" Lucien asked.

"Hostess," Luna replied. "It's better that I don't have both positions. It will keep it so that I don't get too overwhelmed."

"But everyone you hired is qualified for their position Luna. No offense Irys, but have you even been a hostess before?"

"No I haven't," Irys admitted. "But what I have are the very same qualities any person with experience would have. I just haven't been able to use it."

"Enlighten me," Lucien said, sitting at the edge of his desk.

"Mr. Ray, what I-"

"Lucien," He cut in. "I'm not that damn old." Irys chuckled.

"Okay fine. Lucien. First what I have to offer you and your business is this." Irys smiled brightly and motioned to her smile. Just that, Lucien was captivated. Her teeth were sparkly white, and those cherry gloss lips were plump and framed her face so well. Truly, that smile brightened up the room.

"No doubt about it your hostess needs to be warm and inviting. My face is the first your diners will see, and coming out for a night to eat they need to feel welcomed. My smile and my personality can do that well. As a massage therapist I can get very hands on, and I've learned quickly how to get work done, and how to deal with customers in order to keep them coming back. I am not prissy nor am I prone to getting dirty when hard work needs to be done." Lucien already admired her.

"What's more is that I need a job Lucien. I'll keep it real about that. But because I need this job for my own livelihood, I know I'll make sure I do what it takes to perform this job well enough to keep it. If after a few dinner services it doesn't seem like I'm all of that. Then you can let me go no hard feelings. But don't turn me down without giving me a shot first."

"Can you say the restaurant name?" Lucien asked her. "Because no one here can say it. Not even Luna, who like me was raised by French parents."

"To my defense our parents didn't really speak that much French with us." Irys smiled at them.

"It's pronounced Tou-jour," Irys said slowly. Lucien snapped his head in her direction. The way she said it was how it was supposed to be said. But it was more than just practicing how to say it.

"Hold up," Lucien smiled. "*Parlez-vous François?*" He said, asking if she spoke French.

"*Qui, je parle francais,*" Irys smiled. Lucien looked completely surprised. Most people were when they knew she was bilingual and had no connection to the languages she spoke besides just wanted to learn them.

"And," Irys continued, "I also speak fluent Italian, and Spanish."

"No shit," Lucien said. "So do I. Oh my god Irys you're incredible." Lucien couldn't hide how impressed he was. It was clear this woman was more than just her looks.

"So if it helps your decision Lucien, I can practically speak to anyone who comes to your restaurant, according to the demographics of this area. Even the deaf."

"You know American Sign language?" He asked. Irys nodded.

"Now that's something I need to learn," He admitted. "Luna, you didn't tell me your friend was smarter than you," He teased.

"Oh shut up," She snapped, hitting him with her purse. "You're gonna hire her or what?" Even though Luna was over their conversation, she was happy her plan was beginning to work. The both of them were interested in each other.

"How about you work the dinner service tonight? See how you like working here first. Then we can decide after that."

"Um sure. What time does the service start?"

"7," Lucien said.

"Okay great. I can go home and change into something appropriate."

"You'd look good in anything I suppose. Even what you have on now." Lucien looked her up and down again.

"You gonna stop looking at me like that," She smiled.

"Stop looking like that and I will," He murmured. Irys took a deep breath and looked at Luna. The feeling she had inside her was the complete opposite of what she felt this morning, and she really and truly needed a break from all that havoc.

"I'll see you later then," She said to Luna. "Thanks so much for getting me to come here."

"Like I said, I got your back. Don't worry about it."

"Thanks Lucien," She smiled. Lucien returned the smile as she left the office. Even when she was gone, Lucien's eyes lingered after her longingly. What was it about this woman? Besides her incredible beauty? When he finally took his eyes from the door, he looked over at Luna. She was staring a hole into him.

"What?" He asked.

"What did you mean when you told me the other day that Irys was cute?" Lucien shrugged his shoulders.

"I meant just what I said. She's cute. What are you really trying to ask me?" He inquired.

"Nothing I'm just trying to figure out why you staring her down like she's a snicker bar or something."

"Same reason you be staring at Joe like he's a Twix or something." Luna bit her bottom lip.

"I wonder if he's got caramel filling," She groaned.

"Ew. Get out of here," Lucien ordered. "I can't hear that crap."

"Don't act like you wasn't thinking something like that about Irys." Lucien looked at his sister.

"You know, you should learn something from her. She speaks a language you don't that's the language of our parents."

"Mom and dad hardly spoke French around us!" Lucien went into his desk draw and popped out his glasses. He put them on so he could look over some paperwork. His head was beginning to buzz, and when he had headaches it made it hard for him to see.

"You need to take your insulin," Luna said. She knew when he put his glasses on that only meant his head was bothering him and her brother only got headaches when his sugar was getting too high.

"I will," He answered not looking at her.

"You do this, then you complain that I'm babying you," She snapped. "Because now I have to administer your insulin for you!" She went to reach for his shirt.

"Get away from me," He snapped. "I can do it myself and I will!' He batted her hands away.

"Man, you need a woman. Cause she the only one you gonna let take care of your ass." His mind conjured up Irys's beautiful face. He imagined her soft hands against his skin as she would be the one to inject his body with his medicine. It was almost a turn on thinking about it. But he immediately shook his head. One, Irys would never do such a thing. He just met her. And two, he highly doubted he'd ever tell a woman he thought was cute that he was a type 1 diabetic. Especially not after what he went through with Rosa. Just because Luna was staring at him, Lucien took out his needles, then went into his mini fridge for his insulin. He took it right there in front of her so she would leave him alone. When she left the office, Lucien sat back and just relaxed. Occasionally his eyes would flicker to the time in anticipation for 7pm, when the doors would open, and Irys would be back.

****

When Irys arrived home, she told her mother about her new job offer. It would take Irys out of her home for the night, but she had another health aide that was her backup for Diana who worked odd hours and times. Working at night for that aide was perfect for what Irys had in mind. For extra pay, Diana agreed to stay that night since it was too last minute for the backup aide.

"May I ask where you're going?" Rosa stood in the doorway of Irys's room with her arms crossed.

"I'm going to work," She replied.

"Wearing that?" Irys was wearing a spaghetti strapped black dress that clung to her figure but was knee length enough not to make her look like a hooker. She'd put her big afro in a high bun, and put on simple earrings.

"Would you like something?" Irys asked her.

"I thought you would be cooking dinner." Irys gave her sister a fake smile.

"No, I can't cook dinner. Know why? For one, I'm not your maid. And get this, the man you were fucking the other night cleaned by bank account out, so now I have to get a second job to make sure me and my mother don't starve to death because I don't have any money to buy groceries." Rosa laughed.

"You could use a starvation diet. It'll help you lose some weight." Irys grunted under her breath and tried to keep her emotion in check. But when she looked at Rosa and saw that goofy ass grin on her face, something just snapped. Gritting her teeth, Irys balled her hand into a fist. She cocked back and with quickness punched Rosa dead in the mouth. She fell to the ground easily, crying out as she grabbed her mouth.

"You fat bitch!" Rosa cried out, holding her bleeding lip. Irys leaned over the fallen woman.

"Remember you're in my fucking house," She gritted. "I don't need or want you here. So best believe you better start acting like you got some sense before my fat ass starts breaking some of your skinny ass bones." When Rosa tried to sit up, Irys pushed her back onto the ground. She stood then slammed her bedroom door shut and walked over Rosa's body and headed out of the house. She'd already told her mother goodnight, so Irys just left. She felt like she was suffocating. Violence was never something she resorted to. So the fact that she could think of nothing but hitting her sister, it really worried her. Was it overreacting to say that she felt an evil within her? It was as if she knew she was a good person, but life didn't. It took away her baby, and then she was left with a man who used her, and a sister who treated her like trash. Someone like her shouldn't be so nice. People used it to walk all over her. And she hated it.

Driving to the restaurant, her mind was filled with continuous thoughts about everything that upset her. So much to the point where it literally felt as if she was walking around with a dark cloud above her head.

There was a line outside in restaurant already when Irys arrived. She tried to put a smile on her face so no one would see she was clearly upset. But walking inside, her smile didn't make it to her eyes. She just nodded at the other workers and said nothing.

"Hey you ready for this?!" Luna asked, walking up to her.

"Yeah, sure," Irys said weakly. Luna looked at her in the face.

"Irys, whatever happened you need to let it go. We've got work to do. Lucien may be nice, but when it comes to his restaurant he doesn't play. And if you don't impress him, he won't keep you around. If it counts, you look sexy as fuck. If I didn't like the dick so much I would wife you up." Irys cut her eyes at Luna. She couldn't help the smile that infiltrated her face.

"You're stupid," Irys said. "You cute too, but you a little skinny for me."

"Bitch," Luna smiled as she walked away. Irys stood alone waiting for Lucien to come and give her some direction. He was in the kitchen doing his thing, preparing for service. Irys noticed that each person that walked by her, gave her a look. After about the fourth person she was wondering if something was on her face. But then she realized they were looking at her body. What if she was overdressed? Was this dress too much for her figure? Worry seeped over her as she began looking down at herself, trying to hide her curves with her arms.

"We're all ready to go," Joe informed Lucien. Lucien nodded.

"That's the new host?" One of the line cooks asked coming over. Lucien looked over towards the front where Irys was waiting. His jaw nearly dropped at seeing her. She was so gorgeous he couldn't even fathom how gorgeous she was. With her hair up, her neck and shoulders were more prominent especially with the spaghetti straps of her dress. She was a full figured woman, but her neck and shoulders still had a delicacy and slenderness to them. Her breasts were plump but it wasn't spilling out of her top and making the dress inappropriate.

"Damn," Paul, the line cook continued on. "She's thick as hell." Lucien snapped his head towards the man.

"Don't talk about her like that," Lucien snapped. Paul backed up with his hands up.

"Sorry boss," He said. Shaking his head, Lucien looked back at Irys. She was standing there in all her beauty, but there was just something that was off. It wasn't the same woman that Lucien talked with today. Her smile was virtually gone, and she was holding her arms around herself as if she was uncomfortable or embarrassed about something. Lucien didn't like that look on her face. Without a word, he left the kitchen. He'd been waiting to see her ever since she left, and now that she was back there was a part of him that felt calm.

"Hey Irys," He greeted. She jumped.

"Oh crap," She smiled. "Sorry I was caught off guard."

"No worries," He said. She swallowed hard and looked down. From what he gathered, Irys wasn't the type to shy away from something. And in the times he'd spoken with her, she always looked him in the face. Something was wrong.

"Can I talk to you for a moment?" He asked.

"Sure, you're my boss. Or well, not my boss but could be my boss," She hurried out. Lucien smiled at her. He took her soft hands and led her all the way in the back of the restaurant where they could speak in private and no one would cross their path.

"How are you feeling?" he asked her.

"What do you mean? I feel fine," She lied.

"Irys your face is an open book. Meaning if you're happy everyone will know. If you're upset everyone would know too. I just met you and I can tell something is wrong." Irys sighed.

"Lucien I want to be here and I don't want to drown you with my problems."

"Don't come at me with that. It's okay. Talk to me." Irys sighed and rubbed her eyes.

"How do I look Lucien? Because people keep staring at me. The cooks, the servers, they just give me a look when they pass by me and I can't help but think that they are thinking that I'm just a fat girl trying to fit into a small dress and I swear-"

"Wait stop. Did someone here call you fat?" He asked firmly.

"Uh no, no not outright. They just keep staring."

"People will stare Irys. That's their problem. But if anyone and I don't care who it is, if they work here for me and they call you out of your name, especially fat, you let me know right away. Because that's something I will not tolerate. Not now, not ever." The fierceness of his voice gave her comfort. Comfort that if anyone tried to bully her he would be there to protect her. If only she could take him home with her to protect her against her family.

"With strangers it doesn't affect me. But when it's family it can get a little depressing," she admitted. She looked down, afraid to see his reaction. But the moment she did, he put his finger under her chin and made her look at him.

"Your beauty is out of this world Irys. I've seen bombshells that wear a size two and is nowhere compared to your beauty. From what I can gather Irys, you have a rich soul, filled with this goodness. That's more attractive to me than anything else. My opinion may not matter Irys, but if it's worth something I wanted you to know that." Irys's heart thumped hard. Staring into his unwavering eyes, she was lost. How could someone she just met give her a sense of comfort like he was doing?

"That smile you showed me in my office. That's what I want to see. That brightness that made me forget all about my worries, and it just made me happy. Smile for me." Irys continued to look at him. He was rubbing her chin since he'd never let her go. She smiled at him.

"Really?!" He joked. "Is that the best you can do? Come on! I know you wanna show everyone else your teeth look better than theirs. Don't be shy girl." Irys burst out laughing at him.

"There's that smile!" He exclaimed. "Now keep it there."

"Thank you," Irys said.

"If you ever want to talk about something don't be afraid to come to me. I don't mind listening."

"A man that likes to listen," She said. "What an anomaly. Are you still single?" She blurted out. When his eyes went wide she covered her mouth.

"Don't answer that! I'm sorry I didn't-"

"Yeah I'm still single," He cut her off. "And I'm guessing Luna told you that."

"Um, yeah…"

"Don't worry about it Irys," He smiled. "I know women gossip. And clearly you're asking because you're interested," He winked. Irys was going to protest but she knew she couldn't. She was indeed interested. But a man like him wouldn't be interested. She was still convinced he was only saying those nice things to her because he felt like he had to. But she was seriously second guessing that idea, when as she walked away she caught a glimpse of how he stared at her. It sent chills up and down her spine.

Working as hostess was more fun than she thought it would be. She loved talking with the guests and by her luck, a Haitian family came out to eat that night and she was able to display her French to get them seated and helped them order. Each time she looked towards the kitchen, Lucien winked at her.

By the end of the night, when the place was completely empty Irys sat around one of the tables having some water. Lucien was sharing out food for all the workers to take home if they wanted. Irys was still too much on a high to even consider eating at the moment. She was just happy that something was working out in her favor despite Derek and Rosa trying to bring her down.

Luna entered the kitchen where Lucien was only to find him there looking out at Irys. The longing in his eyes was unmistakable. He really had it for this woman. Her best friend.

"You okay bro?" Luna asked him.

"You ever get the feeling that there's a whole lot of hurt behind that amazing smile of hers?" Lucien asked dreamily. Luna looked out at Irys.

"There's times that I've only ever seen Irys smile. But I don't know. These past few weeks she's been struggling. She doesn't talk about it, and she tries to smile but I know something has been going on with her. I brought her in to work because she really needs the extra income. Something happened to her this morning, and I don't want to get into details because that's her business but she's struggling. I know she won't take it but I have to try and give her some money. She doesn't have any."

"None?!" Lucien asked.

"It's bad," Luna said.

"You don't have to give her anything Luna, I'll take care of it."

"You should ask her out," Luna said.

"Excuse me?" Lucien asked, looking at his sister.

"You should ask her out," Luna repeated. "Like on a date."

"I don't know anything about her."

"That's what the date is for Lucien. Duh. Damn you can just tell you haven't been single for a while."

"Tell me you don't wanna spend a little alone time with her." Lucien cleared his throat.

"I do," Lucien admitted lowly. "Is she single?" He questioned.

"Like a dollar bill," Luna smiled. "You should make a move." She patted her brother on the back before walking away. Lucien looked out at Irys again. She was pulling her hair down from it's bun, and fluffing up her afro. Lucien forced himself to stop looking at her. He left the kitchen and went upstairs to get his checkbook.

Back in the dining room, she was still sitting there sipping on a glass of water. Lucien walked up to her slowly.

"I know you're here this time. I can smell that sweet ginger," She said looking up at him. Lucien smiled and sat down next to her.

"Yeah if there's one thing I love eating is things with ginger in it," He smiled.

"And it actually smells really good. Very aromatic or at least the candy you made."

"Thanks sugar." Irys gave him a look.

"So are you exempt from calling me out of my name? Like you said to me earlier?"

"Of course I'm not Irys. I'm sorry I don't mean to make you uncomfortable."

"I'm only teasing you Lucien. You can call me sugar." Lucien smiled at her and pulled out the check he wrote for her.

"Here, this is for you." She took the check but upon seeing the amount she shook her head.

"No I can't take this," She gasped. "My hourly rate is only 17 dollars, that times 4 is not 200 dollars Lucien."

"I know that Irys. But this isn't your check for working. This is your check because Luna said she's concerned about you as if she's concerned then I'm concerned and we want to help. I know it's not much but she told me you wouldn't accept anything more than this."

"I don't know if I can accept this," Irys said shaking her head.

"Take it Irys. If it makes you feel better, you can pay me back. Just get back on your feet sugar."

"I'm gonna kill Luna for telling you my issues," Irys said shaking her head. She didn't want Lucien to know how bad things really were.

"No worries. Luna didn't say anything. She just told me you needed help that's it. Much like I'm hoping she didn't tell you why I was single only that I was." Irys sighed in relief.

"No she didn't give me the details. She's good at that ain't she? Managing to gossip without giving details," Irys smiled. Lucien tucked a piece of Irys's hair away from her face.

"You did really well today and I'd love to have you as my hostess." He handed her the check. She took it reluctantly.

"Thanks Lucien. I'm excited to work here." She looked down at the check. "You know in a strange way this is the first time a man has ever given me money. Well except for my father." Heavens knew that Derek had never even so much as bought her a single rose. Now in hindsight she questioned her motive for actually hooking up with the bastard.

"In that case I'm glad to be your first," He said. The both of them stiffened and looked at each other because of how his statement sounded. Lucien bit his lip not sure how to fix his mistake. Why would he even say something like that to her? Or anywhere close to it? If she wasn't sitting so close to him he would hit himself in the face.

"I didn't mean that the way it came out," Lucien said quickly. "I'm sure you're experienced and-" Irys continued looking at him. "Unless you're not experienced. Oh my god, are you a virgin? Wait no that was a very intrusive question. You don't have to answer that. I mean unless you want to. You wouldn't have to be embarrassed about being one, we were all one at one point, and losing it is a once in a lifetime experience, unless you're not a virgin and I'm just rambling because I can't-" Irys finally burst out laughing unable to hold it in any longer. Lucien buried his head in his hands embarrassed. Was he this bad at talking to women?

"I can't believe this," He gasped. Irys's vibrant laughter filled his body. He felt her small hands pulling at his hands taking them away from his face. He was met with her sparkling smile.

"You're a little rusty at speaking with women aren't you?" She asked. "Welcome to being single," She smiled.

"I'm not usually this awful." He pouted.

"Oh don't be embarrassed. It's actually really cute. Those are the imperfections that make us who we are."

"Thanks for being nice. But I know you're gonna run back to Luna and tell her and then she's gonna come to me and make fun of me endlessly."

"Why would she do that?" Irys asked. Lucien rolled his eyes.

"Because she's my big sister."

"Well that makes sense," Irys smiled. She rubbed the back of his hand. "If it makes you feel better I can tell you something embarrassing about me."

"Sure."

"I'm experienced sexually, but I've never had an orgasm." Lucien's brows raised. He turned his body towards her so he could look at her better.

"If you've never had an orgasm sugar, then you're not experienced." When her eyes heated and they flickered for a moment down to his crotch, he nearly lost himself. His libido that was inconsistent because of his diabetes was raging now, and no matter what his sugar was, he was getting horny. It was surprising actually, almost to the point where it scared him. He was hardened over nothing really. Nothing but simple words, and just the look she gave him. Trying to diffuse his rising arousal, he stood.

"Let me get ready to close up the kitchen," He said.

"Oh, okay," Irys said. She stood. "I should get on home myself. Thanks for the money and everything. I'll um-see you tomorrow. Tell Luna I'll see her tomorrow."

"Let me walk you out." Lucien offered to walk her out, but he maintained his distance. He could not afford for this woman to see his erection. Because if she did, and she gave him another one of those looks, he was going to rip her clothes off in an empty room and show her what it was to have an orgasm. That could be dangerous for the both of them.

Chapter Eleven

Surprisingly, Irys wasn't tired when she awoke the next morning for her shift at the spa. She was actually rejuvenated and she couldn't wait until later on tonight when she'd be back at the restaurant. And it wasn't just because she loved being the hostess either. She wanted to see Lucien again, but she also had to think about the way that their night ended before. She thought they were getting deep into a conversation, but at the last moment he just pulled back abruptly. That was a reminder to Irys that she needed to relax herself. If she had to, she would just have to watch him from afar.

As she prepared herself some lunch for the day, Rosa came into the kitchen in a huff. Irys looked directly at her, noticing her swollen lip.

"You should put ice on that," Irys said. Rosa sucked her teeth and looked at Irys.

"This is not funny!" She snapped. Irys snickered and package her PB and J sandwich.

"That's what you get," Irys said. "Maybe next time you'll be a little bit more considerate."

"Whatever." She went to the fridge. Irys watched her closely and saw when she pulled out the special containers.

"No Rosa, that's for mom," Irys snapped, taking the containers from her and putting them back. "I got extra cash last night so I went out this morning and got some food. When I get more I'll buy groceries. But this is all mom has to eat for the day. Please do not touch it."

"So what the hell am I going to eat?" Rosa asked.

"Gee, I don't know. If maybe you'd get a job and help me with groceries then you'd be able to eat. But since that's off the table then you better figure something out." She gave Rosa a stern look before gathering her things to leave. Sooner or later she needed to get Rosa out of her house.

Irys worked through the day, wishing time would hurry forward. And because Luna worked right next to her, every time Irys looked at the woman, she couldn't stop thinking about Lucien. He and his sister shared the same eyes, and it just made Irys long for the man even more. It was so very strange for her to be infatuated with him when her life was seemingly in shambles. It didn't make sense, but yet still it was happening. Irys had to do a lot not to ask Luna how her brother was, simply because she wanted to know what he was up to or doing. Around lunchtime, Irys and Luna clocked out together to take their hour breaks.

"I'm gonna go by Lucien and get some food," Luna said as they walked out the spa. "What'd you bring to eat?" She pointed at Irys's bag.

"Peanut butter and jelly," Irys said. Luna thought Irys was joking at first but the woman was serious.

"What, is that like your snack or something?"

"No," Irys snapped. "You know what happened Luna. I used the money Lucien gave me to get food for my mom. Until I can get groceries I just have to keep it simple." Luna shook her head.

"You should have killed him when you had the chance Irys. You can eat some real food at Lucien's. He already had it prepared. Come on." Irys was beginning to think that she wouldn't be able to survive without the help of Luna.

Seeing Lucien and actually having his food was way better than her little Peanut butter and jelly sandwich. At this rate however she was staring at Lucien more than she was eating. He was only wearing a t-shirt and jeans as he was getting gritty with prepping fish in the kitchen. His biceps curled and buffed up with each movement he made.

"Stop looking at my damn brother and answer your cell phone," Luna snapped. Irys shook her head, bringing herself back to reality. Her phone was indeed ringing.

"Hi Diana," Irys greeted.

"Hey Irys. Just wanted to let you know there was no food here for your mother. I didn't know what you wanted me to give her for lunch but I just came back from ordering some takeout. Hopefully that's okay?"

"Yes, yes it's fine. But that's not possible, I left four containers of food in the fridge for her!" Diana paused.

"Oh. Those containers are actually now in the sink." Irys grunted.

"I swear I'm gonna kill her one day! I'll pay you back soon as I get home Diana. So sorry."

"Irys you know she doesn't have to live here right?" Diana asked.

"She has nowhere else to go."

"Yeah well if she keeps this up and keeps taking your money and not even caring to leave food for her ailing mother, then you're gonna find yourself without a place to go either."

"I know," Irys whispered. "I know." She ended the phone call feeling defeated.

"I gotta go Luna," She said getting up from the booth.

"Where you going?" Luna asked.

"Anywhere but here. See you at work." Irys didn't know what she was about to do, but she just needed to get away from everyone.

Lucien was cleaning Tuna as fast as he could so he could get to spend a little time with Irys while she was here. But the moment he sliced the fish and was just about done, he looked up to see her walking out of the restaurant hurriedly. Lucien washed his hands and left the kitchen to try and catch her, but she was already out the door. Luna came running up to him.

"Is she okay?" He asked.

"No. She just got off the phone with the woman that looks after her mom. Apparently there's no food in the house."

"What?" He gasped.

"Earlier she told me she used the money you gave her last night to make sure only her mother had meals. She was going to eat a peanut butter and jelly sandwich if I didn't bring her here Lucien. And then she got that phone call and just ran out of here. I don't know what's going on at her house, but it ain't easy on her." Lucien looked around the kitchen.

"Where does she live?" Lucien asked her. Luna gave him her address. He pulled out his wallet.

"I'm gonna take care of it sis. You get back to work and make sure she's okay."

"What are you going to do?" Luna asked.

"Don't worry about it Luna. Can you just make sure she's okay?!" The urgency in his voice gave Luna pause. She knew then that something serious was happening with her brother when it came it Irys.

The moment Luna left, Lucien began packing up the food he'd prepared for the workers for later on. He'd make some more of it later that was no problem. He just packed up what hot food was there, then searched the walk in closet for anything else Irys could use. After packing everything up on the counter he called over Paul.

"I need you to do me a favor," He told the man. "Can you deliver this food somewhere? I would do it, but I need to get cooking to replace it for later."

"Of course no problem boss." Lucien wrote down Irys's address.

"Can you also stop by the grocery store and just pick up 100 dollars of groceries. I don't care what it is, but I trust as a cook you'll be able to pick and choose what's best."

"I got ya."

"You can stay on the clock Paul, and here's an extra 50 dollars for doing this for me. I really appreciate it." Paul clapped him on the back before gathering some of the items to bring out to his car. Lucien helped him with the rest of the items and watched as he drove off. He wasn't sure where this compulsion to take care of Irys came from, but it was just there beating feverishly through his body and he wasn't satisfied until he knew she would be okay. Now he only wished he had her phone number so he could hear her voice just to reassure himself.

Luna walked back into work to see Irys there. She was sitting in a corner silently, just looking through her phone. Their lunch break was over, but their next scheduled client wasn't for another 15 minutes. Luna was almost afraid to ask her friend if she was alright, knowing damn well the woman wasn't okay. She didn't know what Lucien was doing, but he needed to do it quickly. Irys looked as if she was on the verge of a breakdown. When Irys's phone rang, Luna paid close attention to the conversation.

"I told you that food was for mom. How could you just turn around and ignore that?" Irys asked. Rosa scoffed on the other line.

"Derek was hungry, so he ate it. That's what happens when you fuck a man so good."

"You're an awful person," Irys whispered, on the verge of tears.

"Aw is the baby sad?" Rosa teased. Irys could do nothing but hang up. She sucked in a deep breath refusing to let her tears fall. When she looked, Luna was staring at her worriedly.

"I told you my sister moved in with me. So she's been a pain in the ass since then. She won't work and she obviously doesn't care for anyone but herself."

"She ate your mom's food?" Irys nodded.

"I have no problem eating sandwiches or canned food just to make sure my mom has what she needs. And I told her that I didn't have any more money for groceries and that food was all there was for mom. Still, she just ignores that."

"Why do you let her live with you Irys?" Luna asked.

"Because she's my sister you know .And I-I can't be like her and care about nothing but myself. But my niceness is apparently what's making my ass suffer." Luna didn't even know what to say.

"I want to ask you something Luna," she said. "And I'm only going to put it into prospective so it can relate to you and Lucien."

"Okay sure."

"What if you were interested in a woman? You and that woman dated for a couple years then you broke up with her. You're over her completely and you have no feelings for her whatsoever. But then that woman decides that she doesn't want to be a lesbian and starts dating men again. Only she starts dating Lucien and having sex with him. Is it okay for Lucien to date your ex? Or do you think it shouldn't matter because you have no feelings for her anymore?"

"That's some trippy shit Irys," Luna said. "But if so was the case I'd be upset yes. Not because I have feelings for the woman, it's just because you're not supposed to do something like that to your family you know."

"I caught my sister having sex with my ex. And while it made me crazy at first, I couldn't help but feel I was in the wrong for being mad. I broke up with him, and he moved on with his life. Only he'd doing so with my sister. And in my damn house right under my nose."

"If it would have happened to me and Lucien, I doubt that Lucien would ever date someone I dated. Because if I had a complaint about that person, he's the first one I would tell. If that person hurt me, he wouldn't dream of being with them. Things are possibly different for you and your sister because you told me the two of you aren't close. Me and you are more of sisters than you and her. And I wouldn't ever sleep with Derek because I'm the one you come to when you have issues with him so I know he's a world class dick. Your sister may not give a fuck about that."

"How do I get myself to not care?" She questioned.

"That's something you have to answer yourself Irys," Luna said softly. "But might I suggest something. Your sister is playing dirty, I think you should return the favor. Let her know that even if you're nice, you're still not to be fucked with."

The sound of Irys's phone ringing cut their conversation. Irys really didn't want any more bad news but she answered the phone.

"Hey Irys, just letting you know all the groceries came and the food," Diana said. Irys's brows furrowed.

"What food and groceries?" Irys asked. "I didn't have any food sent over."

"Oh well, a man by the name of Paul came by. He brought some food that was already cooked, and then a whole bunch of groceries. He said it was for you and your mom. Should I not have taken it?" Irys thought quickly. The only person she knew who would have food delivered to her home was Luna, or her brother.

"No, no it's fine Diana. I know where it came from. Just a little surprised. I'll see you when I come home to change before my night shift."

"See ya then." Irys hung up the phone and looked at Luna.

"You guys didn't have to do that," She said.

"Do what?" Luna asked.

"A whole bunch of groceries and food was delivered to the house. I know it was your idea and Lucien was the one that had it sent over." Luna smiled.

"Actually. It was Lucien's idea. I only told him you needed help. This was all him."

"You know, that man is something else." Irys said.

"He loves helping people. But he has a keen interest in you."

"No he doesn't," Irys said. "Last night we were talking and it seemed to go well, and then I don't know if it was me, but he kind of just drew back."

"Don't worry about it. Trust me, I'm his sister I know everything about that man. And like I said, he's interested." Irys nodded but she didn't seem convinced. Luna needed to have a talk with her brother about this. Hearing that Irys's own sister was sleeping with her ex was confirmation that Irys was going through much more than she was letting on. She knew Irys didn't have feelings for Derek, but honestly the only way for her to get over what Derek and her sister was doing was to find her own happiness with someone else.

Irys and Luna split for the day, with Irys going home to change after their day at the spa, and Luna heading straight to the restaurant. She had her clothes to change, so she would just do it there. Once there she headed straight for Lucien's office. Finding him there checking his sugar.

"You didn't ask her out did you?" Luna questioned. Lucien gave her a look.

"No I didn't," He answered.

"I thought we agreed you would."

"We didn't agree to anything. And I doubt I should be asking her out when she has a whole lot of shit on her plate right now."

"That's exactly why you need to ask her out Lucien."

"When are you going to stop trying to control me?" Luna shook her head. She held her hands up and left the office. Clearly she would have to do things herself, or her plan to get them together would never work.

The moment Irys got to the restaurant that night, she immediately looked for Lucien. Of course he was already in the kitchen with everyone else. Luna watched as Irys approached Lucien and hugged him without any explanation. Lucien was shocked at the hug, but once that dissipated he had an 'oh shit' moment. A moment where he realized Irys was in his arms, and he was holding onto her soft supple body. Dear lord she smelled so good. But just as Lucien was about to get lost in her aura, she pulled away.

"That's for sending that food to my house. I don't know how else I can thank you."

"It's no problem Irys."

"Wait a minute," Paul chimed in. "I was the one that hand delivered everything." Irys smiled at him and went over to him. She also gave him a deep hug. Luna watched as her brother's face hardened. His brows creased, and his jaw tightened. She had to refrain from gasping out loud. She almost didn't recognize the look on his face, and she couldn't let it go.

"What are you mad at?" She whispered to him. He looked at her sharply.

"I'm not mad," He gritted. He crossed his arms. Yes, he wasn't mad. But jealous, yes he was. The feeling was too new in his body and he couldn't even reason with it. Just seeing another man hold onto Irys's curves made his head ache. The only thing he could think of was punching Paul in the face. And the longer he held onto her, the more Lucien wanted to hit him.

"So what are you?" Luna asked. "You're clearly not happy."

"I just know he better let her go in two seconds," Lucien snapped.

"Enough of that lovey dovey crap," Luna said loudly clearly seeing her brother was about to blow his fuse. Irys let go of Paul and backed up. Lucien was staring a hole into her. Clearing her throat she began to leave the kitchen.

"I'm gonna get ready for tonight," She said. She gave Lucien one more smile before leaving the kitchen completely.

"That's your friend right Luna?" Paul asked.

"Yeah."

"You know if she's single?" Paul asked. "She's a little on the thicker side, but that don't matter to me. I may just ask her out." Lucien glared at Paul. Luna couldn't help but to just laugh.

"Wow," She said looking at her brother. "She's single Paul but I think she's interested in someone else," Luna said.

"Eh, it's still worth a try."

"Good luck with that." Luna patted her brother on the shoulder. That look was still on his face, so he was still very upset. Clearly he was jealous because he wanted Irys to himself. Luna wouldn't be his big sister if she didn't make sure that happened.

For a couple days, Luna watched the interactions between Lucien and Irys each time they were together. She noticed one thing. The both of them were always smiling or laughing. Yet still, each time Luna inquired, Lucien had never asked her out. On a Wednesday morning when the restaurant was closed until the night, and both Luna and Irys was off from the spa, Luna decided to make the moves her brother wouldn't.

"Hey Irys," Luna greeted once the woman answered the phone. "Are you doing anything today?"

"No not really, I'm just relaxing here."

"I was thinking we could go hang out at the wings and things spot. Get a couple drinks and have something to eat. I am dying here by myself."

"Oh that sounds good as hell. What time you want me to meet you?"

"At 4? That good?"

"Yes, I can call the weekend aid to get here in no time. I'll see you then." Luna hung up the phone. Waiting exactly three minutes, she then dialed Lucien.

"Hey sis," He greeted.

"Hey Lucy. Are you doing anything?"

"No, just me and Salsa at home."

"If you're not too cool, I would love to spend some time with you. We can go to wings and things for some food."

"I'm never too cool for you sis," He smiled. "It sounds good. I can meet you there."

"I'll be there at 4," She said.

"Okay, see you later Lue." Once she ended the call she had to physically pat herself on the back for a job well done. Now she was going to spend her day off cuddling with Joe on the phone.

Chapter Twelve

Just before Irys left her house to meet up with Luna, she made sure both the pantry and the fridge doors were locked tightly. After Luna gave her the advice to start playing dirty, Irys took it. She changed the lock on the pantry ensuring that only she and Diana had the key to get inside, then she bought a huge chain and lock to tie around the fridge door handles. When Rosa saw them, the look on her face made Irys giddy. She didn't care if it was mean or over the top. If it wasn't for Lucien her mother wouldn't be eating and that's all she cared about. What Rosa did was uncalled for and now it was Irys's turn. Now she'd see where Rosa was going to get food from.

Before she left, she gave the aide a key to both the locks and made sure she explained why she kept them locked in the first place. The last thing Irys wanted was an investigation at her house for neglect, but the aide understood completely. Irys just felt satisfied that she was leaving her home and didn't have to worry about Rosa ruining something again. Now at least she could enjoy a simple day out with her friend.

It was 4pm on the dot when Irys pulled up to the spot. She parked in the lot and went around the front to wait for Luna. It was the perfect day out so she figured they'd get a table outside to enjoy both the weather and the food. She kept checking her phone as time went by to see if Luna would message her but Luna never did. After ten minutes she had to wonder where the hell the woman was. Getting up from the table she'd taken, she went to search for Luna. Only, instead of finding Luna, she spotted Lucien near the entrance. She had to pause for a moment to just stare at him. He was wearing jeans with a black button down top. The look was very casual, but Irys found it completely sexy. The sleeves were rolled up showing off his biceps and his jeans fit his body perfectly. The curls on top of his head were perfectly coiled and his shapeup was lined to perfection. Irys had to take a moment to gather herself before she actually went up to him.

Lucien was out front of the place Luna wanted to meet him at for ten minutes when he realized she wasn't here at all. He tried calling her but it only rung out. His sister was known to be late at some things but she always alerted him when she was running late. Now he was just standing there like a lost puppy not sure what to do. That was until he caught of glimpse of red coming at him. When he looked over, sure enough Irys was walking through the crowd towards him. The light colored jeans she was wearing clung to her curves like white on rice. Her top was a red chiffon with spaghetti straps that also fit her figure well. Her hair was in its curly fro, and Lucien knew it would smell of coconuts or something fruity. She smiled at him when their eyes met.

"Hi," She greeted. They both went to hug each other, but they both hesitated as if second guessing whether they should be hugging or not, so then they both ended up pulling back. Lucien cleared his throat.

"What are you doing here sugar?" he asked. "I'm meeting Luna here for some food and drinks." Irys gave him a look.

"That's funny because I'm supposed to be meeting Luna here for some food and drinks." The both of them nodding realizing just what was going on.

"Luna set us up." Irys said.

"I can't believe she did this," Lucien grunted shaking his head. Irys stepped back and looked him up and down.

"You know I can go back home. You don't have to be so chapped at spending time with me." Lucien's eyes went wide.

"No sugar that's not what I meant," He said taking her hand. He pulled her close. "I want to spend time with you."

"So what's the problem?" Irys asked.

"It's just that I wanted to be the one to ask you out. Luna kept bugging me to take you out and I told her I would ask you when the time was right. With her doing this, it's like it takes the power out of my own hands. And she won't ever let me forget that she had to be the one to get us together instead of me doing it. That's where she takes her big sister role to the maximum. If she knows I want something she won't wait for me to get it myself. She's gonna personally make sure I get it no matter what."

"I guess she's just really determined," Irys smiled.

"It doesn't matter now I suppose. What does is that we're here together. And I'm hungry."

"Yes me too, I'm starving." Lucien didn't let go of her hand as she showed him where she'd gotten a table. They sat down across from each other. Irys had to admit she was nervous. Was this a date or were they simply just hanging out? She wasn't sure but she was going to try and keep her cool. When the waiter arrived, Irys ordered a virgin Daiquiri while Lucien ordered a Corona.

"A chef with your exquisite taste enjoys wings and beer?" Irys asked, when their order of honey wings came to their table. Lucien took a gulp of his beer.

"I'm a man before I'm a chef," He smiled. "And the man in me loves wings. Beer I only drink on occasion."

"And I hope you don't mind but I eat wings like you're supposed to eat wings. I don't care if I'm sitting across and incredibly handsome man either." Lucien laughed at her

"I ain't mad at that. I mean I'm a chef, I enjoy food and I love it when I can enjoy it with other people too."

"As you can tell, I enjoy food a lot." Lucien gave her a soft look.

"Have you ever been skinny?" He asked her bluntly. Irys tried not to be offended since she knew he wasn't trying to be mean.

"Actually no I haven't. All my life I can just remember being thick. It's just how I am."

"So then don't apologize for something that you are Irys. People like you make it so people like me can live their dreams you know."

"What do you mean?" She asked.

"People who love food sugar. If people didn't love food, then I wouldn't be a chef. I wouldn't have a restaurant to cater to people and live out my food dream. And if I might add you don't seem like a woman who is uncomfortable in her body."

"Actually I'm not. I used to be. Of course going through high school I was bullied and people fat shamed me. But one day I looked in the mirror and I told myself I loved myself. I fought back against the bullies and once they saw that their words didn't affect me, they just stopped teasing me. Since then I've learned to appreciate my body. If anyone doesn't like it then that's their problem."

"That's very inspirational," He said. "I was mostly ignored through high school so it was no problems for me. But the other day you said something about your family making you feel ashamed of your body."

"My sister is a witch. Even to this day she'll call me fat and tease me and do whatever it is she can to make me feel like complete shit. Somedays I can ignore it. Somedays I can't. I suppose it just hurts more when people who's supposed to love you, doesn't." Lucien reached for her hand. He kissed the back of it tenderly.

"It's crazy how burdened you are by all of this, but you have this luminous smile that lights up any room you walk into. Anyone could be evil and mean because of what they go through. But not you. I admire you a lot for that Irys."

"Don't make me cry Lucien. We're supposed to be stuffing our faces with wings, and then possibly licking the sauce off each other's faces!" Lucien cracked up.

"Bet I can eat all these before you can." He challenged.

"Good luck with that!' Irys picked up a wing, and they both raced to see who would finish theirs first. Lucien didn't think Irys had it in her, but sure enough she went to town on her wings. Of course his appetite was bigger so he did win the race.

"Look at your face," Lucien teased. He used his finger to wipe away some of the sauce, then he put that same finger in his mouth, sucking the sauce off. Irys chuckled and wiped her mouth off then took a sip of her drink.

"You know what we should do," Irys said. "Let's take a picture and send it to Luna."

"I love that idea." Lucien moved over to her, sliding his chair so they were sitting next to each other. Irys took out her phone and held it up in the air, with the camera on so they could take the selfie. Staring at their picture Lucien just loved the way they looked together. Their smiles were real, reminiscent of the good time they were already having with each other and the day had only just begun.

"I like that picture," Lucien said. Irys finished sending it to Luna then turned to look at Lucien. He was leaning in close to her.

"I like it too," Irys answered softly.

"We look good together," He whispered. Irys leaned in closer to him, feeling his invisible pull.

"Yeah we do." Lucien pushed her hair back, ready to kiss her perfect lips. Before he could get any closer, her phone rang loudly. They jumped back from each other, the loud ring frightened the both of them.

"It's Luna," Irys said looking at the phone. Lucien nodded and moved his chair back to where it was. Irys answered the phone and chatted for a little while with Luna about what they'd been doing. But thankfully Irys only gave short and sweet answers, then she was kicking Luna off the phone.

"Sorry about that," Irys said. "Where were we?" she asked.

"I believed that perhaps we were going to kiss," Lucien said. "But my dear big sister ruined that moment."

"Yeah she did." Even if it seemed they both wanted to kiss it was awkward now and none of them knew how to reinitiate a kiss. Lucien was thinking about just lunging at her and just going for it. He didn't care. All he wanted to do was tongue her the hell down. He was distracted by the thought of not getting to kiss her when his watch beeped, making him jump. Irys looked at him curiously.

"Do you have to be somewhere?" She asked. Lucien looked down at his watch and turned off the alarm. He dreaded taking his sugar right now, because he hadn't carried any of his insulin with him. So if his sugar was high he was going to have to leave Irys to go home and take his medicine.

"Um. Not that I had planned. Can you give me a second?" He asked, standing up.

"Sure, sure." Irys watched as Lucien walked away hurriedly. She thought he was going to the bathroom but instead, he walked through the tables outside, and headed back towards the parking lot. She was curious as to where he was going and what he was doing, but she just sat back and enjoyed her drink, completely upset that they hadn't kissed.

Lucien hurried back to his car where he kept his test strips and meters. Pulling out the pack, he jabbed his finger with the strip and inserted the strip into the meter.

"Fuck," He grunted. His sugar was high. Too many damn wings. He hadn't calculated how much he should have eaten with his insulin that he took this morning, which was all his fault. He just got lost in Irys, he completely forgot he couldn't just eat randomly. Wiping his finger with an alcohol pad, he cleaned everything up and put his meter and strips away. Now how do you tell the amazing girl you're out on a date with that you had to go? Lucien wondered how that conversation would go.

"Hey Irys, I need to go home before I start getting dizzy and incoherent and I can't drive because I need to take my insulin." Lucien shook his head and scoffed. He hated this shit. And then walking back to the place and seeing her beautiful face smile at him when she saw him return made his gut churn with uneasiness as he was about to tell her he couldn't stay. It was so bad he was considering staying and letting whatever happen, happen. But on second thought, he didn't think passing out on this girl was going to be good pillow talk.

"Are you okay Lucien?" She asked.

"Um yeah I just, I actually have to go," He said.

"Oh." The disappointment on her face cut through his heart. Jeez, he hated disappointing her.

"It's not your fault at all Irys. I just have to take care of something."

"No, no it's fine. You're fine." Lucien motioned to the waiter to get the bill. While he paid for their food, Irys's disappointment never left. He really hated doing this to her.

"Can I walk you to your car?" He asked.

"Actually. No." She said. Lucien felt that sting. "I'll see you tonight. Thanks for paying." And with that she just walked away. Lucien didn't even bother going after her. Annoying her was the last thing he wanted to do. And he'd already contributed to that by leaving in the first place. Rubbing his temples, he quickly left so he could get home before he got too sick to drive.

Irys didn't mean to be so upset, and she didn't know why she cared that much that he left, but she did. He was perfect so far. Everything he said to her, everything he did, and then to just cut the date short and leave she felt as if perhaps he was just forcing himself to be there in the first place. Then after she dogged some wings, he was ready to go. Maybe he was able to be nice to her because of her size, but perhaps actually being with her gave him a little hesitation. Maybe he was just too perfect that Irys wanted him bad, but she also had to open up to the idea that things might just not work out.

Irys was so troubled by his leaving that it stuck with her throughout the whole day. Even so that when she pulled up to the restaurant for the dinner service that night she was almost afraid to go in. Why was she afraid to face him all of a sudden? The reality of being rejected by a man stung.

"Stop being such a drama queen," Irys shook her head at herself. She needed to get a damn grip and stop being touchy about every damn thing. Holding her head up, she walked into the restaurant ready to work. Lucien had given her a time card, so she punched in, in the breakroom with all the servers, then went out to the dining room to get herself prepared. She knew Lucien was in the kitchen, and she couldn't help it that her eyes were drawn directly there. She found him staring right at her. He gave her one of those big comforting smiles. All Irys could do was grimace and just nod before hurrying over to her post.

"I am so excited to hear about your date," Luna squealed, joining her at the front. Irys sighed.

"Nothing to hear," She admitted.

"What?! After that picture you sent me?! Come on, I know he's my brother but I want the details. Did you guys kiss?" Irys looked at Luna and rolled her eyes.

"No," She answered sourly. "We didn't kiss." Luna's mouth fell open.

"Why the hell not?!"

"Well we were going to but then-you know what, how about you go ask him? He's the one that just up and left without really an explanation."

"As a matter of fact, I will." Luna left Irys and charged right to the kitchen to confront her brother. Only Lucien saw her coming from a mile away.

"Don't start with me Luna," He warned.

"Why did you leave her?" She asked. Lucien didn't answered. "Okay so answer this. Why didn't you at least kiss her? Are you that slow Lucien? Do I have to hold your hand to get you to do everything you should be doing?"

"First of all I didn't kiss her, because your nosey ass called just as I was about to! So thanks for ruining that moment. And I don't need you to do anything for me Luna. Just stop butting into my business." Lucien was already annoyed because Irys was clearly still unhappy with him. He couldn't get over it and he just wanted her to be happy again.

"Well guess what little brother. She's my best friend, so that makes it my business. Get used to it. And you need to go and make this right."

"Finished?" Lucien asked. Luna just rolled her eyes and left the kitchen. She was annoyed but she knew her brother was going to make things right. The look on his face told Luna everything she needed to know, and he wasn't happy that their date had ended the way it did too.

If there was one thing Lucien realized he didn't like, it was when Irys wasn't her usual happy self. Sure, she smiled at the diners and talked casually with them, but Lucien could just see the calculation in her eyes that meant she was thinking too much. Not to mention she wouldn't even look at Lucien. Honestly, it was just unacceptable. And the moment the last ticket was served out to a table, Lucien left the kitchen. He disposed of the ginger candy he was eating and marched right up to her.

"Come with me," He said sternly. She gave him a defied look, but still she followed him. Lucien led her up to his office where he closed them inside. He took off his chef jacket, then went into the bathroom and washed his hands. When he came back he faced her.

"I told you earlier I didn't mean to just up and leave like I did, and I apologized."

"Okay," Irys shrugged.

"Don't be like that Irys," He stated. "Why you giving me the cold shoulder."

"Just because you said you were sorry doesn't mean I accept the fact that you left. I'm-I'm sorry myself but I'm in a very sensitive state that I'm not normally in but you just-you make me feel this way. And I'll be damned if I think you want something, but then you pull away from me leaving me hanging."

"That's not my intention Irys. I told you I wanted to ask you out in the first place."

"So what? That could have changed when you saw me dog those damn wings."

"Irys you're such a nice person. But I swear I'm gonna cuss you the fuck out if you mention your weight again and me having a problem with it." Irys was startled at his anger. But then she was also a little bit turned on. He looked at her sternly.

"I don't care about your weight," He said slowly. Still, she pouted and crossed her arms.

"And I was dogging those wings with you, and I licked sauce off your damn face. The only thing I did wrong was leaving you suddenly. And it wasn't something I could avoid." Irys believed him now but she was still concerned because he wouldn't even tell her why he had to leave.

"Well what happened?" Irys asked. Lucien knew the question was coming. And though he didn't want to be a liar, he wasn't going to tell her the truth.

"I had to take care of something."

"I know that Lucien. But what was it that you had to take care of?" She could see he was uncomfortable with telling her the truth. That made her wary.

"Honestly Irys, I can't tell you. Not right now. And I'd rather be honest and tell you I don't want to tell you what I had to do, than lie to your face." It made Irys mad, yes. But she also had to give him credit for choosing to tell her to mind her business rather than cook up some lie. It showed that perhaps she was worth something if he didn't want to lie.

"Fine," She stated. "I'll accept that. As long as you're not admitting to something horrible."

"It's nothing like that Irys." She held her hands up, submitting to him. Lucien could see she was still unsure about everything. He couldn't say he blamed her.

"Don't give me that look Irys," He said. "I just want you to believe what I'm telling you." While she thought about what he said he went over to one of the cabinets in the corner of the room. He opened one and pulled out a fresh t-shirt. He walked back over to her, stripping off his old t-shirt.

Irys lost her train of thought as her brain fizzled at seeing him undress. He pulled the shirt he was wearing over his head, revealing his bare chest. Irys cleared her throat as she stared at his perfectly sculpted body. She knew he was in shape, but she didn't know he was sporting a 4 pack. His pants were a little low, showing off the top of his Hanes underwear, and what looked like it would be an incredible V-line. How could a man like him ever want a woman like her?

"I know you're sorry and I believe you," She sputtered out, licking her lips. Lucien looked up and caught her staring longingly at his body. He quickly donned on his new t-shirt, but she didn't stop looking at him.

"What are you thinking?" He asked her.

"You are very, very attractive Lucien," She admitted. Lucien walked up to her slowly until they were inches apart.

"So are you," He countered.

"I know you said you would cuss me out, and I believe you Lucien, but how am I supposed to believe that a man like you, wants a woman like me?" She questioned.

"I just want you Irys. It's quite simple actually."

"Yes but how do I know for sure that-" Lucien took hold of the side her of face and neck, he closed that short distance between them by connecting their lips. Irys gasped in shock but it only took one peck for her to moan and succumb to him. He pecked her lips at first before he deepened the kiss, pushing his tongue inside her mouth. He tasted like that sweet ginger candy he always ate. His kiss was slow and melodic as if their tongues and lips were dancing in perfect tune with each other. Irys didn't even think she was that great of a kisser, but with Lucien all thought went out the window and she just allowed herself to *feel*.

Her lips were so plump. And not only did they look like cherries, they tasted like cherries too. He was lost. Lost to the world when it came to kissing her. His body was hard, and everything in his mind was telling him that he needed to make love to her right there and right now. He'd never felt like this before. Not even with Rosa. This was just on another level. He hated to pull away from her, but he had to before things got out of control.

"Now do you know?" he whispered. Irys was too lost in the haze of his kiss to even answer him coherently.

"Um-maybe-kisses are generic you know. They can be misleading and-" Lucien rolled his eyes. He pushed his hips forward, embedding his arousal into her stomach. She gasped and jumped.

"Oh shit!" She gasped.

"Now do you know for sure that I want you?" he questioned.

"Yes," Her answer was a high pitched squeal. Lucien backed away from her.

"Good," He stated. "And if anytime you should feel like you need some more convincing, don't be afraid to ask." Irys gulped loudly and just nodded.

"I don't want my sister getting us together again so I'm using this time to ask. Would you like to go out with me?" Irys blushed.

"Yes I would," She smiled. "But when would we go? At nights we're both here."

"We can go Sunday night. I'm going to be trading some shifts with Joe. He's going to take charge as head chef on some nights. Sunday with it being a lighter crowd I think we can both have the night to ourselves."

"Okay that sounds good. Should I-should I expect another wing place?"

"No sugar, expect more than that." Irys was excited. This was a real date. "Can I actually have your number?" He asked.

"You're my employer you have it already," She said.

"I thought it'd be creepy if I took it to text you about personal stuff instead of work. So I thought it was safe if I just asked you for it. You know, you're a wise ass right?" Irys laughed at him.

"Gimme your phone." Lucien handed it to her and watched as she entered her phone number. "Now text me so I can have your number too." Lucien did what she said excited to have her phone number.

"If you ever want to talk or anything I want you to text or call me Irys. Even if just for something simple, I want you to trust me enough to vent to me."

"You sure you want that? There's a whole bunch of shit that happens with me sometimes."

"I don't care Irys. I want you to talk to me, I don't like to see you upset. Got it?"

"Yes master," She smiled.

"Wise ass," He scoffed. "Let's go before Luna comes searching for us with her nosey ass." He took Irys by the hand and let her out of the office. But the moment they reached the dining room, he let her hand go and went off into the kitchen. It was okay that no one knew what was going on with them. Because the tingling of her lips was validation that Lucien was serious about her. After Derek, and then her miscarriage, and with all the problems Rosa was causing her, it was a relief to actually be entertaining a man with genuine interest in her.

Chapter Thirteen

"So, when were you going to tell me you and Lucien are going on another date on Sunday?" Luna pegged Irys on a Friday morning as their shift started at the Spa. Irys gave her a look.

"I was going to tell you today," Irys answered.

"But why didn't you tell me the moment he asked you?" Luna asked.

"Because I didn't think I had to," Irys smiled. "Jeez Luna relax. I'm not gonna do anything bad to your brother."

"I'm not worried about that Irys, I know you're a sweetheart. I just feel so invested. I mean, my best friend with my brother? How could I not be excited?!"

"Well I was going to tell you today. And I needed help with finding an outfit! He says we're going someplace nice but I don't want to overdo it."

"I think we should get you a new outfit. Nothing you have in your closet. Lucien could be the real deal for you." Irys thought of the kiss they shared in his office.

"Yeah, he could be," Irys murmured.

"Wait," Luna gasped. "What did you guys do; what's that look on your face?"

"It was nothing Luna. We just kissed that's all."

"That's all?!" She gasped. "A kiss is a big step!" Irys smiled, feeling giddy knowing that it was a big step they'd made.

"I know it's a big step. But are we going too fast? I mean-"

"I don't want to hear it," Luna interjected. "It happened and you both loved it so just carry on. Now I'll think about an outfit you can wear and give you some ideas later."

"Sure," Irys smiled.

True to her word, Luna came back later on in the day with ideas for her outfit. Finally agreeing on something, they used their lunch break to drive over to the shopping strip 15 minutes away to pick up the items Irys had put on hold, online. She was excited to actually be dressing to go on a date that she knew was going to happen this time. Derek had taken her on dates when they first met, but afterwards he didn't bother trying to go anywhere with her. This was new territory that Irys couldn't wait to explore.

By the time Irys purchased the outfit she didn't have time left to try it on before it was time to return from their break. Irys just hoped it was actually true to size and fit her perfectly. Other than that, she just had to wait until Sunday night to finally go on a date with Lucien. But first she got to spend two more days at work with him, still able to enjoy his time.

When she arrived to work that evening at the restaurant, Lucien already had food packaged and ready for her. He was extremely busy putting together some last minute things, but he still stopped to acknowledge her presence there. No matter what Irys could always feel the warm presence of his gaze all around her. And indeed when she looked he was offering her a pleasant smile and a wink. Just those small things made Irys gooey inside. Their time at the wing spot was already fun, she could only imagine the great time they would have together again. And hopefully this time longer.

****

"Damn baby," Derek grunted as he came again, spilling his seed down Rosa's throat. He'd rocked her world in the bedroom, but what turned into just relaxing on the living room couch turned into an oral sex session. The aide was walking around still taking care of their mother, but once 10pm hit and she was sleeping, the aide left promptly. She told Rosa what to do in case her mother woke up again, but Rosa just brushed her off and pushed her out of the house. The moment they were finally alone, Rosa got down to business getting on her knees in front of him. Derek had no complaints when he was getting all the sex he wanted by the only woman he wanted in the first place. After releasing in her mouth, Derek pulled her onto the couch and laid her down. Making quick work of her skimpy shorts, he pulled them down and off her legs. He pushed his pants down further as he laid in between her legs.

Rosa was content with having sex with Derek, but while she was just content she wasn't completely happy. In most cases in made her long for Lucien even more. Like now to be exact. Here Derek was laying on top of her trying to find her entrance as if he was fishing without a fishing rod. She rolled her eyes in the darkness of the living room.

"Wrong hole!" She snapped at him when he began pushing at her anus. Grunting, she stuck her hand between them and grabbed hold of his erection. She aligned it with her opening and inserted it herself. She would have never had to take control with Lucien. He was always in control and he knew what he was doing. Now Derek was grinding inside her and moaning in her ear as if he was putting in real work. Rosa sighed and just laid there, letting him have her body even though she remotely felt nothing. Sometimes it would be okay and she was able to get off, but it was becoming incredibly old. She kept Derek around because she wanted the money he gave to her, and it was the only way she was able to survive. Irys had locked up all the food sources leaving Rosa alone to fend for herself. Derek was her only means of making it, but even his money was drying up. It seemed as long as she kept having sex with him he found ways to get her money.

The sound of the door opening permeated through Derek's heavy moaning. Rosa tried to push him off, but he held her down and continued thrusting within her not even caring about who might be entering. Or it may have been that he knew exactly who was entering and just didn't care. His thrusts got harder, forcing grunts from Rosa's throat as Irys's footsteps came directly at them.

Irys dropped everything she was holding when she entered the living room. The first thing she saw was Derek's bare ass as he pounded into Rosa's body. She was grunting loudly with her legs wrapped around his waist. Irys stood there having a case of déjà vu from the first time she'd caught them. Only this time they were bold enough to be having sex in her living room and on her couch. Irys switched on the living room light, but that didn't deter them whatsoever. It actually made Derek go harder and grunt louder. This time, Irys wasn't going to stand there and watch them. Derek let out a loud shout as his back stiffened and he found his release. Irys grabbed the first thing she could get her hands on which was a picture frame and launched it directly at his head.

Derek cursed loudly when something hard hit the back of his head, ruining his release. He quickly pulled from Rosa's body as she pushed him off. Snaking out from underneath him, she grabbed her shorts to put them on. Of course it was Irys who'd interrupted them and Derek could care less.

"What in the hell are you doing throwing shit at me?" He growled as he stood pulling up his pants.

"How-how dare you be doing that shit on my couch out in the open?" Irys stammered.

"Cause we fucking can," Derek snapped. "Don't tell me you jealous still." Irys didn't know what she was. All she could do was stand there a mass of confusion.

"Are you gonna react like this all the time?" Rosa asked her. "Cause it's getting old."

"You're having sex in my house with my ex, how do you think I'm supposed to feel?" Irys questioned.

"I don't care Irys. You broke up with him. I'm single and he's single, and we're adults we can do whatever the hell we want. And I happen to live here and I can have my man as company whenever I please. So you're just going to have to get over it." Irys started towards Rosa with her hand cocked and ready.

"What'd I tell you about talking to me like that?" Irys asked lowly. "Didn't I tell you to watch how to talk to me?" Rosa began backing up, seeing the deadly look on Irys's face.

"I'm just telling you the truth Irys. Either you can take it or you can't." Irys decided she couldn't take it. She whipped her hand back, and brought it forward with her palm open to connect to Rosa's cheek. Only when the reality of what she did came at her, Irys snapped from her haze. She covered her mouth as Rosa fell to the ground.

"The fuck are you doing?!" Derek yelled. He ran over to Rosa to comfort her. Irys continued to back up.

"Why are you so jealous of me?!" Rosa cried out as Derek helped her up. "It's not my fault you look like that and I look like I do. It's not my fault that Derek wants me either! You can't brutalize me for your own shortcomings!"

"You know that's not what I'm doing," Irys whispered. "You keep provoking me Rosa. So that's what you get!"

"You better not come near her again Irys. You lay a hand on her and I'm gonna do the same thing to you Irys. And you know I will!" Irys glared at him.

"You can go ahead Derek, but you also know that I won't go down easily. Forget I fucked you up the last time you tried to hit me?"

"I let you off lightly," He scoffed. "I'm warning you, don't touch her again. Because this woman is worth more than you want to believe she does."

"So what are you gonna do? Marry her? Start a whole family while still living in my damn house?" Irys snapped.

"Well this is the kind of woman I'd want carrying my baby Irys." That did it for Irys. She shook her head and practically ran out of the living room. She grabbed the things she'd dropped on the ground and hurried off to her bedroom. Locking herself in her solace, she turned the lock on the door to make sure no one could get inside. She felt panicked, she felt upset, she was hurt, and she was angry. For Derek to say her pregnancy essentially meant nothing because he wanted a woman like Rosa truly cut deep. But the fact that they had angered her again enough for her to resort to violence was the part that scared Irys. Why did she care so much about what they did? Because in the end it was her choice not to kick Rosa out.

Undressing hastily she went straight to the bathroom where she tried to drown her sorrows in a hot shower. But all that did was mask the tears that fell from her eyes. She couldn't understand why someone could be so damned evil. And what was worse, Irys was going to soon be falling evil herself. All she could think about was exacting revenge and making them hurt as much as she was being hurt herself. But it wasn't her. None of this was her. Everything was weighing heavy on her and she just needed something to free her from all this trouble.

Getting out of the shower, she barely dried her skin off properly before she donned a t-shirt. Grabbing up her phone she started a new message to send to Lucien. She didn't know what to even say to start things off so she resorted to just emoji's. She was angry, she was upset, and she was confused so those were all the emoji's she sent to him. She wasn't even sure this was the right thing to do, but he was the only thing she could think of at the moment. Waiting for him to respond, she cut off all the lights and get in bed. It was a little after midnight and after all the cleaning up he had to do at the restaurant Irys wasn't even sure she should be bothering him. He must have been drop dead tired. Deciding she shouldn't trouble him Irys got ready to tell him she'd sent that to him by accident and it was really Luna she was talking to. But as she was typing those words, her phone began ringing and his name in large letters popped up.

"Hello?" She whispered into the phone.

"Hey Sugar, what's the matter?" He asked her gently. Just the sound of his voice calling her sugar seemed to make everything better already.

"I-I'm okay now Lucien. I didn't mean to bother you. It's late and I know you're tired."

"Oh stop that. I'm fine. You obviously texted me because you weren't alright. Don't be afraid to talk to me sugar." Irys sighed. If there was one thing she wanted to do right now it was spilling her guts to get things off her chest. So she just trusted Lucien's words and got to talking.

"When I came in tonight I found my sister having sex with my ex." Lucien audibly gasped.

"Are you serious?!"

"And this isn't the first time I've caught them doing it either. The problem is this time they were out in the open, humping on my damn couch! And it ticked me off because they could care less about how I would feel about it you know! In fact they were shoving it in my face that they were hooking up and none of them saw anything wrong with it. I just got so mad that I hit my sister!"

"Sugar I know you're not that type of person. Do not let someone turn you into something you're not. If they want to be spiteful Irys, let them be. Because the universe has a funny way of working, and they in time will get what they deserve. So if they want each other, then let them have each other. Obviously he's your ex for a reason you know? Unless of course you still have feelings for him." When he said the last part Irys heard the jealousy in his voice. Irys didn't want any confusion with that,

"No Lucien. Absolutely no feelings for him whatsoever! That's why I'm confused as to why I get so upset when I see them."

"It's your mind playing tricks on you sugar. I'm sure with the awful things they must be saying to you, it makes you care about what they are doing. I guess perhaps you just need something to not make you care about them."

"I know I need something," She admitted.

"Don't worry about it. I'll figure it out with you. But in the meantime you need to not fall into their web and become this evil person. Your heart is too rich to succumb to evil okay? Trust me on that."

"I trust you."

"Remind yourself that he's your ex for a reason and he means nothing to you. If your sister wants his trouble. She can have him."

"You know at first I was with him because I felt as if he was the best man alive, you know? And then one day he showed his true colors and since then I couldn't really ever paint him in this fabulous light anymore. I broke up with him and he told me there would never be another man who'd want my fat ass-" Lucien's heart constricted when he could hear the tears in her voice. Soon she stopped talking and Lucien knew it was because she was crying.

"Irys," He said softly. She sniffled.

"Yes?"

"Do you need me to come and see you?" He asked gently. He just wanted to hold her to stop her from crying. Especially over a man who wasn't worth a penny.

"No-don't-it's okay. I just-I'm going to stop crying over him."

"It's not him you're crying over. It's the hurtful words he said that upsets you. It's obviously untrue that no one would want you Irys. I hope you can see that." She wiped the tears from her face. She was on the phone with a man who had asked her on a date. Of course what Derek said was untrue. It had to be.

"I know," she whispered. I've never felt this much emotion before. First I think I'm okay, and then I get super angry, and then I'm super emotional crying and shit. For two people who could care less about me in the first place. My sister hates the fact that we're blood related, and my ex threatens to put his hands on me if I ever hit his new girlfriend again." The alarms went on for Lucien. A man who was threatening to hit a woman was also a man not afraid to hit a woman.

"Wait? He threatened to touch you?" Lucien asked. "All because you slapped your sister for disrespecting you?"

"Can you believe it?"

"He's hit you before?" Lucien asked sternly. Irys knew admitting the truth might makes things worse, but she was spilling her guts at this point.

"Yeah he has. But I promise you the minute he did I was whopping his ass up and down my bedroom, and I kicked him out right after. So even if he does hit me again, he knows he's gonna get a fight in return." Lucien was quiet for too long. Irys thought for a second they had lost connection.

"Lucien?"

"I'm here sugar," He said, anger dousing his voice. "And I don't mean to scare you with my anger honey, but I'm not pleased another man had the audacity to hit you. You said he was with you sister when you got home. Is he still there?"

"Yeah I suppose he is. I didn't hear anyone leave."

"Good. Make sure he doesn't leave," He ordered.

"Why?" She questioned.

"Why you think? I'm coming over there to put a foot in his ass for hitting you in the first place Irys. I'm not just gonna play cool like that grown ass man didn't put his hands on you. And if it's one thing that will piss me off Irys is some man thinking he's god's fucking gift to a woman and hitting her because he thinks he can fucking get away with it. I don't think so. I'm coming over there to fuck him up!" Irys was too shocked to say anything. She loved his protection, but the last thing she wanted was a big fight at her house.

"No Lucien," She said.

"No? Are you protecting him?!" He gasped.

"You know I'm not!" She snapped. "It's just that, my sick mom is here and I don't want her to be startled by any fighting Lucien! And besides, you were just talking to me about not letting people put evil into my heart. I can say the same thing for you. I'm not gonna let you come out here to kick the ass of man that ain't worth it, for you to possibly end up in jail. Trust me Lucien even though it wasn't right of him, I had him on the ground crying the moment he put his hands on me." Lucien was quiet again trying to retain his anger.

"I'm only laying back because you want me to Irys. But I swear if he hits you again I won't let it go. And I don't care where I end up." Before Irys could speak, the sound of his dog barking filled their conversation.

"I'm fine go away from me Salsa," Lucien snapped.

"What's wrong?" Irys asked.

"She can tell I'm upset."

"Aw she just wants to help. Don't snap at her," Irys cooed.

"She's like a child Irys. You know when you're angry and you don't want to be angry around kids so you send them away? That's what I'm trying to do, but she won't leave me alone." Salsa began barking again. Lucien looked down at his dog. She began butting her nose against his stomach. Lucien pet her head to assure her that he was okay, but when she began sniffing him, he knew it was more than him being upset that kept her close.

"She just loves you too much to be away from you," Irys teased.

"With me at the restaurant all day I guess she just misses me a lot." Irys heard Lucien moving around followed by some beeping.

"What are you doing?" Irys asked him,

"Mind your business," He teased. Lucien quickly checked his sugar. Seeing he was low, he grabbed a bottle of orange juice from his fridge and retreated to his bedroom to lay down again.

"I can't wait for Sunday," Lucien told her. "Opening my restaurant was the only thing I've looked forward to. It's good to have something else I'm excited about doing."

"Trust me I feel the same way."

"Let's make a deal," Lucien said. "On Sunday we're not going to talk about exes or mean sisters, or how fucked up people have been to us. We're just going to talk about us. We're going to for one night forget all the shit that troubles us, and just have fun with each other. Deal?"

"Deal," Irys smiled. "But if you're not gonna talk about your ex Sunday night, then you need to talk about her now. I wanna know what kind of idiot let a man like you go." Lucien cracked up.

"She didn't let me go. I let her go."

"Why?" Irys asked.

"Because the only person she was in a relationship with was herself. Bottom line, we both wanted two different things and I just didn't feel like it was necessary to keep the relationship going."

"Did you miss her once she was gone?" Lucien thought about how to answer before he actually did.

"Honestly I did miss her. But for all the wrong reasons. Much like your ex, she also convinced me that I was lucky to have her and I wouldn't find anyone better than her. I didn't believe it at first. But then the first couple nights being alone I started to believe the things she told me. I was a little bit depressed and I kind of sunk into a black hole."

"Did you overcome it? Or are you still battling it?"

"I'm not completely happy Irys that's true, but I also learned that just because someone says something like that to you, doesn't mean it really true. She wanted so bad to be with me Irys. And I asked her why. You know what she said to me?"

"Your money?"

"She wanted my money yes. But then she told me she didn't want to give me up because I knew how to fuck." Irys gasped. "And I completely get it. I'm not a prude when it comes to sex. I know that sex is important when it comes to relationships because it what people do to express how they feel for each other. If I'm insanely attracted to a female I'm eventually going to want to experience her body. But for a woman who I've been dating for years to tell me that the only reason she wants to stay with me is because I knew how to fuck her good that was completely unacceptable. I'm not a perfect man Irys. But I'd like to think that I have more to offer a woman than just good sex." Irys understood what he meant completely. But she'd be wrong if she didn't admit to herself that she couldn't stop thinking about how good in bed he was.

"If it's worth anything, you have given me something that I couldn't get from anyone else, and it wasn't sex."

"It is worth something Irys. Anything you say to me will always be worth something." There was an awkward pause.

"So…you're good in bed huh?" Irys asked.

"I'm great in bed actually," Lucien corrected. The both of them started laughing again.

"Seriously though, your ex was mean for saying that to you, but you should be grateful she did. Because I'm sure you don't want to live your life with someone who can't appreciate the wonderful man that you are."

"How sweet are you," Lucien said.

"The sweetest," She smiled.

"Just like that mouth of yours. That I didn't get to kiss before you left by the way."

"Didn't know you wanted to," She said.

"Didn't know you wanted to," Lucien mocked her. "Don't play that with me you knew I wanted to. But no worries. Sunday coming I'll get my cherry kisses."

"That almost feels like a threat," Irys laughed.

"Then consider it one. Cause I'm completely serious." They got quiet again, their breathing the only thing audible for a moment.

"Are you tired Lucien?" She asked softly.

"A little bit."

"Me too. But I-I feel safe with you on the other line."

"Go to sleep sugar. I'll stay on the line with you."

"Thank you," She murmured. Lucien was completely at peace, listening to her soft breathing until sleep consumed the both of them.

Rosa woke the next morning with Irys already gone. That meant Rosa wouldn't be able to get anything to eat. It frustrated her to have to live like this, but she didn't have any other place to be. Not wanting to be around Derek at the moment, Rosa got dressed and left the house. She knew Lucien wouldn't react well to seeing her, but she needed to see him. After their last encounter she didn't know what would happen between them, especially since she got angry and hit him in the balls. But she knew Lucien couldn't forget about her completely. Like she did before, she went out to the restaurant and just waited for Lucien to show up. This time she didn't attempt going anywhere to eat. Even though her stomach was growling beyond measure, she just stuck it out. After an hour of waiting, his car came into the parking lot. Immediately she could see him looking after her car curiously since no one else should have been parked there. Rosa immediately hopped out of the car to intercept him. The moment he stepped out of his car and saw her, he stopped short. Rosa already knew he was unhappy to see her, but she'd already committed to coming here so she wasn't going to leave without talking to him.

"Lucien," She called out. Lucien gazed at Rosa almost not able to recognize her. She looked as if she hadn't slept in days. Not to mention she was thinner.

"What's up?" Lucien asked approaching her.

"Um, I hope you're not too mad about how I kicked you the last time."

"Why would I be mad at that?" Lucien asked sarcastically. Rosa only nodded not able to defend herself against it. She was completely at fault.

"I know you probably don't want to see me, and I haven't been that great of a person," She said. "But I am seriously struggling. And I was wondering if maybe-"

"Are you on drugs?" He asked sharply, not liking the bags under her eyes or her weight loss.

"No I promise I'm not. I just haven't really been eating. I don't care if it's a banana or something I'm just really hungry." Lucien felt no type of feeling towards her. He wasn't angry for the things she said to him, and he wasn't stuck on her being the only thing he needed in regards to having a woman. It was almost as if she was just another stranger. But since he knew her and he didn't have any feelings towards her, he wasn't averse to helping her.

"Come with me, He said. "But don't think because I'm helping you out this time that you can make this a daily thing."

"I won't," She yipped. Lucien looked back at her as she followed him into the restaurant. He could tell she wasn't living on the street because despite her tired features, she smelled clean and her clothes were clean.

"I don't know why you just don't get a job," Lucien told her. "Instead of having to wonder where your next meal is coming from."

"It's not that simple you know," She pouted. Lucien only offered her a sigh. Pointing to a stool in the kitchen he told her to sit down, then he went into the walk in fridge to find something to reheat for her. After taking out some pasta and setting it on the counter, he took out bowls, and plugged in his waffle machine to make her two quick waffles. While he did that she kept quiet and just looked at him. Lucien actually liked it that way and hoped she wouldn't start talking to him.

While both the pasta and the waffle were cooking, Lucien took his phone out. Earlier that morning he'd awoken to Salsa's whining but he also awoke to Irys's soft breathing too. He wanted to try to wake her up to tell her good morning, but he decided to just let her sleep. Since then he hadn't spoken to her, and he found that he missed their contact. Knowing she was probably caught up with a client and not able to text Lucien sent her a quick message to let her know that he was thinking about her and couldn't wait to see her later. Delightfully she did answer him promptly.

I'm excited to see you too. I appreciated last night so much. Even though you snore. Did you know that? Lucien actually laughed out loud. As he began texting her back, he was interrupted by her incoming call. Lucien picked it up.

"I do not snore," He stated.

"How you gonna tell me? You were fast asleep."

"Because I just know," He said. Irys laughed at him.

"Listen I can't really talk. I just wanted to hear your voice and to rub it in your face that you snore."

"You're so mean," Lucien smiled. "But I'll see you later." She made a kissing sound before hanging up. Checking on the food, he noticed Rosa was staring a hole into him.

"What?" He asked.

"Are you-are you seeing someone?" she asked. Rosa could tell by the tone of his voice, and his body language that he was perhaps talking to a female.

"I can't see how that's any of your business," Lucien said. He plated her waffles then gave it to her with a topping of syrup. He turned the fire off from the pasta then package the food in a to go container for her to have later.

"Because I still want you, you know that."

"And I know that you don't want me for the right reasons. That's why we will never work out Rosa. You just have to accept that." Though he was saying that, Rosa couldn't accept that. The idea that he had already moved onto another woman made her extremely jealous. How could she just let that go? Even if she disagreed, Rosa kept quiet and just finished her food. She wasn't going to argue but she knew she wasn't just going to let it go either.

"Thanks for all of this," Rosa told Lucien as he walked her to the door. He was sending her off with a stomach full of food, and a container filled with food too. Outside, she turned and looked at him.

"You're welcome," He said. Rosa nodded.

"Can I ask you something?" she asked.

"What's up?"

"Have you been having sex with that girl?" She questioned. Lucien wished he could tell Rosa that he was having sex with Irys. But then again, even if he wanted to push it in her face, he didn't think he actually could. He was never that type of man.

"No," He answered simply, which was the truth anyway. The relief that exuded from Rosa's features gave him pause. She shouldn't be so concerned about what he did and the fact that she was sent up a red flag.

"That's a relief," she breathed.

"I don't know what to even say Rosa. But honestly, just let it go. You're free to have sex with anyone you want, as I am free to do the same. Simple," He shrugged. Sure she was free to have sex with anyone she wanted, but Rosa didn't want any woman in Lucien's bed. Especially knowing how good he was in bed. That was all hers. She just didn't know how to get him back.

"I care about you too much to just let it go." Lucien stuffed his hands on his pockets. Rosa leaned forward and kissed him on the cheek. After nodding again, she clutched the bag he'd given her and walked off hastily. He didn't know what he was going to do with that girl.

****

Sunday night Lucien waited in front of the restaurant for his date with Irys. Irys told him she'd drive, but instead he had a car pick her up, and then Lucien himself would drop her home. It was weird for him just to be standing here waiting to go on a date. Even though he and Rosa were together, they didn't really date. It felt good to be going out, and he was more nervous than anything. The wing spot was fun, but this place was as fancy as it gets and from talking on the phone with her, Lucien learned that she loved any kind of food experience and if she never had anything before she'd like to try it. This time, he had his insulin in his car in a Styrofoam container with ice packs to keep it cold so he wouldn't have to just up and leave her if things went wrong. But specifically for today he munched on little things, so his sugar was low and he actually needed to eat. Glancing at his watch is was 8pm on the dot. By the time he was looking up, a car pulled up to the curve and the driver got out. When he opened the rear doors, he helped Irys step out. Lucien could only stand there for a hot minute just lost. She was wearing a gold speckled dress that clung to her curves and flowed all the way down to the ground. The left side of the dress had a split, revealing her thick thigh. The dress had sleeves that were long and elegant along with a deep v cut in the center that showed off her voluptuous chest. As she stood there, someone wolf whistled at her. Lucien snapped out of his trance and went up to her quickly, looking around to see who the culprit was.

Not knowing who did it, he quickly took Irys in his arms so people could see she was actually with someone.

"You look amazing," He complimented her. "Just so delectable." Irys giggled and held his hand as he led her up to the restaurant.

"You look pretty hot yourself," She smiled. Wearing a pair of slacks with a black t-shirt, and a blazer on top he looked too suave to be on a date with someone like her. But sure enough, he held onto her as if he wanted everyone to know she belonged to him. The feeling was very much needed for Irys's confidence.

"This place is amazing," She said as they sat down at their booth. The jazz singer on stage was doing a mesmerizing number. Lucien gave her a look.

"Not as amazing as your place of course," She corrected. Lucien chuckled.

"It's fine sugar. I know I'm not the cream of the crop. And really all I can focus on is you. You just-you're just so gorgeous."

"Stop making me blush," She smiled.

"Fine," He laughed. "Order whatever you want."

They ordered their food, and while they awaited its arrival, they talked over glasses of wine.

"So what made you get into working at the spa?" Lucien asked her. "I know Luna loved going to spas, never dreamed she would actually work in one." Irys laughed at him.

"Well I love working with my hands. And well, the spa is kind of a place where people come to feel good. I want to work there to give people a good time in their own bodies you know?"

"I get it," He said. "I got a massage from Luna once." Irys gave him a look.

"How did that go? Because you're naked once you get inside those rooms and she would have massaged your butt," She giggled.

"Exactly! So it didn't really go too well," Lucien laughed. "So she massaged my shoulders and then we spent the rest of the half hour playing spades on the massage table." Irys laughed out loud and took a sip of her drink.

"I am so envious of the two of you. I mean I wish I had a sibling I was that close to."

"Don't dwell on what you don't have Irys. Because I'm pretty sure Luna is more than a friend to you."

"Yeah she is. That girl has been there for everything."

"Right. So forget about the negativity. It's fine not to have something because in life you'll eventually get it in another way, shape or form."

"You're completely right. So enough about me. Tell me why you named your place *Toujours*. Doesn't that mean 'always' in French?"

"That's exactly what it means. And I name it that because my family is something that I will always have. And they put as much into believing in me as I put into my passion for cooking. So without my parents or Luna I wouldn't have anything."

"That's so sweet," She said. "Luna told me your parents passed but not how. What happened?"

"Old age," Lucien said. "After they retired they said they wanted to move back to France. Of course Luna and I couldn't go with them so we just let them go. We spoke on the phone every day, we video chatted and it went that way for years and years. Finally one day my mom didn't answer her phone. So I called my dad and he didn't answer his phone either. What do you do when you're worried about your parents but they're in a whole different country? Nothing. Me and Luna just waited around. Finally we got the call. My dad had a heart attack and my mom was so grief stricken her heart gave out a month later." Irys covered her mouth.

"That's so sad," Irys said. "My mom is counting down her days. But what she only thought would be a couple days turned into months that turned into years. All she tells me most times is that she can't wait to meet her husband again. And though she's sick and frail, her mind is so strong. I can't imagine her even passing away you know? But I'm also sad for her because I know she wants to be with her true love."

"Sometimes you have to let life take its course. Being with my mom after my dad died was hard. And I told her I'd do anything to see her stop hurting. And just a couple days after I said that she had her heart attack too. I was kind of relieved she wasn't in pain anymore, but I still felt as if I needed my mother. After she passed I learned that both their wills held a certain amount of money for both me and Luna to achieve our dreams. And with that I knew what I had to do and I just did it. What are yours though? Your dreams?"

"I can't really say I have any," Irys said. "I love working at the Spa, and that's my place. I guess I can say something I really want to do is travel. That's why I know all these languages. I hope to one day use them in the actual country. I just want to see the world and be part of it. With my mom being sick, travelling is the last thing I could do. So I just have to wait until it's my time."

"I'll take you anywhere you want to go," Lucien whispered. They locked eyes as an unspoken promise was made between them. Irys was afraid to ask any questions because it was as if he was agreeing to be in her life, as something much more than friends.

The rest of their dinner was spent laughing and sharing embarrassing stories and learning things about one another. Like their previous time together, Lucien's watch began beeping cutting through their conversation. He excused himself from the table and left her for a few moments before he finally returned. When he did return he was drinking a lot of water without eating anything else. It was a little weird to her at first but he made her forget about that the moment he began speaking again. Then she was lost in his stories. Their date seemed so complex, yet so easy to enjoy. Towards the end they agreed not to even speak English, and they enjoyed the fact that they both knew the same foreign languages. Honestly it made Irys feel more connected to him. And plus he was sexy as all hell speaking both French and Italian.

When it was finally over, Irys hated to have to leave but all good things must come to an end. As she waited outside for the car to come pick her back up, Lucien took her hand.

"I didn't order the car to come back for you," He told her.

"Why not?"

"Because I'm old school and I want to take you home myself." Irys paused. She didn't mind the ride home, but she also did not want her sister to be lurking out the windows and see who she'd been out with. Rosa had a tendency to ruin things and this, Irys didn't want her to ruin.

"You think that's a good idea?" she asked.

"I'm not gonna ask to stay the night I promise," He smiled. "Just let me do as my dad taught me and take you home after an incredible date." Irys allowed him to lead her towards the parking lot. It felt so natural holding his hand and walking.

"Actually," Irys said stopping.

"What's up?"

"Are you in a rush to leave?"

"Is there something else you want to do?" he asked.

"Just to go for a walk," She said. Lucien looked out at the calm streets.

"I'm sure they don't mind my car in the lot for much longer. Let's talk a walk." Lucien didn't let go of her hand as they continued onto the street. There was a couple of men who gave Irys second glances and he didn't want her to appear available. That possessiveness he felt all of a sudden was scary but he just knew how he felt about Irys. He'd never been drawn to a woman like this.

"I see you," Irys said to him.

"What you mean?" He asked.

"I see how you look at the men who pass us," She looked over at him with a smirk on her face. "I know you want to defend me but its okay. I've gotten used to getting stares from people because of my weight. I realize that people are uncomfortable sometimes." Lucien stopped walking, keeping hold of her hand to jerk her to a stop. He made her turn around to look at him.

"You think I'm staring back at those men because they don't know how to accept your weight? And I'm trying to protect you?" Lucien questioned.

"Yes."

"Well you're wrong," He said. "I'm staring at them because I feel a sort of jealousy, or well possessiveness when other men look at you. And when they look at you Irys, I don't feel like it's because they're uncomfortable. I feel like it's because you're a sexy woman and naturally men look. Me staring makes sure they know you with me. And honestly Irys, you're not as fat as you make yourself out to be."

"Lucien I shop in the plus size section."

"So what? You're not the average size woman. And that makes you special. Besides," He pulled her close and wrapped his arms around her waist. "You have much more to hold onto," He breathed. Irys chewed on her bottom lip trying her hardest not to tongue him down in the middle of the sidewalk. Since her miscarriage she hadn't been aroused and Lucien was changing that for her.

"You say that now," Irys breathed. "But wait until I'm naked."

"Is that an invitation?" Lucien asked, brows raised. Irys scoffed and pushed off him. She continued walking and he followed.

"Stop playing," She laughed. It was kind of hard for Irys to admit that a man like Lucien actually wanted to see her naked, or even have sex with her to begin with.

"I can't see why you'd want to see me naked when there's all these other women around," She glanced at a woman walking by them, who was tiny and fit.

"You know what I think?" Lucien asked, shoving his hands in his pockets. When she shoved away from him, she hadn't attempted to hold his hand again.

"Enlighten me."

"You said you learned to love your body and you accept the way you look but I don't think that's true." Irys stopped walking and turned to look at him.

"Excuse me?" She asked.

"How are you going to tell me what I do and don't feel?" She snapped at him.

"Don't be upset with me Irys. I'm not saying it to make you feel bad. I just want you to understand."

"Understand what?" she asked.

"How can you love your body if you keep saying negative things about it? A confident women would want me to see her body. A confident women wouldn't wonder why I want her instead of some size 2." Irys rolled her eyes and sighed.

"Yes I know you're right. And I am comfortable with my body. It's more about if you're comfortable you know."

"Clearly I am," Lucien said. "And sometimes sex with skinny girls hurt." Lucien reached out his hand and waited for her to take it. She did so with a smile.

"Was your ex skinny?" Irys asked him.

"Yes, and I've bruised my pelvis a couple times, thrusting too got damn hard against her." Irys covered her mouth and snickered.

"My ex was a little bigger than you but not too much. Just a little more stocky but he was still kind of fit."

"And he's never made you orgasm because?" Lucien inquired. Irys shrugged.

"I'm not sure." Lucien looked her delicious body up and down. Man if she was that type of girl Lucien would have had her in an alleyway by now.

"Don't worry your pretty little head about his inadequacies," Lucien said. "You'll get it good one day." Irys actually trusted his words when he spoke them. And it was believing them that had her heart rate going up. Obviously he was going to keep having this effect on her, proving just how much she was actually into him.

They walked and talked for a whole hour before finally returning back to his car. Along the ride back to her home she felt the effects of the walk, trying to pull her into sleep. For being in Lucien's car for the first time she was awfully comfortable. His scent was all around her, and with his soft R&B music the inside was just cozy. He held her hand as he drove and that was all Irys needed. They didn't talk at all on the drive back. That was just the mood. They were comfortable with that however.

When Lucien pulled up to her home she groaned not wanting to leave him. He looked over at her and smiled.

"It hurts me too sugar," He said as he got out of the car. He came around to her side and opened the door for her to help her out. Lucien made sure to keep her in his arms so she didn't go anywhere.

"Tonight was great," He said. "Learning so much about you makes me feel so full."

"I appreciate you taking the time to want to know me Lucien. I haven't had that before."

"So when's our next date?" he asked. "Because you know it can't just end here. I need more of you."

"I have a question. You're a chef. But can you make everything?" She questioned. Lucien gasped.

"I'm almost insulted!" He laughed. "Of course I can cook anything. And if I can't make it out of my head I can follow a recipe perfectly. Why?" he asked.

"I'm going to challenge you."

"Oh, so you want me to prove I can cook anything?" He questioned. Irys nodded.

"Okay fine with me. So let's do this. You tell me anything that your little heart desires, and I'll make it for you at my home. If you're comfortable I'll invite you there and that can be counted as our next date."

"I'm more than comfortable with that," Irys whispered. "I just hope you can make whip cream from scratch because I love some cream on my desserts." Lucien closed the distance between them.

"I can give you two types of cream if you want it," He breathed. "You only need to say the word."

"I've got cream to give you too," She said. "But you've got to work for that."

"Don't play with me Irys," He warned. "Because I will work for it, and I will get it." He lift her chin and collided against her mouth with his. Her breathy moan that filled his mouth was indication she wanted to kiss him as much as he wanted to kiss her. Her mouth was the softest he'd ever kissed. The plumpness of her lips just kept egging him on to continue kissing her. With his tongue deep in her mouth, this deep of a kiss was sending sensors of something more to his body. It reacted in a way as if he had a woman in his bed kissing her before their bodies connected. And now he was bone hard in his pants, and his hands were itching to slide underneath her dress.

Irys was lost in his kiss, letting him completely take over. She wasn't one to submit, but for Lucien he just overpowered her sensually. Being taller than her, he controlled the tempo of the kiss and caged her against his car. She could feel the tension in his body as if he was fighting with himself. Even though she wasn't sure what he wanted to do Irys still wrapped her arms around his neck to communicate with him that he had her completely under his power. Drawing him closer when she did so, he moaned into her mouth and let that tension leave his body. His hands travel down to her waist before moving down to her legs, caressing her body through her dress. Pushing against him, she paused for just a second. She began to draw away while trying to look down at their joined bodies.

"What's the matter?" Lucien breathed, kissing her chin. He gazed into her eyes.

"Your hands are on my thighs," She said. Lucien nodded. Irys swallowed hard and looked between them. That long stiff muscle she felt against her body couldn't be what she thought it was. It must have been because his hands were nowhere near her stomach.

"Is that your penis?" She gasped. Lucien cracked a smile.

"Yeah sugar it is. You got me excited," He said. Lucien moved his hips away from her body. But that shocked look never left her face.

"Stop looking at me like that," He smiled.

"It's just that, I felt it before but only for a minute when you pushed it against me. But then now I got to feel the whole thing."

"So what?" He asked.

"It feels like an arm!" She gasped.

"Running scared?" He asked her, nipping at her earlobe. Irys's knees trembled. She closed her eyes and bit her lip.

"Yeah right," She smiled. "Big girls can take more than the average." This time she sucked on his earlobe making him weak.

"I don't want to leave you yet Irys but I know if you don't go I'm gonna tear your pretty dress off." Irys gave him a peck on the lips before he completely backed off. He straightened his erection in his pants and took her hand. He only helped her up onto the sidewalk before she let his hand go and continued walking up to her front door.

"Hey Irys," He called out. She turned and looked at him. "Just because we had this date tonight doesn't mean I am tired of you. So if you feel lonely all you have to do is call me."

"I'm going to take you up on this offer," She smiled. "After I take a shower and cool off. Just send me a text so I know when to call you."

"Of course sugar." He winked at her and hopped back into his car. Irys squealed in delight and hurried into the house. She closed the door and leaned against it. But when she heard his car driving off, she sighed with a big smile on her face and sunk to the ground against the door. The happiness that filled her body felt as if she'd just drank a whole liter of Pepsi and the caffeine was bubbling inside her.

"What the hell's up with you?" Rosa asked her. Irys jumped and looked up realizing her sister was hovering over her.

"Nothing," Irys said getting up.

"Where you coming from dressed like that? A date or something?"

"Why do you care?" Irys asked. She gave her a sister a look and walked by her. Like she said before, she wasn't divulging any part of Lucien to her sister. Rosa had already taken Derek without even considering how Irys would feel, and her and Derek weren't even together. Imagine if Rosa knew Irys wanted Lucien? It'll make it much worse if Rosa tried to get her hands on him. And honestly, Irys would lose her ever loving mind.

"Because I was waiting for you to get home to unlock the fridge. I'm hungry." Irys went straight to the kitchen and unlocked the fridge so Rosa would leave her alone. She watched as Rosa took out the things she wanted to eat, and then Irys locked it back up.

"I learned my lesson you know. You don't have to keep it locked."

"I'm not sure I believe that," Irys said lowly. "Anyway, goodnight." She went deeper into the house to get to her room but before going inside she deviated to her mother's bedroom to peek inside. When the door creaked open, her mother's eyes opened.

"Irys?" She said.

"Oh mom I didn't mean to wake you," She said stepping inside the room. "Especially this late."

"No matter girl. Just come give your dear mother a hug. Where have you been looking this pretty?" Irys went over to the bed and leaned over to hug her mother. She sat at the edge of the bed.

"I actually went on a date." Kendra gasped at her daughter.

"A date! Oh my god please tell me all about him!"

"Well, his name is Lucien and he's the sweetest guy I have ever met."

"So when will I be meeting him?" She questioned.

"When the time is right mom. And I don't want to jump the gun with this one."

"Okay fine. But the moment you know you want this man to be in your life I need to meet him."

"You will mom I promise. Now get back to sleep. I'm gonna go to bed myself." She kissed her mother goodnight, tucked her in then left her bedroom. She knew Lucien would be texting her soon so she went to take her shower so she'd be ready for him. Having a wonderful night with him on their date, and then talking with him all night long on the phone until they both fell asleep, it was all perfect for Irys. And she wasn't afraid to admit that Lucien had her falling for him hard.

Chapter Fourteen

"So how was it?" Luna asked her friend the moment Irys stepped into work. Irys was wearing glasses, but when she took them off, Luna saw the exhaustion in her features.

"Are you hung over?" Luna answered.

"No! I just didn't get that much sleep." Luna rubbed her hands together and grinned.

"You guys were doing it like hamsters all night weren't you?" She questioned. Irys gave her friend a look and pushed passed her.

"I swear you beamed down from another planet," Irys said. "But no. We did not have sex last night."

"Why the hell not?"

"Because that was our first date!" Irys exclaimed. "And I'm only tired because we were on the phone talking all night. But that's it. No sex." Luna shook her head.

"I had to get you guys to hang out alone, in the first place. Now it looks like I gotta get ya'll to fuck each other."

"Whoa!" Irys shrieked. "No Luna! You will do no such thing! I can have sex with a man without your help thank you! I don't even want to know how you would get us to have sex in the first place. You're such a creep!" Luna burst out laughing. She was seriously taking joy in this.

"Psycho," Irys smiled. Even though she was tired because her lack of sleep she was happy that it was because she was up all night with Lucien. And she just couldn't wait to experience more.

For the next two weeks Irys and Lucien fell into a sort of rhythm. They talked each other to sleep every night, and they either woke up to each other's soft breathing, or a text. For a couple of nights Irys was actually awoken by the sound of Salsa barking. Sometimes it was 6 in the morning, other times it was 3 in the morning. When that happened the phone would usually hang up quickly as if Lucien was trying to keep from waking Irys up. When she would mention it the next day he usually told her not to worry about it. Irys thought nothing more of it then, figuring it was just his Salsa's behavior and nothing more. Each time they both had a break during the day they would either meet up or talk on the phone for their lunch break. Irys had gotten used to not bringing any lunch with her to work because Lucien would be asking her to come to the restaurant to eat.

But every day no matter what time it was, his watch would beep and he would disappear before coming back. Each time he had a different attitude when he did. Either he was fine, or he was subtly irritated. After these days of talking so much and being in each other's company, Irys thought he would share any problems he had with her, but he just didn't. It concerned her for what she thought she could mean to his life. She didn't want to be like his ex, just using him. She wanted to actually be there to help him and boost him up when he was down. Only if he would let her in. She was after all trying to prove she could be something more to him.

On a Friday afternoon, Luna and Irys was once again leaving for lunch break and heading over to the restaurant. Already she knew something was different with Lucien. His texts weren't comforting or had that warm fuzz in them. It was just robotic and generic. She didn't want to judge anything based off something like a text, but she just had a feeling. But her feeling was only confirmed when she walked into the restaurant. Lucien was working in the kitchen with a serious expression on his face. She thought he was just concentrating but when he looked up at her, he had to force himself to smile in her direction. Irys didn't like that at all.

She went over to the table she usually sat, and waited for him to come to her. In minutes he was at the table with her plate of food. Irys stood to greet him.

"Hey Luce," She smiled leaning in to kiss him. He gave her a small peck, which wasn't the usual, before moving away from her. Irys cleared her throat and sat down. Their usual engaging conversation didn't happen since he just stared at her eat.

"I get the feeling something is wrong," Irys said. Lucien just shrugged at her. "You can of course tell me what's wrong. I won't crucify you or something. I can help."

"You can't help my problems," he said shortly. Irys put her fork down, not liking the irritation in his voice.

"Well if you don't want to talk to me then don't just sit there and stare at me!" Lucien only crossed his arms. He didn't want to talk to her no, but he also didn't want to leave her. He needed to see her face before he completely exploded on himself. With his sugar first being too high, and then being too low, and then being way too high he was frustrated beyond reason the whole day. Now his head was pounding slowly and he could barely see straight. Pulling his glasses from his pocket, he put them on his face to try and make his sight easier.

"You wear glasses?" Irys asked him.

"Obviously," He said. But the moment he said it, he wished he didn't. Everyone in his family knew when he was too high, his attitude would be high too. That's why Luna hadn't even approached him today. He just wished he wasn't taking it out on Irys but it wasn't something he could help.

"I didn't mean it like that," He gritted out trying to make the situation better. Instead of answering him she just went back to eating. But he noticed she hadn't even touched her Branzino.

"Why aren't you eating that? Is it not good?" he asked her. Irys put her fork down.

"I don't like Branzino," She admitted.

"Oh, sorry it's not good enough for you." He said.

"I don't mean it like that and you know it Lucien. But you know what. I'm just gonna go back to work. I'll pick up a sandwich on the way. The last thing I want to do is be here when you don't want me to be." She started getting her things ready to leave but Lucien stopped her.

"Sit down," He ordered. He gave her a piercing look, convincing her to sit. He motioned over to Joe to have him bring her something else to eat from the kitchen. They weren't exactly dating but everyone knew he had a thing for Irys and they didn't question him.

"Is Salmon better?" he asked. Irys nodded. "Sorry we don't have much else. Its seafood night tonight and I didn't prepare anything else but that."

"It's fine Lucien I like it." He crossed his arms and sat back just watching her. He was fine with that until his watch started beeping again. He'd set the times for it to go off more frequently since he was so erratic for the day. He was constantly checking his sugar.

"I'll be right back," He said. Irys tossed her fork down.

"Now wait. I always ignore it and just take whatever answer you give me, but I want the truth now Lucien. Why do you keep running off when your watch beeps? Is it an errand? A phone call? What do you always set a timer for?"

"It's personal."

"Oh. That's what it is?" she questioned. "Because I shared my life story about my mom and my sister and my ex. But that was okay for you right? Now I'm trying to know more about you, and your life is too personal? Look, I don't know what you want from me Lucien but how can you not trust me to let me in, but want me to trust you?"

"It's not that I don't trust you Irys. I just wish you'd stop asking about it, okay?" His watch beeped again. He turned it off and looked at Irys. She wasn't pleased.

"Look, I'm not feeling too well today. I can't really sit here and argue with you." Her facial features finally softened. She stood to give him a hug. Lucien accepted the gesture, embellishing the feel of her in his arms. But that was all taken away the moment his watch beeped again. He moved away from her immediately.

"Let me help you Lucien," She said.

"I already said you can't help. I need to take care of something. Be back in a second." Without another word he just left her. Irys tried to piece together why he would be leaving randomly every time his watched beeped but she honestly didn't really know what to think. She just knew she wasn't going to stick around because this wasn't the Lucien she wanted to be around. She quickly grabbed her items and got ready to leave. It was Luna who bumped into her before she could walk out.

"Leaving without saying anything?" Luna asked her.

"Sorry girl. I just-Lucien's upset and I don't wanna be around him like that. He refuses to let me help him so I don't see the point in staying here."

"He's just having an off day Irys. We all have off days. Don't be too mad at him." Irys looked around. She still didn't see Lucien emerge from the back so she looked back at Luna.

"I know he's your brother Luna. But I'm also your best friend. So even though you love him, would you tell me if he's doing something he shouldn't because it's not right?" Luna gave her a look.

"What are you implying?"

"Well, sometimes his watch would beep and he'd run off. Whenever he comes back I would ask him what's the matter and he would never answer me. Point blank he doesn't want me in his business. I just think the beeping is a timer and I'm not sure if he's trying to maintain another relationship or something with someone else…" Luna gasped.

"No! I wouldn't have to tell you something like that because Lucien wouldn't dare be dating two women at the same time. That's not the type of man he is! You should know better!"

"I know I'm so sorry. I just don't know what else to think! He won't let me in and it worries me. I thought we were at a place of trust with each other but this changes everything. We certainly have a long way to go if he won't let me in."

"Don't think too much about it. He's just anxious because of what happened with his ex and it might be hard for him to just let go. I'm telling you Irys. He'll come around. But I know for a fact he wants to keep you around." Irys nodded.

"I'll see you back at work okay? I'm just gonna walk all the way back." Luna watched Irys walk out of the place. She thought by now Lucien would have told her what he was dealing with. She'd avoided her brother because she knew he was irritated but for this she couldn't leave him alone.

She marched back to his office where she burst inside. He jumped in surprise, sticking himself hard with his needle.

"What the hell!" He snapped. He took the needle from his abdomen and wiped it down with an alcohol pad.

"Why didn't you tell Irys you have diabetes?" She asked.

"Because I don't want to Luna."

"It's been over a month you two been talking I assumed that you would have at least told her about what's going on with you. So when you go around treating her like a dick she'd be able to understand why you have mood swings. Before she left she literally asked me if you were keeping another woman!" Lucien heard only one thing from Luna.

"What you mean before she left?"

"She's gone. She said she's gonna walk back to work. She doesn't want to be around you because you don't want her to be able to help you. And she doesn't want to deal with your attitude. I don't blame her either." Lucien slammed down his needled he still held clutched in his hand. He quickly packed everything away so he could go after Irys. But Luna stopped him when he lunged for the door.

"Luna move," He snapped.

"No Lucien. You're testy and she'll sense it. Just stay back and calm down. Apologize to her when she comes back tonight alright." Lucien hated when his sister was right. He just had to swallow that pill and take it easy.

"Fine," He said. He threw himself onto his couch and just tried to relax. He knew it was right to tell her the truth, but he just couldn't. If Irys shunned him or thought less of him because of it he wasn't sure how he was going to handle it. With Rosa it definitely played with his psych. But then with Irys he imagined it would only be worse because of how he actually felt about her. He just didn't want anything to change with them. But his attitude wasn't going to make anything better if he didn't get a hold on it.

Lucien knew Irys didn't even want to deal with him when he sent her a text and she just didn't answer it. He felt that coming. They weren't even officially together so he couldn't really crucify her for not answering his text. She didn't really have to. It just sucked that she didn't. Preparing for service that night he just couldn't stop thinking about her. Before she arrived back to the restaurant for her shift, Lucien pulled Luna to the side.

"Feeling better?" She asked touching his face.

"Yeah I'm feeling better," He sighed. "And I'm sorry for the way I treated you too. I know my attitude isn't the best-"

"Lucien," She smiled. "I've known you all your life and I was there the moment you became sick. You don't need to apologize to me."

"Yeah I know I need to apologize to Irys. I just wanted to ask you something."

"Sure."

"How soon is too soon to want to actually be in a relationship with someone?" Luna's eyes went wide.

"It's that serious huh?" She asked.

"I just really want us to be together, I don't know, I just have this feeling. And I want to be with her, but is it too soon?"

"Have you even had sex with her yet?" Luna asked. "Because from what I know you didn't." Lucien glared at his sister.

"No we didn't have sex yet."

"Right. So pop in some Marvin Gaye and get it on. Then a relationship will surely follow. Especially if you get it on particularly well. But that relationship won't last Lucien if you don't tell her about your sickness." Luna pat him on the shoulder and walked off. Lucien sighed and watched Luna walk off towards the front. It was then he saw Irys entering. The two women hugged each other. As usual Irys was wearing a black dress that made her look so delectable. Lucien didn't want to wait to talk to her, but he had a lot of things to complete and he didn't want to be distracted when he spoke to her. But he made sure that when she looked at him, he actually delivered her a genuine smile. His heart was only able to calm down when Irys returned the smile. Even that sort of cut the tension between them, and it relieved Lucien. He couldn't get through this service fast enough just to talk to her. He would have never thought he wanted to do something as bad as he loved to cook. Because now he loved his food, but he'd rather have Irys in his arms.

Irys saw the change in Lucien the moment she walked into the restaurant. When he smiled at her she actually felt the genuine nature of it. It gave her hope that whatever was the matter with him earlier he'd gotten over it. Irys was upset because he wouldn't tell her about why he left when his watch beeped, but on the other hand they weren't in a relationship. If he didn't want to tell her, he really didn't have to. She just had to be used to the fact that he didn't have to tell her, and she had to be okay with it.

At the end of the night when the place was finally cleared out, she sat in her favorite booth and put her foot up. She didn't mind working these two jobs but there were times where she just didn't even want to get out of bed. Now all she wanted was her bed, but she was kind of wishing she had someone to lay with. Or more accurately she wished she could lay with Lucien. And thinking of him, she saw him take off his chef coat just by the doors that led to the kitchen. Irys stared at him until he looked over at her. With just a simple motion of his head, Irys understood that he wanted her to follow him. She got up slowly and walked behind him as he went towards his office. When he climbed the stairs, he waited at his office door for her to come up and motioned her inside first. He shut the door behind him and leaned against it.

"Are you feeling any better?" Irys asked him.

"No, not really," He said.

"Why not?"

"Because I know you're upset with me."

"I was before but I'm not now," She said. "I realize that you don't really have to tell me things if you don't want to you know. It just hurt a little that you want to know all my deepest secrets, but I can't know yours. Almost as if you're protecting yourself in case I up and decide I hate you and never want to see you again."

"I don't mean to do that to you Irys. But know that I'm not interested in any other women right now. It's just me and you. Don't be insecure about that." Irys smiled at him and nodded sensing his sincerity.

"I'd like to see if you can cook coquets; any kind, with roasted duck and any kind of sweet inspired soufflé for dessert." Lucien tilted his head giving her a look. Then he remembered about their deal for him to prove he could cook anything for her.

"You got it sugar," He said. "I don't need recipes for any of those. Sunday night again?"

"This time I'm going to drive myself there," She said. "No offense of course."

"None taken," He smiled. "Am I forgiven enough to kiss you?" he asked. Irys smirked at him.

"Cook me a perfect dinner and you'll get your kiss," She smiled. "Time for me to go home Luce," She said. Lucien moved out of the way, staring her down. She was so damn gorgeous he almost felt like stealing a kiss but he wanted to stay on her good side so he just let her go. He knew he could make everything she wanted to perfection, so he knew he'd get a kiss sooner or later. But maybe something more if he played his cards right.

Chapter Fifteen

"Where you going now?" Rosa asked Irys seeing she was getting ready to leave the house Sunday night. Usually she was home.

"You don't get to ask me what I'm doing and where I'm going. Just like I don't get to ask you," Irys said.

"First you're complaining about being broke but now you have all the money to keep these health aids here at all kinds of hours when you feel like up and leaving." Irys rolled her eyes.

"Case you haven't noticed, I work all week, all day. That's why I can afford care for my mother." Irys rolled her eyes at Rosa and went to her mother's room. She was sitting up in bed watching her favorite game shows.

"Hot date tonight?" She smiled at Irys.

"No," Irys blushed. "Just dinner at his house. I dared him to make me some duck."

"Oh at his home huh? So is there going to be any magic happening?" Irys gasped at her mother.

"Ma! No!" She laughed. "None of that!"

"Oh please Irys. Don't act like no little saint. You've been going on dates, talking all day and night to this man. He seems to be playing his cards right, so just give him a little bit of sugar."

"I can't believe my own mother is telling me to give it up."

"Who else is going to tell you? I say go for it. You don't have nothing to lose. Well maybe 15 minutes if he sucks. But what the hell." Irys put her head down and laughed at her mother. Tears almost came to her eyes.

"I can't even with you right now," Irys laughed.

"Are you insecure about it?" Kendra asked.

"I am a little bit," She admitted. "I mean first with my body, and then with the miscarriage I haven't-"

"Don't let that cloud your mind honey. I know it's hard but life has to be lived. You can do it I know you can. Obviously he loves your body if he's been this interested in you. And you love your body too." Irys nodded in agreement.

"Just make me a promise," Kendra said.

"Anything."

"After you two do take that step, and you feel like things are turning serious, I want you to bring him here to meet me." Irys smiled at her mother. She would love for Lucien to meet her mother, but not with Rosa here. She didn't even want Rosa to lay an eye on Lucien. Not with how she was fucking Derek like there was no issue.

"I have a better idea," Irys said. "I'm going to take you to his restaurant so you can have some great food and then you can meet him," Irys said.

"That's perfect my dear. I just hope I am well enough."

"You will be, Irys pledged. She hugged her mother deeply.

"Enough of this. Don't keep that man waiting. Go have a good time."

"Let's hope he lasts longer than 15 minutes," Irys joked. It was her mother this time that burst out laughing as Irys got up to leave the room. Even though she wanted to get it on with Lucien she was still nervous about just the idea that it could happen. But the best bet was not to even think about it happening and just let the night play out.

****

Lucien just finished setting the table when he heard a car pull into his driveway. Salsa was already at the door ready to see who was coming inside. Lucien kept it as simple as possible. With just two candles on the table, and a glass of wine. He wanted it to feel nice but not too fancy. The food was almost done, and she was on time like she always was. Lucien went to the door to greet her. As usual she looked lovely, and it made Lucien's heart flutter in his chest. Wearing a fitted maxi dress Lucien's mouth was already salivating.

"Hey sweetie," he greeted. He kissed her on the lips lightly before leading her inside.

"Wow," Irys said as she followed him into the house. "This place is really nice." His house made hers look like a room out of a motel.

"It's nothing much," He said.

"And the food smells so good!"

"Well you're just in time for the appetizer." Before he could lead her into the dining room, Salsa was at her legs, sniffing and barking happily.

"She likes you," Lucien said. "My ex, she did not like not one bit." Irys smiled and pet the dog who followed her as she walked behind Lucien. He led her to the dining room where he pulled out her chair for her to sit down, and then poured her a glass of champagne.

"Salsa behave," Lucien warned the dog before he left the room. Salsa sat in the corner before laying down.

Irys didn't want to think about having sex with him. But he looked so damn good. Wearing simple slacks and a t-shirt she couldn't take her eyes off him. Even when he walked out of the living room she found herself following him with her eyes. She was so pulled to him that she ended up getting up from her chair, grabbing her wine glass and following him to his kitchen. The spacious kitchen with its high ceiling took her breath away. That plus the huge island in the center.

"You call this place nothing much?" She questioned. Lucien turned around and looked at her. He smiled.

"It was a gift from my parents. Have you ever seen Luna's house? Now that's something."

"We spend so much time together at work we've never been to each other's houses. But now that I know that I will definitely be visiting her more. Can I help with anything?" She asked seeing him pull something from the oven.

"No sweetie I got it," He said. He carried three platters in his hand expertly and stared back towards the dining room. Irys followed him looking at his tight ass in his pants. Irys tamed her arousal and focused on the amazing food he cooked for her.

Every piece of food she put in her mouth made her moan and groan. She couldn't even believe how good it was. She didn't care if she looked like a pig.

"Honestly Lucien, you're such a good cook. I can't even believe it." Lucien looked at her with lust filled eyes. He didn't know if he was turned on because she was enjoying his food or just because of her. Maybe he just liked feeding her.

"Ready for desert?" He asked her softly. The way he said that had Irys blushing.

"Are you talking about actual desert? Or are you talking about something else?" she questioned. He only winked at her as he got up from the table. That left her completely clueless. She looked after him and waited for him to come back. For a moment she thought he was going to come in there buck ass naked, with whip cream over his privates, but he returned with the soufflé she asked for.

"Oh, real desert," She said. He gave her a look.

"You'll get that soon, don't worry about it," He said. She was eager for what that meant. But in the meantime she enjoyed her soufflé. That was perfectly fluffy, perfectly creamy, she couldn't get enough.

"I'm going to gain so much more weight dealing with you," She scoffed.

"I love feeding you and watching you enjoy my food," Lucien said. "Call it obsessive."

"Easy for you to say," She said. "How come you didn't have any of the desert?" She asked. Lucien paused thinking of an excuse. He wanted to eat it, he just couldn't.

"I uh-I like making it but I don't like eating it," he lied.

"Oh? Why didn't you say something? I could have choose something you liked to eat too."

"No sweetie this was about you, not me. Did you enjoy everything?"

"More than you know," She said. He took her hand and led her out the dining room and to the living room. The lights were dim in there as they sat on his large couch. He pulled her legs into his lap and massaged her feet.

"Let me find out you're good at something else too," She groaned. Lucien looked up at her.

"I'm good at a lot of things Irys," He smiled. She rolled her eyes at his cockiness. "Can I ask you something?" She nodded.

"I know you had issues with your ex and stuff. Does that make you hesitant to be in a relationship with someone again?"

"Of course it does. But most of it is just mental. The things he said to me and whatnot I just have to believe it's not true. Worst part though is thinking that I don't want someone else to do the same thing he did to me. Especially by someone who I have complete feelings for and isn't afraid to admit that." She gave him a look.

"Are you hinting something at me?" he questioned. She shrugged with a small smirk at her lips. "Well there's no reason I should ever do to you what your ex did to you."

"I'm sure I'm not your ex either," Irys said.

"No you're definitely not." They went quiet for a moment. He continued rubbing her feet. She felt like this was where she belonged and this was just an average night between them.

"Do you ever want to have kids?" He asked her suddenly. Irys tensed immediately. She hadn't even mentioned her losing her baby or even thought about it since she began talking with Lucien.

"Does that question make you nervous?" He asked, sensing the change in her.

"No I just haven't thought about it. But now that you ask, I would like to have children. After I get through all the traveling I want to do."

"My ex didn't want to have kids. And I did. Not that I'm asking you because I want to put a baby in you I just-"

"Baby in me?" She laughed. "How can I think that when you haven't even made love to me yet?" Lucien looked at her.

"I can change that." He let her feet down and scooted next to her. Their lips connected in a heated passion. This tongue kiss was different than any other one that they had before. Lucien pulled her into his arms, draping her leg over his waist and holding onto her tightly. He grabbed a handful of her voluptuous ass. His mind began to race at how it would be to experience her body. Already just touching every curve she had he was amped up and ready. But apparently it was only his mind that was amped up. Out of the corner of his eye he saw Salsa come into the living room. She just paced uneasily by him. But he didn't need Salsa near him to know something was off. For all the handful that he had of her ass, and how much her mouth felt good on his, and for how much he knew he wanted to make love to her, he knew it wasn't going to work. He wasn't getting hard. He was doing everything to will his libido into place but it just wasn't going. His sugar was too high. Upset at himself he pulled away from her and separated their bodies.

"Sorry," He said as he stood up. "Come Salsa," He ordered. He didn't want her to start barking so he took her back to the kitchen immediately so he could check his sugar. It was high.

Knowing he'd fucked up his chance at being with Irys, he was cursing at himself as he got out his needle and cleaned his finger where he'd drawn blood. He put the meter away roughly.

"What are you doing with that?!" Irys gasped. Lucien looked up sharply. Irys was staring at the needle he was holding, fear written across her face.

"Irys I-" She shook her head and backed up.

"Thanks for dinner. But I'm leaving now." She shook her head and hurried towards the front door.

"Irys it's not what you think!" He called after her. But she didn't stop. She hurried out of the house and hopped in her car. She drove away as if he was some monster she was trying to get away from. Lucien punched the wall and cursed out loud. What in the hell had he done?

****

Irys was distracted as she sat at her desk the next day. Her appointments didn't start for another hour so she didn't have anything to do but prep. Luna was constantly peering over her shoulder or looking at her but Irys didn't want to talk. Not after what happened last night with Lucien. She couldn't quite wrap her head around that situation. And she couldn't stop thinking about it no matter how she tried.

"So me and Joe haven't been on an official date. We've just been talking a lot throughout the day on phone. I feel like I know him, but then I don't really know him. What should I do?" Luna said. When Irys didn't answer her Luna cleared her throat. Irys blinked.

"Oh um, I think you two need to be together like on a date or something. People can be different than what they are through phone you know."

"Yeah I know. I am really attracted to him though. I can tell you that much."

"Yeah…" Irys's voice trailed off. Luna rolled her eyes.

"Alright what the hell happened between you and Lucien? Because he's sort of avoiding me too, and Lucien never avoids me." Irys just shook her head.

"Tell me," Luna urged. "Was he not good in bed or something?"

"Luna stop playing," Irys urged.

"So then tell me what's up."

"Look, there's no real easy way to say this Luna. And I feel so bad that I just up and left him last night but I didn't know what to do."

"What to do about what?"

"We were heated and I thought we were finally going to actually have sex. But then he just pulls away and he just leaves. I follow him and see him with a needle in the kitchen. And I got freaked out and I just left!" Luna gasped silently. She knew the problems Rosa brought to Lucien about his diabetes, but she didn't expect nothing of that from Irys.

"So are you saying that you up and left without even talking to him? This is the guy you've been lusting after and now all of a sudden things have changed?"

"That's why I feel horrible! I freaked out and I just ran. I've never been into it with someone on drugs. I don't know if I should help him or run far away."

"Drugs? Irys what in the hell are you talking about?" It hit Luna then that Irys still didn't know about Lucien's diabetes. She thought the needle meant Lucien was on drugs. Luna rubbed her eyes and sighed. She walked away from Irys and went outside. She dialed Lucien immediately.

"What you want Luna?" He asked the moment he answered.

"I told your dumbass to tell Irys about your condition. Now look at what the hell happened."

"I don't need to hear your shit okay? I've been trying to call her all morning but she's blowing me off. She doesn't even want to talk about what happened last night."

"Well you need to find a way to talk to her. Because she thinks you're on crack because of your needle!"

"But I need to think of something to tell her!"

"How about you tell her the truth? Irys is not Rosa! Get that through your head." Luna hung up on him ending that conversation. When she went back inside she couldn't even look at Irys. She had nothing to say.

"Are you mad at me?" Irys asked her. "For just walking out on him?"

"At the end of the day, that's ya'll business. So the two of you need to sort that shit out yourselves." Just as she said that Irys's phone went off. Lucien was calling her. She quickly silenced it. Until she knew what she was going to say to him, she couldn't speak to him yet. But he didn't give up. He called her again, and again until she finally picked up.

"Lucien I'm at work I can't talk right now," She said.

"I know that Irys but I know you have five minutes to talk to me."

"No I don't." Irys hung up the phone then. He seemingly got the point because he didn't call back. Irys breathed a sigh of relief. For right now she just wanted to work, and then later she'd deal with Lucien.

Lucien sat at his desk for most of the time he was in the restaurant. His sugar was perfectly fine. Which was ironic that everything else around him wasn't fine. Even being around food wasn't making his mood any better. He wanted Irys and nothing was changing that at the moment. So he decided he needed to make things right. After all if he wanted her to be his woman he had to come clean with it. Deciding not to sulk in his office, Lucien went down to the kitchen and whipped up some lunch for Irys. He figured she wasn't even going to come to him for lunch so he was just going to go to her. He just needed to come forth with everything and stop all the secrets. He just hoped she wanted him once he did tell the truth.

Once he packed up her food, he left Joe in charge and headed out to the spa. He didn't even bother practicing what he was going to say to her. Because he knew the moment he got in front of her everything was going to slip from his mouth like slush and he probably wasn't even going to be coherent. Keeping a level head. That's all he needed to do.

It was only after 1pm when he pulled up to the Spa. He stood at the large windows at first gazing in. He spotted Irys at a desk. Her hair was in a high puff and she was wearing yoga pants and a t-shirt. So simple but yet Lucien was captivated. Before he could move, he spotted Luna staring right at him with her arms crossed. Just the look on her face let him know she was about to be annoying.

"Look at this shit," Luna said, glaring out at Lucien from the window. "All this time I been working here and he hasn't ever brought me lunch before!" Irys's head snapped up. She jolted up from her chair to see Lucien just outside with a bag of food.

"Oh no," She said. She pushed past Luna and headed directly outside to see him. His fragrance stopped her short for a moment and she had to force herself to behave.

"You can't be here," She said immediately. "This is my place of employment Lucien. We can't talk about anything." He just dazed at her.

"I brought you lunch," He said. He stretched out the bag to her. She cautiously took it.

"Thanks. But you really have to go." She gave him a stern look and went back inside. She was just putting the food on her desk when he entered the place.

"Lucien! I'm being serious! You can't be here! And I have an appointment in like five minutes! We don't have the amount of time we need to talk."

"I'm not leaving here until we speak. And we have enough time. A whole hour should be just right."

"A whole hour?" She questioned.

"I'm your next appointment," He said. Irys gasped and went to her computer. She brought up the information on the appointment and sure enough it was him. She slapped her forehead.

"Nice one," Luna chuckled. Irys huffed.

"Shut up Luna." She pouted. "Come on," She ordered Lucien. He followed her towards one of the back rooms. They entered the candle lit room where she threw him a towel.

"Strip," She said.

"It would please me to do so sweetie but I only booked your time because I want to talk to you. You can give me a massage some other time." Irys crossed her arms. She went over to the table and hopped onto it, sitting down.

"So?" She asked. "What you wanna say?"

"There's things I have been keeping from you."

"Don't say it so simple like taking drugs isn't a big deal! Lucien I don't even know what to think. You know I'm so into you but I can't just tolerate drugs. It's not healthy and-"

"Be quiet for just a second," Lucien interrupted her. Irys was shocked at his interruption but it did make her shut her mouth.

"I'm not on drugs. Well I am on drugs, but not crack. That's ridiculous."

"You're not gonna lie to my face Lucien. Have a little bit more respect for me!"

"Use your brain Irys. Do I look like someone on crack?" Irys crossed her arms and pouted.

"It would explain why your watch always beep and you run off. Or when you are fine one moment then agitated the next and upset after that then fine again."

"No that's not because of cocaine sweetie."

"So explain it to me Lucien! Explain that damn needle! Because if you weren't taking drugs what were you using it for?!" Lucien leaned against the wall directly across from her. He stuffed his hands into his pockets.

"And I don't care if it's not cocaine. You just said you take drugs. How is that still good?"

"Even if it's to save my life?" He asked.

"What do you mean?" She questioned.

"That needle. It was for insulin Irys. I've had diabetes since I was 10." Irys was shocked to say the least.

"Don't just make something up because you think I'm weak enough to believe everything you say," She whispered. Lucien slowly lifted his shirt revealing the insulin pump he had on his stomach. The small tubes connected from his skin to the machine clipped to his belt that would automatically deliver his insulin to his body.

"I hardly ever wear it because I do a lot of things during the day and don't want to actually accidentally have it pulled out. But I figured I needed something for you to get to believe me. And well I didn't bring any insulin with me." Irys slipped down from the table and walked over to him. She touched his toned stomach and the machine then followed the tubes and the patch on his skin.

"When I have mood swings that's either because my sugar is too high or its' too low. When I run off on you it's because I'm trying to hide the fact that I have diabetes. When my watch beeps, it's because I have to remind myself to check my sugar. I always do it away from you because I'm embarrassed to do it in front of you." Irys didn't know what to say just yet.

"Now look," Lucien said. "I know this is a lot to take in but I'm a grown ass man I don't need to lie to you, especially about this. I may have been keeping it from you, but I wouldn't make it up. This thing between me and you, I'm not playing around. I want you. So right here right now, you either want me or you don't. Make your choice."

"I-I want you too," Irys said. "But you know there's so much other things we have to discuss right? Why-why would you keep it from me?"

"My last relationship ended off of the woman I thought I wanted to marry telling me I'm deficient because of my condition."

"Lucien you know I would never say that to you!" She gasped. "I thought you would know I wasn't that type of woman."

"I wasn't secure in myself Irys. I found I wanted you so bad that it scared me to believe you could turn me away just like she did. But I realize you and her are two different people. And Luna has been on my ass to get me to tell you and I simply couldn't. But after last night I just didn't see how to escape without just telling you the truth so there it is."

"I don't know what to say," She murmured. Lucien pulled her closer. He wrapped an arm around her waist.

"Don't say anything," He whispered. He lowered his head and kissed her softly, before going in deeper with his tongue. Her open receiving of his kiss let him know that she wanted him as much as he wanted her.

"You know what that kind of kiss does to me Lucien. Stop it," She breathed pulling her mouth from his.

Lucien gazed at her, running his thumb over her plump lips. He sighed at her pure beauty. He was relieved to have that secret off his chest but he was still a little apprehensive about things. His diabetes would affect their relationship if they chose to enter one. And it was that thought that made Lucien nervous. Irys wouldn't disrespect him because of his condition he knew that for sure. But that also didn't mean she was going to agree to date him either.

"Can I ask you something?" She squinted. "That you'll be completely honest about?"

"Go for it," Lucien said. "While I'm still an open book," He chuckled. Irys smiled shortly.

"Um last night. With how we were kissing, and what we were talking about I thought that we were going to actually…you know. But then before when we used to kiss I would feel your arousal, but last night I didn't feel anything. Was it because of me? Were you not turned on or something." Lucien took her hands.

"I was turned on sweetie. Believe that. And I wanted to do it with you. I just…my body physically wouldn't allow me to."

"What do you mean?"

"During my teens and early 20s and whatnot, sex wasn't an issue for me. Whenever I wanted it I did it and that was it. But when I turned 30 I started experiencing some issues with my erections. When my sugar isn't in the right spot sometimes I can't get erections. With age that's just a part of me that my diabetes will effect."

"Are you on treatment for it?"

"No I'm not. I just try to stay fit and keep my sugar in check. Though if it gets too frequent I know what I'll have to do."

"That sucks," Irys said. Lucien shrugged.

"I know that. You don't need to tell me."

"I don't mean it that way Lucien. You know I won't make fun of you for that. It affected me too. I wanted to get fucked."

"You can get that shit right now for all I care," Lucien said crossing his arms. Irys's eyes flickered down to his groin and sure enough she could see the print of his hard on.

"You see-I would-I would ride that but I'm at work! I can't do that at work!"

"Well I'm here for a massage. My dick is a part of my body. And you riding it is a massage."

"You know that don't cut it Lucien."

"Can't blame me for trying."

"Do you even like…come like normal?" Lucien's brows creased and he gave her a look. She knew that was a dumb question. And now she felt like a complete jackass.

"What kind of question is that?" he asked.

"I don't know. I thought that there would be something different about the way you orgasm. But it's dumb. I'm sorry Lucien."

"Yeah. It was." Without another word he leaned off the wall and headed towards the door. Irys slapped herself on the forehead once he walked out of the room.

"Don't be an idiot," She scolded herself. She hurried after him to see he was getting stopped by Luna. Of course she was trying to figure out what happened between them.

"Hey," Irys said. "Just going to leave without a kiss goodbye?" Lucien turned to her. Clearly he was displeased by what she said. And Irys needed to make it up to him.

"I still owe you a massage," Irys said. "I'll come over tonight after dinner service."

"Inviting yourself over huh?" He asked.

"Yeah I am actually." He looked her up and down.

"Don't plan on going home tonight," He said starkly. Irys swallowed and nodded. Lucien turned to Luna and gave her a kiss on the cheek.

"There's some food in the bag for you too sis," He said. "Make sure you both eat up." He gave Irys once last look before he turned and walked out of the place. That left Irys and Luna looking at each other.

"Don't plan on going home huh?" Luna asked.

"Please don't," Irys said, going to her phone to get the aide situation dealt with seen as she wasn't going to go home tonight.

"So are you and him okay? Did he tell you everything?"

"Yeah he did tell me."

"And? How do you feel about it?"

"There's lots I still don't know. And things I know I need to understand. But I do know that he's such a kind and caring man and I'm attracted to him. That much hasn't changed." Luna smiled, and it wasn't just a regular smile. It was almost like relief and true happiness.

"I'm really happy to hear that," She said. Irys smiled at her and dug into the bag of food.

For the rest of her time at the spa she was much more relaxed than how her day started. Not saying she wanted Lucien to be sick, but she was relieved he wasn't doing drugs or something. But when she thought about it, his condition did little to hinder him. If she hadn't caught him with the needle she would have never guessed that was why his watched beeped all the time. But what she thought she saw on the outside could be very different from what actually was happening with him. It would just take her learning and experiencing the things he went through. It might have been daunting for anyone else but Irys knew she could handle it.

When she left the spa that evening, she went straight home, almost giddy as she packed herself a small bag. She changed into a dress for her shift at the restaurant afterwards and then went to kiss her mother goodnight. She was excited to hear what happened with Irys and Lucien the night before and Irys had to break that news to her that nothing happened. The sadness on her mother's face made Irys feel like she really wanted this thing with Lucien to work. Between her mother and Luna, Irys and Lucien had people rooting for their relationship. And perhaps it would be sealed after this night.

Chapter Sixteen

Lucien watched from the kitchen as Irys interacted with people at a table who had called her over. Dinner service was over and they were pushing out deserts but for that Lucien didn't necessarily need to do anything since he prepared the deserts from earlier. Joe took control to get the deserts out to each table depending on what they ordered. So in that time, Lucien made like a creep and watched Irys work. He loved having her there because he wanted to be close to her, but workwise she was damn good at her job. Almost all the reviews the restaurant got included a compliment to the hostess. As if she could feel his eyes, Irys turned and looked directly at him. He'd been caught staring plenty of times so he just shrugged knowing he got caught. Irys turned completely and began walking back towards the kitchen. He figured he was going to get a mouthful.

"Chef Lucien," She called sweetly. Whenever she entered the kitchen with his staff around he was never just Lucien to her.

"Yes Irys?"

"There's a lovely couple at table 12 who'd love your company for two minutes. Do you have time?"

"Always time for the diners. I'll follow you." Irys gave him a small smile and led the way out to the dining hall. The older couple was ecstatic to see Lucien come out of the kitchen. And when Irys began speaking French, Lucien was more captivated by her than his customers. He snapped from his daze and spoke with them about the food. It was great interacting with them, but Lucien was ready to get the hell out of there to take Irys back to his house.

By the time the place was cleared out and they were able to leave it was going on midnight. But this time Lucien wasn't going home alone. Even though they drove in separate cars to his place, Lucien could feel Irys's presence with him.

When they reached his home, she parked next to him in the double driveway. She got out of the car and went to her trunk where she was pulling out her bags and something large.

"What's that?" Lucien asked taking it from her to carry it.

"I said I owe you a massage. That's my massage table." Did she seriously think he was going to be into a massage tonight? Especially when he wanted her so bad?

"Oh yeah sure. A massage." While she carried her bags, Lucien carried the table inside. Salsa greeted him as usual but the dog paid more attention to Irys than she did to Lucien. That was a first. Irys played right into her hands by petting her and scratching her behind the ears.

"I'll leave the table in here. Want to take your bags to the bedroom?" She nodded. Lucien led the way to his bedroom. She was walking slowly because she was looking everywhere mesmerized. But when he got to his bedroom she had stopped at his guest room.

"Here right?" she asked.

"If we were like 15 and this was my parent's house. Get your butt over here." She giggled and walked over to him.

"Well when you put it like that." She looked around the room. "Wow now this is what I call a master bedroom." She placed her bags at the foot of the bed and walked around the spacious room.

"The bathroom is that door over there," He said pointing.

"Good. I'll actually take a shower now. After the spa all day and then the restaurant I need a warm shower. Once I'm done I'll set up your massage."

"I'll make you something refreshing and light to eat for when you're done."

"Aren't you tired of cooking?" Irys asked him.

"No," He chuckled.

"Figures." She turned around putting her back towards him. "Unzip me please." Lucien obliged without any issue. He pulled the zipper of her dress down slowly, admiring the creamy skin of her back. He noticed she had a lot of deep brown beauty marks across her skin. He wanted to kiss all of them. He would. He just had to wait.

"I'll leave you to it," He said. He backed out of the room and closed the door before he lost control. He wanted to start sexing her down immediately but he almost felt like he needed to at least act civilized.

While she showered, Lucien chopped up some fruits for her then made a quick whip cream. Since he had some frozen fruits he'd chopped up earlier that week he used to make his smoothies, he decided to use them now to whip up a quick an easy sorbet that was light and refreshing to go with the fruit salad. Once he mixed it all up, he set everything in the fridge until she was ready to eat it. He settled into the living room to wait for her but he only had to wait a few moments before he heard her coming down the hall. He stood as she entered.

"Damn Irys," He gasped, seeing her dressed in the short silk spaghetti strapped nightgown. It stopped a little above mid-thigh, showing off her thick thighs.

"Too much?" she asked. "I brought a t-shirt."

"Nonsense," He shushed her. She came over to him and flopped down on the couch. Her hair was in a neat bun, but not for long.

"Let me get what I made you," He said. He left the kitchen and returned with the items. She took it happily.

"Have that while I take a shower myself. Then I'll be back."

"Wait, you won't eat this with me?" She asked.

"Ah no. I can't." He replied. "Sugar problems." He added.

"Oh."

"Don't worry about me though. Just eat it. I'd be upset if you didn't." He kissed her on the cheek before going to the room for his shower.

Irys stayed in the living room alone and ate the fruit. It was perfectly balanced and with the sorbet to add that freshness she wasn't feeling too full from a heavy meal. Once she finished eating, she began setting up the table along with some candles and her oils. She had worn this nightgown because she wanted to make it clear of what she wanted. He seemed impressed by it, and intrigued so she was counting on him getting what she wanted. She stood by the table waiting for him to return. When he did, she was the one stuck for a moment. He was wearing nothing but his boxer briefs.

"Hop on the table," Irys said patting it. He came over and hopped on the table. She could smell his old spice intensely. She loved it. He stretched out on his stomach. When the hot oil touched his back his dick jumped. But then when she touched him he was beginning to swell.

"Wow, you're pretty tense," She said as she ran her hands over his back.

"Not like my job is relaxing," He answered. She began rubbing intensely, freeing up some of the tenseness in his muscles. Lucien groaned, as she eliminated his knots. He didn't know how much he needed it.

"Does that feel better baby?" She asked softly. The tone of her voice had him flipping his eyes open. He turned his head and looked up at her.

"What?" she asked. Without answering he sat up completely and swung his legs off the table. He grabbed Irys towards him and kissed her deeply. Her small sound of shock filled his mouth as he kissed her. But she still sunk into his kiss, wrapping her arms around his neck. His hand crept up her nightgown grabbing a handful of her ass.

"Wait," She breathed, pulling away from him. "Are you going to have any problems?" She questioned. Lucien pushed her back slightly and hopped down from the table. He wrapped his hands around the back of both of her thighs and picked her up. He wrapped her legs around his waist and dug his groin into her core. She yelped in surprise.

"Doesn't feel like a problem does it?" he questioned.

"No it does not." Aside from what she could feel of his arousal, she was shocked he was able to pick her up. While she held onto him he took up the two candles and blew them out before carrying her through the house to his bedroom. He closed the bedroom door slightly but not all the way. He set her at the edge of the foot of the bed. He leaned down and began kissing her again. He kissed her so deeply she found herself laying back with him on top of her. With Derek she was in control most of the time. In the case of initiating sex and getting him aroused and keeping herself aroused, she had to do everything. And then when he was good and ready to penetrate her, he would go ahead with those strokes she realized now were only for his pleasure and not hers. Here with Lucien, she felt odd just lying there while her panties were getting wet by the way he kissed and sucked at her neck. She knew by the time he was done, she was going to have plenty of hickey marks. He continued down her neck until he reached the mounds of her breasts. Slipping her breasts from the confines of the nightgown, he sucked on her nipples. The low groaning in his throat let Irys know he was having pleasure himself too. After sucking on her nipples he rose up and pulled her nightgown down completely. When he stood over her and just gazed at her, Irys didn't know what to feel. There was no darkness, nowhere for her to hide. There was just an incredibly handsome man, staring down at her nakedness. She told herself that she could handle it, but when he reached to pull her panties down she jumped up.

"Wait," She breathed.

"What's the matter?" He asked a look on concern on his face.

"I-I haven't done this in a little bit," She said.

"Don't worry about that," He said leaning over her again. He kissed her softly guiding her to lay back down.

"I'll take care of you," He whispered against her lips. He distracted her with his kisses enough to get her panties down.

Lucien couldn't wait to see her naked. The moment her panties were off, he sat up promptly just to take her in. She had a small square patch of hair on her womanly core intrigued him. He couldn't stop looking at the plumpness of her, imagining himself stroking her. But he had to take care of something first.

"You're very beautiful," He complimented. "I must say."

"Am I prettier than your ex?" She asked softly. Lucien lifted her legs and pressed them back against her chest. She was easily flexible.

"Yes, you are," Lucien admitted. He bent over and drew his tongue over her pink insides. He moaned in pleasure when her hips jerked.

"You taste better than her too," He added, opening her lips to delve his tongue deeper. Irys's mouth flew open when his tongue made contact with her clit. He rolled his tongue over it slowly before using his lips to suckle it. Her back bowed as shivers ran through her body. She was already soaking wet, so now she was a fountain as he licked her clit repeatedly. She came hard when he thrust his tongue into her channel, stroking her while his finger played with her clit. As she came, he sucked her juices up.

"Damn," She breathed. He rose up, biting his bottom lip. He winked at her as he backed away.

"Scoot up to the top of the bed," He ordered. Irys did what he said slowly. It was her time to watch as he pulled his underwear down. His large arousal was heavy in front of him, filled with veins with a plump head. Definitely bigger than Derek but was it going to be good? She watched as he searched through his top drawer for a moment before he finally pulled out a condom. He ripped the packet open with his teeth and crawled back into the bed with her. When he hovered over her, Irys paused to take a deep breath.

"It's just me and you here," He said. "Not your ex, not mine. Just us." He reached down and pulled the latex over his erection.

"Me and you," Irys breathed. Lucien rested himself on one elbow as he aligned his barrier coated erection with her pink insides. He slipped inside but felt her resistance immediately. She truly hadn't done anything in a while, he could tell. He kissed her neck to distract her as he slowly forced his way inside her.

Irys scraped his back with her nails as the thickness of his cock filled her all the way up. She could feel him all the way to her stomach, a place where Derek never was.

"Why does it feel like you're about to come?" Lucien asked her, bracing himself on both his elbows now, hovering over her. He could feel her walls quivering and he wasn't even moving.

"Because I am," She breathed. Lucien pulled out and pumped back inside filling her completely. She let out a loud and long moan as her eyes fluttered close. Her walls tensed and snapped as she came hard. He cursed and buried his head in the crook of her shoulder as he stroked her continuously, forcing her into another orgasm. She felt so damn good, even with the barrier between them. And the fact that he'd managed to get her to orgasm off of one stroke only emphasized how much pleasure she'd been missing out on. He picked his head up and kissed her deeply as he continued stroking her.

"Damn Irys," He muttered against her lips. "You keep coming and I won't last long," He admitted. Irys couldn't help it. There was something about the way his hips moved, as he grinded within her that was sending the waterworks out of her.

"I-I can't stop," She cried out. "Fuck you feel so good."

"He didn't make you come a lot did he?" Lucien grunted.

"No. He didn't!" Lucien rose up. He tucked her legs against her chest again, holding himself up on the back of her thighs, he swung his hips freely, working his way as deep in her as he could. He doubted if her ex ever took the time to really feel her, to really pleasure her.

Irys pressed at his abdomen when he went too deep. But Lucien kept plummeting inside her, rocking her core to the limit. She couldn't even believe she was actually having sex with this incredibly sexy man, and he was making her come all over herself. Lucien hissed as she came again, and her walls clenched him. He pounded her until her orgasm completely ebbed, before he pulled out of her and let her legs down.

"Look," He said. She looked down to see the condom was dripping with her moisture.

"Haven't come like that in forever," She breathed. "But now it's your turn." She sat up and pushed him over. He rolled onto his back, and she mounted him. He'd given her enough confidence that her weight was no issue, so she felt good on top of him. And when he grabbed her ass and lift his hips up to get inside her eagerly she was boosted even more. She grinded on top of him before bracing herself to bounce up and down on his shaft. He was so long he wasn't slipping out of her like Derek used to. He met her thrust for thrust and he popped a breast into his mouth. She was going to come again.

"That's it baby, come," He groaned. Her body stiffened as the orgasm towered over her. Lucien rolled them onto their sides, hooking her top leg in the crook of his arm and lifting it. He continue thrusting in her as he kissed her deeply. She was gushing with juices and the only thing Lucien wanted to do was rip the condom off, but he wasn't going to pull out he knew that much.

"Shit!" Lucien gritted his teeth as she came again, this time he was going with her. Her high pitched moaning filled his ears as he filled the condom with his orgasm. Irys took several deep breaths to calm her racing heart. Lucien held onto her tightly then kissed her mouth softly.

"Don't even think about going to sleep," He said. "I'm not done with you yet." Irys scoffed.

"Don't need to push it Lucien. My pussy isn't going nowhere."

"After that workout I just gave it. It better not." Irys laughed and rolled over. He let her go seen as he had to get rid of the condom anyway. While he was in the bathroom he wet a washcloth and brought it back out to her, to wipe her up. He was only wiping her up but then he got distracted and before he knew it, his finger was inside her, flipping at her g-spot.

"Ever squirted before?" he asked her.

"No-no!" She gasped out. Lucien dug deeper curled his fingers harder and faster until she was squirting on his hand. He watched with a smirk on his face as she had a full body orgasm in response to her squirting. He wiped her up again.

"Now you have," He smiled. Irys gasped and looked up at him. She couldn't even believe it. He threw the washcloth in his hamper and laid down next to her. He wasted no time grabbing her up and holding her closely. He ran his finger across the tattoo of the word *free* on her side below her breast.

"How come you got that word tattooed on you?" He asked softly.

"My sister bullied me more than anyone else about my weight. When I finally learned to love myself I wasn't tied down to bullying anymore. And I was just…free."

"You are such a beautiful person Irys. Not just physically. You have such a good heart."

"You do too," She smiled at him. Irys snuggled into his chest, taking in his old spice scent and letting it lull her to sleep. After so much orgasms, sleep came no problem.

But sure enough it was only 2 in the morning when Irys felt herself rising to another orgasm. Her eyes popped open and she was coming all over his dick again. He continued grinding inside her, not letting up even though she just came. Irys wrapped her legs around his hips as he dug deep inside her.

"You feel so goddamn good Irys," He breathed. "I couldn't help but be inside you again." Irys was too busy moaning her head off to answer him. How he was making her come this much was a mystery. And it didn't end until he jerked to a stop. He dug himself deeper as he came into the condom again.

"You're gonna kill me," Lucien groaned.

"Me?! I wake up to an orgasm and it's my fault?!" She giggled.

"Because you lying next to me and you smell so fucking sweet and you felt so good I just had to get back in there."

"Sorry I'm so good," She laughed. He kissed her on the nose.

"Okay sleep. I won't bother you no more. Well, until the morning at least." Irys curled back in his arms after he threw away the second condom. Wow he went in for seconds without her having to prompt him to do so. That was new to her too. Somewhere in her heart she felt like she was going to fall in love with this man deeply.

Irys was deep in sleep again but this time it wasn't pleasure that woke her. The sun was just starting to rise and she heard the door creak open. She was about to jump in fear until she realized it was only Salsa. She walked over to the other side of the bed and began whining at Lucien. Irys jumped a little when Salsa barked loudly. Lucien jumped up however. When he awoke Irys closed her eyes figuring he would take care of whatever Salsa needed.

"Okay hush I'm coming," He said. She felt him get up.

Lucien looked over at Irys. Her eyes were closed so he hurried out of the room with Salsa following him. He didn't want her to be annoyed that he had woken her up. Salsa followed him all the way to the kitchen where he pulled out his meter to check his sugar. He knew something was off because he was beyond thirsty. He chugged down a whole bottle of water but that didn't seem to quench his thirst. He cussed as he turned on his meter.

"Are you okay?" Irys's soft voice sounded out. Lucien turned around sharply.

"I'm fine sweetie. You can go back to bed." He turned around to continue what he was doing but he didn't hear Irys leave. Sure enough when he looked, Irys was still standing there.

"You don't have to hide it from me," She said. "I want to see." Lucien wasn't sure how comfortable he was about it, but Irys wasn't taking no for an answer. She walked over to the island and sat down. Lucien sighed and didn't turn away. He pricked his finger and waited until his meter read his sugar.

"It's too high," He told her. "Which means I gotta drug myself up. Sure you won't run off this time?" Irys rolled her eyes. She watched as he went into the fridge and pulled out a small vial. He took needles from a drawer and used one to pull up the insulin. He wasn't wearing a shirt so he just pinched his side and injected himself.

"That's why when we fall asleep on the phone and I hear Salsa barking in the middle of the night. She trying to get you to wake up." Lucien nodded.

"Yeah. Which my ex didn't handle very well. She hated it."

"I don't mind it Lucien. I know you may be uncomfortable with certain things especially being how it was with your ex, but I'm not going to be a bitch to your because of this." Lucien leaned over the island and kissed her lightly on the mouth.

"This might scare you Irys. But in all honesty, you're making me fall in love with you." Irys was scared. Not for any other reason that she was falling for him too.

Chapter Seventeen

Rosa heard when Irys's car pulled up in the driveway. She patted Derek on the back telling him to rise up, but he didn't. She just sucked her teeth and let him continue to eat her out even though she was feeling nothing. He finally rose up but he did so with his dick in his hand ready to enter her. Just then, Irys walked through the front door. She looked directly at them on the living room couch. Rosa prepared herself for another fight with her sister about her ex.

"Oh, good morning," Irys greeted. "Hey Derek." She smiled and continued into the house. Rosa gasped. No argument? Nothing? It was like she didn't even see what they were doing. Rosa pushed Derek off her and went after Irys.

"Sorry you had to see me and Derek fucking again. But his appetite is insatiable."

"What you apologizing for?" Irys joked. She rolled her eyes and looked at her phone. Lucien was checking if she got home safely. She wished that she had just stayed with him and went to work from his house but she wanted to come and check on her mom first.

"Thought you'd be mad."

"Do I look mad?" Irys asked. She looked at Rosa who looked at her.

"No you don't."

"Glad that's settled." Irys just had the time of her life last night with man she wanted. How could she even focus on Derek right now? In fact, she really could care less.

"I'm gonna see mom then get ready for work." She smiled at Rosa and walked off. Rosa just stood there. Something was up. No way was Irys just ignoring her and Derek.

"Are you seeing someone new?" Rosa called after her. Irys just giggled and continued without stopping. Oh yeah, something was up. And Rosa wanted to know what.

****

Luna walked into work to see Irys smiling her face off. She was sitting at the desk with a compact mirror touching up the makeup on her neck. Luna dropped the coffee she was carrying for Irys on the desk.

"Whatcha tryna cover up?" Luna asked. Irys jumped and gave her a smile.

"Your brother likes to leave evidence," She giggled. She showed Luna the hickey marks. "I managed to cover it up most of it though, just making sure it was still covered up." Luna crossed her arms and gazed at Irys.

"I don't mind the hickey's at all. But man the orgasms that I got I can't-"

"Girl!" Luna snapped. "I know I'm nosey but I don't wanna know all the details." Luna saw the blush on Irys's face. She was obviously smitten and happy about her ensuing relationship with Lucien.

"So this thing with you and Lucien. It's serious now?"

"I believe it's getting there." Luna nodded. She leaned over, placing her hands on the desk. She went eye to eye with Irys.

"I'm completely happy for you. I wanted this to happen between the both of you. But I'm gonna warn you Irys. You do some bullshit that breaks my brother's heart, I don't care what kind of friend you are to me; I will make your life a living hell. I don't play when it come to my brother." Luna glared at her intensely before smiling.

"I'm glad to know my brother knows how to work it in the sack!" She winked and walked off. Irys sat there in complete shock. She and Luna were close friends but she knew that Lucien meant the world to her and a friendship wouldn't protect Irys if she did anything to wrong Lucien. Not that she would in the first place. He was just so perfect for her. And Irys honestly couldn't believe what they were developing into. Even now, she couldn't help but daydream about what he was doing and how his day was going. If that wasn't her falling in love, then Irys didn't know what was.

She was happy to share anything with Luna about her time with Lucien. But when she got home to change for her shift at the restaurant it was Rosa who was prying into her business. That was the one person she was not willing to share any information about Lucien with. Not after what she did with Derek.

"I don't even know where you work. How come you never offered me a chance to get a job with you?" Rosa questioned.

"Are you kidding me? The last thing I would do is get you a job and then you turn around and make me look like a fool when you start to screw shit up! And why all of a sudden you give a damn about what I'm doing?"

"It looks like you met someone new. Just trying to see what's up."

"That's none of your business. And who says I met anyone?" Irys scoffed. She grabbed her purse to leave, but Rosa wouldn't get out of the way. Irys glared at her.

"Move, or be moved," She threatened. Rosa backed out of the way slowly. She watched as Irys left the house in yet another pretty black dress. No matter how many times she'd called her sister fat, Irys was always still gorgeous. Going to the door, Rosa stared at Irys getting in her car. She really wanted to know what her sister was up to.

****

When Irys pulled up to the restaurant Lucien was outside waiting for her. She couldn't get out of her car fast enough to be in his arms. He hugged her tightly, breathing in her sweet perfume as he kissed her neck.

"How was your day?"

"It was really, really good. What about yours?"

"My sugar been all over the place which I suspected it would be. But seeing you makes me feel loads better. Know what I mean?"

"Yeah I do know. I feel the same too," She blushed. Lucien leaned over and kissed her again.

"I feel like taking you for a round in my office," He said against her lips. "You look beautiful."

"Don't get me started Lucien. Please" She breathed. Lucien looked at her neck.

"Covering up my marks?" He asked.

"Well, I didn't think it was professional coming up in here with all these damn hickeys!" Lucien kissed her neck.

"No!" She giggled. "Save it for later." Lucien grunted and pulled away.

"Fine if that's what I have to do. I made you a special meal." He took her hand and led her inside the restaurant.

"People will start to think that you're giving me special treatment," She said.

"I don't give a damn," He said. He didn't know if anyone else knew it for certain but they all had a clue there was something up with him and Irys. Lucien wasn't trying to hide it either. He wanted people to know Irys was all his. Every last supple and delectable inch of her was all his.

When they went inside, Luna grabbed Irys away from him and took her to the table where he had her food laid out. Lucien let them go and resorted to the kitchen where he had his own work to do. Even prepping for the service he was so enthralled with Irys he looked up to make sure she was okay about fifty times within an hour.

"So you and Irys?" Joe asked, leaning against the counter next to Lucien. Service was starting in a half hour and everything was ready to go.

"Yeah, me and Irys," Lucien said.

"I can dig it. She's a looker."

"What about you and my sister?"

"It's in the works."

"Don't tip toe around her. Luna hates that shit."

"Thanks for the tip. But um, I know about you and Irys. Does everyone else?"

"I didn't broadcast it, but I thought it was obvious."

"Apparently not for everyone." He nodded his head behind Lucien. Lucien turned to see Paul all up in Irys's face. She was smiling at what he was saying while he was trying to hand her his cell phone.

"Son of a-" Lucien grunted. He left the kitchen promptly and walked right up to them. He tapped on Paul's shoulder. Paul turned around sharply.

"What's up?" He asked casually. "You kinda messing up my game boss," he chuckled. "I was just telling Irys how gorgeous she was looking. Right Irys."

"Yes, yes you were," Irys said. He went to push a strand of hair from her face but Lucien grabbed his wrist stopping him.

"That's all mine Paul," He said. Paul looked between him and Irys.

"Wait are ya'll?"

"Yeah we are. So watch yourself playa. Back up from her." Lucien pushed him away and let go of his wrist. Paul put his hands up in submission and backed away.

"My bad." He continued to back away. Lucien looked at Irys and crossed his arms.

"Listen. I'm not a jealous man. Or at least I wasn't in my past relationship but when it comes to you things are different. We both need to understand what we're going to tolerate. And that shit there that just happened. Nope. I'm not gonna tolerate that." Irys just gazed at him, confused and turned on.

"But I didn't do anything," She said.

"You should have shut that down the moment he came up to you."

"Wait, wait. You make it sound like I was cheating on you or something? That we're an actual couple?" Lucien's brows creased.

"So are you saying we're not a couple then?"

"Well no! But I didn't know we were official. You didn't ask me or say anything!"

"We made love like we did last night and you didn't know we were serious?"

"It's dumb but yeah. I guess I thought you'd ask me."

"Well then Irys, are you mine or not?" He leaned over and kissed her to help her along with her decision.

"I will be, after one thing," She whispered.

"What?" He questioned.

"My mother. She wants to meet you," Irys chuckled.

"That's nothing. I'll meet your mom. Just set it up." He kissed her again before going to walk off. Irys pulled him back.

"And just so you know. Paul ain't got shit on you. No one does." Lucien winked at her before she let him go. When he got back to the kitchen Paul was standing there with his arms crossed.

"You lucky as fuck with a girl like her," Paul said.

"Yeah I know that," Lucien said. He looked at all his chefs. "And just in case some of ya'll stuck on stupid like Paul was a second ago, Irys is my woman. I'm not petty but if you fuck with her imma fire your ass."

"Heard that," Joe laughed. Lucien nodded.

"Aright. Time to open up!" Lucien shouted. When he looked out towards Irys, she blew him a kiss before getting ready to open the doors to his restaurant.

Chapter Eighteen

"I want to take you home again," Lucien said as they stood in front of their cars. Service was over and the restaurant was closed up.

"I want to go with you. But I didn't ask the aide to stay with my mom any longer. So I have to get home."

"It must be hard having an aide take care of her all the time. If you need help Irys all you have to do is ask me."

"Having this job with you helps me plenty Lucien. You don't have to do anymore." She wrapped her arms around Lucien and hugged him tightly before giving him a deep kiss.

"Okay baby, stop before I drag you back to my house. I don't want you driving out so late, so time to go."

"I'll call you as soon as I get home okay?" Irys said. Lucien gave her one last kiss before helping her into her car. He closed the door and stepped back as she backed up. He watched her drive off until he couldn't see her taillights anymore.

It felt like Irys was leaving a piece of herself behind the further she drove away from Lucien. She honestly wished she could spend the night with him again, but she had to keep in mind she had her responsibilities to tend to. And her mother would always come first.

When she got inside her home, the first thing she did was head back to her mother's room. The aide was just putting the blanket over her as her mother was falling asleep.

"Thanks Diana," Irys whispered.

"You're welcome. See you tomorrow." As she left the room, Irys sat at the edge of her mother's bed.

"Guess what?" Irys whispered. Kendra looked at her with low eyes. "Lucien said he'd love to meet you." She smiled weakly.

"Perfect," She smiled. "I can't wait."

"Sleep," Irys cooed. "I'll see you in the morning." She tucked her mother in and when she was fast asleep, Irys slipped out of the room and hurried to hers so she could call Lucien. She wanted Lucien to meet her mother soon. It was the approval Irys wanted for her man. She knew her mom would love him anyway. That was a given.

She was off from the Spa in the morning so she made the plan with Lucien that night that her mother would be visiting the restaurant to meet him. He was perfectly fine with that plan, but by morning the plan was falling apart. When Irys awoke, she made breakfast like she usually did and took it to her mother's room. Only this morning her mother wasn't waiting happily for her. She was in and out of sleep and weak.

"Ma?" Irys questioned, setting the platter down.

"Sorry dear. Your mother is very tired this morning." Irys helped her sit up and then brought the food over. She couldn't take her medication unless she had something to eat. The way things were going, her mother was too weak to go anywhere.

"Oh ma, I was going to take you to see Lucien. But you're too weak. And I don't want you traveling at all."

"I'm sorry my child. But why can't the young man come here?" She questioned.

"I don't want him anywhere near Rosa ma. Like seriously. Because I will kill her if she tries anything on him." Kendra chuckled weakly.

"You and your sister always have been fighting and I have no idea why."

"She's sleeping with Derek ma," Irys admitted. Kendra gasped.

"Are you serious?"

"Yes. I catch them all the time. But no matter it is what it is. I have Lucien and I want to keep him. And Rosa, she's a parasite I don't want her sticking onto him. But I want you to meet him so I just have to do something about it." She thought long and hard about it. She needed some kind of lie to make it work so that Rosa either left, or locked herself in her room until Lucien came and left.

After her mother finished breakfast, Irys took the platter and left the room to wash the dishes in the kitchen. Rosa was there sitting around the table having a bowl of cereal.

"I'm gonna need you out the house for the day," Irys told her.

"Excuse me?" Rosa asked.

"My landlord is coming over today. So you can't be seen because my rent will go up. So I need you out the house. Unless you have money to make up for the higher rent?"

"Where the hell you want me to go?" She asked.

"I don't know. But you need to figure it out. You have until 1pm." Rosa rolled her eyes. She messaged Derek immediately. She needed money. He only agreed to give her money if she agreed to sex him up. As she rolled her eyes she wrote to him how she couldn't wait to ride him. Course she didn't care about any of that. He didn't give her any pleasure so this was purely for the money. At least when it came to Lucien the sex was the bomb. But whatever, that's how it was.

By one, Rosa was leaving the house, probably going to fuck Derek or something. But Irys could care less. She had butterflies in her stomach because Lucien was coming to her house. Well, she had butterflies every time she saw him, period. And when Rosa was finally gone, she sent him the text that he could come. While he was on his way, Irys have her mother a sponge bath, did her hair and painted her nails. A special request from her mother.

"This man must be special. You've been smiling ever since he said he was on his way."

"I can't help it," Irys said. "That's what he does to me." The bell rang. "That's him!" She kissed her mother on the forehead and hurried to answer the door.

Lucien stood on her doorstep with bags of food. He was wearing jeans and a short sleeve button down that fit him perfectly.

"I was wearing just a t-shirt, but I didn't know if your mom would appreciate that. So I just out this on instead," He said.

"You look sexy as fuck," She gasped, embracing him in a rush and kissing him deeply.

"That's a record," Lucien said pecking her.

"Huh?"

"You got me hard in under a second," He chuckled. He fixed himself in his jeans. Irys laughed at him and helped him with the bags.

"Simmer that thing down. You can't hide an anaconda that easily." Lucien gasped at her.

"Stop it," He laughed. He followed her inside.

"It's not much. But this is my home."

"Oh hush. It's very nice," Lucien said. And he was being honest. The way she decorated the place spoke to her freeness. His house was barely decorated at all.

"I'll come back for the food later. Come on." Irys took his hand and led him to her mother's bedroom. When she entered, her mother perked up in bed.

"Hi," She greeted.

"Hi Mrs.-"

"Don't start that crap with me. Call me Kendra," She scolded. Lucien walked closer to the bed to take the woman's hand. She and Irys looked just alike and from the looks of it, they shared the same personality.

"Sorry Kendra," He smiled. "My name is Lucien."

"Now you are a good looking man. No wonder Irys don't stop smiling." Lucien looked over at Irys who slapped herself on the forehead.

"So how serious is this?" Kendra asked. "Because I can't allow my girl to be tied down to another deadbeat."

"It's as serious as ever. I don't plan on wasting her time and I don't think she wants to waste mine either. We were both in need of something real and I think we found it."

"What's one thing you like about my girl?"

"Mom come on seriously?!"

"Irys please. Let me and the man talk."

"I'm gonna share the food out," Irys said turning and leaving the room. Kendra looked back at Lucien. His handsome features soft and caring.

"Tell me," She said.

"When I first saw her, it was her beauty that threw me off. I was distracted by it. But then actually speaking with her, and that fierce determination she has, it was refreshing."

"My daughter has a way with determination. But sometimes she gets down. And usually I'm the only one she looks to for advice. And it's never a problem. But with you in her life I want you to be there for her like that."

"I plan on it," He said. Kendra patted his hand. "Do you also speak three languages?" Lucien asked.

"Oh no. I just speak Spanish because of my first husband. When Irys got into high school and she realized I spoke Spanish she wanted to do the same thing. But my dear child didn't stop at that. She wanted to learn French and Italian, and then ASL. All of which she did."

"That's amazing of her. She told me she wants to take a trip to see the world especially the countries of those languages. I just hope she doesn't leave me behind when she does," Lucien joked. Kendra smiled even though a sadness came over her face.

"What's wrong?" Lucien asked.

"I know my girl has all these things she wants to do, and I'm literally tying her down. If not for me being sick she would be in Paris right now gazing at pastries through the windows of pastry shops."

"I know that Irys loves you and she wouldn't think of it like that."

"I just want her to experience the things I know she wants to. Especially when it comes to you. I don't want to hinder you guys' relationship."

"You won't hinder anything Kendra." She smiled at him and continued holding his hand. Irys came back into the room with a platter of food. Lucien stood up to help her carry everything in.

"Tryna steal my man, mama?" Irys teased, seeing they were holding hands when she walked in.

"Please child. Remember who gave you those looks of yours."

"My daddy," She chuckled.

"While we're on the topic, Lucien," Kendra said. "I'm not getting any younger. I want some grandchildren." Kendra waved her hand at the both of them.

"Ma!" Irys shouted. "Really? The topic of kids right now?" Lucien was cracking up even though Irys was freaking out.

"Think this is funny?" Irys asked with a hint of a smile on her face.

"Kinda," He smiled. He looked at Kendra. "Don't worry Kendra. I won't wear a condom the next time," he winked at her. Irys slapped him playfully across the chest.

"Lucien!" She laughed. "Don't make those kind of promises!" He grabbed her around the waist and kissed her.

"You know you can't resist me," He murmured. Kendra looked at Irys and Lucien embracing and she knew her daughter had found the right man.

For the rest of the afternoon, they talked about pretty much everything. The food Lucien brought was on point like it always was, and Irys loved that her mother was actually enjoying a different kind of food for once. What's more was that she actually felt like her mom really liked Lucien.

"Sweetie I gotta get going now," Lucien said looking at his phone.

"Are you alright?" She questioned.

"I don't have my insulin with me, and I need to start prepping for tonight."

"Insulin?" Kendra asked.

"Yeah. I've been diabetic since I was a kid," Lucien admitted.

"Oh that's so terrible. You're still a fine young man," She said.

"Thank you Kendra. It was so good meeting you." Lucien leaned down and hugged her tightly.

"Are you two seeing each other tonight?" Kendra asked.

"No ma, I didn't ask Diana to stay overnight to look after you."

"I can stay alone for one night child. Please go have a night with your man." Irys looked unsure.

"Ma I don't know."

"Do what I said girl. Spend the night with him. Make my damn grand babies." Irys shook her head but she still smiled.

"Fine," She smirked "I'll pack some things now and leave with you so that we don't have to drive in separate cars." Both Irys and Lucien kissed Kendra goodbye before they left the room. Even though her mother wanted to stay alone Irys knew she couldn't. So she called the back-up aide to come over. Once the aide agreed to come, Irys took Lucien down to her bedroom so she could pack up some of her things. He sat at the edge of her bed and watched her, completely smitten with her. He almost wanted to forget working tonight and just spend the night in her arms.

"You know I can stay here with you sometime," He offered. Irys looked at him cautiously.

"What you mean?" She asked.

"If you can't get someone to stay overnight with your mom, there's no problem that I stay here with you. That's if you want me to." Irys got nervous for a split second.

"Oh no it's fine Lucien. As you can see my mother likes for me to get out," She said quickly. She wouldn't mind him staying here at all, if it wasn't for Rosa. There was a whole new protective side to her when it came to her man, and she wasn't going to allow Rosa near him.

"Sure?" he questioned, as if he didn't believe her.

"Yes. Okay I'm all done. The back-up aide is going to come though. Even if she wants to mom shouldn't be alone." They only had to wait an extra 15 minutes before the aide arrived at the house. Once she did Irys was comfortable with leaving.

Lucien carried her bags for her, and after another goodbye to her mother they were leaving the house. He helped her into his car and they were off. Irys didn't like keeping secrets from him, but she didn't want to just flat out say that she didn't want him here because of her sister. Because then he'd give her his sweet words and promise that he wouldn't pay her sister any attention, and then he'd force her to let him stay the night. Irys couldn't deal with that so she just kept her mouth shut. Besides, she liked sleeping in his bed.

****

Irys waited patiently by the door for Lucien to get his things. They were the last to leave. The place was dark as she waited by the door.

"Lucien!" She called out to him. He didn't answer but after a few moments she heard his feet coming towards her.

"Sorry sugar. I was just putting my insulin away." Irys took his hand and they walked out of the restaurant. She watched as he set the alarm then closed and locked the door with the key. She didn't know why she felt a sense of completion. Closing the restaurant up with him late, and then holding his hand as they walked to his car where she'd be going home with him. As they drove to his house he was quiet. He just held her hand as he drove.

When they arrived to the house he opened the door for her and led her inside his house. She could see on his face he was tired but there was also something else too.

"Lucien?" She questioned.

"Just tired sugar." Irys accepted that answer and left him alone. While she waited in his bedroom he took a shower in the master bathroom. When he came out, he only had a towel around his waist. Irys pretended to be looking through her phone while she looked at his body. The towel was so low she could see the wisps of his pubic hairs. She cleared her throat and got out of the bed. He was tempting her. She knew it. So she tempted right back. She took her shower but instead of wrapping herself in a towel she came out as naked as she was born. Lucien was on the bed but he looked right at her. She dried herself off then slowly rubbed lotion over her skin.

"Really?" he questioned. She smirked at him. "And even as tempting as you are right now, I can't." She crawled into the bed.

"Yeah?" she questioned. She cuddled next to him and kissed him.

"Yes I can't," He breathed, pecking her lips. "My sugar is low. I won't have the energy to keep up with you."

"It's okay baby," She said. "Cuddling is fine with me too." Lucien sensed she was okay with it, but he wanted more than just cuddling. He wanted in her body again.

"I want to give you more," He said.

"It's fine." Irys looked at him. "Do you have some more fruits? Like last time?" she asked.

"Yeah I do. Want some?"

"With some whip cream if that's fine."

"Sure." Lucien got off the bed and left the room to get some fruits from the kitchen. Irys stayed where she was, still completely naked and not looking to put on clothes. He returned shortly with the bowl and a can of whip cream. He handed her the bowl and the can and got back in bed.

"Why aren't you eating?" he asked after a moment.

"Because it's not for me," She smiled. Lucien was confused. "I did some research. And well, when you're sugar is low and you want to make love, you have to do a little improvising. We need to get your energy up to par with some food. And well, fruits are filled with sugar. So the question is…"

"What?" He asked. Irys laid back and sprayed each of her nipples with the whip cream before topping it with a strawberry.

"Do you want to eat the fruits off my body?" she asked huskily. He couldn't even believe this. If he had told Rosa his sugar was too low or too high, she would have an attitude with him the whole night. But this, this was something different. Lucien liked it. Without saying anything else, Lucien leaned over and took her supple breast in his hand. He licked off the whip cream before eating the strawberry off. Besides the fact that it was helping him, Lucien loved the way she moaned and her body squirmed under him. After sucking off the fruit and whip cream from her breasts, he just about sprayed the whip all over her and sprinkled the fruits everywhere. She wanted to give him a feast, and he was going to take it. He took his time licking every crevice of her until he got down to her core. She was dripping with arousal. Lucien speared her open and took that first swipe of his tongue. He groaned and sucked her clit softly, loving the texture of it in his mouth. Her body rocked and shivered as she came in his mouth.

"You are a dangerous man," She breathed, looking down at him. Lucien crawled up her body with a smirk on his face.

"You are a dangerous woman," He countered. He pulled his underwear down and off as he stayed on top of her. She opened up for him as he nudged his way inside her. Her walls captured him and gripped him tight as he buried himself to the hilt. Resting his weight on his elbows at each side of her head, he swung his hips in a smooth rhythm, making love to her body as he kissed her deeply. The feeling of her on his bare skin amplified every feeling he thought he felt before for their first time. Only this was better, and he felt himself not only digging deeper inside her, but deeper into her heart. He wanted a permanent place in there because she was surely etching a permanent spot in his heart. And when he pulled his lips away from her, it was because they were both gasping in their oncoming orgasms. She pressed her heels into his ass, and to him that meant one thing.

Irys came hard and even more so when she felt Lucien release his hot release inside her. She didn't know what she was doing not making him pull out but she was just lost in the moment and she couldn't help it. She had a miscarriage and maybe she ws trying to replace her loss with someone she was falling deeply for. And everything was completely different from what she had with Derek. And she felt that with Lucien everything was real, and it was right.

Once they caught their breaths from their lovemaking, Lucien stayed hovered over her with a smile on his face.

"Thank you for that," He breathed. "Because most women wouldn't get it."

"You don't need to explain anything to me," She smiled. He rose up off her, and helped her up. He lift her in his arms and carried her to the bathroom, where they took a long hot shower together. But simply showering didn't last long before Lucien kissed her at the right spot and she was wet all over again. Her fruit trick worked wonders because he made love to her all damn night long.

Chapter Nineteen

Lucien awoke to the smell of biscuits. He sat up quickly and looked around. The space next to him was vacant. Salsa hadn't bothered him all night. His sugar must have been okay. Stretching, he pulled on a pair of shorts and went to the bathroom to brush his teeth. The smell of food made his stomach growl heavily. And when he opened the bedroom door it was more fragrant than ever. Stepping into the kitchen, he smiled when he spotted Irys bending over and looking into the oven. She was only wearing her panties and one of his shirts that fit her tightly because of her curvy figure.

"What are you doing?" He questioned. She bounced up and turned to him.

"Good morning," She smiled. She walked over and kissed him. Lucien held onto her.

"I'm the cook," He reminded her.

"Yes. And I'm sure you can cook way better than me. But I still can throw down in the kitchen. And my biscuits with eggs and bacon are the best. Besides when was the last someone cooked for you?"

"Valid point," He said. Irys took his hand and brought him to the island and forced him to sit.

"Do you have to check your sugar?" she asked.

"Yeah I do," He responded. She pulled out his meter and strips from the drawer and gave it to him. Lucien eyed her curiously as he took his sugar. He was in his normal numbers.

"I'm good right now. I just have to take insulin for the amount of food I'm going to eat now, just so my body breaks down the sugars." Irys nodded and shared out his breakfast. He found it odd, yet refreshing that she cared about diabetes. Rosa didn't give a damn what so ever.

And after he ate her tasty breakfast, which was really good, she watched as he retrieved his insulin from the fridge and injected himself.

"How come you're so interested?" he asked unable to help himself. She seemed offended by his question.

"Excuse me?"

"I don't mean to be rude sugar. It's just that my ex wasn't into all this shit. And you, you are."

"That's because I'm not your ex that's first. And second I'm your new girlfriend. You mention your ex again and I'm going to think you're not over her." Lucien was shocked at her tone.

"I am over her," He said.

"Good. And the reason I want to know if because what if you get sick. Am I just supposed to stand around looking dumb not knowing how to help you?" Lucien understood her point.

"Okay, I get it," He said. "Sorry sugar." He kissed her deeply. She ran her hand over his cheek and gazed into his eyes. He was lost in her eyes as much as he was lost in hers. And in each other's arms was where they stayed before they would have to get ready to work. Since she still didn't have her car, Lucien agreed to take her to work, and then pick her up from the Spa when it was time for her to head over to the restaurant. She loved how cohesive they were working together in their new relationship.

****

Rosa was more than sick of Derek. All night he'd been in her and she had enough. She rushed him out of the house just to get some alone time. But in a matter of hours he was calling and texting her repeatedly. Rosa ignored it all. With him annoying her she was just ready to have Lucien back. She expected Irys to be home but again she'd slept out and wasn't telling anyone where she was. Rosa didn't even know why the hell she cared anyway. She needed to get Lucien back and that was it. When Irys was still a no show for the morning, Rosa figured she was at the Spa anyway. She left the house to see Lucien again. It was midafternoon at what she thought the perfect time was to see him. Lucien however was inside the restaurant and looked to be buried in a mountain of things to do and she didn't want to interrupt. So she would wait. She stayed in her car to wait for the right time. She didn't know when it would be, but she wasn't going to leave without talking to him again.

Derek kept texting her, almost begging her to speak to him. After two hours, Rosa finally gave up and just answered one of his calls.

"What?" She answered.

"Why you ignoring me baby? What I do?"

"Derek me and you can't be doing this. It was fun but now I need to go back to my man. Hell, you're living on a friend's couch and you don't have any money to support me. What am I gonna do with that?"

"I can get money Rosa. I swear. My friend just told me about this job he's gonna do and I can work with him." Rosa was distracted by Lucien walking out of the restaurant.

"Look, I can't talk to you right now," she said.

"Baby I'll get some money-" Rosa hung up the phone on him and left her car immediately.

"Lucien!" She called. Lucien turned around at the sound of that voice. He sighed and rubbed his eyes.

"Yes?" he asked as Rosa ran up to him. She jumped in his arms and hugged him, then tried to kiss him.

"Whoa, back off," He said. "If my woman ever saw that she'd be pissed."

"You woman?" Rosa asked.

"Yeah. Turns out there is a woman out there who wants me. Even with me being diabetic. And I'm late picking her up. Later Rosa." And just like that he just left. Rosa stood there, mouth hanging open wondering what the hell she'd just done. Did she really just lose her man to someone else? As he drove away Rosa went back to her car. But she wasn't leaving. She was going to wait until he came back. She wasn't going to let it go this easily.

"Sorry I'm late sweetie," Lucien said when Irys hopped into his car. Luna was waiting with Irys too.

"It's fine," She smiled. Lucien kissed her deeply before driving off. He was concerned about Rosa for only a moment. The instant he saw Irys he forgot completely about Rosa. And that's how it should be. He wasn't going to worry about his ex when he had a woman who was all his. A woman that he felt confident around. When he pulled back up to the restaurant he saw Rosa's car but he didn't even give her a second thought. He went around to the passenger side of his car and helped Irys out.

"Is this only because we just started dating? Or are you gonna do this all the time?" she asked, grabbing his hand and hopping out of the vehicle.

"Hmm, it depends on my mood," Lucien joked. Irys plucked his nose.

"Come on lovebirds," Luna said. "I didn't hook you two up to become a third wheel and shit." Lucien pecked Irys on the mouth before draping his arm over Luna.

"Feel better?" he teased. While his arm was over Luna, he held Irys's hand as they walked into the restaurant.

Rosa was gripping the steering wheel so hard she was burning her palm. No way did her fat bitch of a sister grab up her man. Seeing Irys kiss Lucien made her grunt and growl in anger. This wasn't going to stand. Rosa wasn't letting this shit happen. Not on her fucking watch. She peeled out of her parking space and motored down the street. She was so angry the only thing she could think of doing right this second was trashing Irys's house. She was gonna tear it up from floor to ceiling so Irys had to come home and clean every bit of it up. But the moment she pulled up, Derek was sitting on the steps.

"You know what. You gonna leave me the hell alone!" She snapped at him. "I'm not in the mood today?!"

"What the hell is your problem?" he asked.

"That bitch Irys is messing around with MY man!" She shouted. "Who the fuck does she think she is?!"

"Wait a minute, someone actually had sex with that whale?" Derek asked.

"Yes! And that someone is my man!"

"How can she be fucking someone while she's pregnant? Fucking slut."

"Pregnant?" Rosa gasped.

"Yeah! I left that bitch because I told her I didn't wanna have no baby with her. She refused to get an abortion and I left her ass. Don't know who's gonna help her raise that kid but it ain't me. I guess maybe that's why she's fucking. She gotta shop around for a new daddy."

"I can't believe this," Rosa whispered. "I bet Lucien doesn't even know she's pregnant. Hell, who would know she's pregnant when she's fat anyway. Listen you still gotta go. I need to deal with this shit."

"I only came to tell you about the money I'm gonna be making."

"I don't care Derek. Don't tell me about it, I wanna see it. Show me the money and then we can move on." She didn't actually mean it, but if she could take his money she was fine with that. And besides, she was going to get Lucien back anyway. After what she was going to tell him about Irys, he was going to come running straight back to her.

Even though she was fuming, she kept it buried inside her. So when Irys came home that night all happy and shit, Rosa just gave her a fake smile and said nothing else. It all made sense now why Irys didn't care about Derek. She was getting off on Rosa's man. It was so frustrating not to rip the whole house apart, but Rosa kept her cool. She was going to get her payback. She just kept her mouth shut. The next day when Irys was off to work, Rosa was jumping into action. She phoned Lucien around 11 in the morning, hoping he had some free time.

"What's up?" he asked the moment he answered.

"Hey Lucien," She tried to sound sweet. "I was wondering if maybe you had some time for us to meet up."

"Look Rosa, you can't keep this up. I don't want to meet up with you. There's nothing to say."

"Lucien it's important. And you're going to want to hear what I have to say."

"I'm sure it's not all that bad. I gotta go-"

"Either you agree to meet me privately or I'll come up there and make a scene. I'm pretty sure you don't want your girlfriend thinking there's still something between me and you."

"You've got to be kidding me," He sighed. "Whatever Rosa. Come by the restaurant in 20 minutes. If you're late forget about it."

"Good. See you then." Rosa smiled to herself as she hung up then when to get some clothes on to meet him.

Lucien knew that if Irys knew he was meeting up with his ex she wouldn't like it. But he would much rather talk to Rosa privately than have her come down to the restaurant and cause a scene. He went up to his office to check his sugar. He was fine, but he didn't have any needles.

"Luna," Lucien said when Luna answered her phone. "I have to take care of something, can you go to the pharmacy for me?"

"No," She scoffed.

"Come on Luna! I'm not in the mood to play with you."

"I'm not playing either Lucien. You have a whole woman at your disposal. Ask her to get your medicine."

"Actually, you're right." Lucien hung up the phone and called Irys.

"Hey sugar, do you mind doing me a favor while you're on lunch break? Before you come over to the restaurant?"

"Yes, what's up?"

"I don't have any more of my needles here. Could you go to the pharmacy and pick some up for me? It's not a prescription. Just ask one of the workers for needles 31 gage, half CC and they get it for you. It's about 3 dollars for a pack of ten."

"31 gage, half CC. Got it. Will you be okay until my break?"

"Yes I'll be good. Thanks sugar. I'll give you a big kiss when I see you."

"You'll give me more than that," She whispered. She kissed him through the phone before hanging up. He felt so happy with her and Rosa hanging at his back was a little annoying. But he just wanted to see what she had to say so she could leave him alone. Twenty minutes later he was standing in the parking lot waiting for Rosa to show up. And she showed up like she always did. Wearing heels and a short skirt, she look her usual self but Lucien realized that anything he found attractive in her before, he just didn't now.

"What you need to say?" Lucien asked, getting straight to the point.

"You shouldn't be with that girl," She said.

"See, this is what I'm not doing. I'm not gonna stand here and listen to you go on about this. Me and you are over. And it's never happening again. Just accept that and you'll be able to move on."

"But-"

"That's enough Rosa. And I mean it. I've moved on, and I'm happy." He shook his head and walked by her to get back inside the restaurant.

"Then I hope you'll be happy when she has her baby," Rosa called out. Lucien stopped in his tracks. He turned around slowly to look back at her.

"What'd you just say?" he asked. Rosa smirked, clearly snaring his interest.

"Irys. She's pregnant. And I'm pretty sure it's not yours."

"How do you even know her name?" Lucien asked walking back towards her.

"We have the same mother, but not the same father. Our resemblance is quite fleeting."

"You're Irys's sister?" Lucien couldn't believe it. And thinking about all the things Irys told him her sister did to her, made sense when he thought about Rosa. But he couldn't believe that this was just coincidence.

"She told me what a bitch you were and I didn't even think it was you. And now it all makes sense," Lucien said.

"Yeah well bitch or not, she's still lying to you," Rosa said. Lucien crossed his arms. He wasn't going to believe anything Rosa said based off how much Irys had been through with her in the first place.

"And I know that look on your face," Rosa spoke up. "And whether you believe me or not is up to you. Irys is pregnant by her ex. When you kicked me out, I went to live with her. Her ex, he tried to get frisky with me. I know he hits Irys and she denies it but I called him out. He ended up hitting me and then he tried to seduce me. When I told Irys she thought I was just trying to take him from her. He only made it worse because then he left her, claiming he wanted me. I didn't have sex with him or anything but that didn't stop Irys from being upset. The night you left me Lucien I told her everything about you. And next thing I know, her man leaves her because he wants me, and then she's dating you? I confronted her last night. And she laughed in my face and told me you and her were in a happy relationship and that you were going to help her raise her baby. I just wanted to talk to you to see if it was true."

"I didn't know she was pregnant..." Lucien said lowly.

"Okay well. Now you know." Rosa backed up and sighed. "Later Lucien." She walked by him and left the parking lot. The seed was planted on one side, and now to plant it on the next.

She drove off from the restaurant and went straight to the spa where Irys worked. If that fat bitch thought she would just have Lucien to herself, she was sadly mistaken. Rosa pulled up to the spa and parked round back. She marched towards the front but before she could throw the door open and enter she spotted Luna sitting at the front desk.

"Shit!" Rosa back pedaled quickly. Luna couldn't see her. She went back to her car and decided to just call Irys.

"I know it must be the apocalypse or something to have you calling me," Irys joked.

"Look, I'm not in a joking mood. I'm in the lot behind the spa. I need to talk to you immediately." Irys didn't even know what to think. Rosa never sounded this serious before.

"I'll be right out. Lucky I'm going on break anyway." She hung up the phone and stood from the desk.

"Luna, I'll meet you at the restaurant," Irys told her.

"Okay. Don't forget his needles. Then I'll feel bad for telling him no." Irys smiled at her as they went separate ways. She appreciated the fact that Lucien trusted her to ask her to pick it up for him in the first place. But before she could, she had to deal with whatever Rosa wanted.

"Now what would have you coming to my job?" Irys asked her when she walked up to Rosa.

"Lucien. That's who you've been dating?" She said immediately.

"How-how did you know? Have you been following me or something?" Rosa scoffed.

"Lucien is my ex Irys. He's the one I left when I moved in with you. And I wasn't following you. He's the one that called me, gloating about how he was fucking you. He's trying to make me jealous enough to come back to him. So now I feel like an idiot because my sister is out here getting played by my ex."

"Wait just a minute. Don't act like I should feel sorry for you because you didn't give a damn about fucking Derek."

"Fine okay, I fucked him. But I was really hurt by not having Lucien. But the fact that he's using you to get back at me is just wrong. And I don't know I figured maybe you should know."

"So all of a sudden after all the shit you done to me, I'm supposed to believe anything you say?"

"Think about it Irys. Why would he be fucking you in the first place? Knowing he had me first? What would make him want you but just revenge? Get real Irys. And I can be a horrible ass person but one thing you can't say about me is that I don't keep it real. So think about that shit. Looks like we're the same. I fucked your ex, and you fucked mine. Only thing is you're the one getting played." Rosa looked her up and down before going back into her car. Irys just stood there for a moment. Could it all be fake? Was Lucien really that type of man? No. No he couldn't be. She wasn't about to believe anything Rosa said. Not knowing the kind of woman Rosa was. She was simply just going to ask Lucien about his past with Rosa. Then she'd take it from there. But before she went to the restaurant she drove out to the pharmacy to get his needles first.

Lucien was pacing in his office, thoughts running rampant when Luna arrived. Ever since Rosa left he couldn't stop thinking about their conversation. So the moment Luna came into his office she could tell something was on his mind.

"What you thinking about?" She asked him. Lucien took a deep breath before answering her.

"Luna did you know Irys was pregnant?" He asked promptly.

"Oh shit, you're actually making me an auntie?"

"No Luna not like that. Rosa came to see me today. She said Irys is pregnant by her ex."

"How the hell does Rosa know Irys?"

"They're sisters apparently." Luna was too shocked to say anything at first. But the more she thought about it the more she realized she'd never been to Irys's home or introduced to her sister.

"She spoke of her sister but I've never been introduced or even to her house."

"And when I suggested that I stay over her house she was against it completely. But I don't know. Does that mean she was hiding something from me?"

"If she was, I didn't know anything about it. I wouldn't hook you up with someone who was pregnant by someone else."

"Yeah well, Rosa says that she wanted me because her ex and Rosa were fucking. Apparently Irys is using me to be her baby's father and to get back at her sister." Luna sat there silently, anger slowly rising insider her. Just the thought that Irys could even do something like this to her brother was making her livid.

"I'm gonna kill her," Luna said lowly.

"Luna no. I don't even know if this is true!"

"I don't care." Luna stood from her chair and left the office. She didn't want to cause any drama inside the restaurant itself so she waited outside for Irys to pull up. Luna didn't care if that was her best friend. If she tried to pull one over on Lucien, she was going to have to answer for it.

Lucien stayed close to Luna because he knew when she was upset she was likely to do anything. And when she saw Irys's car pull up into the parking lot she charged towards it. Lucien followed close behind her. Luna was right there the moment Irys got out of the car.

"So what's the deal with Rosa? She's really your sister?" Luna asked. Irys looked back and forth between Luna and Lucien.

"Yes she is but-"

"But what?" Luna snapped. "Irys I told you not to mess with my brother! I thought you were different!" Luna pushed Irys back.

"What the fuck are you talking about?!" Irys snapped. Lucien separated the two women.

"Luna you can't put your hands on her," He ordered. "Especially if she's pregnant."

"Pregnant?!" Irys looked at him sharply. "What are you talking about now?"

"Rosa told me you were pregnant by your ex Irys," He said. Irys blinked. Rosa found out she was pregnant but apparently she left out the little information that she'd miscarried.

"Yeah well Rosa told me that you were only fucking me to get back at her because she left you. And that there was no way you'd want a girl like me after having a girl like her."

"You know that's not even true Irys," Lucien said.

"You're right," Irys nodded. "I knew it wasn't true. I couldn't believe nothing Rosa said because I knew you couldn't be that type of man. But here I am being confront by the both of you. So it's obvious the both of you think I'm some type of manipulative bitch." Luna backed up a little, doubt beginning to fill her body.

"No it's not that Irys. It's just that I don't know what to think and if you're pregnant-"

"You think I would be pregnant and not say that to you? And not mention it after our first date? Like hey, I'm gonna push a 7 pound baby out my vagina in a couple months but that's okay with you right? Rosa has done a lot of shit to me. And I knew not to believe anything she said about you. And if you dated her Lucien, you should know that she cares about no one but herself. So I don't know how you could let someone like her tell you something like that about me and you actually believe it." Lucien was starting to realize how screwed up this all was. How could he even doubt Irys?

"But why would she say you were pregnant? Out of all the lies she could have told? Why that?" Luna asked. Irys crossed her arms.

"Answer her," Lucien prodded. The fact that he was doubting her didn't make Irys mad. It upset her. Knowing this man she was in love with thought she was manipulating hurt like no other. Irys shook her head. She wiped the tears from her eyes.

"Because I was pregnant," She admitted. "Luna, when I came into work that day and my lip was busted it was because Derek had hit me. He hit me because he told me to get an abortion and I refused. I got him back good for it but in the end he still won out." Irys choked up. She rocked back and forth.

"I was going to raise my baby by myself with no problem. I didn't have any regrets in Derek leaving me. But then one day I just- I started bleeding. And before I even met you Lucien, I was sitting in the emergency room with a doctor telling me I had just lost my baby."

"That's why you missed those days of work," Luna supplied.

"Yes that's why I missed work. Because I just lost my fucking baby and I had no one. I felt embarrassed to tell you Luna so I kept my mouth shut. And then at the end of it all I just came from the emergency room to a sister who could do nothing but yell at me and calling me names for leaving her to take care of our sick mother for more than an hour."

"Irys I'm so sorry-"

"I don't wanna hear it Luna," Irys snapped. "If you were my friend you wouldn't have done that to me. You wouldn't stand here and accuse me of something like this."

"It's just that-" Irys shook her head. She reached into her bag and pulled out Lucien's pack of needles.

"Fire me if you want to Lucien. I don't care. But we're done." She threw the pack of needles at him. He let it hit his chest and fall to the ground. Wiping her eyes and sniffling, she got right back into her car and pulled off swiftly leaving two people she thought cared for her behind.

Chapter Twenty

Irys threw Rosa's clothes in trash bags. Again her face was painted with tears as she couldn't help but break down. But this time she wasn't going to continue being weak. Rosa was finished walking over her. Irys was sure of it. First she was fucking Derek and now she managed to get in between her and Lucien. Honestly it wasn't even Rosa's fault for that. Sure she planted the seed, but it was Lucien who decided to let it grow. She was so upset and frustrated she didn't even know what else to do. She continued slamming Rosa's clothes in the bags and moving it to the front door. Once all the bags were lines up she threw them outside along with every other item that belonged to her. She slammed the door shut and turned the lock. Irys paced directly in front of the door waiting for the moment that Rosa would arrive. She was heated and the last thing she could think about was being her regular old nice self.

So the moment Rosa turned the key in the lock and entered, Irys was ready for her. She snatched her key from Rosa's hand and pushed her back out the house. Rosa landed on her ass on the grass. Irys stood over her as she scrambled back to her feet.

"What the hell is going on?" Rosa snapped. "Why is all my shit out here?"

"Because you ain't my problem anymore," Irys countered. "You lied to Lucien and you definitely lied to me. Why don't you want to see me happy huh? You fucked around with Derek and now this? What have I ever done to you?"

"Lucien was mine first! And you can't have him!"

"Yeah well he wasn't yours anymore! I didn't even know he was your ex Rosa! But he told me plenty about his past relationship and thinking about it, it fits you perfectly. You took it upon yourself to ruin something I had going perfectly for me! And you ain't gonna stay in my house no more causing me all this fucking trouble!"

"You're the one that's pregnant!" Rosa snapped. Irys pushed her again.

"NO I'M NOT!" She screamed. "I had a miscarriage and you would have known had I thought you cared about anyone else but yourself! After the shit I been through with Derek, Lucien was perfect. He wanted me for me and that's it."

"You can't date my ex Irys. You're the one pissed off because I fucked Derek and now you wanna date my ex?"

"You know what?" Irys asked. "Karma is a bitch ain't it? Get your shit and get off my property. You ain't gone in ten minutes I'm calling the cops. Because you're officially trespassing." Irys looked her up and down before backing up into the house and slamming the door shut. She watched out the window as Rosa paced for a couple minutes before finally piling her things in her car and driving off. Irys wiped her eyes and ran to her mother's bedroom.

"What is all that noise and yelling?" Kendra asked.

"I told Rosa to leave," Irys sniffled. "She told Lucien I was pregnant, and he believed her."

"Well did you tell him about the miscarriage?"

"No, I didn't."

"You can't blame him for being curious and wanting to know if it was true or not Irys. It's only natural."

"But it was almost like he was blaming me or something."

"You need to go and talk to him Irys. No sense in letting a good man like that go over this nonsense." Irys flopped down in the chair next to her mother's bed. Even if she was hurt she knew she wanted nothing more than to talk to him.

"It won't work anyway," Irys pouted. "Because Lucien is Rosa's ex." Kendra gasped.

"Seriously?"

"Yes mom! And I gave her shit for fucking Derek. I can't turn around and keep messing with this man."

"That's true Irys. But I think the situation is different. Rosa and Derek, that wasn't nothing but sex. You and Lucien you know it's much more than that. And if you love him Irys, you have to fight for him."

"I just don't know," Irys sighed. She placed her head in her hands to think. She felt her mother run her hand through her hair. It was comforting until Irys' phone began ringing. She took it from her pocket and just looked at it. Lucien was calling her.

"Answer that phone child," Kendra ordered. Irys sighed and did as she was told.

"What do you want Lucien?" She asked.

"You thought you would get rid of me that easily?" He countered.

"Oh you wanted to believe what Rosa told you so I guess you wanted me to leave."

"A part of me didn't believe it Irys. But I'll be honest and admit that I did have some kind of doubt. It was wrong of me and it was wrong of Luna to accuse you like that. But I promise you Irys I want you in my life."

"You're my sisters ex. Even if I did forgive you we can't date."

"Stop it. Yes we can."

"How can we?"

"Because me and Rosa wasn't right. I wanted to force myself to be with her because I thought I couldn't be with anyone else. But me and you Irys, what we have is right. It's real. I'm not gonna let Rosa come in between that. Not again." Irys was quiet. She sniffled involuntarily.

"Are you crying sweetie?" he asked.

"I was," She said "But I'm okay now. Listen…just give me some time okay. Can you do that?"

"I will try," He said. "And I hope you know Luna is really sorry too."

"Yeah well, she has to tell me that herself doesn't she? I gotta go Lucien." Without waiting for his response, Irys hung up the phone.

"You're gonna take him back," Kendra said.

"I know I am," Irys whispered. "It just still hurts."

"I know baby." Kendra patted her hand and sighed. Irys stayed in her mother's room and watched her fall asleep. Once she was out, Irys pulled the covers over her and left the room. For the rest of the evening Irys stayed in bed and watched romance movies while eating chocolate and popcorn. So typical. But she couldn't help it. Luna sent her a couple texts but Irys didn't answer them. She knew Luna was too protective for her own good. That's why she saw the bad in people before the good when it came to her brother. For right now, Irys didn't want to talk to anyone.

****

It was weird when she went into work for the spa the next day. She didn't even so much as look at Luna. But Luna looked at her. And she kept looking at her all shift. It wasn't until they were leaving for the restaurant that Luna finally approached her.

"Look I know you pretty much don't want to talk. But I know I just have to tell you this in person. I really am sorry. I let my protectiveness get in the way of seeing what was true and what wasn't. If you never want to be a friend to me anymore I get that. But just don't take my mistake out on Lucien. If I don't deserve you, I know for sure that he does." Luna gave her a small smile and backed away. Irys sighed and let her go. She knew going to the restaurant right now to work was going to be hard.

Of course the moment she saw Lucien she wanted to run to him to get a hug and a kiss. She fought the urge and took her eyes of him. She managed to keep herself busy with work but then when she got that you look beautiful text she nearly lost it again. After staring at the text forever she finally took a glance at Lucien. He was fileting a fish and even that was sexy to her. She rubbed her eyes. The only thing holding her back was knowing he dated Rosa. What if he thought about how different she and Rosa was each time she took her clothes off? Irys shook her head. She knew she shouldn't think like that. Especially after the way he made love to her body. Not to mention how he licked every part of her down with whip cream. That wasn't the action of someone who was concerned about her weight. She was just confused.

At the end of the night, she just about ran out of the restaurant, afraid that if she stayed any longer she would be all over Lucien like jelly in a PB and J. She hurried to her car and drove home fast just wanting to be locked away in her room away from all this temptation.

On her way home, she picked up a box of pizza. It was late she knew but she refused to eat anything Lucien had made her so she was starving. She paid Diana and gave her a hug goodbye as the aide left. Her mother was still awake, so Irys took a quick shower and changed into a t-shirt before going into the room with her mother.

"I hear you had a good day," Irys said to her as she walked in the room.

"Yes. Yes. Diana took me for a small walk so I could enjoy the sun. I'm tired now. What's that pizza?"

"I already know you want a slice," Irys laughed. If there was one thing her mother liked, it was a slice of pizza. Irys opened the box of pizza and laid it on her lap. When she was younger this was how they ate pizza. Her mother took a slice up slowly and bit into it.

"How's Lucien?" she asked.

"I don't know," Irys shrugged.

"Oh child. Stop playing!" Kendra scolded. "I want you to be with him."

"Mom I just don't know."

"Well know this. He makes you happy. When he told me about what drew him to you he spoke so happily about you. I felt his truth. And besides I know you want to travel the world and I can see you and him doing those things together. Irys he's going places. And he wants you at his side. And I want you to be free and not stuck here with me."

"Cut that out ma, you know I'm not worried about any of that. I love you being here and I'm fine with it. If I'm supposed to travel I will. If me and Lucien are meant to be then it will happen." Her mother took her hand and looked at her deeply.

"Promise me something," She sighed.

"Anything."

"Promise you won't be one of these chicks out here stuck on stupid when there's a man that loves you but you won't just accept him."

"I am not stuck on stupid!" Irys gasped. Kendra rolled her eyes.

"You more than stuck," She said. "Just promise me."

"I promise." Irys laughed. "I can't even believe you," She chuckled.

"I'm just saying Irys. I love you to death but you tripping right now. Got that sexy ass man and you acting all confused and whatnot." Irys gasped again. Kendra looked at her curiously.

"You never told me how he was in bed."

"Because you're my mother and I cannot divulge that type of information," Irys chuckled.

"Well was it good?"

"It was more than that mom. Way better than that in fact."

"Like I said. Stupid," Kendra scoffed. "Good looking man, a well set future, ambition, wants to be with you, and he's good in bed and you over here confused. If you don't get it together girl."

"Okay, okay, okay," Irys sighed. "I'll have lunch with him tomorrow and we'll talk. I know I want him I guess I'm just making him wait it out."

"I'll take that," Kendra smiled.

"You need to get some rest," Irys said. She stood and closed the box of pizza. "I'll make you some waffles tomorrow."

"You should get Lucien to come over and make me some," She teased.

"Ha ha, very funny," Irys smiled. She kissed her mother goodnight and gave her a hug.

"Love you," Kendra told her.

"Love your crazy behind too," Irys chuckled. She tucked her mother in before turning down the lights and leaving the room. She put the pizza in the fridge and retired to her bedroom. There waiting for her was a message on her phone from Lucien.

I'm here alone and all I want is to have your warm body in bed next to me. Have a good night sugar. And remember how bad I want you Irys.

Of course it made Irys all gooey inside. Who was she kidding? She was going to have this man and she knew she would be happy with him. It hurt that he doubted her to begin with, but he was obviously regretting the fact that he did that to her.

It took forever for Irys to get to bed but finally she drifted off to sleep with Lucien heavy on her mind. The thing that her mother made her promise was also prominent in her mind. Maybe she was stuck on stupid. But like she said, she would give him one night before calling him.

****

Irys awoke the next morning with her phone buzzing next to her ear. She slowly came out of sleep and looked at her phone. She was getting messages repeatedly and they were all from Lucien. Rubbing her eyes, she sat up with her phone in hand and looked at the messages. She actually laughed as she read each one. He was talking to her normally as if they weren't in this place they were in right now. And then he sent her pictures of Salsa, proclaiming that the dog missed her and wouldn't be able to go on without her. In one of the pictures he included himself, shirtless and Irys actually whistled getting drawn into his physical appeal. Yeah, she was dumb if she didn't take this damn man back. Irys left the messages unanswered because she knew she was going to call him later anyway. Best to keep him on his toes. And since she promised her mother she would she wasn't going to keep leaving him in the dark.

She got out of bed and went to freshen up and put on her favorite sweat suit. She gave herself two large French braids before she was ready to go about her day. Her mother was usually up by 9 and with it being 10 already Irys figured the woman should be starving right now. But when Irys left her room and walked by her mother's room she didn't hear the sound of the soap operas her mother watched every morning. Irys back pedaled.

"Ma I'm going to make-" Irys paused as she opened her mother's bedroom door. A shrill scream left Irys's mouth when she saw her mother's ghostly complexion and stone still body lying in the bed. Irys backed up but tripped on something, sending her falling to the ground. She back pedaled on her ass trying to get out of the room as fast as possible.

"No, no, no!" She screamed. She wanted to go and shake her mother awake but she was too afraid to go back into the room to deal with the fact that she wasn't going to wake up. Irys didn't know what else to do but there was only one other person she could possibly run to at a time like this.

****

Luna watched her brother eat his food drearily. Nothing she said would be enough to get him out of his mood. Point blank he just wanted Irys back.

"So the pictures didn't get to her?" Luna asked.

"No," He sulked. "I thought for sure Salsa would get her." Lucien shook his head. "This is the last time I'm gonna ever make this mistake again. It's horrible. I can't function like this."

"I just say you just go to her house and get her. Irys likes to keep herself closed off. Like she didn't tell me about her miscarriage."

"If I go there she might call the damn cops on my ass," Lucien said. "Because I won't just-" The sound of his phone ringing caught his attention. He looked at the face on the screen and immediately popped up from his chair.

"Irys, sugar!" He greeted. But the response he got back wasn't what he expected. Irys' voice was choppy and barely coherent as she sobbed into the phone.

"What's wrong?" He asked urgently. "Irys take a deep breath and talk to me. What's the matter?"

"My mom," She sobbed. "I need you Lucien. I-I-"

"Don't say anything else baby I'm coming right now." Lucien hung up the phone

"What happened?" Luna asked.

"I don't know. Something is up with Irys. I gotta go."

"Maybe I should come," Luna said.

"No sis, let me just be there for her alone. I'll call you later. You can hang out here if you want." Lucien rushed into his bedroom and jumped into a pair of sweatpants. He threw on a t-shirt and stepped into his sneakers. He was in such a haste to leave he didn't even think twice about checking his sugar, or bringing his meter with him. He bolted from the house and straight into his car. There was only one thing that could leave Irys emotional like that and Lucien was fearing the worst on this one.

He sped to Irys's home. When he arrived, the front door was closed but it wasn't locked. He entered easily, finding Irys pacing in the kitchen.

"Sweetie?" he called to her. She stopped pacing and gasped when she saw him. She rushed to him and fell into his arms. Lucien held her tightly.

"What happened?" He asked her.

"She's gone," Irys whispered. "In the bedroom." She stepped away from him and pointed to her mother's bedroom. Lucien walked to the bedroom slowly. The door was wide open and when he looked inside sure enough Kendra was in the middle of the bed looking as if she was asleep. But the whiteness of her face said otherwise. Lucien sighed. He was looking forward to spending more time with that woman and showing her all the things he could give to her daughter. Shaking his head, Lucien backed out of the bedroom and returned to Irys. She was hugging herself. Her face was drenched in tears and her eyes were big and puffy.

"We have to call the police Irys," He said. "So they can remove her body."

"I'm not ready for that," She sobbed shaking her head. Lucien held her.

"You probably won't ever be ready baby. But she needs to get taken care of. We can't leave her like this." Irys nodded realizing he was right.

"I'll make the call okay? Go in the bedroom and relax a little let me take care of it." And that's what he did. While Irys stood in the doorway of her bedroom, Lucien called the police and explained the situation. When they came to her house he took control, leading them to the bedroom and speaking with them. Irys didn't have to say a word. And when the mortician came for her body, Irys was able to hide away, not yet strong enough to see her mother like that. Lucien took care of it all, and he was there to comfort her. When her mother's body was finally loaded into the truck she was able to come from her room. She held onto Lucien as they walked outside. They told her where they were going to carry her body.

"Is there a funeral home you'd like us to contact to send her body to?"

"Um-uh..no I don't know. I-"

"We don't know anything now this is kind of sudden, but I'll be in touch," Lucien spoke up for her. That was all that needed to be said. As the cops and the mortician drove away Lucien and Irys went back inside.

"Does she have life insurance Irys?" Lucien asked her. Irys thought for a moment.

"Um. I think so. I just need to find the paperwork." Lucien held her face and wiped her tears.

"I'm here baby. Remember that," Lucien said. Irys nodded her head. She led the way to her mother's room. Thankfully there weren't many things to go through to find what they were looking for. Her mother kept all important papers in her night table drawer and they were all neatly piled inside. Irys gave Lucien half and she took the other half. While he began looking through the paperwork first, Irys busied herself changing the bed sheets and making the bed as if her mother was going to return at any moment. Once she was done she began looking through her half of the papers.

"I found her will," Lucien said quietly. He handed Irys the closed envelope. She took it but didn't read it until she was able to find her life insurance.

"Here's the insurance," Irys said. She looked through the papers and had to admit to breathing a sigh of relief. Without this she wasn't sure how she was going to afford laying her mother to rest.

"There's enough in the policy to give my mom a proper funeral," Irys said.

"Whatever it is baby I can help you no matter what." Irys took a deep breath and nodded at him. After that Irys really couldn't say anything. She opened her mother's will slowly so she could read it. Tears clouded her vision as Irys envisioned her mother writing each word. She was splitting her savings, which wasn't much between both her and Rosa. She told Irys what dress she wanted to be buried in and where. Right next to Irys's father. Once she finished reading Irys stood and went to her mother's closet to find the dress her mother wanted to wear.

"I guess I should start packing all this stuff up," Irys said.

"No baby," Lucien said. "She just passed away you don't need to do that right this minute. Give yourself time." Just as he said that his watch began to beep. He immediately turn it off, but Irys already knew what that meant.

"It's okay Lucien. Thank you for coming over. I know you didn't have to."

"Actually I did," Lucien said. "And I didn't bring any of my things with me in my rush. So I do need to go home."

"I'll see you around then."

"Don't be silly Irys. They'll need a day and a half to get your mom's body to the funeral home you choose. I'm not leaving you alone. You called me for a reason."

"So what?"

"There is no so what baby. You're my woman. And the thought of not being with you again literally made me want to claw my brains out for being so dumb in the first place. Get a few things and come stay with my at my house baby. You can stay for as long as you like honey. But you need to come with me now. I know you don't want to be here alone."

"I don't," She whispered.

"Okay so come on. I'll take the papers. You get a small bag packed." Irys left her mother's room with Lucien behind her. As she passed the kitchen she went into the fridge and gave Lucien a banana and a bottle of water.

"I'm not sure it will help," she said. Lucien smiled at her.

"Actually it would. I left before I could actually eat," He said. "Thanks baby." Irys smiled and hurried off to her bedroom to pack a small bag. Yes, she did call Lucien for a reason and she figured this was why. She just needed him. And with her mother gone, Lucien and Luna were going to be her only family that cared about her. So she was through pushing them away.

"Ready," She said quietly once she was done packing. Lucien threw the banana peel away and finished off his water. Without saying anything he took her hand and led her out of the house. Irys looked back before she got into Lucien's car, sadness taking over her body. She couldn't believe her mother was actually gone.

"It's okay," Lucien said rubbing her shoulders.

"How did you ever get over this when your parents died?" She asked him.

"You never really get over it Irys. But you learn that living is the only thing that they'd want you to keep doing. A woman like Kendra, she wouldn't want you to be sulking around after too long. Especially knowing she thinks you have a lot to live for." She sighed and rested her head against his chest.

"Let's get you out of here." Lucien opened the car door for her and helped her inside. Through their drive back to Lucien's house, she was completely quiet. Each time Lucien looked over at her, she was wiping her eyes. He reached into the glove compartment to find her some tissue. He kept hold of her hand afterwards just to give her a small measure of comfort for now.

Luna was waiting at the door when Lucien pulled up to his home. He parked in the driveway and went around to open her door for her. She tried to dry her eyes as much as she could before getting out.

"Irys," Luna greeted. "How-how are you." The women hadn't been talking for a while now and it was probably awkward for the both of them.

"Hey Luna," Irys greeted.

"Is everything alright?"

"Um-" Irys cleared her throat. "My mom passed this morning." Luna hugged her without any further word. She helped Irys into the house forgetting that Lucien was right there. He went to get Irys's bag and her mother's papers before following them into the house. The women were talking quietly among themselves so Lucien went straight to check his sugar. Salsa rushed from his bedroom and instead of coming to him she went straight to Irys. She was trying to jump up on Irys, licking her face and wagging her tail excitedly.

"Told you she missed you," Lucien joked. Irys laughed and hugged the dog. Surprisingly the dog was giving her comfort too and she was soaking it in before she fell into another fit of tears. She walked to the living room where she fell into the couch. Salsa jumped up next to her and laid in her lap. Luna followed her too but Lucien stayed in the kitchen. She didn't know what he was doing until she could smell food.

"I'm real sorry," Luna said.

"It's fine Luna. I knew she had to go at some point she was only getting sicker. I just wasn't ready I guess."

"No, I was saying sorry for the way I treated you before. With accusing you of doing something to deceive Lucien."

"Oh that. Look its fine now. I was mad let's face it but truly you and Lucien is all I've got now. So I can let that petty shit go."

"You're right."

"But there is one thing I'm gonna say."

"What?" Luna asked.

"I know you're his sister and nothing can break the bond you two have. But I am his woman Luna. And when it comes to certain things I'm gonna have to ask you not to butt into our business. When it comes to our relationship it's something that me and Lucien have to figure out. If you stay out of it I think that gives you a position to not have to choose sides again. I don't want to exclude you out of everything. But there must be boundaries." Luna crossed her arms.

"Well that's something that Lucien needs to agree to as well. Because if he chooses to divulge information to me, that's his fault not mine."

"I agree!" Lucien called from the kitchen. Luna huffed and held her hands up.

"Okay fine. I'm too invested in his love life I admit that." Lucien came into the living room and shooed Salsa away so he could place a plate of food in Irys's lap. He stood there awkwardly for a minute. Then he whistled at Luna.

"Move," He shooed her. Luna rolled her eyes and got up, realizing he wanted to sit next to Irys.

"We should go to a funeral home shouldn't we?" Irys asked him. "Pick out a casket and such?"

"It's still early baby," Lucien said. "We can do that in a couple hours. I think you should still just relax. I'll call the insurance company to report the death. Then we'll take it from there. Eat." Irys settled back and began eating. Right now with him, she was actually able to relax. And throughout the day he was going to be in her corner when she needed him to be.

After Irys ate something and took a small nap, Lucien took her to a couple funeral homes before they decided on which one was the best. They picked a casket and arranged for her mother to be picked up by that funeral home when the mortician was finished with her. By the time the day was over, they had everything sorted out along with a date for the funeral. The insurance company was going to kick in funds for the insurance once everything cleared and her death was ruled as natural causes. So that night, she was in bed with Lucien wide awake.

"You need to sleep," Lucien told her.

"Should I tell Rosa?" Irys asked.

"Why wouldn't you?" He questioned. "That's her mother too."

"Yeah but Rosa never wanted to even take care of her. She barely talked to her."

"So what? That's still her mom. You need to have a clear conscience. Tell her about the funeral. Whether she decides to show up or not is up to her. At least your conscience will be clear." Irys laid across Lucien's chest. He could feel the wetness of her tears against his chest. Knowing she didn't need him to say anything, Lucien just held her tightly and vowed not to let go.

It was easy for Irys to fall asleep, but it wasn't easy for her to stay asleep. Her eyes were tired from all her crying but every time she had them closed all she could see was her mother's ghostly face in her mind. She looked so peaceful but for some reason it just scared Irys down to her bone. She was just used to her mother's face looking flush and full of life.

"Don't let him go," In her dream her mother's mouth moved and Irys heard her voice, but her eyes never opened. And she didn't look responsive. So how could she be talking? Irys reached forward and tried to touch the woman's face but she just completely disappeared. Irys let out a gut wrenching scream and shot up from the bed. She began crying all over again realizing her mother was really and truly gone. Lucien jumped out of his sleep when he heard Irys wailing. He immediately grabbed her up and held her tightly.

"I'm so sorry," She cried. "I-I didn't mean to yell I just saw her in my dreams."

"It's okay sugar. It's okay." He kissed her forehead and rocked her back and forth. He rested back and pulled her on top on his chest.

"Don't you apologize for feeling. I know it hurts." He continued kissing all over her face.

"But you know I won't ever leave you right?" He asked. "That I'll always be here for you." Irys nodded her head against his chest. She knew he would be there for her, and even if it was in her dreams her mother told her not to let him go, so she wasn't.

****

After her mother passed it was hard for the first couple days but she knew she had to get things done. She needed to arrange the funeral and send out invites to her mother's closest friends. The easy part of it was that all of Irys's relatives had already passed on so there was not a lot of people to invite in the first place. Like Lucien said, Irys was the bigger woman and actually called her sister.

"Hey we should meet up, I gotta talk to you," Irys said when Rosa answered her phone.

"About what? I shouldn't even be talking to you after you kicked me out! Now I'm staying at this bum ass motel because Derek can't afford anywhere else. How could you do this to me?!" She screeched.

"Oh cry me a fucking river," Irys said blandly. "Meet me by Lucien's restaurant." Irys hung up the phone after that. She didn't care to hear any of her sister's rant. Lucien looked at her when she hung up the phone.

"What?" she asked. Lucien couldn't fault her for her mood seeing the circumstances, but this was a part of Irys he never experienced before.

"Are you alright?" he asked her.

"I'm burying my mother in two days. Do you think I'm alright?" she snapped.

"Don't catch an attitude with me Irys," He said sternly. That seemed to get her to realize she was acting out. She looked away from him and crossed her arms. After a moment she turned and looked at him.

"Sorry," She pouted.

"It's fine sugar. Come here." She slid off the stool she was sitting on and went over to him. He cupped her face in his hands and kissed her lips lightly.

"I know you're upset," He said. "But you betta watch your mouth," he teased her.

"Or else what," She smirked. He bit her bottom lip.

"You can find out now or later. Your choice." Irys wrapped her arms around his neck and kissed him deeply. She knew he was only trying to make her feel better and it worked tremendously. Anytime she got to hug and kiss his sweet lips she was able to feel comfort. And knowing what was coming in a couple days she was going to need all the comfort she could get.

After spending the morning with Lucien at his place they traveled to his restaurant together. Rosa was already there waiting outside dressed like a slut as normal. The moment Irys and Lucien walked up to the front door, Rosa threw herself at Lucien.

"Hi baby!" She greeted hugging him tightly. Irys just stood there and looked at the both of them. Lucien quickly took Rosa's arms from around him and pushed her off. He took Irys's hand and let her into the restaurant first before letting Rosa in. It was still early but the other cooks would be showing up soon to start prepping for that day's dinner service. The three of them sat around a table.

"So Lucien how have you been?" Rosa asked him reaching out to touch his hand. Lucien moved away quickly then sat back and put his arm around Irys's shoulders.

"I've been great," He said. He sensed Irys's tenseness so he leaned over and kissed her on the cheek.

"Just ignore her," He whispered in his ear. Irys took a deep breath then nodded.

"Rosa this is about mom. She um…she's gone." Rosa looked at her sister.

"Well it's about damn time," Rosa cheered. "So, did the hen leave me any money?" Irys's mouth fell open as tears ran down her face again.

"Rosa that's our mother," She said. "You must have some type of remorse or something!" Rosa just shrugged.

"Did she leave me any money or what?" Irys just shook her head. She pulled out the copy of her mother's will and the amount of money Rosa was going to get.

"Her funeral is in two days. Here's the location." Irys gave her all that information but she didn't care about nothing but the money. It cut Irys deep but what did she expect? Rosa cared about no one but herself.

"It's not much but I guess it'll do for something." Lucien saw Irys begin to unravel at her sister's inconsideration.

"Rosa have some respect," Lucien spoke up. "For this one time at least be courteous. Don't you see how hard this is for Irys?"

"All my life it's always been Irys this and Irys that. But it was never Rosa needs this or Rosa needs that. I was always the outsider when Irys's father moved in. And now as an adult I'm supposed to give a damn about her still? I don't think so. Especially after she stole you from me?"

"Something is seriously wrong with you," Lucien said.

"But yet still you loved fucking me. And I imagine when you close your eyes when you're inside this whale it's me you see in your head and not her." Irys stood abruptly shaking the table. Lucien stood with her, seeing the heat in her eyes.

"Don't," He said immediately knowing well Irys was about to knock Rosa the fuck out.

"She talks to me like that and you don't want me to snatch her fucking wig off?" Irys sneered turning angry eyes on him.

"Because I don't want you to sink down to her level," He said.

"It's not about that!" Irys snapped.

"Whoa little sis, relax," Rosa said standing up. "The truth hurts I know. But you should have known well that Lucien probably can't help thinking about me. I mean look at me and look at you." Rosa moved from where she was standing and strutted next to Lucien. She ran her hand over his chest and down to his stomach.

"My number hasn't changed Lucien so if you need to call me you always can." She was seconds away from groping his crotch and that's when Irys lost it. She pushed Lucien out of the way and punched Rosa straight in her face. She fell back immediately falling on her ass.

"Who the fuck you think you are?" Irys asked her. Rosa began that fake crying and trying to back away so Irys wouldn't hit her again, but Irys wasn't going to let her get away. She grabbed the front of Rosa's shirt and pulled her to her feet. She slapped her in the face and kept hold of the shirt so she wouldn't fall back again.

"I try giving you the benefit of the doubt Rosa. I tell you OUR mother is dead and you've got the nerve to sit here smiling and asking how much money she left you. And then you wanna sit here and insult me by touching on what's mine?" Irys slapped her again.

"Irys let-" Lucien tried to cut in but Irys wasn't going to allow it this time.

"You wanna be single?!" Irys shouted at Lucien, turning angry eyes to him.

"No," He snapped.

"So back the fuck up and let me handle my business. Butt in again. I dare you." Lucien hadn't seen Irys this angry before and even if he didn't want her to sink to Rosa's level he wasn't going to chance getting on her bad side too. So he did the only thing he could do and just backed the fuck up.

Irys looked back at Rosa. Her lips were already bleeding but that was minimal compared to all the hurt Rosa had caused Irys over the years.

"Newsflash Rosa," Irys continued, "Lucien ain't ya man anymore. He's mine! And I can guarantee, no as a matter of fact I can promise you that he's not thinking about your skinny, need a big mac meal ass when I'm riding his big fat dick until he's toes are doing the goddamn electric slide." Lucien gasped at Irys's vulgarity but nothing she said was a lie.

"And look, you can come around any fucking time you want to Rosa, I ain't got no problem with that." She went from just holding Rosa's top to wrapping her hand around Rosa's neck. She squeezed.

"But if you come around me or my fucking man and start talking out of your mouth and disrespecting me, you're gonna see my hands again. And if you ever, *ever* touch Lucien inappropriately again I'm gonna break your fucking arms off. You got me?"

"Yes-yes," Rosa whimpered since she couldn't talk because Irys was choking her. Irys let her go and watched as she fell to the ground coughing. Irys looked at both her and Lucien before she walked off so she could cool down. She went up to Lucien's office and sat in his chair and slowly swiveled left to right to calm down.

She didn't know what was going on downstairs but Lucien came up to the office ten minutes later.

"She's gone," He said. Irys just nodded. Lucien went over to his desk and leaned over it. He kissed her softly.

"I'll never condone you being violent Irys, but I gotta say you were sexy as fuck handling your business." Irys cracked a smile and chuckled.

"I'll always be that nice kind hearted person but I'm through being disrespected and treated like that especially by Rosa. It would have been nice if you did more to defend me but you'll pay for that later." Lucien groaned.

"Don't be like that baby. You know I don't be thinking about her ass." Irys made a face.

"Don't care," She teased. "So tonight don't even think about touching me. If you do, I'll break your arms."

"Aye you can't pull that one on me Irys. I'll fuck the shit out of you." Irys giggled knowing he was right. She liked the idea of denying him as punishment but she honestly didn't think she could. He turned her on too much. And with her excessive sadness over her mother's passing she was all over him and was probably going to keep being all over him too. She stood and walked around the desk towards him. He scooped her in his arms and hugged her tightly.

"You're my woman Irys. And nothing can change that remember."

"Thanks for being here for me," She said resting her head on his chest. Without him she didn't know how she would be pulling through.

****

Irys decided she was just going to wear shades. Whether it was happy tears, or sad tears she just couldn't stop crying. When her mother's friend spoke about her at the funeral Irys couldn't help but be sad and happy at the same time. Her mother looked so pretty in that casket, in the dress that she wanted to wear because it was Irys's father's favorite dress. The service was sweet and well done. Lucien stood by her side looking so handsome in his suit. Even though Irys told Rosa about the funeral Rosa still was a no show. She figured after she whooped her ass that Rosa would have the decency to come to her mother's funeral.

Lucien was running errands all day going back and forth between the restaurant and the funeral home. He decided to close the restaurant for the day and allow for Irys and everyone who attended the funeral to come to the restaurant for the reception after the funeral. Since he made the majority of the food he was up early in the morning to make sure everything was set before he finally went to the funeral with Irys. He knew she needed him on this day more than any other so he stuck by her side to give her comfort. It was hard seeing the woman you were falling in love with hurt so deeply. Especially because it wasn't anything he could take away from her or fix. It wasn't like he could bring her mother back or take her pain away. Nothing would do that except time. The only problem was that all the commotion and looking after Irys meant that he hardly had a time to even think about his own health. And to be honest he really didn't care anything about himself in that moment. He just wanted to be there for Irys to make sure she wasn't going to completely lose control.

While everyone was saying their last goodbyes next to the casket that's when Lucien spotted Rosa coming in. Lucien stood next to Irys holding her around the waist as she bid her mother goodbye. She wiped her tears and watched as her mother was lowered in the casket. Lucien rubbed her arm and whispered in her ear.

"Rosa's here," He said. Irys looked up and indeed her sister was standing in the doorway. Irys took a breath and walked up to Rosa with Lucien and Luna at her side.

"I didn't know if I should have come in or not. But I was here I just never came into the room," Rosa said.

"Well, we're taking her down to the cemetery now. If you're coming that's for you to decide." Irys said.

"She left me money so I guess I could."

"Our mother's funeral, and this is what you're interested in," Irys said.

"Fine. Be like that. I'll go by the cemetery. But after that, with the money mom left me I'm gonna move out of town and start over. I won't be getting in your way."

"Sure," Irys said. "You're free to do whatever you want."

"Come sugar," Lucien said to her. He kept his arm around her and led her away from Rosa and out of the building. Rosa looked on longingly but said nothing else.

At the cemetery, Irys put roses on her mother's casket but after that she had to walk away. She couldn't see the casket be lowered. There was a sense of completion for her because at the same time she buried her mother, she was able to say hello to her father and lay new flowers in front of his headstone. Her parents were finally together again.

****

"Man I feel like I got hit by a bus," Irys said, once they got back to Lucien's house. She threw herself on the couch and sighed hard. The reception lasted longer that she thought but she didn't want to rush anyone out of the place. Plus they all loved Lucien's food. But truthfully she didn't want to be around all those people anymore. She just wanted to be with Lucien now.

"Ain't that the truth," Lucien said. When Irys took off her glasses he saw how puffy her eyes were.

"Look the funeral is over everything is done. Now I just want a big tub of ice cream and some cartoons."

"Anything you need my lady," Lucien said. He retrieved the ice cream for her and sat with her to watch cartoons. His vision was a little blurry from his sugar but the headache he was used to by now. But instead of complaining about it he just continued to cater to Irys to make sure she was alright.

By the time the sun went down that day the both of them had changed clothes and taken showers. After his shower, Lucien went to get Irys so they could go to bed. She'd enjoyed her ice cream and cartoons were still playing on the screen but Irys was knocked out. But now with the sun down, Lucien wanted her in bed next to him. He didn't want to wake her but he was getting weaker and weaker as the day drew on.

"Irys," Lucien whispered. She stirred a little.

"Hm?"

"Come up to bed with me," He said. He could see she wanted to, but she was still in her sleep. Lucien kissed her on the forehead. He reached under her and scooped her into his arms. Even though he was weak he tried his best not to fall over. He moved as quickly as he could carrying her up to his bedroom. He laid her on the bed and in no time he had fell asleep next to her warm body.

When Irys blinked her eyes open everything was dark. She could feel Lucien next to her so she knew she was in his bed. Her bladder was screaming at her to get up but she felt so lazy. Obviously having an accident next to the man you were in love with was a no-no, so she forced herself to get up and go to the bathroom. Good thing he had one in his bedroom and she didn't have to go far. As she got up, Salsa came into the bedroom. Irys smiled at the dog and went into the bathroom. While she sat on the toilet she heard Salsa whimpering. That happened before Salsa began barking. Irys wasn't bothered by her barking since she was probably trying to wake Lucien up. It had happened before when Irys slept over so she was used to it. But Salsa didn't stop barking. Irys finished with her business and got up from the toilet. As she washed her hands, Salsa came rushing into the bathroom. She barked at Irys and quickly ran back out of the bathroom. Irys followed the dog promptly. She was back at Lucien's side of the bed, whimpering and pacing.

"Lucien?" Irys rushed to him and turned him over. She gasped sharply when she saw his eyes were rolling in the back of his head.

"No!" Irys shouted. "Not you too!" Salsa barked and began jumping up against the wall. When Irys looked at her, she saw that the dog was hitting something on the wall with her palm.

"911, how can I help?" A voice sounded. Irys was filled with shock. It was true Salsa was trained to perfection when it came to Lucien's health.

"Hello, is anyone there?" The voice sounded.

"Yes! Yes! I'm here. My boyfriend, he's diabetic and he's eyes and rolling over. I don't know what to do!"

"Okay Ma'am I'm sending an ambulance. You need to check his sugar. Can you do that?"

"Yes." Irys fumbled around finding Lucien's meter in the night table draw. She'd watched him do it so many times it was no problem for her now. She pricked his finger and checked his sugar.

"It's 160," Irys said.

"Okay. That's way too high. Are you able to administer his insulin?"

"I've never done it before!" Irys exclaimed, panic consuming her.

"Don't panic okay? The ambulance is there." True enough the ambulance was wailing out in front of the house. Irys didn't want to leave Lucien's side, but she had to in order to let them in. Salsa stayed with Lucien guarding him. Irys led the EMT'S back to Lucien's bedroom. She stayed out of the way watching as they worked on him.

"Where's his insulin?!" they shouted at her. Irys ran into the kitchen and retrieved his insulin for them. She watched again, as one of the EMT's supplied his insulin. Irys bit her nails, her heart beating heavily. Salsa stood next to her and she had to give the dog credit. With or without her here, Salsa was going to get her owner help no matter what.

"Why isn't his eyes returning to normal?" Irys panicked.

"Just give him time," One of the EMT's said.

"We have to transport him to the hospital just until he goes back down to normal." Irys nodded and walked over to the bed slowly. Salsa hopped onto the bed and began licking Lucien's face. One of the EMT's touched her collar and looked at the pendant.

"Salsa the service dog," He said. "Looks like you got yourself a guardian." Wasn't that the truth?

While the EMT's strapped Lucien to a gurney to get him out to the ambulance truck, Irys threw on a pair of sweat pants and a t-shirt so she could follow them. She and Salsa got in Lucien's car and drove behind the ambulance. She petted Salsa trying to calm the dog down. She was still a little anxious and Irys could sense that. In fact, Irys was anxious too. It struck her how serious his condition could turn and it scared her to death.

When they pulled up to the hospital, she realized Luna needed to know what happened. She called her quickly.

"Whhyyyy?" Luna groaned into the phone.

"Lucien's in the emergency room," Irys responded.

"What?!" Luna's voice became alert.

"We just got here. I thought you should know. We're at-"

"I know what hospital it is. He always goes there. Be there in 15 minutes." Irys hung up the phone and proceeded into the hospital.

"Hey, no dogs," Someone told her.

"She's a service dog," The EMT spoke up for her. The lady nodded her head signaling Salsa could come inside.

Irys walked behind the EMT's as they wheeled Lucien in. Once in the emergency room they took him straight to a room then the EMT's left him to speak with the doctor. Irys sat next to Lucien's bed and looked at him. Salsa hopped up on the bed and laid at the foot of it across his legs. They sat there for what seemed like an hour before Lucien groaned. Irys snapped her head in his direction to find that his eyes had returned to normal and he was gazing back at her.

"Why didn't you take your insulin?" Irys asked him. "Or check your sugar? Or-I don't know do something before this happened? There must have been signs Lucien. And you ignored them all?!" Irys didn't mean to sound so accusatory but she was scared.

"I don't know," He replied gruffly.

"That's not a good enough answer Lucien! You-I-" Irys shook her head. She wiped her eyes.

"I thought I was losing you. And after losing my mom, I can't manage living without you Lucien." He grabbed her hand and held it.

"If you want to be with me Irys you have to know that things like this will happen. I never mean for them to. It just does. I wouldn't want to be without you either." Irys rested her head against his chest.

"I'm gonna be here for you Lucien. To make sure you never leave me. But I need to know everything. I felt so useless I couldn't even give you your insulin. So you need to teach me everything. And I mean it." He rubbed her back.

"I'll show you baby don't worry about it."

"Damnit Lucien!" Luna gasped rushing into the bedroom. Joe came in the room behind her. Lucien looked at them both.

"Well I wasn't sleeping alone, and he wouldn't let me come by myself so…"

"I asked you not to sleep with my sister until you proposed to her," Lucien stated evenly. Joe was quiet.

"I-Lucien I'm not out to hurt your sister-"

"Hush up," Luna snapped at Joe. "Lucien you have no say in my personal relationships. Remember just the other day you were telling me I needed to stay out of your relationships? Well the same thing goes for you. If Joe wants to give me orgasms, which I haven't gotten to experience yet thank you very much, then he's more than welcome to give me those orgasms. And you don't get a say in that. Besides, if you feel that way I don't see you proposing to Irys."

"Whoa, don't pull me in this," Irys said sitting up.

"And you're in no position to scare the man that I'm interested in. You're in the hospital for Pete's sake." Lucien just sighed and turned his head.

"Whatever Luna," He said.

By the time Lucien's sugar was normal and he had regained some of his strength, they had been in the emergency room for two hours. As they got ready to leave, Irys helped Lucien get dressed while everyone else waited outside of the room.

"Luna is right you know," Irys said. "Can't ask that man not to be with Luna intimately without proposing."

"Yeah I know. And it's true I haven't proposed to you. But if you gave me that ultimatum then I would Irys."

"If it has to be an ultimatum Lucien, how authentic could it be?" Lucien only sighed knowing she was right.

"Do you want a wife one day?" Irys asked him.

"You know that I do."

"Right. And I want a husband. So shall we move in the right direction Lucien I think we can both get what we want. I don't need to deny you of sex to get that. And besides it would be denying myself also. I love me an orgasm or two." Lucien snickered and hugged her tightly.

"I can agree with that," Lucien smiled.

Chapter Twenty-One

With having Lucien, moving on from her mother's death was somewhat easier. It was hard for her to go home at times, but most nights she didn't feel the need to. She hated sleeping away from Lucien anyway. In the two months that her mother had passed, Irys found more of her items being transferred to Lucien's house. Not only were they staying together most of the time, they were working together too. That was what Irys loved the most. Going to work and seeing her man run his restaurant gave her a feeling like no other. She loved seeing him cook and she loved his claim to her. At no point in time was he ever embarrassed to say that she was his woman. And he wasn't shy about giving her kisses before any service started.

"I know you told me to stay out of your relationship," Luna said to Irys. "But you'd tell me if you were pregnant right?" They were getting ready to leave the spa and go down to the restaurant for the night service.

"Of course I would tell you Luna. What you think I'd carry around your niece or nephew and not say anything?" Luna gave her a look. They got into her car then she dug into her purse. She pulled out a box of pregnancy tests.

"I found this in Lucien's bathroom last night. Wanna tell me about it?" Irys snatched the box away from her.

"As you can see, it's not opened so there's nothing to tell you about."

"But you bought it for a reason. Does Lucien know?"

"I bought it because your brother lost control and came inside me. That's just me being prepared if I miss my period."

"Humph, if you say so." Irys rolled her eyes and laughed at Luna. She knew the woman couldn't stay out of Lucien's relationship no matter how hard she tried.

"What were you even doing searching the bathroom?" Irys asked. Luna shrugged with a smirk on her face.

"I had a dream so I got suspicious. That's all." Irys shook her head. Luna would never stop being crazy.

Like he always did, Lucien was waiting for the women outside of the restaurant. He didn't wait for Irys to come to him. He had her in his arms the moment she stepped out of the car. He kissed her neck and her lips.

"See now that's why you can't pull out. You're a sucka," Luna teased.

"You told her?" Lucien exclaimed still holding onto Irys protectively.

"She found my pregnancy tests."

"Look, I don't even care. She's mine I can come in her if I want to," Lucien stated, plucking Luna's nose.

"Just know I want a niece," Luan teased. As they began bickering back and forth, Irys laughed at them. Her phone buzzed in her purse. She pulled it out, and moved away from Lucien to answer it. It was a number she didn't recognize. She knew something was up when she answered and there was a machine asking her if she accepted the charge.

"Yes," Irys said. She waited a moment as the phone connected.

"Irys?!"

"Derek?" Irys asked. "Where the hell are you?"

"I'm in jail Irys. And I need bail money. It's ten grand to get me out."

"Where the hell you think I'm gonna get ten grand from? And what the fuck did you do?"

"Well I was trying to make some money to show Rosa I can take care of her. Turns out I was pulled into a whole scheme and they're talking about grand larceny and money laundering and all that shit. I don't belong in a place like this. So you need to help me out." Irys was quiet for a moment.

"No I don't need to help you with anything. Why don't you call Rosa?"

"She won't take my calls. Please Irys I need you."

"Now you need me," Irys chuckled. "Well I can't help you Derek. Because I'm a fat bitch who you hated enough to want to abort your kid and for you to get with me only to sleep with my sister. So you can rot in that little jail cell Derek. Don't call me back." Irys hung up the phone. She stayed where she was for a moment not even believing Derek had called her from jail.

"Who was that?" Lucien asked her.

"It was Derek," She said. "He's in jail and he wants me to bail him out."

"And what did you tell him?"

"Basically to fuck off," Irys said.

"Good girl," Lucien smiled. "You've got me now. You don't need to ever think about that dick. He's good where he's at. And I know you have a big heart Irys, but you don't need to feel bad for him."

"I don't," She said. "Well in a way I do. But not bad enough for me to do something about it personally." Lucien turned her to face him.

"You deserve happiness Irys. Thinking about anything involving Derek weighs you down in a way that doesn't allow you to be happy. Just let it go baby." Irys took a deep breath and then let it out. She nodded and smiled at him.

"Letting it go," She said.

"Good. Now let's go inside. I can't cook without my lady there with me." Lucien looked her up and down.

"What?" Irys asked.

"Are you losing weight baby?" he asked. "I noticed it last night too. Though I got caught up focusing on making you come, but nevertheless I noticed it."

"Well I lost a couple pounds yeah. You cook healthy and well you feed me right. And I get in some exercise."

"You're not one of those people on that show you watch all the damn time Irys. You're not 600 pounds and you're healthy. There's not a damn thing wrong with being a thick woman. And I quite like you the way you are. If you want to lose weight that's fine, I'll still love you the same. But don't lose the weight because you think you have to."

"You don't notice it Lucien, but when we're walking together I see women look at us. I see them trying to figure out why you're with a woman like me."

"Did you hear what I just said to you?" Lucien asked her. Irys nodded. "No, did you really hear me? I love you. That's just it." He wrapped his arms around her and kissed her.

"Okay. Now I really did hear you."

"Good," He smiled. "Let's go." Lucien took her hand as they walked into the restaurant.

The service went smoothly, and as usual each diner loved their meal. Lucien didn't talk much about his finances, but Irys wasn't blind. She saw how many tables got turned in one night, and she knew he was making a lot of money. She wasn't sure about the cost in terms of the taxes on his building, or the amount of money needed to buy daily supplies, plus pay his staff, but apparently it was enough. Not to mention whatever Irys wanted, he got for her. All she could say was that things were going well for Lucien. And that's all he ever wanted. To be able to make a living doing something he loved.

"Excuse me, hostess," Someone called. Irys looked over and went to their table.

"How can I help?" Irys asked with a smile. The older couple smiled back at her.

"My husband and I was wondering if we would be able to talk to the chef after dinner service."

"Oh of course. He always comes out and speaks with his guests. I will let him know you're particularly interested." Irys smiled at then before walking away. She went into the kitchen where Lucien was in the corner drinking water.

"What's up sweetie?" Lucien asked.

"There's a couple out there who wants to speak with you."

"Then I should go talk to them huh," Lucien smiled. He pecked Irys on the lips before he left the kitchen to go speak with the elderly couple.

Irys watched from the kitchen, smiling with pride as her man spoke with the couple. She had no clue what they were saying but she knew it had to be good based on the look on Lucien's face. They spoke longer than Lucien would speak to any guest but at the end, Lucien shook both their hands, and walked away.

"What was that about?" Irys asked him when he came back to the kitchen.

"They liked the food," He said. But Irys could tell there was something more. He had a faraway look in his eyes that made her know he was thinking about something heavily.

"Lucien is something the matter?"

"No baby it's all fine." He kissed her on the cheek and proceeded with work. Even if he tried to remain normal, Irys had a feeling something was up.

She didn't mention it again however. And neither did he for that matter. They went home that night and acted normally. The next morning Irys woke up to a Saturday morning breakfast. Lucien smiled and greeted her like he normally did so Irys thought it wasn't worth mentioning anything from last night.

"Do you have plans for the day?" Lucien asked her. "Before service?"

"Well I needed some more clothes I was gonna go home and get some. Then I think I was just gonna wash my hair, and that's all really." He nodded and looked around uneasily.

"Okay, what the hell is on your mind?" Irys questioned.

"Why do you keep going back and forth to your house to get things and bringing them here?"

"Because I need stuff. I mean, unless you don't want me to keep brining my shit here? I can just get my shit and stay at my own house." Lucien slammed his hand down on the island.

"That's not what the hell I meant," He snapped at her. Irys sat back and crossed her arms.

"I meant, how come you just don't stay here?"

"Like what? Live here?" Lucien crossed his arms too and raised his brows.

"Yeah. Like that," He stated.

"Because…because you never asked me to move in with you. I'm not gonna assume you want me to live her for real. I mean, when we argue I go back to my place until we both cool down. If I live here then there's no room for that."

"Irys please. There's four bedrooms in this house I'm pretty sure if you're mad at me you'll have someplace to go. But is that what you think? You won't move in because you want to be able to get away from me?"

"No Lucien. I haven't moved in because you didn't ask me to." He uncrossed his arms and rocked back on his heels.

"There's something that couple last night told me that I need to talk to you about," He finally spoke.

"What does that have to do with anything we're talking about now?" Irys was completely confused.

"That couple last night came all the way from France to come eat at my place. Apparently a French cuisine restaurant in America is news to people in France."

"Okay and?" Irys asked.

"They're food enthusiasts. They go around the world eating all kinds of food. Last night they told me they bought a building in France with the purpose of opening a restaurant. Turns out they're not as good cooks as they imagined and they haven't been able to find anyone to take over the property or a cook who wants to take a job there. So they proposed to me last night that I should open another restaurant in France, in the building they bought. They want to sell it to me." Irys gasped.

"Can you...can you afford it?"

"Honestly no. The building I can buy sure. But the cost of starting up a restaurant, especially in another country is a lot Irys."

"So you told them that?"

"Yes. But then they told me that the building is fully furnished. So I have all the kitchen equipment I would need. They said all I would need is a deposit to get started. Doing a deposit can ensure than I would still have enough money to hire a kitchen and dining staff. Then I would begin paying them back at the end of each month based on my sales. So technically if my restaurant does well I can easily pay them the full amount in a couple months."

"Are you considering doing this?" Irys asked. "I mean, it can work. And it does sound like a good deal?"

"You sound a little skeptical."

"Well who would take over the restaurant here?"

"I spoke with Joe. He's completely capable and willing to do it. And I feel comfortable leaving my restaurant in his hands."

"So you want to go?" Irys said lowly.

"I do actually. Very much so. It's something I never thought was possible, but if it's offered to me in this way why shouldn't I take that leap?"

"I agree. You should go for it. Um-" Irys cleared her throat. "I guess I should get my stuff out of here since you'll be gone." Irys got up prepared to walk out. She knew she couldn't deny him of that but she didn't want to be without him.

"Irys no," Lucien said cutting her off. He stood in front of her. He held her face and kissed her tenderly.

"I was asking why you didn't move in with me because I wanted to see how committed you were to just being with me. Because if you wanted to move in with me then you wanted to give up everything to be with me."

"Babe I'd give up my house to be with you yeah. That's nothing," Irys said.

"Irys I want to be with you. This opportunity won't come by again and I don't want to lose it."

"I know you don't baby. And I'm not blaming you for leaving. It's fine."

"You're not getting it baby." He took her hands and held it. "I want to leave to France, but I want…actually I NEED you to come with me Irys. I want you on this journey with me." Irys gasped.

"So I should…just leave everything and come with you?"

"When we met you told me you wanted to travel the world. You speak three languages just to be able to one day visit those countries. So why not now? Why not come to France with me?" Irys thought for a moment. Her job wasn't a big deal to leave. And she did want to travel the world. But most importantly, she wanted to be with Lucien. And she wanted to take this journey with him.

"I'd do anything to be with you. Period. So I guess that's two tickets you're gonna have to buy," Irys smiled. Lucien grabbed her up and swung her around. He kissed her on the mouth. When he set her down he gazed into her eyes.

"You don't know how much it means to me to have you in my life Irys," He said softly. When she looked into his eyes she got lost. Lost in the love he exuded. To think she could be herself completely with a man and he would love her as much as she loved him.

"Can't believe I'm going to France!" Irys squealed. "Oh my god I need a whole new wardrobe!" Lucien smiled at her as she rushed off to their bedroom. He couldn't help but smile. The woman of his dreams was an actual reality, and he was sharing something with her that was part of his life.

****

"I'm gonna miss you," Luna said hugging Lucien tightly. "Can't believe you actually are doing this."

"Yeah me either. But it's happening."

"And I didn't even get an invite!" She exclaimed.

"Guess he just had someone better to take," Irys teased, coming over from the bag check.

"You know if I didn't love you myself I'd be incredible angry you're taking my brother away," Luna smiled. She gave Irys a big hug.

"Luna I need you to stay here because if you don't who else is gonna keep everyone in check?" Lucien asked. "I know you will keep everyone in shape."

"Damn right I will," She said turning and slapping Joe on the butt. Lucien shook his head.

"In front of me Luna?" he asked. She giggled and hugged Joe.

"Don't worry about it boss. I will keep everything to standard," Joe spoke up. Lucien shook his hand.

"Babe, last call to board," Irys said. Lucien hugged his sister once more time and whispered in her ear.

"In a couple months I'll be sending for you."

"What for?"

"You'll see." He tightened his hug for a minute more before letting go. He smiled at his sister then turned to leave. Only when he turned, his woman was smiling at him and a complete feeling of bliss filled him. What else did a man need? Lucien reached for Irys's hand and held it tight.

"Did you check your sugar?" she asked.

"15 minutes ago. It's right in the middle, perfectly normal."

"Then we're ready to go," She smiled. Lucien looked at Irys.

"Yes, we're ready to go." Lucien kissed her again, before they both boarded the plane heading to Paris, France.

Epilogue

5 months later…

Lucien waited under the bright lights of the Eiffel tower for Irys to arrive. It was a late Sunday night and the restaurant was closed for the night. It was one of the rare nights where the restaurant was actually closed. In the past five months, Lucien had worked his butt off and Irys was at his side. He hated having debt, so paying back Mr. and Mrs. St. Pierre. and within five months his restaurant had made enough money not only to pay them back, but to keep him and Irys afloat living in another country. It didn't hurt that the restaurant back home was keeping up to pace, and that money was helping him too. Where he was at in life was where he always wanted to be and then some. And in this whole thing he had Irys at his side.

The first restaurant opening was a complete failure. They only had 10 tables out of a place that seated 50. And that same night Irys rubbed Lucien's shoulders and convinced him how he wasn't a failure. Even if only ten tables were served, all ten tables loved his food. It was the boost Lucien needed. And it wasn't just the advice she gave. She was there to taste all his concoctions and when they were rightfully bad, she told him the truth. When he was too busy to check his own sugar she reminded him. Just the night before he'd fell asleep because he was drained from the rush of the service. He'd completely forgotten about checking his sugar or taking insulin. But he awoke to her pricking his side as she suppled his insulin then kissed him and told him to go back to sleep. A woman like that you just didn't let go. And Lucien wasn't planning on it.

Hearing Salsa bark, he looked up to see Irys finally coming towards him. Luna was with her. He'd flown her down like he promised to in the first place. Even though Luna was there all Lucien could see was Irys. She was wearing a fitted red dress that hugged her curves in the way that Lucien loved. Her hair had grown longer and bigger, a curly mass that he loved rubbing his hands through at night. Not to mention she didn't have to wear makeup to be appealing. She just was. And seeing her in that limelight as she walked towards him, all other women faded away. She made every women in this world nonexistent to him.

"Sorry we're late," Luna said. "We got carried away eating macaroons." Lucien gasped and looked at Irys.

"You ate someone else's macaroons?!"

"I'm sorry baby I couldn't resist. But I'll have you know that it didn't taste better than yours."

"Well that's a relief." Irys sighed and looked up at the Eiffel tower.

"I can't believe we're actually here," She said. "I haven't spoken so much French in my life before this. Now I can't get enough."

"Next we'll be in Italy, and then Columbia, or Mexico, or even Costa Rica. Possibilities are endless. Especially because I just came back from paying the St. Pierre's the last of the loan."

"Finally! I'm happy that's not weighing on us anymore."

"Me too. Because that means I can spend my money on something else. Something rather important actually."

"I hope that something shares a similar DNA and name starts with a letter L too," Luna chimed in. Lucien rolled his eyes but he couldn't help but smile at her.

"Actually Luna, you're right. With the way you and Joe handled everything I knew I had to pay you back in a big way. And by the time we come back home to America I was thinking I can help fund your Spa. How's that sound?" Luna's mouth just dropped. She petted Salsa and tried to say something.

"You don't have to speak I get it," Lucien said. He turned and looked at Irys. "But you woman, you deserve something too."

"No I don't Lucien. Stop talking like I've done something incredible."

"But you have Irys. You've made my existence as a man real. Living my dreams is one thing. But doing it with a woman like you is another. Making it so that I can't see no other woman but you is incredible Irys. And I want to make sure that you understand how much you've made me fall in love with you." Lucien pounded his chest. "I've never been in love before. I thought I was, but it was nothing compared to this. And there's probably nothing better for me right now than this feeling I have inside. And without you Irys Black, I would be nothing."

"So...so what are you going to give me then?" Irys whispered on the verge of tears. "You've given me your love already Lucien, there's nothing else I want from you." Lucien gave her a tender smile, before he was lowering himself to the ground. Irys clutched at her heart as he went into his pocket for the ring case. He opened it and looked back up at her.

"You deserve to be more than just my girlfriend Irys. You deserve to be my life time companion. You deserve me wholeheartedly. I want to be your husband Irys. Because I want you to carry my last name. I want you to carry my children. And I want you to be mine. Forever. So Irys Black. Will you marry me?" Irys nodded slightly as tears brimmed her eyes. And in each language she knew, she shouted the words, 'yes I will marry you' at the top of her lungs. Lucien slipped the ring on her finger before standing up and hugging her tightly. He held her face and kissed her deeply. Irys pulled around and wrapped her arms around his neck.

"I hope you meant all that gooey stuff you just said. Because my maternity clock is ticking and if I'm not pregnant in two years I will be one unhappy wife. You got that?"

"Baby I'll get you pregnant right now. Don't play with me," Lucien joked. They were caught up in their own world until they felt Luna hugging them both.

"Ya'll better make room for me up in here," she said coming in between their hug. Lucien laughed and moved so Luna could slip in between them.

"So I'm the wedding planner right sis in law? Damn that sounds good as hell to say!"

"Yes it does," Irys smiled. "But can I get my fiancé back?" She made a face. "Now that's what sounds good!" Lucien pushed Luna out of the way to hug Irys again.

"Yes, I wanna hug my fiancée," Lucien said. "Damn that does sound good. Feels good too."

"Wanna know what feels good too?" Irys asked him seductively.

"What?" Lucien asked.

"Take me home and you'll find out."

"Oh hell," Lucien gasped. He lifted Irys in his arms and began strutting away from the Eiffel tower with purpose.

"Wait for me!" Luna called out. But Lucien didn't hear her. All he heard was the high spirited laughter coming from his wife to be.

The End

Stay updated on everything Jade Royal by liking my Author Page and following me on Social Media outlets
INSTAGRAM: *Shewrites_jaderoyal*
FACEBOOK: *Jade Royal*
AUTHOR PAGE: *https://www.facebook.com/Author-Jade-Royal-412988942467908*

JADE ROYAL

CPSIA information can be obtained
at www.ICGtesting.com
Printed in the USA
LVHW02s1845280518
578746LV00002BA/447/P